Jacqueline Winspear

Jacqueline Winspear was born and grew up in Kent. The Maisie Dobbs Mysteries have won acclaim from readers and reviewers alike, and have been nominated for many awards. The other titles in the series – *Maisie Dobbs*, *Birds of a Feather* and *Pardonable Lies* – are all published by John Murray.

Praise for the Maisie Dobbs series

'In Maisie Dobbs, Jacqueline Winspear has given us a real gift. Maisie Dobbs has not been created – she has been discovered. Such people are always there amongst us, waiting for somebody like Ms Winspear to come along and reveal them. And what a revelation it is!'
Alexander McCall Smith

'A fine new sleuth for the twenty-first century'
Elizabeth George

'Immensely readable . . . a vivid
Mail on Sunday

'A heroine to cherish'
New York Times

'Even if detective stories aren't your thing, you'll love Maisie Dobbs'
New Woman

'A new Maisie Dobbs mystery is always a cause for celebration . . . fiendishly entertaining'
Time Out

'For readers yearning for the calm insightful intelligence of a main character like P. D. James's, Maisie Dobbs is spot on'
Boston Globe

'Feisty, working-class heroine Maisie is a deliberate throwback to the sleuthettes of old-fashioned crime writing . . . The well-plotted story, its characters and the picture of London between the wars are decidedly romantic'
Guardian

Also by Jacqueline Winspear

Maisie Dobbs
Birds of a Feather
Pardonable Lies

MESSENGER OF TRUTH

A Maisie Dobbs Mystery

JACQUELINE WINSPEAR

JOHN MURRAY

First published in Great Britain in 2006 by John Murray (Publishers)
A division of Hodder Headline

Paperback edition 2007

A CIP catalogue record for this title is available from the British Library

B Format ISBN 978-0-7195-6739-1
A Format ISBN 978-0-7195-6864-0

Designed by Victoria Hartman

Printed and bound in Great Britain by Clays Ltd, St Ives plc

Hodder Headline policy is to use papers that are natural, renewable and
recyclable products and made from wood grown in sustainable forests.
The logging and manufacturing processes are expected to conform to the
environmental regulations of the country of origin.

John Murray (Publishers)
338 Euston Road
London NW1 3BH

Dedicated to
My Cheef Resurcher
(who knows who he is)

I am no longer an artist interested and anxious.
I am a messenger who will bring back word from the men
who are fighting to those who want the war to go on forever.
Feeble, inarticulate, will be my message, but it will have a
bitter truth, and may it burn in their lousy souls.

—Paul Nash, Artist
1899–1946
Paul Nash served with the Artists' Rifles and
the Royal Hampshire Regiment in the Great War.

JANUARY: You enter the London year—it is cold—
it is wet—but there are gulls on the embankment.

—from *When You Go to London,* by H. V. Morton,
published 1931

PROLOGUE

Romney Marsh, Kent, Tuesday, 30 December 1930

The taxi-cab slowed down alongside the gates of Camden Abbey, a red brick former mansion that seemed even more like a refuge as a bitter sleet swept across the grey, forbidding landscape.

"Is this the place, madam?"

"Yes, thank you."

The driver parked in front of the main entrance and, almost as an afterthought, the woman respectfully covered her head with a silk scarf before leaving the motor car.

"I shan't be long."

"Right you are, madam."

He watched the woman enter by the main door, which slammed shut behind her.

"Rather you than me, love," he said to himself as he picked up a newspaper to while away the minutes until the woman returned again.

THE SITTING ROOM was warm, with a fire in the grate, red carpet on the stone floor and heavy curtains at the windows to counter draughts that the ancient wooden frame could not keep at bay. The woman, now seated facing a grille, had been in conversation with the abbess for some forty-five minutes.

"Grief is not an event, my dear, but a passage, a pilgrimage along a path that allows us to reflect upon the past from points of remembrance held in the soul. At times the way is filled with stones underfoot and we feel pained by our memories, yet on other days the shadows reflect our longing and those happinesses shared."

The woman nodded. "I just wish there were not this doubt."

"Uncertainty is sure to follow in such circumstances."

"But how do I put my mind at rest, Dame Constance?"

"Ah, you have not changed, have you?" observed the abbess. "Always seeking to *do* rather than to *be*. Do you really seek the counsel of the spirit?"

The woman began to press down her cuticles with the thumbnail of the opposite hand.

"I know I missed just about every one of your tutorials when I was at Girton, but I thought . . ."

"That I could help you find peace?" Dame Constance paused, took a pencil and small notebook from a pocket within the folds of her habit and scribbled on a piece of paper. "Sometimes help takes the form of directing. And peace is something we find when we have a companion on the journey. Here's someone who will help you. Indeed, you have common ground, for she was at Girton too, though she came later, in 1914, if my memory serves me well."

She passed the folded note through the grille.

Scotland Yard, London, Wednesday, 31 December 1930

"So you see, madam, there's very little more I can do in the circumstances, which are pretty cut and dried, as far as we're concerned."

"Yes, you've made that abundantly clear, Detective Inspector Stratton." The woman sat bolt upright on her chair, brushing back her hair with an air of defiance. For a mere second she looked at her hands, rubbing an ink stain on calloused skin where her middle finger always pressed against the nib of her fountain pen. "However, I cannot stop searching because your investigations have drawn nothing. To that end I have decided to enlist the services of a private inquiry agent."

The policeman, reading his notes, rolled his eyes, then looked up. "That is your prerogative, of course, though I am sure his findings will mirror our own."

"It's not a he, it's a she." The woman smiled.

"May I inquire as to the name of the 'she' in question?" asked Stratton, though he had already guessed the answer.

"A Miss Maisie Dobbs. She's been highly recommended."

Stratton nodded. "Indeed, I'm familiar with her work. She's honest and knows her business. In fact, we have consulted with her here at Scotland Yard."

The woman leaned forward, intrigued. "Really? Not like your boys to admit to needing help, is it?"

Stratton inclined his head, adding, "Miss Dobbs has certain skills, certain . . . methods, that seem to bear fruit."

"Would it be overstepping the mark if I asked what you know of her, her background? I know she was at Girton College a few years after me, and I understand she was a nurse in the war, and was herself wounded in Flanders."

Stratton looked at the woman, gauging the wisdom of sharing his knowledge of the private investigator. At this point it was in his interests to have the woman out of his hair, so he would do and say what was necessary to push her onto someone else's patch. "She was born in Lambeth, went to work in service when she was thirteen."

"In service?"

"Don't let that put you off. Her intelligence was discovered by a friend of her employer, a brilliant man, an expert in legal medicine and himself a psychologist. When she came back from Flanders, as far as I know, she convalesced, then worked for a year in a secure institution, nursing profoundly shell-shocked men. She completed her education, spent some time studying at the Department of Legal Medicine in Edinburgh and went to work as assistant to her mentor. She learned her business from the best, if I am to be honest."

"And she's never married? How old is she, thirty-two, thirty-three?"

"Yes, something like that. And no, she's never married, though I understand her wartime sweetheart was severely wounded." He tapped the side of his head. "Up here."

"I see." The woman paused, then held out her hand. "I wish I could say thank you for all that you've done Inspector. Perhaps Miss Dobbs will be able to shed light where you have seen nothing."

Stratton stood up, shook hands to bid the woman good-bye and called for a constable to escort her from the building. As soon as the door was closed, while reflecting that they had not even wished each other a cordial Happy New Year, he picked up the telephone receiver and placed a call.

"Yes!"

Stratton leaned back in his chair. "Well, you'll be pleased to hear that I've got rid of that bloody woman."

"Good. How did you manage that?"

"A fortuitous move on her part – she's going to a private investigator."

"Anyone I should worry about?"

Stratton shook his head. "Nothing I can't handle. I can keep an eye on her."

"Her?"

"Yes, *her*."

Fitzroy Square, London, Wednesday, 7 January 1931

Snow had begun to fall once again in small, harsh flakes that swirled around the woman as she emerged from Conway Street into Fitzroy Square. She pulled her fur collar up around her neck and thought that, even though she did not care for hats, she should have worn one this morning. There were those who would have suggested that the almost inconsequential lack of judgment was typical of her, and that she probably wanted to draw attention to herself, what with that thick copper-coloured hair cascading in damp waves across her shoulders – and no thought for propriety. But the truth was that, despite drawing glances wherever she went, on this occasion, rather like yesterday morning, and the morning before, she really didn't want to be seen. Well, not until she was ready, anyway.

She crossed the square, walking with care lest she slip on slush-covered flagstones, then halted alongside iron railings that surrounded the winter-barren garden. The inquiry agent Dame Constance had instructed – yes, *instructed* her to see, for when the abbess spoke, there was never a mere suggestion – worked from a room in the building she now surveyed. She had been told by the investigator's assistant that she should come to the first-floor office at nine on Monday morning. When she had canceled the appointment, he had calmly suggested the same time on the following day. And when, at the last minute, she had canceled the second appointment, he simply moved the time by twenty-four hours. She was intrigued that an accomplished woman with a growing reputation would employ a man with such a common dialect. In fact, such flight in the face of convention served as reassurance in her decision to follow the direction of Dame Constance. She had, after all, never set any stock by convention.

It was as she paced back and forth in front of the building, wondering whether today she would have the courage to see Maisie Dobbs – and lack of pluck wasn't something that had dogged her in the past – that she looked up and saw a woman in the first-floor office, standing by the floor-to-ceiling window looking out across the square. There was something about this woman that intrigued her. There she was, simply contemplating the square, her gaze directed at first up to the leafless trees, then at a place in the distance.

Sweeping a lock of windblown hair from her face, the visitor continued to watch the woman at the window. She wondered if that was her way, if that window was her place to stand and think. She suspected it was. It struck her that the woman in the window was the person she had come to see, Maisie Dobbs. Shivering again, she pushed her hands deep inside the copious sleeves of her coat, and began to turn away. But then, as if commanded to do so by a force she could feel but not see, she looked up at the window once more. Maisie Dobbs was staring directly at *her* now, and raising her hand in a manner so compelling that the visitor could not leave, could do nothing but meet the other woman's eyes in return. And in that moment, as Maisie Dobbs captured her with her gaze, she felt a warmth flood her body, and was filled with confidence that she could walk across any terrain, cross any divide and be held steady; it was as if, in lifting her hand, Maisie Dobbs had promised that from the first step in her direction, she would be safe. She began to move forward, but faltered as she looked down at the flagstones. Turning to leave, she was surprised to hear a voice behind her, petitioning her to stop simply by speaking her name.

"Miss Bassington-Hope . . ."

It was not a sharp voice, brittle with cold and frozen in the bitter breath of winter, but instead exuded a strength that gave the visitor confidence, as if she were indeed secure.

"Yes –" Georgina Bassington-Hope looked up into the eyes of the woman she had just been watching in the window, the woman to whom she had been directed. She had been told that Maisie Dobbs would provide a refuge wherein to share her suspicions, and would prove them to be right, or wrong, as the case may be.

"Come." It was an instruction given in a manner that was neither sharp nor soft, and Georgina found that she was mesmerized as Maisie, holding a pale blue cashmere wrap around her shoulders, stood unflinching in windblown snow that was becoming an icy sleet, all the while continuing to extend her hand, palm up, to gently receive her visitor. Georgina Bassington-Hope said nothing, but reached out toward the woman who would lead her across the threshold and through the door alongside which a nameplate bore the words MAISIE DOBBS, PSYCHOLOGIST AND INVESTIGATOR. And she instinctively understood that she had been directed well, that she would be given leave to describe the doubt-ridden wilderness in which she had languished since that terrible moment when she knew in her heart – knew before anyone had told her – that the one who was most dear to her, who knew her as well as she knew herself and with whom she shared all secrets, was dead.

ONE

"Good morning, Miss Bassington-'ope. Come on in out of that cold." Billy Beale, Maisie Dobbs's assistant, stood by the door to the first-floor office as Maisie allowed the visitor to ascend the stairs before her.

"Thank you." Georgina Bassington-Hope glanced at the man, and thought his smile to be infectious, his eyes kind.

"I've brewed a fresh pot of tea for us."

"Thank you, Billy, that will be just the ticket, it's brassy out there today." Maisie smiled in return at Billy as she directed Georgina into the room.

Three chairs had been set by the gas fire and the tea tray placed on Maisie's desk. As soon as her coat was taken and hung on the hook behind the door, Georgina settled in the middle chair. There was a camaraderie between the investigator and her assistant that intrigued the visitor. The man clearly admired his employer, though it did not appear to be a romantic fondness. But there was a bond, and Georgina Bassington-Hope, her journalist's eye at work, thought that perhaps the nature of their work had forged a mutual dependence and regard – though there was no doubt that the woman was the boss.

She turned her attention to Maisie Dobbs, who was collecting a fresh manila folder and a series of coloured pencils, along with a clutch of index cards and paper. Her black wavy hair had probably been cut in a bob some time ago but was now in need of a trim. Did she not care to keep up with a hairdressing regime? Or was she simply too busy with her work? She wore a cream silk blouse with a long blue cashmere cardigan, a black skirt with kick pleats and black shoes with a single strap across to secure them. It was a stylish ensemble, but one that marked the investigator as someone who set more stock by comfort than fashion.

Rejoining Georgina, Maisie said nothing until her assistant had seen that the guest had tea and was comfortable. Georgina did not want to confirm her suspicions by staring, but she thought the woman was sitting with her eyes closed, just for a moment, as if in deep thought. She felt that same sensation of warmth enter her body once more, and opened her mouth to ask a question, but instead expressed gratitude.

"I'm much obliged to you for agreeing to see me, Miss Dobbs. Thank you."

Maisie smiled graciously. It was not a broad smile, not in the way that the assistant had welcomed her, but the woman thought it indicated a person completely in her element.

"I have come to you in the hope that you might be able to help me. . . ." She turned to face Maisie directly. "You have been recommended by someone we both know from our Girton days, actually."

"Might that person have been Dame Constance?" Maisie inclined her head.

"However did you know?" Georgina seemed puzzled.

"We rekindled our acquaintance last year. I always looked forward to her lessons, and especially the fact that we had to go to the abbey to see her. It was a fortuitous connection that the order had moved to Kent." Maisie allowed a few seconds to pass. "So why did you visit Dame Constance, and what led her to suggest you should seek me out?"

"I must say, I would have had teeth pulled rather than attend her tutorials. However, I went to see her when . . ." She swallowed, and began to speak again. "It is in connection with my brother's . . . my brother's —" She could barely utter another word. Maisie reached behind her into a black shoulder bag hanging across the back of her chair and pulled out a handkerchief, which she placed on Georgina's knee. As the woman picked up the pressed handkerchief, the fragrant aroma of lavender was released into the air. She sniffed, dabbed her eyes and continued speaking. "My brother died several weeks ago, in early December. A verdict of accidental death has been recorded." She turned to Maisie, then Billy, as if to ensure they were both listening, then stared into the gas fire. "He is — was — an artist. He was working late on the night before the opening of his first major exhibition in years and, it appears, fell from scaffolding that had been set up at the gallery to allow him to construct his main piece." She paused. "I needed to speak to someone who might help me navigate this . . . this . . . doubt. And Dame Constance suggested I come to you." She paused. "I have discovered that there was little to be gained from badgering the police, and the man who was called when my brother was found seemed only too pleased when I told him I was going to talk to an inquiry agent — I think he was glad to get me out of his sight, to tell you the truth."

"And who was the policeman?" The investigator held her pen ready to note the name.

"Detective Inspector Richard Stratton, of Scotland Yard."

"Stratton was pleased to learn that you were coming to see me?"

Georgina was intrigued by the faint blush revealed when Maisie looked up from her notes, her midnight-blue eyes even darker under forehead creases when she frowned. "Well, y-yes, and as I said, I think he was heartily sick of me peppering him with questions."

Maisie made another note before continuing. "Miss Bassington-Hope, perhaps you could tell me how you wish me to assist you – how can I help?"

Georgina sat up straight in the chair, and ran her fingers back through thick, drying hair that was springing into even richer copper curls as the room became warmer. She pulled at the hem of her nutmeg-brown tweed jacket, then smoothed soft brown trousers where the fabric fell across her knees. "I believe Nicholas was murdered. I do not think he fell accidentally at all. I believe someone pushed him, or caused him to fall deliberately." She looked up at Maisie once more. "My brother had friends and enemies. He was a passionate artist and those who expose themselves so readily are often as much reviled as admired. His work drew both accolades and disgust, depending upon the interpreter. I want you to find out how he died."

Maisie nodded, still frowning. "I take it there is a police report."

"As I said, Detective Inspector Stratton was called –"

"Yes, I was wondering about that, the fact that Stratton was called to the scene of an accident."

"It was early and he was the detective on duty apparently," added Georgina. "By the time he'd arrived, the pathologist had made a preliminary inspection. . . ." She looked down at the crumpled handkerchief in her hands.

"But I am sure Detective Inspector Stratton conducted a thorough investigation. How do you think I might assist you?"

Georgina tensed, the muscles in her neck becoming visibly taut. "I thought you might say that. Devil's advocate, aren't you?" She leaned back, showing some of the nerve for which she was renowned. Georgina Bassington-Hope, intrepid traveller and journalist, became infamous at twenty-two when she disguised herself as a man to gain a closer view of the lines of battle in Flanders than any other reporter. She brought back stories that were not of generals and battles, but of the men, their struggle, their bravery, their fears and the truth of life as a soldier at war. Her dispatches were published in journals and newspapers the world over and, like her brother's masterpieces, her work drew as much criticism as admiration, and her reputation grew as both brave storyteller and naive opportunist.

"I know what I want, Miss Dobbs. I want the truth and will find it myself if I have to. However, I also know my limitations and I believe in using the very best tools when they are available – price notwithstanding. And I believe you are the best." She paused briefly to reach for her cup of tea, which she held in both hands, cradling the china. "And I believe – because I have done my homework – that you ask questions that others fail to ask and see things that others are blind to." Georgina Bassington-Hope looked back at Billy briefly, then turned to Maisie once again, her voice firm, her eyes unwavering. "Nick's work was extraordinary, his views well known though his art was his voice. I want you to find out who killed him, Miss Dobbs – and bring them to justice."

Maisie closed her eyes, pausing for a few seconds before speaking again. "You were very close, it seems."

Georgina's eyes sparkled. "Oh, yes, we were close, Miss Dobbs. Nick was my twin. Two peas in a pod. He worked with colour, texture and light, I work with words." She paused. "And it has occurred to me that whoever killed my brother may well want to silence me too."

Maisie nodded, acknowledging the comment deliberately added to intrigue her, then she stood up, moved away from the fire and walked across to the window. It was snowing again, settling on the ground to join the brown slush that seeped into shoe leather only too readily. Billy smiled at their guest and pointed to the teapot, indicating that perhaps she might like another cup. He had been taking notes throughout the conversation, and now knew his job was to keep their guest calm and quiet while Maisie had a moment with her thoughts. Finally, she turned from the window.

"Tell me, Miss Bassington-Hope: why were you so reticent to keep your appointments? You cancelled twice, yet you came to

Fitzroy Square in any case. What caused you to renege on your contract with yourself on two – almost three – occasions?"

Georgina shook her head before replying. "I have no proof. I have nothing to go on, so to speak – and I am a person used to dealing with facts. There's a paucity of clues – indeed, I would be the first to admit, this looks like a classic accident, a careless move by a tired man using a rather precarious ledge upon which to balance while preparing to hang a work that had taken years to achieve." She paused briefly before continuing. "I have nothing except this." She pressed her hand to her chest. "A feeling here, right in my heart, that all is not as it should be, that this accident was murder. I believe I knew the very second that my brother died, for I experienced such an ache at what transpired, according to the pathologist, to be the time of his death. And I did not know how I might explain such things and be taken seriously."

Maisie approached Georgina Bassington-Hope and gently laid a hand on her shoulder. "Then you have most definitely come to the right place in that case. In my estimation, that feeling in your heart is the most significant clue and all we need to take on your case." She looked at Billy and nodded, whereupon he flipped over a new card. "Now then, let us begin. First of all, let me tell you about my terms and the conditions of our contract."

MAISIE DOBBS HAD been in business as a psychologist and investigator for almost two years, having previously been apprenticed to her mentor since childhood. Dr Maurice Blanche was not only an expert in legal medicine, but himself a psychologist and philosopher who had provided a depth of learning and opportunity that might otherwise have been unavailable to his protégée. Now, with a steady stream of clients seeking her services, Maisie had cause for optimism. Although the country was in the grip of economic depression, there were those of a certain class who barely felt the deepening crisis – people like Georgina

Bassington-Hope – which in turn meant that there was still plenty of business for an investigator with a growing reputation. The only dark cloud was one she hoped would remain at a good distance. During the autumn of the previous year, her own shell shock had reared up, resulting in a debilitating breakdown. It was this malaise, compounded by a rift with Blanche, that had led to a loss of trust in her mentor. Though in many ways she welcomed the newfound independence in the distance from him, there were times when she looked back at the rhythm of their work, at the rituals and processes, with an ache, with regret. At the outset of a case, following a preliminary conversation with the new client, Maurice would often suggest a walk or, if the weather was poor, simply a change in the seating arrangement. "As soon as that contract is signed, Maisie, we shoulder the weight of our load, open the gate and choose our path. We must therefore move the body to engage our curiosity again after taking on the task of administrator."

Now, with the contract signed by both Maisie and Georgina Bassington-Hope and poor weather preventing all possibility of a walk, Maisie suggested the trio move to the table by the window to continue the conversation.

Later, after the new client had left, Maisie and Billy would unfurl a length of plain wallpaper across the table, pin the edges to the wood, and begin to formulate a case map of known facts, thoughts, feelings, hunches and questions. As the work went on, more information would be added, with the mosaic eventually yielding up previously unseen connections pointing to the truths that heralded closure of the case. *If* all went well.

Maisie had already jotted some initial questions on an index card, though she knew that many more would come to mind with each response from her new client. "Miss Bassington-Hope –"

"*Georgina*, please. 'Miss Bassington-Hope' is a bit of a mouthful, and if we are to be here for any length of time, I would rather dispense with the formalities." The woman looked from Maisie to Billy.

Billy glanced at Maisie in a way that made his discomfort at the suggestion obvious.

Maisie smiled. "Yes, of course, as you wish. And you may call me Maisie." Though she was not at all sure she was really open to such an informality, her client's preference must be honored. If she were relaxed, information would flow more readily. Both women now looked at Billy, who blushed.

"Well, if you don't mind, I think I'll stick to your proper name." He looked at Maisie for guidance, then turned to the woman again. "But you can call me Billy if you like, Miss Bassington-'ope."

Georgina smiled, understanding the predicament she had placed them in. "All right, then, Billy – and how about just 'Miss B-H' for me."

"Right you are. Miss B-H it is."

Maisie cleared her throat. "Well, now that we have that little conundrum out of the way, let's get on. Georgina, first I want you to tell me as much as you know about the circumstances of your brother's death."

The woman nodded. "Nick has – had – been preparing for this exhibition for some time, over a year, in fact. His work was becoming very well known, especially in America – there are still a fair few millionaires and they are buying up everything from poor old Europe, it seems. Anyway, Stig Svenson of Svenson's Gallery on Albemarle Street – he's more or less Nick's regular dealer – offered him a special exhibition that comprised both earlier and new works. Nick jumped at the chance, especially as he thought the gallery would be the ideal place to unveil a piece he has been working on, one way or another, for years."

Maisie and Billy exchanged glances, and Maisie interjected with a question. "Why was it perfect for his work? What did the gallery have that made him so excited?"

"Stig had just had the whole place ripped apart and painted – and Nick had already made it clear that he needed a certain amount of room for the new pieces." Georgina held out her arms to help describe the gallery. "Essentially, there are two sort of square bay windows at the front – they're huge – with a door in between, so you can clearly see in from the street, though you cannot view each individual piece. Svenson has – as you might imagine – a very modern, Scandinavian idea of how to use room. It's very bright, every inch of his gallery modeled to display a piece to its advantage. He's had the latest electric lighting installed, and fittings that direct beams in such a way as to create shadows and light to draw buyers in." She paused, to see if her audience of two were keeping up. "So, at the far end there is one huge blank wall almost two floors high for larger pieces, then on both sides a galleried landing, so that you walk in as if you are walking into a theatre, only there are no seats and you are not on a gradient – and it's *completely* white. You can go to either side, up stairs to the landings, but there are screens to divide the room in sections so that you never actually see the whole pièce de résistance – if there is one – until the end. All very clever."

"Yes, I see." Maisie paused, tapped her pen against the palm of her left hand, then spoke again. "Would you describe his 'pièce de résistance' for us?"

Georgina shook her head. "Actually, I can't. As far as I know, no one had seen it in its entirety. He was very secretive about it. That was why he was at the gallery until late – he wanted to construct it himself." She paused thoughtfully, her hand on her mouth, then she looked up. "The only thing I know about it is that it was in several pieces."

"But I thought you said he was working on it when he died. Wouldn't it still be at the gallery?"

"Sorry, what I meant was that he was working on scaffolding, placing the many anchors that would secure the pieces when he brought them in. He had them in storage in London – frankly, I have no idea where."

"Who would know where? Svenson?"

She shook her head. "That's a bit of a mystery at the moment. No one can find the key, and no one knows the address. We just knew he had a lock-up or something somewhere. I know he wanted it all to be kept under wraps until the last moment so that it would draw even more attention – I think he imagined the gasps, if you know what I mean."

"I see, and –"

"The trouble is," Georgina interrupted, "he had already promised most of the collection – except that main piece – to a collector of his work, sight unseen."

"You mean, someone made an offer without first viewing the collection?"

"They'd seen preliminary sketches, but not of the centrepiece."

"Was it a significant offer?"

The woman nodded. "Some tens of thousands of pounds, to my knowledge."

Maisie's eyes grew large and, glancing at Billy, she thought he might pass out.

". . . For a painting?"

Georgina Bassington-Hope shrugged. "It's what people will pay if they think the work will dramatically increase in value. And the buyer has the money, had already paid a deposit, which Svenson retains until delivery."

"Who was the buyer?"

"A man called Randolph Bradley. He's an American living in Paris, though he also has a home in New York. One of those back-and-forth people." She ran her fingers through her hair and looked away.

Billy rolled his eyes. "I think I'll put the kettle on again." He stood up and left the room, taking the tea tray with him. Maisie said nothing. Though she understood his annoyance at such amounts of money passing hands in such troubled times, she was dismayed that he had felt it necessary to leave the room. Maisie made small talk, a series of barely consequential questions, until he returned.

"Several pieces? So, was this 'piece' like a jigsaw puzzle, Miss

B-H?" Billy set a cup of hot tea in front of Georgina and the customary tin mug in front of Maisie. He placed his own cup on the table and took up his notes again. Maisie was relieved that he had been thinking as he made tea, and not just fuming with resentment.

Georgina nodded. "Well, yes, you could say that. Before the war, Nick was studying art in Europe. He was in Belgium when war was declared, and he returned home very quickly." She shook her head. "Anyway, in Belgium he became very interested in the triptych form."

"Triptych?" Maisie and Billy spoke in unison.

"Yes," continued Georgina. "A triptych comprises three parts, a centre main panel with smaller panels on either side. The stories depicted on the smaller panels give more detail to the scene in the main panel, or augment it in some way."

"Bit like the mirror on a dressing table, eh, Miss B-H?"

The woman smiled. "Yes, that's right – though a stained-glass window in a church might be a better description. Triptychs are often religious in nature, though many are quite gory, with scenes of war, or execution of someone important at the time – a king, perhaps, or a warrior."

"Yes, I've seen some in the museums. I know what you're talking about." Maisie paused, making a note to come back to Nicholas Bassington-Hope's background as soon as she had a sense of the circumstances of his death. "So, let's continue with his death – he was at the gallery – what happened, as far as the inquest revealed?"

"There was scaffolding against the main wall. All of the smaller, less important pieces had been placed, and Nick was working on the main wall, as I told you. The scaffolding was there so that he could situate the pieces correctly."

"And would he do this alone?"

"Yes, that was his plan. Though he had help with the scaffolding."

"Wouldn't Svenson have arranged for workers to set up the scaffolding?"

"No." Georgina paused. "Well – yes, usually he probably would, but this time he didn't."

"Why?"

She shook her head. "You don't know Nick. Has to do it all himself, wanted to ensure that his scaffolding was in the right place, that it was strong and that there was nowhere the work could be compromised by the structure."

"And he had help?"

"Yes, his friends Alex and Duncan helped."

"Alex and Duncan?" Maisie glanced at Billy to ensure that he remained attentive. If they both took notes, then nothing would be missed as they studied the cache of information later.

"Alex Courtman and Duncan Haywood. Both artists, Nick's neighbors in Dungeness, where he lived. His other friend, Quentin Trayner, had a twisted ankle and couldn't help. He'd fallen while bringing a boat ashore." She paused briefly. "The three of them always helped one another out. They were all artists, you see."

"And they all lived at Dungeness – in Kent? It's a bit bleak and isolated, isn't it?"

"And freezing cold at this time of year, I shouldn't wonder!" Billy interjected.

"There's quite an artists' haven there, you know. Has been for a few years now. In fact, when the Rye to Dungeness railway closed down – I think in '26 or '27 – they sold off the railway carriages for ten pounds apiece, and a few artists bought them to set up as houses and studios on the beach." Georgina paused and her voice cracked, just slightly, so that both Maisie and Billy had to lean forward to better hear her. "I called it the 'place where lost souls were beached.'" Georgina leaned back in her chair. "They were men of an artistic sensibility who had been drafted by the government to do its dirty work, and afterward all four of them were left feeling sick about it for years."

"What do you mean?" asked Maisie.

Georgina leaned forward. "Nick, Quentin, Duncan and Alex met at the Slade, that's how they forged such a strong friendship. And they had all seen service in France. Nick was wounded at the Somme and was sent to work in propaganda after he'd healed – he was no longer fit for active duty. Alex worked there too. Then Nick was sent back over to Flanders as a war artist." She shook her head. "It changed him forever, that's why he had to get away after the war, to America."

"America?"

"Yes, he said he needed lots of space around him."

Maisie nodded and flicked back through her notes. "Look, Miss – Georgina – I suggest we complete our notes on the actual events of your brother's death today, then let us make another appointment to talk about his history. That will give you time to gather other items that might be of interest to us – journals, sketchbooks, letters, photographs, that sort of thing."

"All right."

"So . . ." Maisie stood up, placed her index cards next to her teacup and walked to the other side of the table to look across at the snow-covered square. "Your brother, Nick, was working late, preparing the gallery's main wall to hang a piece – pieces – of his art, which no one had seen yet. At what time did he arrive to do this work? Who else was with him? And what time, according to the pathologist, did he die – and how?"

Georgina gave a single nod as she sipped her tea, set her cup down again and began to answer Maisie's questions as directly as they were asked. "He had been there all day, since dawn, hanging the pieces. They had set up the scaffolding later in the day, according to Duncan and Alex, who said he told them to return to my flat around half past eight – it wasn't unusual for Nick to bring friends to stay at my flat and they had turned up the night before with their knapsacks. My home is a convenient London bolt-hole for all sorts of people." She paused, took another sip of tea, and went on. "The gallery caretaker, Arthur Levitt, said that he looked in on Nick around nine and told him he was ready to go home. Nick replied that he had a key and would lock up."

There was silence for a moment, a hiatus that Maisie allowed to linger in the air as the narrator sought strength to recount the loss of her brother. Georgina Bassington-Hope pulled at the handkerchief Maisie had passed to her earlier and shifted in her chair.

"Detective Richard Stratton from Scotland Yard was on my doorstep at eight the following morning, with news that there had been an accident. I don't think he usually deals with accidents, but came out all the same as he was on duty when the alarm was raised by Mr Levitt when he came in and found Nick. . . ."

Maisie spoke softly. "Can you tell me how he described finding your brother?"

"On the floor below the scaffolding. Part of the rail was broken and it looked as if Nick had leaned back a bit too far while checking the position of some anchors against a guide that he had already drafted on paper. His neck had been broken and it is thought that he died instantly when he hit the stone floor, probably around ten-ish, according to the pathologist." She shook her head. "Damn him for being so secretive! It was all this business of wanting there to be a big ooh-ahh when the triptych was revealed to the world that killed him. If he hadn't been there alone . . ."

"Georgina, let's summon a taxi-cab to take you home." Sensing a weariness in her client that was not physical but rooted in her soul, Maisie leaned across and placed her hand on Georgina's shoulder. "We'll speak again tomorrow – and perhaps we should meet at the gallery, if it isn't too difficult for you. Would ten be convenient?"

Georgina nodded, feeling the now familiar warmth flood her body again as Maisie touched her. Billy stood up and pulled on his overcoat before making his way out to Tottenham Court Road to hail a taxi-cab. Maisie helped Georgina into her coat and picked up the collection of index cards to pen some additional notes.

"Everything you've described points to an accident. The intensity of your sense that it was not a misstep by your brother that caused his death is compelling to me, which is why I am taking on this case. However, when we meet tomorrow, and in our future meetings – for there will be a few – I would like to know if you are aware of anyone who might harbour an intensity of feeling about your brother, or his work, which might have led to a desire to see him dead, either by accident or a deliberate act."

"Yes, I've been thinking about that, I –"

"Good. Now then. One final question today – may I have details of your family? I will need to meet them."

"Of course, though don't expect to make too much headway – they do not share my feelings and would be horrified if they knew I had come to an inquiry agent." She buttoned her coat as they heard the door slam and Billy make his way back up the stairs. "My parents live on an impossibly large estate just outside Tenterden in Kent. Noelle – 'Nolly' – my older sister, lives with them. She's forty now, lost her husband in the war. She's nothing like the rest of us, very proper, very county, if you know what I mean. She's a justice of the peace at the local magistrates' courts, sits on all sorts of local committees and gets involved in politics; you've met the sort – bit of a know-all. And she heartily disapproves of me. My brother Harry is the baby, the child who came along when everyone least expected it, according to Emsy – that's Emma, my mother. Harry is twenty-nine now and a musician. Not classical, no, much to Nolly's dismay he plays the trumpet in dark places where people have fun and enjoy themselves."

Billy came into the room, a coating of fresh snowflakes across his shoulders. "Taxi-cab's outside, Miss B-H."

"Thank you, B –, Mr Beale." Georgina Bassington-Hope shook hands with Billy, then addressed Maisie. "See you at ten tomorrow morning at Svenson's Gallery on Albemarle Street." She paused for just a moment, plunging her hands inside her coat sleeves once again. "I know you will find out the truth, Maisie. And I know you will find his killer, of that I am sure."

Maisie nodded, moved as if to return to her desk, then turned back. "Georgina, forgive me – one last question, if I may."

"Of course."

"You were obviously close to your brother, you've said as much, but, were you on good terms when he died?"

The woman's eyes reddened. "Of course." She nodded her head. "We were close, so close that we never had to explain ourselves to each other. We just *knew* about each other, to the point of perceiving what the other one was thinking, even when we were miles apart." Georgina Bassington-Hope looked at Billy, who opened the door to accompany her downstairs to the waiting taxi-cab.

When Billy came back to the office, he was shaking his head. "Well, what do you think about all that, Miss?"

Maisie was now seated at the paper drawn across the table to form the case map, working with coloured pencils to add notes to a small but growing diagram. "It's too soon to say, Billy, too soon to even begin to draw conclusions." She looked up. "Come and help me pin this paper onto the table."

Billy smoothed his hand across the paper to remove folds before pinning the edges and studied his employer's preliminary notations as he worked. "What do we do next?"

Maisie smiled. "Well, here's what we'll be doing this afternoon – we're off to the Tate to learn a bit more than we know already about art."

"Oh, Miss . . ."

"Come on, Billy, an hour or two spent in contemplation of the great world of art will do us both the power of good on this grey old day."

"If you say so, Miss. You never know, you might find something nice for them bare walls of yours!" Billy patted the case map as he pressed in the last pin, then moved from the table and collected Maisie's coat, which he held out for her.

"I think the bare walls are there to stay for a while, Billy. Furniture is top of my list for the new flat at the moment." Maisie laughed as she buttoned her coat, collected her hat, scarf, gloves and document case. "Now then, let's go and find a triptych or two. With a bit of luck we'll find an amenable curator who will educate us about the people who can afford to buy such things without even looking at the goods or balking at the price!"

TWO

Maisie and Billy left Fitzroy Square at half past nine the following morning, each wrapped up in a heavy coat, scarf
and hat.

"Nippy, innit, Miss?"

Maisie's eyes watered. "Yes, and the so-called central heating system in my flat is not working properly – mind you, I thought it was
too good to be true."

Billy stood aside for Maisie to go through the turnstile at Warren
Street tube station before him, then they stepped onto the wooden
escalator, one behind the other.

"P'raps the main boiler weren't put in right, what with the
builder goin' bust like 'e did."

Maisie turned around to continue the conversation as the escalator clattered down to the platforms. "Wouldn't surprise me. I
jumped at the chance to buy when the flats came up for sale, but
there's no proper system yet for those collective repairs, such as the
heating that isn't! I have discovered that bankers aren't very good at
being managers of property. They were probably thrilled when buy-

ers came along but didn't really think about what came next, only about recouping their money. Thank heavens there's a gas fire, because my radiators are stone cold!"

Billy put his hand behind his ear. "Aye-oop, Miss, 'ere we go, train coming in." Stepping off the escalator, they ran to the platform and clambered aboard the waiting carriage, each taking a seat before Billy continued. "We've 'ad the fires going nonstop. Doreen's been rushed off 'er feet, what with the nippers going down with one thing after the other. O'course, I don't think that coal smoke is good for you at all, but our little Lizzie is a bit poorly now."

"What's wrong with her?" Maisie had a soft spot for the Beales' youngest child, who was barely two years old.

"Doreen thinks it's a bit of a chill. Both the boys've 'ad chesty colds, so we think that Lizzie 'as copped it now. Poor scrap, even turned 'er nose up at a bit of bread and dripping for 'er tea yesterday."

The train slowed to a halt, and as they alighted to change trains for Green Park, Maisie instructed Billy, "Look, when we're finished here, we'll go back to the office to get everything on the case map, then you should go home early to give Doreen a hand. And keep an eye on Lizzie's cold – there are some nasty things going round and she's young to have to fight some of them off. Keep the windows closed and put some Friars Balsam in a bowl of hot water next to her cot – that'll clear all your noses!"

"Right you are, Miss." Billy looked away. Lizzie was the apple of his eye and he was clearly worried about her. They continued on their way in silence.

As they walked down Albemarle Street, their talk was of the terrible state of London traffic and how it was easier now to ride by tube or travel by "shanks's pony" rather than use the motor car or even a bus. They noticed Svenson's Gallery some yards before coming to a halt alongside the building, for the once-red bricks had been painted bright white.

"Gaw, I bet the neighbors 'ad something to say about that. Bit stark, innit?"

"Yes, I think I much prefer the original brick with a white sign for contrast. This is rather clinical, if you ask me." Maisie looked both ways, anticipating the arrival of Georgina Bassington-Hope, then turned to Billy. "Look, I want you to find your way to the back of the building – there must be some kind of alley, an entrance for deliveries and so on. See if you can locate the caretaker. I want you to get to know him, talk to him about the gallery, see if you can get some inside information regarding Svenson, and also – needless to say – the night of Nicholas Bassington-Hope's death." She paused, reaching into her case. "You might need a few shillings to oil his vocal cords, so take this –" Maisie handed Billy several coins. "We don't want to overdo it, this is man to man, you and him having a chin-wag together – all right?"

Billy nodded. "Consider it done, Miss. I'll come back to the front 'ere to find you when I'm finished."

"Good. You'd better be off before Miss B-H gets here."

Billy cast a glance in either direction and continued on down Albemarle Street. As she watched him leave, Maisie saw him bear the weight of concern for his daughter, as if carrying a burden across his shoulders. She hoped the child would improve soon, but knew the East End of London to be a breeding ground for disease, with its proximity to the damp and filth of the Thames and with houses and people almost on top of one another. She understood that Billy was worried about the cost of a doctor, if it came to it, and how they would manage. Not for the first time, she was thankful that her business was doing well and that she was able to employ Billy – she knew he might be in the dole queue if the situation were different.

"Good morning, Maisie!" A taxi-cab screeched to a halt, and Georgina Bassington-Hope was calling to Maisie from the open window.

"Ah, good morning, Georgina. How was your journey?"

The woman alighted onto the pavement, paid the driver and turned to Maisie. "You wouldn't think it would take so long to get from Kensington to Albemarle Street. Heaven only knows where the traffic comes from – and they thought the horseless carriage would be the answer to London's congestion problems!"

Maisie smiled and held out her gloved hand toward the gallery. "Let's go inside."

Georgina placed her hand on Maisie's arm. "Just a moment –" She bit her lip. "Look, it would be best if Stig isn't told who you are. It would give him an attack of the Viking vapors if he thinks I've asked a professional to look into Nick's 'accident'. He's bound to come out of his office – he's always on the lookout for a sale – so we'll let him think you are an interested buyer."

Maisie nodded. "All right. Now then, I'm freezing out here –"

The two women entered the gallery and were immediately met by Svenson. As befitted his profession, he was impeccably turned out. His grey trousers were pressed so that the front crease appeared sharp enough to cut a mature cheese. He wore a blue blazer-style jacket, a white shirt and pale blue tie with a matching kerchief placed in the chest pocket with a certain panache. Maisie suspected he dressed with immense care, knowing that he must convey the flair of an artist along with the perceived gravity of a businessman.

Svenson ran his fingers through his silver-blond hair as he walked toward the women. "Georgie, darling, how are you bearing up?" He leaned to kiss Georgina on both cheeks, taking her hands in his own and speaking with only the barest trace of an accent.

"I'm as well as can be expected, Stig." She turned to Maisie, withdrawing her hands from his grasp. "This is an old friend from my days at Girton, Miss Maisie Dobbs."

Svenson leaned toward Maisie, and as he took her right hand, instead of the expected handshake, he pressed his lips to her slender knuckles. Like Georgina, she withdrew her hand quickly.

"Delighted to meet you, Mr Svenson." Maisie looked around at the paintings exhibited, chiefly landscapes depicting country scenes. "Your gallery is most impressive."

"Thank you." He held out his hand for the women to walk farther into the gallery. "Are you a collector, Miss Dobbs?"

Maisie smiled. "Not a collector, as such, though I have recently moved and have a few bare walls to do something with."

"Then I am sure I can help you fill them; however, this entire collection was purchased yesterday."

"The whole collection? Goodness me!"

"Yes, as fast as the old families are selling off their collections, so the American new money is buying it up – even in an economic slump, there are always those who continue to do well, who still have money to spend."

"Is it usual for one person to buy a whole collection, Mr Svenson?" Maisie was surprised, but conceded that her knowledge of the art world was limited – two hours at the Tate gallery yesterday afternoon notwithstanding.

"Yes and no." He smiled at Maisie in a way that suggested he had embarked upon such conversations many times and had pat responses up his sleeve ready to present at a moment's notice. "Yes, in that once a collector becomes enthusiastic about a given artist, they look out for more of his work, especially if that artist is on the cusp of a wider fame." Svenson turned to Georgina. "Such as our dear Nicholas, Georgie." He brought his attention back to Maisie. "However, there are also complete collections from certain families or other collectors that are extremely valuable and of great interest when they come onto the market – such as the Guthrie collection here."

"What makes this one valuable?" Maisie was genuinely interested.

"In this case" – he swept his hand around to indicate the paintings throughout the gallery –"it is not only the name of the collector, but their reputation and the interesting blend of pieces. Lady Alicia and her late husband, Sir John Guthrie, never had children and both inherited substantial collections from their respective families. Each was a sole heir. Sir John died last year and Lady Alicia's solicitors have persuaded her to sell in order to set up a trust to support their property in Yorkshire, which I understand has been bequeathed to the county. An American investor was drawn to this collection given its provenance and the fact that some interesting and influential artists are represented here." He smiled again, as if he were about to make a joke. "Not to put too fine a point on it, it's new money buying an instant connection to old money. I am amazed they haven't pressed Lady Alicia to sell the estate, or even her title." Svenson laughed and both Maisie and Georgina indulged the Swede with a brief chuckle.

"Is Nick's work safely in storage now?" Georgina changed the subject.

Svenson nodded. "Yes, indeed, although not for long. A buyer – another American – wants to view and purchase other works not previously exhibited. He's even interested in sketches and partials, and is very keen. I tried to telephone you this morning – in fact, I gave a message to your housekeeper, but you had already left. A confirmatory telegram has been received and I await your instructions. No doubt you will need to speak to your family."

"Does he think he's getting a chance to purchase the triptych?"

"Ah, a thorny subject, especially as we don't know the whereabouts of the main piece at the present time. The buyer has spoken of recruiting a private detective to find the piece, but frankly, I find that rather low, if you don't mind me saying so. I also think our friend Mr Bradley should have first refusal."

Georgina nodded. "Let me have the full details of the offer so that I can discuss it with the family this weekend. I think they may be interested, though I do not wish to include the triptych – Nick was vehement about it."

"Georgie, I must advise you –"

"No, Stig. No triptych. When we find it, I will decide what to do with it." She held up her hand and looked at Maisie, as if to underline the personal value of the piece.

Maisie spoke up, asking a timely question to diffuse the situation. "Mr Svenson –"

"Stig, please."

She smiled accord, then beckoned her companions toward the back of the room, where she pointed to the wall. "Tell me, Stig, is this where the triptych was to be exhibited?"

"Indeed, yes, though do remember, we may not be correct in our assumption that it was a triptych."

"What do you mean?" Georgina's tone seemed short with Svenson as she joined Maisie.

"Nick only ever spoke of the sections or pieces. I – we – always assumed it was a triptych given his work in Belgium before the war, and the influence of Bosch in particular. However, as no one but Nick saw the work, as far as we know, it may be some other arrangement of pieces, like a collage or sectional landscape."

"Of course, I understand." Maisie touched Georgina's arm as she spoke, hoping to neutralize the unbecoming edge demonstrated by her client's earlier remark. "Mr Svenson, how many pieces were there in this exhibition, all told?"

"Counting the sketches and fragments, all of which were included, there were twenty pieces."

"And all in the same style?" Maisie wondered whether she was using the correct terminology, but suspected that Svenson was one of those people who could become quite puffed up in his role of expert and would make the most of her naïveté.

"Oh, no, that was the interesting thing about this exhibit: it comprised works from all stages of Nick's life as an artist. Some were kept back from previous collections, and together with early experimental efforts and new pieces, they demonstrated the arc of his artistic gift. One could see how the professional accomplished artist was formed from an extraordinary raw talent."

"I see. Of course, I know about Nick's paintings from Georgina's descriptions, but have never seen any exhibited." She turned to Georgina. "I do hope this is not too difficult for you, dear."

Georgina smiled, understanding that Maisie had spoken with such intimacy so that Svenson would not doubt the authenticity of their friendship. She replied in the same vein. "Oh no, not at all, in fact, it's all rather lovely, you know, talking about Nick's work when all I have really thought about is that terrible accident."

"So, Mr Svenson," Maisie continued. "I'd love to hear more about the work that was on display before the accident."

"Yes, of course." He cleared his throat and directed his full attention to Maisie, though she felt his proximity was rather too close. She took one step backward as he began to detail the artist's life from his perspective. "First there was his interest in those artists from the Low Countries that he studied in Belgium. What is fascinating was that it was not the technique that interested him as much as the crafting of stories each told in a painting, which then led to another story and another painting. Structure was of great interest to him and his early work was rich with curiosity."

"Did he employ the triptych form even then?"

"No, that came later. What he did, and this was interesting, was to paint fragments of stories on one canvas, so that he achieved a rather avant-garde effect. That phase was youthful, and though it reeked of the novice artist, it was also compelling and caused a stir when first exhibited – at this gallery, I might add, though it was in a collective exhibit."

"Interesting . . ."

"Then, sadly, the war intervened and – as you know – Nick enlisted and was sent to France. I still believe it was his good fortune to have sustained an injury serious enough to bring him home. However, I was rather upset when I heard that he had accepted the work of war artist at the front. Mind you, it was an offer that was probably not up for discussion."

"No . . ." Maisie said only enough to keep Svenson talking. She would interview Georgina again later, and compare notes against what she had already learned about the dead man.

"That, of course, was when he grew up, when he became not just a man, but – I am sad to say – an old man." He sighed, as if genuinely pained. "But his work at that time proved to be more than a record, a moment in time to be placed in an archive. No, it became a . . . a . . . mirror. Yes, that is what it became, a mirror, a reflection of the very soul of war, of death, if such a thing exists. He became driven, his work no longer light or colourful, but dark, with heavy use of those colours one associates with the very bleakest period in one's life. And of course, red. His work from that period was rich with red."

"Did his technique change? I have not seen those works, so I am trying to imagine them." Maisie leaned forward, and though she was aware of Georgina watching her, she paid her no heed.

"There were elements of the old work, the experimentation. Images superimposed, death a shadow in the background. And that was the thing that was most appealing to both the collector with an artistic sensibility and knowledge, and the rather well-heeled neophyte – Nick's work needed no explanation. None at all. You could see his message, feel his emotions, see what he had seen. He touched you. . . ." Svenson turned to Georgina and placed a hand on her shoulder. "Just as Georgina re-created what she saw with her words, so Nick could do the same with colour and texture. What a family!"

"What came next, from your perspective?" As she continued to question Svenson, Maisie noticed that Georgina had stepped aside, away from his grasp.

"As you know, Nick left the country almost as soon as he received his demobilization papers. America was, frankly, the obvious place for Nick."

"Why do you say that?"

"The space. The sheer enormity of the place." He held out his arms to emphasize an expanse he could not properly describe. "And the possibilities there."

"Possibilities?"

"Yes, this is most interesting to his collectors, that his techniques became so influenced by the American schools at the time, and influenced too, by the sheer geography of the country. Look at his sketches, and you will see the bold landscapes, the use of muted and vivid colours blended to achieve a quality of light that is seen nowhere else in the world. He went alone to canyons, to valleys, across prairies. His view of the world was cast from the dirt, filth and enclosure of the mud and blood-filled trench, to the clear air of the American West, especially Montana, Colorado, New Mexico, California. And that's where he began to experiment with the mural, an extension of his interest in the triptych form of earlier years, if you will. Of course, the mural was being used by many of the emerging American artists at the time."

"And all these different styles" – once again, Maisie hoped she had chosen the correct term –"were on display here when he died? And the whole collection is now under offer, as good as sold?"

"Yes, that's right."

"Look, I hope you don't mind me asking – after all, I haven't seen Georgie in a long time, or Nick, so I am interested – but would you call his work offensive in any way, or controversial?"

Svenson laughed. "Oh, yes, it was most certainly controversial in the art world, and the world outside, as you know." His countenance became more serious and Maisie felt him begin to draw back, as if it had only just occurred to him that she should have known all of this if she were as close a friend as Georgina had suggested – and Georgina had hardly said a word for some time. Nevertheless, he continued, though only to bring the conversation to a close. "Nick drew the onlooker into his world with his paintings, then just at the point when you are lulled by a landscape, perhaps sun rising across a mountain lake, he could quickly challenge you with the next piece, a man screaming his way into death, impaled on the bayonet. That was how he presented his work, that was how he wanted to speak of the angelic and that which is evil. He confused people, he threatened." He shrugged, his hands upturned. "But as you know, Miss Dobbs, that was Nick, and he was an angel when one met him, which is why those who were offended would melt in his company."

Maisie looked at her watch, pinned to the lapel of her jacket. "Oh, gosh, we should be getting on, shouldn't we, Georgina? But I would love to look at the upper galleries before we leave."

"Please, be my guest." Svenson gave a short bow toward Maisie, then turned to Georgina Bassington-Hope. "Georgie, a moment of your time, perhaps?"

Maisie made her way to the galleried landing, then spent a moment standing alongside the balustrade to consider the wall where Nicholas Bassington-Hope was to have exhibited his masterpiece. Was it a triptych, as everyone assumed, or had the secretive artist something else up his sleeve? She leaned forward, squinting to better see certain parts of the wall in closer detail. Yes, she could identify where anchors had been placed in the plasterwork, anchors that had now been removed and the wall made almost smooth again. Fresh repairs were clearly visible, and Maisie wondered whether the damage had been due to the scaffolding, which must have dented the wall as it collapsed when the artist fell – if he fell. How high might the scaffolding have been, and which level had Nick Bassington-Hope been working from when he crashed down to the stone floor? From ground to ceiling, the wall must be some twenty-five feet high, not a height that would necessarily cause a life to be lost as a result of a fall, unless the victim were unusually unlucky. *And if someone had pushed* . . . Maisie now looked at the doors on the main floor below, one exit on either side of the wall, leading, she supposed, to storage and delivery areas and to offices. Could someone have made the scaffolding unstable without being seen by the victim? Might such instability have been accidental? There were clearly several possibilities to consider – not least the possibility that Nicholas Bassington-Hope had taken his own life.

"Oi, Miss –"

Maisie looked around. She could hear Billy, but could not see him, and she didn't want to call out his name.

"Pssst. Miss!"

"Where are you?" Maisie kept her voice as low as possible.

"Over 'ere."

Maisie walked toward a painting at the far end of the landing. Much to her surprise, the painting moved.

"Oh!"

Billy Beale poked his head around what was, in fact, a door. "Thought you'd like that, Miss! Come in 'ere and 'ave a dekko at this 'ere trick door. I tell you, my three would love this."

Maisie followed Billy's direction, stepping as quietly as she could. "What is this?"

"I started off in the storeroom – been down there talking to the caretaker, man by the name of Arthur Levitt. Nice enough bloke. Anyway, I found a staircase, came up it and then along this 'ere corridor. They must use this for bringing up the art and what 'ave you from where it's delivered." He crooked his finger again, closing the door that led onto the balcony. "Look through 'ere."

Maisie leaned forward to the point in the door indicated by Billy. "Oh!" She moved slightly, then stepped back. "You can see a good deal of the gallery from here – as well as having access to the balcony that extends along three sides of the room, right around to the opposite side of the wall where Nicholas Bassington-Hope would have been setting up his main piece."

"Do you reckon it's impor –" Billy stopped speaking when raised voices were heard coming from below. Maisie and Billy both remained perfectly still.

"I told you, Stig, you were to deal with me only. You were not to agree to anything with Nolly."

"But Georgie, Nolly said –"

"I don't give a damn what Nolly said. My sister has no business poking her nose into this. She knows nothing about art."

"But she does have a right, after all, as joint executor –"

"I'll speak to Nolly today. In the meantime, I will not allow the piece to be sold with the rest of the collection. Absolutely not. And if I even think of selling

*the remaining sketches and incompletes, I will let you know. You can keep your
rich buyers hanging on for a day or two if they're that interested."*

"But —"

"That is final, Stig. Now, I had better find my friend."

A door below slammed.

"We'll talk about this later," Maisie leaned toward Billy and whispered. "I'll see you out on Piccadilly in about fifteen minutes. Don't
join me until Miss Bassington-Hope has left."

THE TWO WOMEN departed the gallery, Svenson cordially thanking them for visiting, though perhaps not with the theatrical flourish
of his greeting.

"Let's walk along the street here — I have several requests to
make, in order to commence with my investigation."

"Of course." Georgina fell into step with Maisie, unaware that
the woman to whom she had turned for help was now gauging her
intent and her emotional state of mind simply by observing her
physical demeanor.

"First of all, I want to meet your family, so please arrange for us
to visit, using the pretext of our early friendship at Girton."

"All right."

Maisie cast a glance sideways at Georgina and began mirroring
her movement as she walked. She continued listing her requests. "I
would like to see — alone, this time — where Nicholas lived in Dungeness. Perhaps you would be so kind as to furnish me with keys and
his address — or, knowing Dungeness, perhaps there is no actual address, but simply directions."

Georgina nodded, but said nothing. Maisie had noticed her
shoulders sag, her manner suggesting a sense of melancholy and,
perhaps, a feeling of anger. The melancholy might be easily
explained — she had lost a beloved brother, after all — but at whom
was the anger directed? At Maisie, for making the request? At her
sister for whatever gave rise to the crossed words with Stig Svenson?

Or at her dead brother, for abandoning her to a life without her twin?

"I will need details of all previous purchases of your brother's paintings. I understand that artists can be rather fickle when it comes to retaining financial records; however, I will need anything that comes to hand. I want to know who was collecting his work."

"Of course."

"And I want to see his friends, the men he was closest to. Was he courting, as far as you know?"

Georgina shook her head, and gave a half laugh. "Let's just say that Nick was better with his finances than with his romantic life — 'fickle' would suit very well."

"I see." Maisie knew from experience that the more personal aspects of a person's life were seldom understood by immediate family. Hadn't her own father thought it strange that she was not anxious to become engaged to Andrew Dene by now? She smiled in return, and continued. "And I want to see his work, in addition to those things I mentioned before: correspondence, journals — in fact, anything you have that belonged to Nick."

The women stopped when they reached Piccadilly, where each would go their separate way. "Oh, and one last question for you?"

"Yes?" Georgina turned to face Maisie directly.

"When a person close to the victim suspects foul play, they usually have a suspect or two in mind. Would that be true of you, Georgina?"

She blushed. "I'm afraid it isn't. As I told you yesterday, it was just that feeling here." She touched her chest. "That's all I can say."

Maisie nodded, then smiled. "I'd like to go down to Dungeness tomorrow, so perhaps you can let me have keys at your earliest convenience. Then perhaps we can meet in Tenterden on Saturday — probably best if we visit your parents together. Can you arrange it?"

"Of — of course." Georgina paused, somewhat flustered. She reached into her handbag and took out an envelope, which she passed to Maisie. "This is a photograph of Nick, taken in the summer at Bassington Place, my parents' estate."

Maisie took the envelope, and removed the photograph halfway, claiming a moment to study the man whom the lens had caught leaning in an easy, almost somnolent manner against a tractor. Using the size of the tractor as a guide, Maisie thought he must have been about six feet in height, with hair that was a barely controlled mop of curls on his head, the "short-back-and-sides" haircut having little effect on his crown and fringe. He wore wide trousers, a collarless shirt with rolled-up sleeves and an unbuttoned waistcoat. His smile was expansive and Maisie thought that, if her father were to see the photograph, he might comment that the man had the look of a lout, rather than the well-bred son of good circumstance. Though Frankie Dobbs was a working man, a costermonger by trade and, since the outbreak of war in 1914, a groom at the Compton estate in Kent, he had strong opinions on being properly turned out.

Maisie placed the photograph in her bag and nodded to Georgina. "Good. Now then, I must be on my way. Please telephone me as soon as you can so that we can confirm arrangements and your progress with my list. Until then, Georgina." Maisie held out her hand, which Georgina took in a manner that suggested she was regaining some of the strength and resolve that had propelled her somewhat infamous reputation.

When they were some three or four yards apart, Maisie turned and called to her client. "Oh, Georgina – I want to meet Harry as well."

She had timed her final request perfectly.

Georgina flushed. "I – I'll see what I can do, he's . . . oh, never mind. I'll contact him and let you know." Then she hurried away.

BILLY JOINED MAISIE as she watched Georgina Bassington-Hope being swallowed into a flurry of passersby.

"Miss B-H gone then?"

Maisie nodded, seemingly half dreaming, though Billy knew that the glazed eyes disguised a depth of thought that some might have considered quite unnecessary in the circumstances.

"Everything all right, Miss?"

"Yes, yes, I'm very well, thank you."

They began to walk toward Piccadilly underground station. "She shot off a bit sharpish, didn't she?"

"Hmmm, yes, it was a bit quick. But then it gave us some interesting information."

"What's that, Miss?"

"That, concerning Harry B-H, the family – or perhaps just Georgina – has something to hide." Maisie turned to Billy. "Now then, you know what to do this afternoon, don't you, Billy – usual lines of enquiry with your newspaper friends." She pulled on her gloves. "I'll see you back at the office around three. We'll have a talk about our respective findings, then you can go home early – perhaps Lizzie will be feeling a bit better."

THREE

Having already nurtured contacts among the newspapermen who gathered in Fleet Street pubs – and many of those men, reporters, compositors and printers alike, were at the bar by mid-morning following a night shift – the cost of a pint often proved to be a very good investment, as far as Billy was concerned. Following the meeting at Svenson's Gallery, Billy procured information from newspaper reports pertaining to Nicholas Bassington-Hope's death. For her part, Maisie returned to the Tate gallery to meet with the helpful curator, Dr Robert Wicker, with whom she had consulted the previous day. Now they were back at the Fitzroy Square office comparing notes on the day's work.

"I looked through the obituary, and it didn't say anything that wasn't known to us already. There were a couple of write-ups on 'is paintings, otherwise it was all along the lines of 'a rare talent lost' – you know, that sort of thing." Billy seemed to stifle a yawn. "Mind you, there was a line or two in one of them about the sibling rivalry. I thought it was a bit snide myself. In the *Sketch*, it was. The reporter saying that the B-Hs had always competed to see who could get more attention, and that now there was no twin brother, Miss B-H would probably have the wind knocked out of her sails."

"That doesn't mean that there was anything untoward in the competition though. That sort of thing often happens, I believe."

"Too right, Miss. You should see my boys go at it sometimes."

Maisie smiled and was about to speak again, when Billy continued. "Now then, Brian Hickmott, one of the reporters what I know, did say that 'e remembered the story because 'e went over there, to the gallery, as soon as the press got wind of something going on."

"And?"

"Said it was all very strange. Police didn't stay long, just a quick look, a 'Yes, that's accidental death,' then off they all went, much quicker than 'e would have thought."

"Well, it could be that once they had determined there were no suspicious circumstances, their work was done until the inquest. The body could be released to the family that much earlier, and with little in the way of red tape."

"Per'aps. I'll find out a bit more about it though."

"Good." Maisie looked up at Billy, assessing his interest in the case and therefore his attention to detail. His attitude in the initial meeting, where he revealed some resentment toward the client's social standing, had unsettled her.

"Mind you . . ." Billy sat up straighter as he read through his notes, clearly keen to move on to another point so that he could get home early, as Maisie had suggested. "Brian did mention the younger brother, 'arry."

"What did he say?'

"Well, you know that fella, Jix?"

"The former home secretary Joynson-Hicks? Of course, but what has this to do with the younger brother?"

"It's one of them roundabout stories, Miss. You remember that when 'e was in government, Jix was the one who got the police going round to the clubs and closin' 'em down? Right killjoy was that man, we're better off without the likes of 'im."

"Billy . . ."

"Well, turns out that one of the people old Jix 'ad it in for was Harry B-H. The boy might've been able to carry a tune with that trumpet of 'is, but 'e 'ad a reputation for carryin' on with all sorts of people – you know, girls on the game. And 'e kept the villains entertained while they got up to no good at all. The press 'ad their eyes on 'im too, and 'e'd got a few mentions in the linens, you know, when the police'd raided a club on Jix's orders."

Maisie was thoughtful. "Well, it's funny you should say that, but I confess, since Miss B-H first mentioned him, I have had a sense that all was not well with the brother. I mean, as a family, they definitely sound a bit out of the ordinary, but there was a certain hesitation in her voice. Look into it again tomorrow. The club raids subsided as soon as Jix lost his position, so Harry might've been able to keep his job without having to move on. I want to know where he is, who he works for, who he consorts with and, if he's on the edge of the underworld, so to speak, whether he's in any trouble."

Billy nodded.

"I think you might have to go back to see Levitt as well. I want to know the location of Nick's lock-up and Levitt probably knows someone who can tell us, even if he doesn't know it himself. An artist might be secretive about his work, but he's also protective and would want there to be help available if there were a fire, for example – someone else may well have known the location of the lock-up, and I suspect that the major work that he wanted to hang is still there. Mind you, I am wondering what the arrangements were for its delivery to the gallery on the evening of his death – was it loaded on a lorry waiting for Nick B-H to drive it himself once the backdrop was ready? Or did he have drivers at the ready – and had they already left by the time he'd fallen? If so, then what did they do when they couldn't gain access to the gallery?" Maisie had been staring out at the square, seeing only the closing hours of the dead man's life, rather than the trees, people walking across the square or anything another onlooker might have noticed. She turned to Billy again. "There is much to gather, Billy. Let's be ready to put our backs into the case again tomorrow."

Billy nodded, consulted his watch once more, then asked Maisie whether her second visit to the Tate had been fruitful.

"Yes, I think it was. I wanted to find out more about the artist as a person, what character traits define someone who takes on that kind of work –"

"Work?" Billy was frowning. "I can't say as I would call that dabbling around with brushes and paints *work*. I mean, work is . . . is . . .'ard graft, ain't it? None of this daubin' business."

Maisie stood up, leaned back against the table and regarded Billy for what must have felt like an age to him, though it was only seconds. "I think you had better get what's gnawing at you off your chest, because if there is one thing we cannot afford in our work, it's jumping to conclusions about the moral worth of our clients. We must accept who they are and get on with it, putting our personal feelings and beliefs aside. Such opinions reflect prejudices, and we cannot allow smoke from our personal fires to prevent the vision that is crucial to our work."

Billy's lips formed a tight line. He said nothing for some time, then blurted out his words, his face becoming red with anger. "It was when that man yesterday, you know, 'im at the Tate, was tellin' us about that bloke who spent almost 'alf a million – 'alf a bleedin' million – on a picture last year. What was 'is name? Duveen or something? 'alf a million! There's men out of work and children wantin' for a good meal and a man spends all that on a f –" He bit his lip. "Spends all that on a picture. It makes me seethe, it does."

Maisie nodded. "Point taken, Billy, point taken. And it's a good one." She paused, allowing her agreement to soften her assistant's temper. "But here is something to remember, when this sort of thing comes up and makes you angry: that in our work we come across injustice. Sometimes we can do something about it – for example, as Dr Blanche taught me, our wealthier clients pay us handsomely, which enables us to work for those who come to us with little or nothing with which to pay. And sometimes our work can put right an injustice against someone who stands accused, or clear the name of someone who is dead. To accomplish all of this, we have to face aspects of life that are not always palatable."

"So, what you're sayin' is that I've just got to swallow it and get on wiv me job."

Maisie nodded. "Look at the world beyond your immediate emotion, the immediate fury of inequality. Choose your battles, Billy."

Silence seeped between them. Maisie allowed another moment to elapse, then moved to the chair and picked up her notes.

"I thought it would be a good idea to get a better sense of what we are dealing with in our investigation into the death of Nicholas Bassington-Hope. I am keen to know more about those characteristics that are common among artists, that might give us clues as to what moved him, what risks he might take as an individual and what he might do for his fellow man, so to speak."

Billy nodded.

"Dr Wicker was most interesting, explaining that there is a connection between art and the big questions that the artist is seeking to answer, either directly or indirectly, with his work." Maisie met Billy's eyes as she uttered the word *work*. He was listening, and even making a note. "It may be a passion for a landscape that he can bring to life for a broader audience, people who will never have the opportunity to visit such a place. It might be a depiction of another time, a comment on our world, perhaps, let's say . . . life before steam or the spinning jenny. Or – and I think that this may be where Bassington-Hope felt he could communicate a message – it might be some inner or external terror, an experience that the artist struggles to tell us about by depicting the memory, the image, in his mind's eye."

Maisie stood again, rubbing her arms against the encroaching chill of late-afternoon's darkness. "The artist takes it upon himself – or herself – to ask questions and, perhaps, sit in judgment. So, as in literature, the work may be taken at face value, for an audience to appreciate as a form of entertainment, or it can be seen in the context of the artist's life, and indeed, from the perspective of the individual observer."

"So, the artist really is sendin' a message?"

"Yes – and in working on their craft, the dexterity of hand, the understanding of colour, light and form, so the artist builds an arsenal of tools with which to express a sentiment, a view of the world from their perspective."

"I reckon these 'ere artistic types are probably a bit soft."

"*Sensitive* is a better word."

Billy shook his head. "Now that I come to think of it, it must've been rotten for the likes of Mr B-H in the war. You know, if you're a person what lives with pictures, someone who sees somethin' more where the rest of us just see what's what, then what we all saw over there in France must've been terrible for 'im, what with all that sensitivity or whatever you call it. No wonder the poor bloke went off to America and all that land." He frowned, then continued with a sad half laugh. "If 'e came back from the war 'alf as worn out as the rest of us, at least 'e 'ad a way to get it all out, you know, from the inside." Billy touched his chest. "Onto the paper, or canvas or whatever it is they use."

Maisie nodded. "That's why I want to see everything I can that came from his mind's eye and onto the canvas." She looked at her watch. "Time to go home to your family, Billy."

Billy gathered his belongings, then his coat and cap, and left the office with a swift "Thanks, Miss."

Maisie read over her notes for a moment or two longer, then walked to the window and looked out onto the already dark late-afternoon square. This quiet time was *her* canvas; her intellect, sensitivity and hard work formed the palette she worked with. Slowly but surely she would use her gifts to re-create Nicholas Bassington-Hope's life in her mind, so that she could see, think and feel as he might have, and in so doing she would come to know whether, indeed, his death was an accident or a deliberate act, whether it was self-inflicted or the result of an attack.

SOME THREE HOURS later, having seen two more clients, one man and one woman seeking not her skill as an investigator but her psychologist's compassion and guidance as they spoke of fears, of concerns and despair, she made her way home. Home, to the new flat that was quiet and cold, and that did not have the comforts to which she had become accustomed while living at the London residence of Lord Julian Compton and his wife, Lady Rowan Compton. Lady Rowan had been her employer, the sponsor of her education, her supporter and now, in her senior years, she was something of an ally, despite a chasm in the origin of their respective stations in life.

The flat was in Pimlico, which, despite the proximity of neighbouring Belgravia, was considered less than salubrious. However, for Maisie, who was careful with her money and had squirreled away savings for years, the property was affordable, which was the main consideration. A flurry of pamphlets produced by banks for the past decade, extolling the virtues and affordability of home ownership, had allowed her to dream of that important nugget of independence: a home of one's own. Indeed, the number of young women whose chance of marriage ended with the war – almost two million according to the census in 1921 – meant that an adverse attitude toward women and ownership of property had been suspended, just a little, and just for a while.

Certainly, living rent-free at the Belgravia home of Lord and Lady Compton had helped enormously, as had the success of her business. The initial invitation to return to Ebury Place had been inspired by Lady Rowan's desire for an overseer "upstairs" in whom she could place her trust while she spent more and more time at her estate in Kent. The invitation also stemmed from an affection with which Maisie was held by her former employers, especially since she had played an important part in bringing their son, James, back into the family fold following his postwar troubles. James now lived in Canada, directing the Compton Company's interests from an office in Toronto. It was thought that, like many of their class in these troublesome times, the Comptons would no longer retain two or more properties, and might therefore sell the large London home. But Maisie, for one, could not imagine Lady Rowan completely closing the house, thereby putting people out of work.

A skeleton staff had lived at 15 Ebury Place, and Maisie knew that she would miss the young women who worked below stairs, though Eric, the footman-*cum*-chauffeur, had said she should bring her motor car to the mews regularly for him to "have a look at, just to make sure she's running smoothly." But for two months now, she had been living at her new flat in Pimlico, chosen not only for price but for its proximity to the water, the river that ran though London and that Maisie loved – despite her friend Priscilla, who referred to the Thames as "swill."

She had traveled by underground railway this morning instead of driving the MG, so she returned the same way this evening. The cold, the damp and thick yellow smog conspired to nip at her ears, her lips, gloved fingers and even her toes, so she pulled her hat down even lower, navigating her way from the station to the new block of flats by following the flagstones underfoot. Designed with an optimism that was extinguished before construction was complete, the four-story building housed some sixteen flats. Each end of the building was curved to reflect a fascination with ocean travel fashionable in the 1920s, when the architect first sat at his drafting table. En-closed service stairwells to both the right and left of the building were made brighter by porthole windows, and in the center, a col-umn of glass revealed the inner spiral staircase for use by residents and guests. The accommodation requirements of a well-heeled res-ident had been in mind, one who would pay a good rent to live in an area that the developer thought "up and coming," yet the building was still barely half occupied, either by owners who, like Maisie, had seen an opportunity to buy, or by tenants now renting from an absentee landlord who had stretched his resources to acquire four apartments on the top floor.

Turning her key in the lock, Maisie entered the ground-floor flat. Though not a palace, it was deceptively capacious. A corridor gave way to a drawing room with plenty of room for a three-piece suite and, at the far end, a dining table and chairs – if, of course, Maisie had owned a three-piece suite and dining table with chairs. Instead, an old Persian carpet, bought at an executor sale, half-covered the parquet floor, and two Queen Anne chairs with faded chintz covers were positioned in front of a gas fire. There were two bedrooms to the left of the hallway, one larger than the other, and separated by a bathroom. A box room to the right was probably meant for storage, as it housed the gas meter. Maisie had set a stack of coins by the meter, so that she never had to grope around in the dark when the power went out.

Only one bedroom had a bed and, fortunately, the flat was already equipped with some new Venetian blinds, the sort that had suddenly become rather popular a few years earlier. Maisie sighed as she felt the radiator in the corridor, then made her way to the living room without taking off her coat. She took a matchbox from the mantelpiece and lit the gas fire, then moved to the windows and pulled down the blinds.

The compact kitchen, which was situated to the left of the area that would one day accommodate the dining table and chairs, was already fitted with a brand-new Main stove and a wooden table, as well as a kitchen cabinet. The deep, white enamel sink had one cupboard underneath and the bottom half of the walls were decorated in black-and-white tiles all the way around the kitchen. Maisie opened the cabinet, took out another box of matches and lit the gas ring under a tin kettle already half full of water. As the heat filtered upward from the kettle, she held her hands open to the warmth for comfort.

"Blast, it's cold in here!" Though she could single-mindedly rise above many deprivations, as she had in France during the war, there was one thing that Maisie found hard to ignore, and that was the cold. Even as she set about making tea, she would not take off her coat until after she had sipped the first cup. Reaching into the cabinet again, she pulled out a tin of Crosse & Blackwell oxtail soup, which she opened and poured into a saucepan, ready to cook. Admonishing herself for not going to the grocers, she gave thanks for a half loaf of Hovis and wedge of cheddar cheese. And, because it was winter, a half-full bottle of milk set by the back door was not yet sour.

Later, with the drawing room warmer and a hearty supper inside her, Maisie sat back to read before going to bed. She picked up a book borrowed from Boots, where she had stopped to browse the lending library earlier: *A Portrait of the Artist as a Young Man*. She flipped open the cover, pulled her cardigan around her and began to read. Distracted, Maisie only read for a page or two before setting the book down and leaning back to gaze at the white-hot gas jets. Amid the activity of the day, she had neglected to write to Andrew Dene, the man she had been walking out with for more than six months now. She knew full well that she had failed to write because she was bothered, very bothered, by what she should do next.

Andrew was a kindly man, a good person, full of humour and energy, and she knew he wanted to marry her, though he had not proposed. There were those – including her father and Lady Rowan – who thought that, perhaps, her heart still ached for that first love, for Simon Lynch, who lived through each day in a coma-like shell of existence, the result of wounds sustained in the war. Maisie suspected that Maurice Blanche knew the truth was somewhat more complex, that it was not her heart she was protecting, not the memory of a love lost. No, it was herself. Her independence was gained early, more by default than design, and as time went on, like many women of her generation, her expectation of a certain freedom became more deeply ingrained. Her position, her quest for financial security and professional standing, were paramount. There were those who floundered, women who could not step forward to the rhythm of a changed time, but for Maisie the composing of this new life was to a familiar tune, that of survival – and it had saved her, she knew that now. Since the war her work had been her rock, giving structure and form to life so that she could put one foot in front of the other. To marry now would be to relinquish that support – and even though she would have a partner, how could she step away from her buttress if there were an expectation that she give up her work for a life in the home? How could she release her grasp? After all this? And there was something else, something intangible that she could not yet define but knew to be crucial to her contentment.

It was clear to her that she must call a halt to the relationship, allow Dene to meet another. However much she liked him, however many times she felt that they might be able to consider a future together, she knew that the very likable, happy-go-lucky Andrew Dene would ultimately want more than she might ever be willing – or able – to give.

Maisie sighed and rubbed the bridge of her nose between finger and thumb. Yawning, she opened the book again, not at the first page, but at a place in the middle. When she was young, when the urge to learn gnawed at her as if it were the hunger that followed a fast, there was a game that Maurice, her teacher and mentor, had introduced to their lessons – perhaps at the end of their time together or to reignite her thoughts following a weighty discourse. He would hand her a novel, always a novel, with the instruction to read a sentence or a paragraph at random, and to see what might lie therein for her to consider. "The words and thoughts of characters borne of the author's imagination can speak to us, Maisie. Now, come on, just open the book and place your finger on the page. Let's see what you've drawn." Sometimes she found nothing much at all, sometimes dialogue of note. Then, once in a while, the short passage chosen moved her in such a way that the words would remain with her for days.

Pointing to a sentence at random, she read aloud, her voice echoing in the almost empty, still-chilly room. "'Yes! Yes! Yes! He would create proudly out of the freedom and power of his soul . . . a living thing new and soaring and beautiful, impalpable, imperishable.'"

Maisie closed her eyes and repeated the words. "New and soaring and beautiful, impalpable, imperishable. . . ." And she knew that she would rest little that night. Already it was as if Nick Bassington-Hope were beginning to speak to her. Even as she slept, she would strain to hear his message.

CHAPTER 4

Maisie and Billy arrived at the office at exactly the same time on the following morning.

"Mornin', Miss. All right?"

Pulling her scarf down to her chin so that she could be heard, Maisie stamped her feet on the front step, put the key in the lock and pushed open the door. "Yes, thank you very much, Billy. How's Lizzie?"

Billy closed the door behind him and replied as they made their way upstairs, "Still not well, Miss. Running a bit of a temperature, I'd say, and the poor little mite just spits out 'er food. Doreen bought a bit of brisket yesterday, put it in a soup to go round everybody, and Lizzie wouldn't even take some of the broth."

" 'Go round everybody'?" Maisie hung her coat on the hook behind the door, as did Billy. "You make it sound like a tribe!"

"Aw, it's nothing, Miss, not any more than anyone has to put up with these days."

Maisie stood in front of Billy's desk as he placed his notebook on the polished oak surface and reached into his inside jacket pocket for a pencil.

"Is there anything wrong? Look, I know it's not really my business, but are you stretched a bit?"

Billy would not sit down until Maisie had gone to her desk and taken a seat. He shook his head, then explained, "Doreen and me always thought we were lucky, you know, with a two-up, two-down for just the five of us. Reasonable landlord into the bargain. The nippers've got a bedroom, we've got a bedroom, and with cold running water, we don't 'ave to walk down to the pump, not like a lot of 'em round our way." He reached for the tray, ready to make a pot of tea. "Doing well, I am, thanks to you, so we've even been able to afford a few extras – a bit of beef every now and again, a toy each for the kids at Christmas. . . ."

"What's happened?"

"A few months ago, my brother-in-law – that's Doreen's sister's husband, he's a carpenter – lost 'is job. It got bad for 'em, they 'ad to move out because there weren't money for the rent and they were feedin' their boy and girl on bread and Oxo water – and there's another one on the way, y'know, making it all the worse for 'em. So, Jim reckoned there'd be work in London, and they turned up wanting somewhere to live. Now they're sleepin' in one bedroom, the five of us are in the other, and it's like sardines, it is. Jim still 'asn't got work, Doreen's all but 'ad to build a wall around 'er sewin' machine to do the dressmaking she's still got comin' in, and, to tell you the truth, Miss, it's a stretch, puttin' food on the table for nine people every day. Not that Jim's idle, no, the man's wearing out what shoe leather's left on 'is feet walking round all day tryin' to get work." Billy shook his head, then moved toward the door.

"No, don't make tea just yet. Let's sit down and talk about this." Maisie nodded toward the table by the window where the case map was laid out. "Come on."

Billy slumped into the chair alongside Maisie, who was, in fact, somewhat relieved. Only the year before, brought down by the constant lingering pain from his war wounds, Billy's behaviour had become unpredictable, and further investigation had revealed abuse of narcotics – not uncommon among men who had once been inadvertently overdosed on morphine in the dressing stations and casualty clearing stations of the Great War. At least he had not lapsed.

"Are you managing? Is there anything I can do?"

"Yes, Miss, I'm managing, it's just tight, that's all. My Doreen can make food for five go round 'undred and five, if needs be. It'll just be better when Jim gets on 'is feet." He paused. "Poor man fought for 'is country, and now look at what 'e's bein' treated like – it's not good enough, Miss."

"Billy, have you been in touch with the nurse, to come in to see Lizzie?" asked Maisie. It was common for a local nurse, instead of a doctor, to be summoned to see the sick, simply because of the greater cost of a physician.

"No. Fool's choice, really, Miss. We thought she'd be over it by now, but I don't know . . ."

Maisie checked her watch. "Look, I'm driving down to Dungeness later this morning – at least, I will be if I hear from Miss B-H – so I'll detour and go to the house first, just to have a look at Lizzie. How does that sound?"

Billy shook his head. "Nah, Miss, don't you go out of your way – we'll get the nurse round later if Lizzie's not any better by this evening."

Maisie took several pencils of different colours from a jar on the table. She knew Billy's pride and did not want to push. "All right, but the offer's there, you know. You only have to say – and if things get any more troublesome . . ."

Billy simply nodded, so Maisie moved on to the Bassington-Hope case.

"Right then, let's look at where we are. Per our conversation yesterday, it's your job to find out more from Levitt about the gallery,

Nick B-H and that mysterious lock-up of his. See what you can sniff out. And also see if you can uncover more about the younger brother and the credibility of that story about liaisons with a criminal element." She paused. "In the meantime, I'll be having a quick cup of coffee with Stratton this morning before I set off – I'm curious to know why he was so keen to support Georgina's decision to seek my help. If he thought the case merited more investigation, why didn't he do it himself?" Reaching out onto the case map, she began to link several notes, creating circles that she joined with arrows. "On Monday I'll be doing some background research on Miss B-H and her family, and of course, I'll have some impressions from my visit to the house." Maisie consulted her watch. "The morning post should be here soon and I am expecting to hear from her."

"Won't she use the old dog 'n' bone?"

"Perhaps, but I need a key, a map and some specific directions from her."

Billy nodded. "And when're you going to see the family?"

"I am to join her at Bassington Place on Saturday."

"*Bassington Place*. Very posh, if you don't mind me sayin' so. And this is where you meet the rest of the cuckoos, eh, Miss?"

Maisie was glad to hear Billy joking, though he still looked drawn. "Yes, it appears so. I don't think it's over-egging the pudding to call the Bassington-Hopes *eccentric*, given Georgina's description – and what did she call her sister, *Nolly*? I must admit, I –"

The doorbell rang. "Probably be that letter now." Billy left the room, returning to the office less than three minutes later. "Messenger turned up at the same time as the postman, so you've got one thick envelope" – he passed a bulky package to Maisie –"and a few letters from the postie."

Maisie placed the letters on the table and reached for an opener to slit the seal securing the envelope delivered by messenger. As she pulled out the letter, a second envelope in heavy cream vellum fell onto the table along with a key.

"Hmmm, looks like I will *definitely* be going alone to Dungeness, much as I suspected. Interesting . . ." Maisie allowed her words to fade as she began to read the accompanying letter aloud.

Dear Miss Dobbs,

Maisie noticed that, though Georgina had taken the early liberty of using Christian names, in her written correspondence she was rather more formal.

I must beg your pardon for the swift communiqué. I am attending a banquet this evening and have much to do. The attached map and directions will see you safely to Nick's carriage-cum-cottage in Dungeness. Do prepare yourself; it is really quite simple, though he adored the place. Should you encounter a problem with the key or lock, Mr Amos White lives in the old cottage to the right of Nick's carriage as you are facing it, and I am sure he will help. Amos is a fisherman, so will probably be in his shed mending nets in the afternoon. Duncan and Quentin returned to Dungeness this morning, so do look out for them. I believe they will only be there for a day or so.

I will meet you outside Tenterden station at three o'clock on Saturday afternoon, as we agreed. If you are travelling from Chelstone, you will probably come from the direction of Rolvenden, thus you will find the station signposted from the middle of the High Street as you come into town, a sharp turn to the left. It's best that we meet there and then go together to the house.

You will also find enclosed an invitation to a party at my flat on Sunday evening. It's just a few friends. I thought it might give you a chance to meet some of Nick's pals. Do come.

"Gosh . . ." Maisie shook her head.

"What's up, Miss?"

"An invitation to a party at Georgina B-H's flat on Sunday evening," Maisie was rereading the invitation.

"That'll be nice, you know, to get out."

Maisie shook her head. "I don't know how nice it will be, but I will most certainly go."

"Take Dr Dene along – you know, make an evening of it."

Maisie reddened and shook her head. "No, just me, Billy. It's business."

Billy regarded her carefully, his attention drawn to the slight edge in her voice. Though they would never discuss Maisie's private life, Billy could see it was quite clear that Andrew Dene's intentions were toward marriage, whereas Maisie's responses had become generally lukewarm. Now she was going to a party alone, which wasn't something that a woman on the cusp of engagement might do, work or no work.

"Right then, we'd better get cracking. Let's do a bit more work here, see if the cold light of day has brought any new thoughts to our investigation, then go our separate ways." Maisie took out a sheaf of notes made the previous evening and moved toward the case map. She turned to look at Billy. "And remember, Billy – let me know if you need me to see Lizzie."

Billy nodded, and they set to work.

THE CAFÉ ON Oxford Street where Maisie was to meet Detective Inspector Richard Stratton was a rather down-at-heel establishment that she had once described as being "more *caff* than café." She had already packed her leather case for the journey to Dungeness, from which she had originally thought she might go directly to Hastings but then decided to make her way to Chelstone for the evening. She would visit Andrew Dene in Hastings on Saturday morning. It wouldn't take long to drive from the Old Town to Tenterden in the afternoon.

Stratton was waiting at a table by the window and had just sat down. Having removed his hat and coat and placed them on a coat-stand by the door, he was smoothing back his dark hair, which was peppered with gray at the temples. He wore dark-grey gabardine trousers, with a black waistcoat, grey tweed jacket, white shirt and black tie. His shoes were highly polished, though he did not have the sort of accoutrements with which someone like Stig Svenson embellished his attire – there was no kerchief in the jacket pocket, no cufflinks at his wrist. Though he was not a young man – Maisie had thought him to be about thirty-eight or forty – an olive complexion and dark eyes meant that he was often the subject of a second glance from strangers. The detective was not aware of such attention, and the passersby would not have been able to explain why they were compelled to turn, though they might admit to thinking they had seen him in one of those new talkies at the picture house.

Stratton had already bought two cups of tea and a plate of toast and jam. The tea was strong and, Maisie thought as she approached the table, looked as if it had been in the urn long enough to make itself quite at home.

"You could stand a spoon up in that tea." Maisie sat down as Stratton pulled out a chair for her, and smiled. Though they had crossed words on several occasions, there was a mutual respect that had led Maisie to be called to Scotland Yard to consult on cases where her particular skill and insight was thought to be of use in the investigation of a case.

"Keeps you going on a day like this, though. It's been very chilly this past week, hasn't it?"

Their eyes met. Maisie sipped her tea and nodded. "Gosh, that's better."

Stratton looked at his watch. "You wanted to see me, Miss Dobbs?"

"Yes." She placed her plain white cup in the saucer, then paused as she reached for another slice of toast and jam, to which she added an additional half teaspoon of jam.

"Good Lord, would you like some toast with that dollop of jam?" Stratton leaned back in his chair and caught Maisie's eye.

"I'm starving, Inspector." She smiled again, then continued with her explanation. "I wanted to speak to you about the death of Nicholas Bassington-Hope. Of course, I must thank you for supporting his sister's plan to engage my services so that certain doubts in her heart might be put to rest; however, I hope that you can tell me more about the event, from your perspective." Maisie inclined her head, then proceeded to bite into the toast, reaching for her tea as she did so.

Stratton allowed a few seconds to elapse, seconds in which Maisie was sure he was composing a response that would have been acceptable to his superiors, had he been called to account for his actions. And despite the delay in answering, during which she appeared to make herself busy with another slice of toast, she knew that he had likely anticipated the reason for her request that they meet and was therefore ready to share only the barest minimum of information.

"There was – is – no doubt in my mind that Mr Bassington-Hope fell from the scaffolding he had constructed. It hadn't been put up by a builder or other person used to such a task, though he'd obviously had help. It was quite amateurish – in fact, he was asking for trouble." He sipped from his cup. "Terrible waste – it's not as if there aren't builders out of work who would have jumped at the chance of making a shilling or two to give him a hand."

Maisie placed a half-eaten crust on her plate. "I have seen the wall against which the scaffolding was positioned and it appeared that there were anchors in place. I'm not an expert at this sort of thing, but I would have thought that, being an artist, he would have been used to setting up all sorts of exhibits, and, seeing as he worked on fairly large pieces, of actually getting at the canvas to paint. I mean, the man wasn't a fool, he'd been a soldier, had a certain dexterity –"

Stratton shook his head. "That artistic temperament – seen it a lot in my time. He was a soldier over thirteen years ago now, so I am dubious about any lingering practicality that might have been drilled into him at the time. And he was fiercely secretive about his work – as you probably know, they can't even find half of it! No, for his own reasons, he wanted to do everything himself, which led to his death."

"And that brings me back to my original purpose for wanting to see you: do you think there might be even the merest scrap of merit in Miss Bassington-Hope's belief that her brother was the victim of a crime?"

Stratton sipped again from his cup. Maisie smiled, knowingly. *He's playing for time.*

"To tell you the truth, I'm only too glad she came to you, otherwise she would be nipping at my heels. That woman is one of those terrierlike people who, once they have something to chew on, simply do not let go. I should never have been assigned to go to the scene of the accident in the first place, as it was – to me – clearly not a place where a crime had taken place." Stratton sighed. "She did not accept that her brother was the victim of his own ineptitude and seemed set to make a nuisance of herself, just like she did in the war."

"But I thought she did something quite brave in the war – after all, it was a risk to do even half of the things she did in order to obtain background information for her dispatches."

"Oh, dear, Miss Dobbs, is this an old Girton girl camaraderie? I do hope you haven't fallen under the spell of the charismatic Georgie Bassington-Hope, I –"

"Old Girton girl camaraderie? Charismatic? I'm disappointed in you, Inspector."

"It was a figure of speech. She uses her buoyant charm to get what she wants, even if that thing she wants is access to dangerous places she has no right to even contemplate entering – and all to write a story."

Maisie raised an eyebrow. "To write the truth."

Stratton shook his head. "She was a troublemaker, her 'stories' undermined the government's decision to –"

"But hadn't the government undermined –"

"Miss Dobbs, I –"

"Detective Inspector Stratton, if I am to keep Georgina

Bassington-Hope out of your way, to effectively pick up your laundry, then wash and fold it, I should say you owe me a bit more than fifteen minutes in a third-rate caff on Oxford Street." Though she noticed that Stratton's cheeks had become flushed, she continued. "I have a few questions for *you*, if you don't mind."

Stratton looked around at the counter. "I think they've just brewed up a fresh urn of tea. Another cup?"

Maisie nodded. Stratton picked up the cups and walked to the counter. She checked her watch, noting that if she left London by half past eleven, she could feasibly be in Dungeness by half past two. An hour or so of daylight before the grainy dusk of the coast set in.

"This is a bit better." He set two cups of tea on the table, pushing one toward Maisie.

"Thank you." Maisie reached for her cup, and then looked away as Stratton proceeded to put several teaspoons of sugar into his tea, a habit she had observed before but which set her teeth on edge. She turned back as he moved the sugar to the centre of the table. "Now then, I want you to tell me anything you can about Mr Bassington-Hope's death; it's the least you can do if you want me to keep your terrier under control." She paused. "Oh, and by the way, I must say, though I am familiar with her reputation, she didn't strike me as a terrier when it came to keeping her first appointment with me. She could barely garner enough courage to go forward with the interview."

"I can't account for the woman's behaviour. However, I anticipated that you wanted to see me regarding this case." He reached into the large inner pocket of his mackintosh and pulled out an envelope from which he removed several sheets of paper. "You can't take this with you, but you can peruse the postmortem notes."

Maisie reached for the sheets of paper proffered by Stratton, then took several moments to read them carefully. Determined not to rush for Stratton's sake, she opened her document case and removed a few index cards and set them on the table beside her teacup, which she then picked up and held against her cheek until she'd finished reading. She took two or three more sips as she placed the report on the table and flicked through a few pages again, then she set down her cup, reached for a pencil in her case and proceeded to take notes.

"I say, I haven't got all day, you know."

Maisie smiled. Had he not known her professionally for some time now, Stratton might have thought that he was being manipulated. "Just a moment longer, Detective Inspector." Maisie completed her notes, then leaned back. "The predictable broken neck, caused by an unfortunate fall at an awkward angle. Death almost instantaneous, according to the examiner. Now then, how about the bruises to the side of the head and to the upper arm. Is the pathologist sure that these indications of trauma are in keeping with the nature of the fall?"

"Second-guessing the doctor, are you?"

"I should not have to remind you that, not only was I a nurse, but I served a lengthy apprenticeship with Dr Maurice Blanche. I am used to questioning the examiner; it is what I am trained to do."

"The bruises are not severe enough to indicate an alternative cause of death and were, as the pathologist concluded, in keeping with the nature of the accident."

"Hmmm, that's two 'in keepings' – I wonder what else they might be 'in keeping' with?"

"Miss Dobbs, you appear to be suggesting a lack of attention to detail, or perhaps ineptitude. I would not have closed the case had I any doubt –"

"Wouldn't you?" Maisie did not allow the question to linger, and ensured only that it had been voiced. "If I seem confrontational, it is only because my brief from my client – thanks to you supporting the referral – requires me to ask such questions. Indeed, I do believe I could point out several anomalies, but at the same time, I can see why such a conclusion was reached by the attending physician."

"May I?" Stratton reached for the document. "Now, I can't help with anything else, I'm afraid. I am sure you have more questions, but if I had the time to answer – or saw reason to answer – then I wouldn't have closed the case." Stratton returned the report to the envelope, and then to his pocket. "I've got to leave now. Busy day as I'm leaving work early today."

Maisie knotted her scarf and stood up as Stratton pulled out her chair. "Going away for the weekend, Inspector?"

Stratton shook his head. "No, just an evening out. A banquet, actually. Rather looking forward to it."

They left the café, shaking hands before they went their separate ways. Maisie felt compelled to turn and look back as she walked toward her motor car, and as she did so, she saw Stratton crossing the road in the direction of the waiting black Invicta and the police driver who held open the door for him. It was at that moment that she noticed another motor car parked behind Stratton's, and though she could not be sure, she thought that the second motor was a faster, newer model, and of the sort used by the Flying Squad. A man wearing a black hat and black overcoat who had been leaning on the door of the motor car threw a cigarette stub on the ground, then pressed into it with the sole of his shoe. He walked over to Stratton. Leaning toward each other, they spoke briefly, before turning to look in her direction. Maisie feigned interest in the window of an adjacent shop, then when she felt it was safe to do so, cast her eyes once again in the direction of Stratton's motor, just in time to see the two men shake hands and climb into their respective vehicles.

Reaching the MG, Maisie checked her watch. Yes, she would be in Kent before half past two. As she drove, confidently, despite sleet that caused the London streets to become increasingly hazardous, she replayed the meeting with Stratton so that it was like watching a moving picture show in her mind's eye. There were questions to be asked, but if she rushed to answer them at this stage, she might bring to a halt the possibility of reaching a full and complete conclusion to the case in a timely fashion. Her first questions – for Maisie's curiosity rarely seemed to grow without more questions attached, as if it were a giant root with subsidiary tubers feeding – centred around Stratton's delight that she was working for Georgina Bassington-Hope. Did he really want the woman occupied lest she pen some controversial piece regarding police procedure for a newspaper or one of the political journals? Had he reason to continue his investigation into the artist's death without the knowledge of either Maisie or the next-of-kin?

Maisie used the back of her hand to wipe condensation from the inside of the MG's windscreen while thinking about the second motor car and the meeting between Stratton and the man in the black hat and coat. Of course, collaboration between men with different police responsibilities – one dealing with murder, one with gangs, robberies and other such crimes – should not be suspicious; after all, their paths must cross all the time. But she felt a sensation at the nape of her neck, as if a colony of ants were beating a path from one shoulder to the other. The image that now seemed to impress itself upon her was of a cellar with steps leading down into the darkness. It was not an unfamiliar picture, one that often presented itself at the outset of a troublesome case, but Maisie shuddered as she realized that she had already gone beyond the top step. She was clearly in the dark when she took on the case and began her descent, but there was no going back now.

As she left the outskirts of London and crossed the border into Kent, the low afternoon sun finally managed to break through, casting a cut-glass sheen across the Weald. She was glad of a break in the weather, as it took just a hint of clear, bright sky to begin to warm her bones. Settling into what she hoped would be an easy run down to the coast, Maisie looked out across the countryside, the wintery white swath of land interspersed with patches of green where sheep and cattle clustered, their backs against the chill wind. Kent calmed Maisie, had tempered her since girlhood, when she moved from London to work at the Comptons' country estate. Despite that calm, she was unsettled, the image of Stratton and the other man, and their furtive looks toward her giving rise to more questions. Then Georgina and Stratton came to mind. Might they be attending the same function this evening? Together, perhaps? As she changed gears to negotiate a turn, she wondered if there was a plan already in progress, and whether she could be a pawn in the game. But if so, whose pawn might she be? And how serious was the game?

FIVE

Maisie arrived in Dungeness at two o'clock, having made good time. The flat expanse of shingled land, a promontory that reached out into the western limits of the Straits of Dover, seemed to extend from the village of Lydd until one reached the sea. She thought the word *windswept* must have been invented for Dungeness, positioned at this southernmost point of the Romney Marshes, across which gales would howl, even on a good day.

Maisie made her way at a low speed along a track worn by the milk tender. She thought her MG might be the only motor car that had ventured down the road for a while, so quiet was the land, with no sign of even the fishermen. Looking both ways as she crossed the narrow-gauge lines of the Romney, Hythe and Dymchurch railway, she held Georgina's map against the steering wheel and looked down for a second or two as she continued driving. It seemed that most of the old railway carriage homes were to the south, so she turned right past the lighthouse and maintained a crawling pace until she reached the former railway carriage that was the home of Nicholas Bassington-Hope.

Maisie parked, pulled her scarf around her, then opened the MG's door, which she had to hang on to, fearing that it would be swept back by the wind. Once she reached the carriage, she fumbled with the key but, thankfully, did not have to resort to the good graces of Amos White, as she gained entry after only one false turn in the lock. Maisie pressed all her weight against the door to close it again, then secured it behind her. She let out a deep breath, glad that she was finally inside and out of the freezing winter weather.

"Nothing like the marshes to brittle your bones!" Maisie said aloud, as she pulled back her scarf, removed her hat and looked around the dwelling. For a moment, she was surprised, for the converted cottage did not resemble anything she had envisaged.

Without taking off her coat – it was still far too cold – she used her scarf to wipe rain droplets from her hair and face as she walked around the room. In truth, she couldn't really remember what image came to mind when Georgina first mentioned that her brother lived in a converted railway carriage, but vaguely thought of prickly vermillion-red wool fabric on seats, dark wooden walls and doors with signs that read FIRST CLASS or THIRD CLASS. She had imagined the artist living in a glorified goods wagon, as opposed to the tasteful interior she now beheld.

The sun was already going down, but Maisie found matches next to an oil lamp on the sideboard, so removed the flue to light the wick. She was rewarded by a warming light as she replaced the column of glass and then a yellow globe shade that had been set alongside.

"That's better." Maisie placed her document case on the table and walked around the main room. As neat as a pin, the room had been thoughtfully decorated, though Nick had clearly retained the more attractive elements of railway carriage design. The rich wooden bulkhead walls at either end had been stripped, varnished and polished to a shine, as had the floorboards underfoot. Side walls had been painted in a pale cream distemper, and there were dark linen blinds against windows that faced the sea. Two leather arm-chairs, the sort one might find in a gentlemen's club, were posi-tioned close to a wood-burning stove set against the bulkhead to the right of the front door. A stack of dry driftwood had been placed on one side of the red-tiled hearth, and on the other was a large kettle filled with water, alongside several fire tools. A wood-framed bed was set lengthways against the other bulkhead, the rich burgundy counterpane hanging low over the sides to mingle with a Persian carpet woven of what seemed to be every shade of red wool, from claret to vermillion, from maroon to a colour that was almost burnt umber. Opposite the sideboard stood a dresser with upper cup-boards and shelving for crockery and an open space underneath where Nick Bassington-Hope had placed a set of jars and a bread bin, with a heavy bread board placed on the flat working top to pro-tect the dresser. Two more cupboards below held a frying pan, saucepan, and various dry goods and tins of soup. Turning around, Maisie thought the compact room seemed to exude warmth, some-thing she thought was probably essential to life on this part of the coast, whatever the season.

Opening a second door, Maisie found that the accommodation was not one carriage, but two, positioned parallel to one another. A house-size door had been installed, which led to a small vestibule, built to connect the two carriages. Windows on this long side of the carriage had been painted white, then decorated with a mural. Maisie did not linger to consider the story depicted in the series of paintings, instead continuing her survey of Nick Bassington-Hope's home. The vestibule gave way to a studio and bathroom, though there was no running water or plumbing for the residents of Dun-geness. The bathroom consisted of a wooden washstand with a tile splashback and marble top. A jug and ewer were placed on top of the washstand, while underneath a chamber pot was covered with a plain white cloth. Maisie suspected that residents made a quick trip across the shingle to the water's edge each morning to empty the "thunder pot". Upon investigation, a small wardrobe held several items of clothing: three shirts, a pair of blue corduroy trousers, a brown woollen jacket and another jacket of heavy waxed cotton. Reaching farther into the depths of the wardrobe, Maisie felt the rough texture of heavy wool and drew the sleeve of another garment toward her. Nick Bassington-Hope had kept his army greatcoat. Pulling the coat from the wardrobe, Maisie lifted it out and instinctively held it to her nose.

Oh, my God, I should never have done that. She held the coat at arm's length, then walked into the studio to take a closer look. *Oh, dear.* There was still a speckle of mud across the hem of the coat; then, as she pulled the fabric closer to the light, she noticed a broad, aged stain on the sleeve that she knew to be blood. *My God, he kept it all this time.* Maisie closed her eyes and gripped the coat to her, the smell of death lingering among the folds of fabric, as if the garment had absorbed something of what the artist had seen as a young subaltern. As Maisie returned the item of clothing to the wardrobe, her hand lingered on the door handle for some seconds while she tried to extinguish the thought of Nick Bassington-Hope and the greatcoat he could not part with.

It was almost dusk now and Maisie had barely dented the task she had set for herself this afternoon. Having made a note to ask Georgina why Nick's clothing had not been taken from his home, she moved on. She had imagined an artist's place of work to be somewhat untidy, perhaps with drawings here and there, paints weeping from unsealed pots, colour-smeared rags, books and papers strewn across the floor. Looking at the clean, carefully tended studio, Maisie realized that she probably held the same impression as Stratton of an artistic "type." Admonishing herself, she moved around the studio in which Nick Bassington-Hope created the work for which he had been feted.

On the wall that paralleled the first carriage, a special wooden case had been fitted to store the artist's paints. It reminded Maisie of the mail slots at the block of flats that was now her home. Here each wooden pigeonhole had been allotted a certain colour, and within held tubes and small pots of paint in the many hues that could be described as blue, red, yellow, green, black, orange and violet.

Jugs in varying sizes had been set on a gaily decorated wooden tea trolley to hold a collection of brushes, and though each brush showed the staining and wear associated with good use, it had been properly cleaned before being stowed again. An easel stood by the bulkhead close to the bank of windows, and against the new partition that had been fitted to form the bathroom was a chest of narrow drawers that held papers of different weights as well as wood for frames and sections of unused canvas. A basket of stained but clean cloths was set on the floor, and there was also a deep, cushioned armchair by the window. Alongside the chair was a small table with untouched sketchbooks and pencils.

"But where's your work, Nicholas? Where have you put your work?" Maisie asked the silent studio.

Holding the lamp in her left hand, she used her right to open the bottom drawer of the paper chest. Bundles of well-used sketchbooks were stored there, so, still with her coat on, she sat on the floor, set the lamp alongside her, and began to leaf through the books, all of which were signed and dated. She had only just begun when there was a loud thump on the door.

"Oh!" Maisie was startled at the intrusion, but clambered to her feet, and with the lamp in hand went to answer what sounded like an impatient caller.

Opening the door, Maisie faced a heavyset man no taller than she was herself. He wore a long jacket of rubber-covered cloth and a woollen cap atop his greying red hair, which was drawn back in a long, thick braid. His trousers of the same rubbered cloth were tucked into boots that had been turned over at the top. Maisie wanted very much to smile, for she had no doubt as to the identity of this man.

"You must be Mr White." She spoke before he had a chance to open his mouth, to quell any questions he might have about her right to be in the house of a man not long dead.

He stared at her for some time, it seemed, as if taken aback by her forthright manner. Then he spoke, with the rounded brogue of the Kentish fisherman. "Just thought I'd look in, don't want strangers looking into Mr 'ope's matters."

"I'm not a stranger, Mr White. I am a friend of Mr Bassington-Hope's sister Georgina. She asked me to look in as I was in the area."

"Funny area to be in, bit out of the way for the likes of anyone, not a place you pass through, Dungeness."

"No, I know, it was just a bit out of my way." Maisie smiled again, though she felt her polite responses were having little effect on the fisherman. "I know the Marshes and was going to Hastings, so it seemed a good opportunity to help Miss Bassington-Hope."

He shook his head. "Strange lot, them 'ope's. You'd've thought they'd've been down a bit more, not just the one visit. Three of 'em just came in, then left as soon as they got 'ere. Funny lot." He shook his head, moved as if to leave, then turned again. "You'd be best to move that little motor car be'ind the carriage, out to the back. Come mornin' you won't 'ave a roof on that thing, what with the wind." He regarded Maisie without speaking, then continued. "You knowin' the Marshes, I would've thought you'd've parked round the back to begin with."

Maisie checked her watch. "Well, I didn't expect to stay very long." Maisie felt the sting of cold rain on her cheeks, and the lamp flickered. "Gosh, I really should be on my way."

Amos White turned, speaking as he walked away. "Just remember to put that little motor to the lee of the cottage." Then he was gone.

Maisie closed the door behind her and shuddered. Perhaps she ought to stay here in Dungeness, especially as she had barely started her search of Nick's property, though she knew she would feel like an interloper, sleeping in a bed that was not hers, in a house she had not been invited to use as overnight accommodation. There was little time, and already more questions were lining up to be given voice, to be answered. *Who were the three family members? Could it have been Georgina and her parents? Or perhaps the three bereaved siblings?* She looked around the room. Either Nick was a tidy person, or someone else had come in and seen fit to ensure that the house was neat. Someone who had managed to escape the canny eyes of Amos White.

It was when Maisie stepped into the centre of the room again that she allowed herself to push all questions to the back of her mind and studied the mural painstakingly crafted on the former railway carriage windows of the opposite wall. Each window, painted in a base of white to form a canvas, depicted a scene that was pure Romney Marsh, from the trees forced to lean inland by the wind, to isolated churches set in flat hedge-divided fields, with sheep grazing and, above the water-meadows, silvered clouds scudding across a gray sky. Maisie drew the lamp closer and smiled, for as her eyes moved from left to right, from the calm of the marshes to sea crashing against shingle, with some images larger than others to create an illusion of distance along with the immediacy of detail, she saw that the story told in the mural was one that had been part of the coast's history for centuries. In the middle of the tale, day had drawn into night and the scene was of a fishing boat beached. Men were unloading their catch by lantern light, scarves drawn around their heads gypsy-style. Atop a black horse with wild eyes, a man in a tricorn hat and mask wielded a pistol while watching over the haul, which was not cod, nor plaice, huss, rock or haddock, but barrels and chests bursting open to reveal a bounty of gold and spices, silk and rum. Moving along the mural, the men had taken flight toward the church with their booty, where a welcoming vicar bid them enter, enabling their escape to a place beyond the pulpit. The next scene saw dawn break and the excisemen – as feared today as in ancient times – searching for the smugglers, to no avail. In the final scene, situated above the bed's footboard, daylight has returned to the marshes once more. Sheep were grazing, the wind blowing against inland-leaning trees, and the thunderous sky had given way to blue. It was a scene of peace, of calm.

Maisie stood back to look at the mural in its entirety. The infamous eighteenth-century Kent gangs given life, given colour, by the hand of the artist. She moved in toward the wall and held the light to the finely drawn faces, to marvel at the detail, even that of the dog cowering to one side as the horse reared up. Nick Bassington-Hope was indeed talented, that much was evident even in a whimsical scene depicting life gone by in the place where he had established his retreat.

She checked her watch and sighed. She would remain awhile longer, searching. It was already past four and dark outside, but she decided that she could not leave until she had conducted a thorough search of the cottage, even if it meant driving later in less-than-safe conditions, picking her way with care along the rough roads. As the air around her seemed to become accustomed to her presence, it occurred to Maisie that those who came before her might have visited in search of something of great import.

She moved the MG to a place behind the second carriage, where a surprisingly strong lean-to had been constructed and sheltered not only a carefully stacked pile of driftwood, but a privy, and a barrel where water was collected from a clever gutter system. Maisie was able to park under the lean-to, and smiled as she walked around to the front of the cottage. It would seem that, contrary to Stratton's assessment, this was one artist with a very practical streak, if one took into account the work involved in adapting the two carriages – work that she suspected Nick had completed himself.

Locking the door behind her again, Maisie pulled the blinds, made up a fire in the cast-iron stove and put the kettle of water on to boil. As the room warmed, she opened the door to the studio to allow heat to circulate so that she could move around in comfort. She looked around the home that Nick Bassington-Hope had created. No, none of this was the work of a man who would have had a slapdash attitude toward the construction of a scaffolding platform.

RETURNING TO THE sketchbooks she had just opened when Amos White banged on the door, she saw they contained work from Nick Bassington-Hope's early days – charcoal drawings and watercolours that lacked the mature interpretation of later years – and also more recent work that seemed to demonstrate a more confident hand. Maisie looked through the sketchbooks and felt certain that there should be more. Calculating that Nick would have used perhaps more than a hundred, or two hundred books, she began to search again, though there were precious few places for storage in the carriages. It was under the bed that she found a series of apple crates containing more sketchbooks, along with the many works of fiction and nonfiction he had acquired over the years. On hands and knees Maisie pulled out the crates, set them alongside the fire, and, sitting on the floor with the lamp on a side table, she began to leaf through their contents.

Unlike the rest of the cottage, in which everything seemed to have its place, the sketchbooks had not been catalogued or kept in any order, and if Maisie had to guess, she would have concluded that they had been worked through quite recently. Recalling her conversations with Georgina, she wondered whether the Bassington-Hopes had expected to find something that might indicate the location of the lock-up – something she rather wanted to find herself.

Nick's early sketches were of pastoral scenes, of horses in Kentish fields, of farms and oasthouses, of cattle ambling toward the milking shed in late afternoon and of women gathered outside farm buildings, their jackets secured by string, laced boots muddied under heavy cloth skirts with pinafores. Strong as men, they were running newly washed hop-pokes through a mangle, two turning a giant handle, two feeding the sacking through twin rollers. There were detail sketches, a face here, a nose there, the arm of a farmworker or a child's dimpled hand held by the worn, working hand of her father. And then came the war.

Maisie could barely bring herself to look at the sketches, and as she did so her head began to throb, the scar on her neck aching in unison. She could not continue, but turned instead to work completed in the time following Nick's return from France, the time when, still recuperating from his wounds, he was called upon to work for the cause of war in designing propaganda literature. This time the sketches inflamed Maisie. She moved back from the fire, so heated was her response to the slogans revealed as she flicked through the pages. A small boy sitting on his father's knee, and the words, WHAT WAR STORIES WILL YOU TELL, FATHER? A young man with his sweetheart, the woman looking away toward a man in uniform: ARE YOU STILL HER BEST BOY? Then another, a German soldier breaking down the door of a family's home: YOU CAN STOP HIM NOW! Maisie had seen the posters herself in the war, but had never questioned who might have drafted each idea, never thought of the man who had challenged others to join the fight and who compelled those at home to push them toward service.

And here in her hands were the ideas as seeds. For each poster she had seen on a railway station, at a picture house or on a board outside a shop, there were ten, fifteen sketches, if not more, with the design at a different stage of development. At first she felt anger toward the artist. Then she found herself wondering if he'd had a choice, and, if not, how he might have felt, knowing the ultimate, deadly outcome of his work. As the fire inside abated, Maisie moved closer to the stove again and wondered what remorse, if any, might have shadowed Nick Bassington-Hope each day.

The sketches from his time in America were most interesting to Maisie, not only because they illustrated a land far away, but because they revealed a man who seemed to have found a peace of mind. Magnificent canyons backlit by a sun high in the sky; trees of such grandeur that she could barely imagine walking through the forest; then the plains – even in mere sketchbooks, with pencil and charcoal, with pastel chalks, with watercolour, she could almost smell the heat, the breeze pressed against fields of corn or whipped up spray on a river as it was forced downward across fearsome rapids. Again, Nick Bassington-Hope had drawn segments in detail, perhaps one of water rushing across a single rock, or of a branch, perhaps part of an eagle's wing. And there, penciled into the corner of a single page, the artist had written, "I can dance with life again." As Maisie closed one sketchbook and reached for another, she realized that tears had fallen, that the work of an artist she never knew was touching her deeply. His travels to the other side of the world had saved Nick Bassington-Hope's very soul.

Taking up a collection of sketchbooks tied with string and marked CONSTRUCTS, Maisie dried her eyes and was intrigued as she flipped through the pages, for it appeared that not only had the artist planned his murals and triptych pieces with utmost care, but he had anticipated each step involved in exhibiting them, even down to the last bolt and anchor required to secure a piece. So, she was right, he was no fly-by-night who took chances, but a careful executor of his work. One might also remark that such attention to minutiae was an obsession. Flicking through, Maisie noted that the details here were of past exhibits and that there was nothing pertaining to the unveiling at Svenson's Gallery. Had it been removed? Or was it still here? Or at the lock-up?

Maisie pushed the books to one side, rose to her feet and placed her hands on the back of first one chair, then the other. She smiled, for as she touched the chair on the left of the fireplace, it felt warm against her fingers – but not in a way that would indicate proximity to the embers. It was a different heat, a sensation that another person would likely not feel. As she rested her hand on the leather chair, Maisie knew it was Nick Bassington-Hope's preferred seat, that he would have chosen this chair before the other, always. She sat in his place, closed her eyes and, with her hands resting softly in her lap, took three deep breaths, each time inhaling to the extent of her lung capacity before breathing out. Then she sat in silence, with only the crashing of the waves outside and closer crackle of burning drift-wood for company.

Banishing all thoughts from her mind, she waited. In time – though she would not have known how much time, for Maisie had been taught that the moments and hours spent in silence without in-tellectual thought give the seeker the opportunity to transcend such human measurements – an image came to her of the artist in his home, moving from one room to another. The living room, this room in which she was sitting, was cosy and warm, as it was now, though instead of winter, it's high summer and light is streaming through the windows. Now Nick is in his studio, a palette in his hand, his trolley of brushes along with a selection of paints at his side, and he is working. The image blurs, and there he is sitting on the chair alongside the chest of drawers. He is sketching, yet as he puts charcoal to paper, tears fall and he brushes the back of his hand against his red-rimmed eyes. Though it is a bright day, he is wearing the greatcoat, drawing it around him as he works, as he struggles with the emotion his work inspires. He stops and looks around the room, puts his work to one side, paces the floor, then takes a piece of paper from his pocket. He looks at the paper for just a moment, then returns it to his pocket. Then the picture becomes blurred and he is gone. The sea crashes against the shore, the sea-gulls screech and wheel overhead.

Opening her eyes, Maisie rubbed her temples and looked around to regain her bearings. Half past seven! Standing up, she moved as if to go to the studio, but suddenly stopped, for it struck her that to hear seagulls whooping in such an excited state was un-usual at this hour of darkness. Her weekend visits to Andrew Dene's home in the Old Town had given her a sense of the rhythms of coastal life. She stepped to the window, and as she did so, extin-guished the lamp so that she stood in darkness to draw back the blind, just slightly.

Lights went back and forth, and there was a flurry of activity close to the shingle bank where a fishing boat had just been drawn up. Maisie watched as men – there must have been three, perhaps four – unloaded a haul. She had waited many a time for the fishing boats to come in with the morning's catch, but what she was seeing now seemed strange to her. There were no nets, as far as she could see, no barrels for the fish, and it was late for the catch to come in. A rumbling, heavy sound distracted her as a lorry appeared, backing up as far as the driver could take the vehicle to the shingle bank. She squinted; it was hard to see in the dark, though the scene was illuminated by Tilly lamps. Yes, perhaps it was a late catch. Shadows could be misleading, tricksters of light and imagination. And she was weary, with work to do. But not so weary that she would not take precautions to protect herself, even if such protection were not necessary.

Extinguishing the fire, Maisie carried the lamp into the studio where she relit the wick and, with one hand, searched down into the folds of the armchair's seat. Her slender fingers teased out a few pennies and even a florin, a dried-up paint tube and a pencil. Pushing her hands down farther, Maisie was frustrated to find nothing of consequence, when she had been so sure that her meditation would yield the clue she needed. She returned to Nick's living room, pulled on her hat and coat, washed the cup and saucer and placed them on the dresser. Then she waited. Waited until the only light on the beach came from the lighthouse, until the coast was clear and she could leave. With her hand held out to guide her from the carriage, she crept back towards the lean-to and claimed the MG. The engine seemed loud, but – she hoped – was probably drowned out by crashing waves as she again made her way slowly along the shingled track out to the main road.

Her route was one that took her across Kent toward Chelstone. But it was as she left the marshes that her headlamps illuminated, just for a second or two, the back of a lorry as it pulled off the main road and down a lane. She thought that the driver had probably not seen her, though she recognized the lorry immediately. It was the same vehicle she had seen at the beach.

Maisie made a mental note of the place where the lorry had turned, and, as she drove along in the darkness, she knew she would be back.

SIX

Maisie had arrived late at Frankie Dobbs's home, yet despite the hour, father and daughter sat together until the small hours, sometimes saying nothing, at other times speaking of Maisie's work or, as now happened increasingly, talking of the past. Frankie Dobbs would begin a sentence with the words, "Do you remember when . . ." and continue with a story of someone he'd known as a young man while working at a racing yard, or perhaps it was a story about one of his customers, the people to whom he'd delivered fruit and vegetables on his rounds as a costermonger. But since 1914 Frankie had lived in Kent, though his dialect was easily recognizable as being from within the sound of the tolling bells of Bow, marking him as a true cockney.

Frankie no longer asked Maisie about Dr Andrew Dene and whether their courtship might lead to him welcoming a son-in-law to their family of two. As he commented to Mrs Crawford, the cook at Chelstone, just before she retired at Christmastime, "Well, I like the boy – London born and bred, you know. Good sort. Got feet on the ground, and does right by Maisie, but, I dunno, she never seems to . . ." And with that he looked into the distance, so that Mrs. Crawford touched him on the shoulder and said, "Don't you worry about our Maisie. She's different. I've said all along: the girl's different. And she'll find her own way. Always has, always will. No, she's not one to worry about." Though as she spoke, Mrs. Crawford reflected briefly on the many times she herself had worried about Maisie Dobbs.

"There you are, fresh eggs this morning and two rashers of bacon! That'll keep you going, my girl."

"You spoil me, Dad." Maisie admonished her father as he sat down to tuck into his own hearty breakfast.

Frankie looked at the clock. "I've got to get out to the horses a bit sharpish this mornin'. I tell you, we're doing well, with another mare due to foal soon, though it'd sit better with me if it weren't so cold for a young 'un to come into the world. Spend all my time makin' sure the stables're warm." He turned back to his breakfast, dipping bread into fried egg.

"As long as you're not overdoing it, Dad."

Frankie shook his head. "Nah. All in a day's work." Deflecting any further harking back to injuries sustained in an accident the year before, Frankie repeated some gossip heard on the estate. "Well, you've certainly set the cat among the pigeons, haven't you?"

"Me?" Maisie set down her knife and fork. "What do you mean?"

"There's talk that, what with you moving out of Ebury Place, 'er Ladyship won't keep it on because you've left and there's no one she trusts to keep an eye on the property, that she'd be better off mothballing it, you know, until that James comes back to England."

"But she didn't keep it on for me, Dad. I was just there as a sort of overseer, and I admit it was handy. Helped me to get some savings in the bank. I'm sure this is just hearsay, you know how they all talk."

Frankie shook his head. "No, I reckon there's something in it this time. Costs a lot of money to keep a house like that going, and even if they just close it up, it'll save a bit." Frankie paused to take a sip of tea. "But I don't think it's the money, myself. No, I think that 'er Ladyship just doesn't want to spend much time up there in the Smoke. And she doesn't want to be out with them types anymore, you know, them what don't know there's a slump on. Reckon the only people she ever 'eld in account were the ones like old Dr Blanche, them with a bit of nouse." Frankie pushed back his plate, then tapped the side of his head with his forefinger. "She don't much mind what station a person is, as long as they've got something to say for themselves. So I reckon it's on the cards, especially with Mrs Crawford gone to 'er brother and 'is wife in Ipswich. They've already brought that Teresa down to work in the kitchen, but it's not as if anyone wants a big staff anymore, not like it was years ago."

"I hope no one really thinks this is all my fault," said Maisie.

"No, not your fault, love, just all come at the same time. And like you said: people talk." Frankie looked at the clock again. "You're off in a minute, I know, so I'll say my good-bye now. Better get over to the stable."

Maisie kissed her father and waved him off, watching him walk slowly down the path. Frankie hated to see his daughter drive away, so she had expected him to leave before she departed the cottage. It was time he retired, and Maisie was grateful for the fact that Lady Rowan had assured her that the Groom's Cottage would be her father's home for the rest of his life; she had never forgotten that Frankie Dobbs had saved her horses from requisition in the war.

After tidying up the kitchen, Maisie packed her bag and left before nine, with the intention of reaching Hastings by ten o'clock. In the solitude of the journey down to the Sussex coast, she could consider the case of Nicholas Bassington-Hope against the cold light of day. And it was most certainly cold, and bright, for a clearing wind had swept across the south leaving blue skies but frosty ground underfoot.

Maisie liked to work methodically through a case, while at the same time allowing for intuition to speak to her, for truth to make itself known. Sometimes such knowledge would be inspired by something as simple as an unfamiliar scent on the air, or perhaps uncovering information regarding a choice made by one of the victims. And Maisie had found that the perpetrator of a crime was often every bit as much a victim. Yet this case seemed to beg for another approach, requiring her to "work both ways at once" as she had commented to her father, when he had asked her about the assignment that had brought her to Dungeness. Not that she had said anything else about the case, simply that it demanded something quite different from her.

That something different was the need to build up a picture, an image of the victim's life without, perhaps, some of the usual information that might have been available. As she drove, she reflected upon the fact that she had not had the advantage of being present soon after the accident, so the immediate environment was clear of that energetic residue she always felt in the immediate presence of death. She thought she might in any case visit the gallery again soon, alone. Thus far she was only just beginning to fill in the outline of Nick Bassington-Hope's life. She had first to sketch in her landscape, then, as she uncovered new information, she would add colour and depth to her work.

Maisie changed gear as she decreased speed down the shallow hill into Sedlescombe. Her thoughts were gathering pace. Wasn't this whole case like creating one of those murals, building a picture across uneven terrain, telling a story by adding detail to give life and momentum to the masterwork?

She had her broad charcoal sketch of the artist's life, now to the finer points. First Dungeness: had she seen something untoward or had the eerie silence of the coast at night ignited her imagination? Perhaps Nick's carriage-window mural had teased her, led her to see something that wasn't there, as hardworking fishermen brought their catch ashore against the unrelenting winter weather. Perhaps the lorry ahead of her on the road was not the one she had seen at the beach, or perhaps it was the same vehicle going to a warehouse or rural factory where fish were packed in ice for transit to London. Maurice had often warned her that the emotional or unsettled mind could interpret an innocent remark into a cause for argument, could change a happily anticipated event into an outing to be dreaded. And hadn't she been unsettled by the greatcoat, by the weight of a garment that had been dragged though Flanders's mud, with sleeves covering arms that, perhaps, had lent support and final comfort to the young officer's dying men?

As Maisie pulled into the narrow road that led to the outer edge of the Old Town, above the slum of broken-down beamed cottages on Bourne Street, and along to the houses that commanded views across the Channel, she knew that she had a list of detailed sketches to create: the Bassington-Hope family; Nick's friends and associates; those who collected his work and those who hated it; the mysterious lock-up. She wanted to know why her client had argued with Stig Svenson at the gallery. Looking back to that first meeting, she remembered Georgina's observation that if someone had murdered Nick, they might also prey on her. What event, what situation gave cause for such a fear, or was it a throwaway comment meant to egg on the investigator? Was she being played for a fool by Georgina as well as by Stratton?

It was early yet, only two days had passed since the first meeting with Georgina Bassington-Hope, but now there was work to do in earnest – if not for her client, then for herself. For she was now quite convinced that even if Nick Bassington-Hope was killed in a terrible accident, and possibly as a result of his own negligence, it had given Svenson a cause to argue with his client's executor, had resulted in a rift between the Bassington-Hope sisters and was leading to some very strange behaviour by Detective Inspector Stratton.

"Maisie! By golly, I thought I would never see you again – and why, might I ask, are you sitting in your little red car staring out to sea?"

Maisie shook her head. "Oh, sorry, Andrew, I was miles away."

Dene opened the door of the MG, took Maisie's hand and

pulled her to him as she alighted. "You've been avoiding me, I think," he said teasingly, though the statement clearly begged for contradiction.

Maisie smiled, and blushed. "Of course I haven't. Don't be silly." She turned her head toward the sea. "Let's go for a walk. I have to leave at about two o'clock, you know, so let's not waste the morning."

For just a second Dene's expression revealed his disappointment, then he smiled in return. "Grand idea, Maisie. Come on in while I put on my coat." He held out his hand for Maisie to go ahead into the house. "Just a pity you aren't staying until tomorrow."

Maisie did not reply, did not turn back to offer an explanation or even an apology. And Dene did not repeat the sentiment, thinking his words had been caught on the wind and swept away, which, he considered, was probably just as well.

IT TOOK ONLY fifteen minutes to amble down to the High Street and then on to Rock-a-Nore toward the tall fishermen's net shops at the Stade, where the couple stopped to watch a boat being winched ashore. Nets from other boats had been heaped in piles, ready to be cleaned out, mended and stowed for another day's fishing. Though Dene was an orthopedic surgeon at the nearby All Saints' Convalescent Hospital, he travelled to London regularly to lecture medical students on matters concerning injuries to the spine and the rehabilitation of those who are adversely affected by accidents, disease or the wounds of war. A protégé of Dr Maurice Blanche, Dene thought that this connection in common with Maisie might promote their fledgling courtship, but after a promising start, he now wondered if he had not been rather optimistic. This morning he had opened his mouth to speak several times, hoping to open a deeper dialogue, only to remain silent.

Strolling along, Maisie and Andrew Dene watched as the womenfolk of the Old Town sold fish, winkles and whelks to winter day-trippers from London, who would take them home, a special treat with a bit of bread and dripping for their Sunday tea. Then there were those who paid a few pence for a white saucer of jellied eels or whelks to eat while leaning against the counter, a delicacy when washed down with a cup of strong tea.

> *"Lovely plate of whelks, that."*
> *"Have you tried them jellied eels?"*
> *"Nice day, when you get out of that wind, innit?"*

All around them conversations could be heard, but little passed between the pair. Dene was about to try another tack, start another conversation, when he noticed Maisie looking across the Stade at one of the fishing boats. She was squinting, holding a hand across her forehead to shield her eyes from the light.

"What is it, Maisie? Seen one of the boys unload a fish you'd like?" quipped Dene.

She barely moved, still staring in the direction of the boat, then looked back at him. "Sorry, Andrew, what did you say? I was rather preoccupied."

Dene replied in a clipped manner. "If you don't mind me saying so, Maisie, you have been rather preoccupied since you arrived. What's the matter? Can't we even have one afternoon together without you seeing something that sparks a thought that clearly takes you back to your work – or to somewhere other than here, with me, in any case?"

Maisie did not address his comment, but instead asked a question. "Andrew, do you know the fishermen here? Are their names familiar?"

Dene suspected that Maisie had barely even heard him. "I – I . . . yes, I do, Maisie. I know most of the families, simply because I'm a doctor and I choose to live close to Bourne Street, where the ordinary people live." He felt tension rise as he spoke, a mixture of annoyance at her avoiding his observation and fear that she might have used the moment to speak of her feelings – feelings he wasn't sure he was ready to hear. He was relieved when she laced her arm through his and continued to walk in the direction of the men she'd been watching.

"Come on, let's wander back to the tea shop. I'd love a cup before I leave for Tenterden." With that she smiled, though Dene was quick to notice that, although she continued speaking, her attention had been drawn to three fishermen now standing alongside their boat. They were deep in discussion, backs against the wind, heads almost touching. As the couple passed by, Dene saw the men look up in unison, then turn back to resume their talk. Maisie was facing him now, as if, he thought, she did not want them to know she had seen them. They crossed the road.

"So, do you know who those men were, Andrew?"

"Look, what's going on, Maisie? I know it's none of my business, but —"

"Just their names, Andrew."

Dene sighed, not for the first time today. "I don't know the one in the middle with the red ponytail, but the other two are brothers. The Drapers: Rowland and Tom. They run *Misty Rose*, the boat they were all leaning against."

Maisie walked faster now, unentwined her arm and faced Dene again. "Andrew, do you know anything about smuggling along the coast?"

Dene laughed, shaking his head as they reached the tea shop. "Oh, the things you ask, Maisie, the things you ask." Placing coins on the counter for two cups of tea, Dene waited until they were served and had secured two seats at a table before replying. "Of course, smuggling has flourished along the coast from the Middle Ages, you know. Once upon a time it was cloth, fine wool or silk. Spice was valuable enough to be smuggled, then alcohol or even the fruits of piracy. It's all a bit cloak-and-dagger and Dr Syn-ish."

"Dr Syn?"

Dene took a sip of his tea before replying. "You should read a few more adventure stories, Maisie, then perhaps you wouldn't look for trouble." He paused to see if she would rise to the bait, but she continued to listen, without comment. "Dr Syn, the Romney Marsh vicar and smuggler – a tale of devil riders and witches, me 'earties!" He mimicked the voice of a pantomime pirate and was delighted when Maisie laughed at his joke, but she soon became serious again.

"And what about now? What do they smuggle now?"

Dene leaned back. "Oh, I don't know if there is smuggling nowadays, Maisie. Of course, there's talk that those caves up on the cliffs all lead to tunnels that in turn wind their way into Old Town cottage cellars – so you know the smuggling went on, and they had a way out with the spoils, so to speak."

Maisie was thoughtful. "But if you had to hazard a guess, what do you think people might smuggle, if they could?"

Dene shook his head, and shrugged. "I really don't know. I mean, I suppose people smuggle things that are hard to get, and that you can get a good price for. I'm not sure that means alcohol anymore, or spices, or silks and wools." He thought for a moment. "People probably smuggle things for different reasons. . . ." He paused, shaking his head. "Now you've got me at it, Maisie. Speculating over something of little consequence." It was Dene's turn to consult his watch. "You'd better be getting on if you want to arrive at your appointment in Tenterden on time."

They reached the MG in silence. Maisie turned to Dene before taking her seat and starting the engine. "I'm sorry, Andrew. I don't seem to be able to give you what you want, do I?" She looked into his eyes, as if to gauge the effect of her admission, her assessment of their situation.

"We're probably the kind of people who end up wanting the same thing at different times." He smiled, though as his shoulders sagged and he looked down at the ground, it was the smile of a man resigned to a situation, rather than one who knew how he might change it.

Maisie touched his cheek with her hand but did not kiss him. It was just as she was about to drive away, her face framed in the side window of the motor car, that Dene leaned down and kissed her. He drew back, then spoke again. "Oh, and about those smugglers – I would imagine that the only reason for smuggling now is if someone is prepared to pay handsomely for something they desire, something that's hard or impossible to get here. There are people who will do almost anything for something they really want, you know." Dene patted the roof of the car as he stepped back to watch Maisie drive off.

THERE ARE PEOPLE who will do almost anything for something they really want, you know. Maisie repeated the words as she drove toward Tenterden. The third man on the beach, the one Dene didn't know, was Amos White, the Dungeness fisherman. Maisie wondered whether it was usual for the fishermen to meet in this way. *Of course, it must be. Surely the fishermen all know one another, they fish the same territory, probably trade together.* But they had seen her, had found it necessary to comment to one another as she passed. Though they whispered, the tension in their bodies, the way they clustered as if to protect a secret, all served to speak directly to Maisie, as if they had uttered their very thoughts to her, or shouted their conversation above the wind. Yes, she had seen them all before, and so had Nick Bassington-Hope. She knew that now.

THE SKY HAD become lightly overcast by the time Maisie reached Tenterden, but instead of being a portent for rain, the cloud cover shimmered, backlit by a low sun that served to render the fields greener, the bare trees more stark against their surroundings. The conditions were ideal for ice on the roads, perhaps snow later. She had allowed more than enough time to drive from Hastings and had enjoyed a clear journey, so there would now be an opportunity to complete a couple of errands. At the florist she bought a small bouquet of flowers for Mrs Bassington-Hope. Blooms were scarce at this time of year, but greenhouse flowers from the Channel Islands of Jersey and Guernsey were available, though expensive. As she left the florist, Maisie wondered how long the shop might remain in business, as expenditure on items such as flowers was becoming increasingly difficult for everyone – not that the poor ever had money for frivolous extras.

The local bookshop was another business run from premises with limited space. She was curious to see a copy of *Dr Syn*, the book mentioned by Andrew Dene. There were two copies in stock, and Maisie settled into a chair to read the first few pages. If the novel had in some way inspired the artist, Maisie wanted to know more about the story. Before leaving the shop, she made a notation or two on an index card, then slipped it into her shoulder bag as she approached the bookseller to thank him for allowing her to look at the book.

"Maisie!" Georgina Bassington-Hope waved to Maisie when she saw her pull up at the station, then walked over to the passenger side of the MG, opened the door and sat down. "I cajoled Nolly into giving me a lift into town. She had to run a few errands, you know, visit the farm tenants, and so on, but if I ask a favour of her, she acts as if I've petitioned her to go in and feed herself to the lions."

Maisie checked the road, then pulled out.

"No, don't let's go yet, I'd like to have a word first."

"Of course." Maisie drove on for a few yards, parked the motor car, turned off the engine, then reached for the scarf and gloves she'd pushed behind her seat. "Only you won't mind if we walk rather than sit here. I see you're wearing sturdy shoes, so come on, let's go."

Georgina agreed, but appeared rather taken aback. Maisie guessed that she was usually the one with the ideas, the one who made suggestions.

"What do you want to talk about?"

"Well, first of all, Nick's carriage-cottage. Did you glean much from your visit?"

Maisie nodded, composing her reply, while at the same time assessing Georgina's mood. The way she walked, held her hands at her sides, opened and closed her fingers into her palm, then just as quickly pushed her hands up into the sleeves of her coat, all revealed a depth of tension, but what else? As they walked, Maisie came into step with her client, holding her hands and shoulders in the same fashion. She felt that not only was Georgina afraid, but her fear came from an expectation of something untoward. In her work, Maisie saw fear revealed time and time again but had learned that it was experienced in degrees, demonstrated in quite different actions and responses from person to person, from one event to another. Anticipation of bad news resulted in a more depressed aura surrounding the one who was afraid – different from, say, that of one who was fearful of another person, or who feared failing to do something by a certain time, or perhaps the consequence of a given action. Maisie suspected that Georgina was rather afraid of what might be uncovered, and that she was also somewhat regretful of her decision to delve into the cause of her brother's accident. She considered that such feelings on Georgina's part could have come as a result of some new information received, or perhaps a sense she had bitten off more than even she could chew.

"I came away with more questions than answers, to tell you the truth. Mind you, that's not unusual at this stage in an investigation." Maisie paused. "I find that I have become rather curious about Nick's work. He was a most interesting artist, wasn't he?"

Georgina took a handkerchief from her pocket, which she dabbed against the small drops of perspiration on her brow and on either side of her nose. "Yes, he was certainly interesting, and innovative. But, in what way did *you* discern that he was 'interesting'?"

Maisie reached inside her coat and glanced at the old nurses' watch pinned to the lapel of her jacket. "I noticed on one or two pieces that Nick depicted people he knew – their faces – in scenes that they couldn't have posed in. I thought it was interesting that he would do such a thing. In fact – and bear in mind, I know nothing about art – I assumed that, much like a writer who casts a character inspired by a person known to him, yet who then protects that person with a fictional name, so the painter will employ all manner of disguises to avoid revealing the real person in a given scene. Nick seems to have gone out of his way to do the opposite."

"Which piece are you referring to?"

"The mural on the walls of his cottage."

"The smugglers?"

"Yes. It appears he used the fictional character, Dr Syn, from the books by Russell Thorndike, to inspire an illustrated story. Yet when you look at the faces, they are men known to him."

"Oh, of course! You know, I think he only did that the once. I remember him saying that fishermen have such weatherbeaten faces, like rocks chiseled by sea over the years, so he wanted to paint them in an historical context. He said that the sheer look of the men brought to mind the whole mythology of smuggling in the area. Then, of course, he read that book and was inspired to depict the story as a decoration for his carriage – all very appropriate, I must say, being on the edge of the mysterious Marshes."

Maisie nodded. "Yes, I thought it was rather clever. Mind you, I was curious about one thing, you know." She turned to Georgina as they walked back to the MG and noticed beads of perspiration across her forehead.

"Oh, what's that?"

Maisie took her seat and leaned across to open a door for Georgina. She started the engine, then continued. "I've placed the three fishermen who inspired the smugglers in the mural, but not the face behind the character of their fearless leader on his charger." She let the comment hang in the air, looked both ways to check the road, then pulled away from the station and drove toward the High Street. "Left or right?"

SEVEN

The entrance to Bassington Place was flanked by two moss-covered pillars from which rusted iron gates hung open. Maisie thought the gates had probably not been closed for years, judging by the ivy tethering them in place. There was a one-story sandstone lodge, to the left, also covered in ivy.

"Gower, our gamekeeper, occasional footman and general estate factotum lives there with his wife, the housekeeper. Frankly, I wonder why we still have a gamekeeper, but Nolly is determined to raise funds by opening the estate to shooting parties. We've always had the locals, you know, and they all pay a bit to shoot, but Nolly has her eye on bigger things – in fact, she got the idea from one of Nick's clients." Georgina pointed to the right. "Carry on along here, then turn right, over there, by that oak tree."

Making her way along a drive bordered by snow-dusted rhododendrons, Maisie drove slowly to avoid ruts in the road, following Georgina's instructions. "One of Nick's clients?"

"Yes, the American tycoon who is desperate to have the triptych. He said that there are still men with plenty of money over there, and they're all looking for a bit of old Europe. I think that if Nolly were left to her own devices, she'd sell the whole place and my parents along with it – now there's a bit of old Europe for you!"

"Is this it?"

"Yes, we're here. And thank heavens, Nolly isn't back yet."

Maisie slowed the MG even more on the approach, so that she could study the property, which she thought was a magnificent example of a grand medieval country house, if now a little down-at-heel. It appeared almost as if three houses had been joined together, there were so many pitched roofs and even some ornate candy-twist Elizabethan chimneys, clearly added at a later date. The sturdy beams that framed the structure were completed by brownish-gray rendering that Maisie suspected had been laid on top of walls made of ancient wattle-and-daub. Diamond-paned windows had changed shape with the centuries, and here and there the beams were less than true where the ground had settled under the weight of walls and burden of years. Despite its size, the ivy-clad house seemed warm and welcoming, and in its way reminded her of Chelstone.

As she parked the MG, the heavy oak door opened with an eerie sound as cast-iron hinges groaned for want of some oil. A tall man of about seventy years of age approached them, but before he reached the motor car, Georgina leaned toward Maisie.

"Look, I realize I should have let you know before now, but I thought it best to tell my parents I had briefed you to look into Nick's accident. Of course, even though I swore them to secrecy, they told Nolly, who has completely gone off the rails about it. Not that I'm scared of Nolly, but she can be such a bloody nuisance, even though one always feels sorry for her . . . but I'm fed up with dancing around her moods." She clambered from the MG, walked toward her father and kissed him on the cheek. "Hello, Piers, darling, let me introduce my old friend from Girton, Maisie Dobbs."

The Bassington-Hope patriarch held out his hand to Maisie, who immediately felt his warmth and strength. He was tall, over six feet in height, and still walked with the bearing of a younger man. His corduroy trousers were well kept, if slightly worn, and along with a Vyella shirt and a rather colourful lavender tie, he wore a brown cable-knit pullover. His ash-grey hair, which matched that of his eyebrows, was combed back, and his steel-grey eyes seemed kind, framed by liver-spotted furrowed skin at the temples and across his brow. Though Georgina had portrayed her parents as being somewhat eccentric, Maisie had been prepared for unusual behaviour but was surprised when the woman used her father's Christian name. As she observed the pair, she gained an immediate sense of Piers Bassington-Hope and suspected he might well use any appearance of eccentricity to his advantage, should such a thing be necessary.

"Delighted to meet you, Miss Dobbs."

"Thank you for inviting me to your home, Mr Bassington-Hope."

"Not at all. We're so glad you've come and that you've agreed to help Georgina here. Anything you can do to put her mind at rest, eh?"

Bassington-Hope's smile of welcome was genuine but could not camouflage a grey pallor that pointed to the man's sorrow at losing his eldest son. It didn't escape Maisie's notice that he used his smile, punctuating his words to great effect, as if to suggest that any investigation was purely for Georgina's emotional well-being, an indulgence of her unsettled state. She suspected that, as far as Nick's father was concerned, the matter was closed, with no further questions on his part. She wondered how Nick's mother was bearing up under the weight of the family's loss.

"Come along, Mrs Gower has put up a tea, the like of which we have not seen in years! Your favourite this weekend, Georgie – Eccles Cakes!" He turned to Maisie. "Our children may well have grown, but Mrs Gower feels a certain need to fill them up with their favourite foods when they make a weekend visit. Nolly's here all the time, poor girl, but of course, if Nick were here . . ." The man's words trailed away as he stood back to allow the women to enter the drawing room before him.

Even before she reached the drawing room, Maisie thought she would need a week to absorb her surroundings. Had this been Chelstone, or perhaps one of the other grand houses she had visited in the course of her work, the decor would have been more reserved, more in keeping with what was considered good taste. There were those adherents of Victorian mores who covered every table leg in sight and who filled every room with heavy furniture, plants and velvet curtains. Others adopted a softer approach, perhaps using those older pieces of furniture but blending them with brighter curtains and light, cream-painted walls instead of a forbidding anaglypta. Then there were those who had plunged headfirst into what the French had termed *Art Deco*. But for most, the decorating of a house was often a question of balancing personal taste with available funds, so even in the grandest homes, a blend of furniture and fittings illustrated the family's history as well as investment in a few new pieces – a gramophone, a wireless, a cocktail bar. But this, the decor in the Bassington-Hope house, represented a departure she found at once stimulating and a little alarming.

In the entrance hall, each wall was painted a different colour, and not only that, someone – perhaps a group of people – had left their mark by adding a mural of a garden of flowers and foliage growing up from a green skirting board. It appeared as if ivy had snaked in from the exterior of the house. On another wall, a rainbow arched over a doorway, and even the curtains had been dyed in a variety of patterns to match the artistic frivolity around her. An old chaise longue had been recovered in plain duck, then the fabric painted in a series of triangles, circles, hexagons and squares. Avant-garde tapestry wall hangings and needlepoint pillows of red with yellow orbs or orange with green parallel lines added to the confusion of colour.

The drawing room seemed to be named more for the activity that went on there than as a place to which guests would withdraw for tea or drinks. The walls were painted pale yellow, the picture rail in deep maroon, while the skirting boards and doors were hunter green. When she had the opportunity to look more closely, Maisie saw that the beveled edges of the panelled doors were finished in the same burgundy, along with the window frames.

Georgina's mother turned from her place in front of one of two easels set alongside French windows, wiped her hands on a cloth and came to welcome Maisie, who thought she was as colourful as the house itself. Her grey hair was coiled and pinned on the top of her head in a loose braid, with wisps coming free at the back and sides. A paint-splashed blue artist's smock covered her clothing, but Maisie could see the lower half of a deep-red embroiderd skirt. She wore hooped earrings, and bangles of silver and gold on her wrists. She looked like a gypsy, reminding Maisie of the Kalderasa immigrants who'd flooded into London's East End some twenty years earlier, bringing with them a mode of dress that had been adopted by many of those tired of dour, lingering Victoriana.

"Thank heavens Georgina found you. With Nolly driving, we thought she might insist on completing her errands first before running Georgie to the station to meet you. We were worried you'd be left in the lurch." Emma Bassington-Hope clasped Maisie's hand between both of her charcoal-stained hands. "As you can see, Mrs Gower has laid out a magnificent tea – did you tell them, Piers? Come along, let's sit down to our feast and you can tell us all about yourself." She turned to her daughter and husband. "Throw those books on the floor, darlings."

Becoming comfortable on a settee covered in floral fabric, she beckoned Maisie and patted the place next to her. Georgina and her father seated themselves in armchairs that reminded Maisie of old gentlemen in the midst of an afternoon nap. The settee springs had softened in the middle, so that, despite the large feather cushions, Maisie couldn't help but lean toward her hostess. It was as if the settee was conspiring to bring her into the woman's confidence, which wasn't a bad thing, as far as Maisie was concerned.

"Emsy, Maisie is here on business, remember. She will have to ask you some questions."

Maisie smiled and raised a hand. "Oh, that's all right, Georgina. Later. There's plenty of time." She turned to Emma Bassington-Hope, and then to Georgina's father. "You have a lovely house, so interesting."

Georgina poured tea and passed cups to her guest, then her mother and father before offering cucumber sandwiches. Emma continued the conversation with Maisie.

"Well, it is a wonderful house for people who love to paint. We're surrounded by the most exquisite countryside – we grow all our own vegetables, you know – and we have all this space to experiment with. And Piers and I have always been proponents of the notion that our canvases do not have to be squares constructed of wood and cloth." She pointed at her daughter. "Why, when Georgie was a child, she would compose whole stories on the bedroom walls, then Nick would come in and illustrate them – we still have them, you know. Couldn't bear to paint over them, and now, of course, it's even more . . ." She held her hand over her mouth, then reached for the edge of the painter's smock and pressed it against her eyes.

Piers Bassington-Hope looked down at his feet, stood up and walked to the window, stopping alongside his wife's artwork, where he picked up a charcoal and added to her piece, then crushed it between his thumb and fingers. For her part, Georgina studied her hands, and glanced at Maisie, who had made no move to comfort the woman, whose shoulders moved as she sobbed into the smock. After some moments, moments during which Georgina's father had opened the French doors and walked outside, Maisie reached across, taking the older woman's hands in both of her own, as Emma had held Maisie's hands when they were introduced.

"Tell me about your son, Emma."

The woman was quiet for a while, then sniffed and shook her head, though she was looking directly at Maisie. "This is quite unusual for me, you know. I have barely met you, yet already I feel as if I am here with someone I have known for a long time."

Maisie said nothing, waiting, still with her fingers cocooning the woman's hands.

"I've been lost, quite lost, since the accident. Nick was so much more like me, you see. Georgina's like her father – he writes, you know, and he's also accomplished in other ways: designing furniture, drawing and composing music. That's where Harry gets it from, I would think. But Nick was an artist through and through. I saw that even in boyhood. His work was so sophisticated for a child, his sense of perspective, the level of observation, acute. I remember thinking that not only could the boy draw a man working in a field, but he seemed to draw the very thoughts the man held within him. It was as if he could tell the complete story of the field, of each bird, of the horse, the plough. I could show you his boyhood drawings and paintings, and you would see – his heart and soul were poured into every line of charcoal on the paper, every sweep with sable and colour. Nick *was* his work." She choked on a sob, then leaned forward toward her knees, her forehead now touching Maisie's hands as they continued to clasp her own. So earnest was her grasp that Maisie herself felt drawn to lean forward, to acknowledge the mother's trust in allowing her tears to fall, and to gentle her by resting her cheek against the back of the grieving woman's head. They remained so for some moments, until Maisie felt the dreadful keening subside, whereupon she sat up, but did not move her hands. Some moments later, when Emma Bassington-Hope raised her head, Maisie drew back her hands and looked into the woman's eyes.

"Goodness me, I . . . I . . . do excuse me, I . . ."

Maisie spoke, her voice soft. "Say nothing, there's no need." She paused. "Would you like to show me some of Nick's work, tell me more about him?"

IT WAS PERHAPS an hour later that Georgina's mother and Maisie returned to the drawing room. During that time, Maisie had received a tour of the house, seen that every room was decorated in a different colour and style and had concluded that this family seemed to typify everything she had associated with the word *bohemian*. The Bassington-Hope parents had clearly adopted a way of life that would have shocked the elders of their time, but they were not alone in their day in seeking an authenticity through which to explore their creative sensibilities. They had been fortunate to inherit land and property, resources that enabled them to pass on the indulgence to their children, who had no reason to believe that any door was closed to them, though Maisie was now intrigued to see if such an assumption was shared by the eldest child.

More of Nick Bassington-Hope's work was on display around the house, though Emma pointed out that Nolly had sold a few pieces, gifts to his parents, even before Nick's death. It was an action that, apparently, had caused Nick to argue with Nolly and had later incurred Georgina's wrath. The parents had acquiesced at the time, realizing that the family trust was presently looking more than a little underfunded. During their conversation, Maisie became even more curious about Harry, as his name was seldom mentioned.

Maisie and Emma returned to the settee, where the demonstrative woman had taken Maisie's hands in her own once again. She was talking about Nick's wartime service, explaining how he had felt the need to "do his bit" for King and country, and had joined the Artists' Rifles at the outset of war in 1914.

"I think it was having been in Belgium before the war, he felt that he should. Of course, we were completely against it – after all, Nick was a sensitive boy." She smiled. "Now if they had given a rifle to Nolly or Georgie, I might not have worried so much, but then Georgie went in, anyway, and rather got herself in trouble with the authorities. And as for Nolly –"

" 'As for Nolly' what?" The door slammed, and a tall, fortyish woman wearing a tweed walking skirt, brown leather shoes and a brown woollen jacket strode into the room. Pulling a beret from her head and running her fingers through mousey-brown hair cut in a sharp bob, she cursed the snow that had begun to fall again and glared at Maisie as she helped herself to tea and a scone. With features more pointed than Georgina's, Noelle Bassington-Hope appeared terse and inflexible, and it occurred to Maisie that worry and tension had taken a toll on her looks.

"Go on, Mother, confess all, 'as for Nolly' – what?"

"Oh, don't be boring, Nolly. Miss Dobbs is our guest." Georgina fumed at Nolly as she and her father had entered the drawing room through the French doors, just in time to hear the elder sibling demand an explanation of the overheard conversation.

Maisie held out a hand to Noelle, though she realized that she did not know Noelle's married surname. "Mrs . . ."

"Grant. You must be Georgie's inquiry agent, not that there's anything to inquire into." She took a bite from her scone, set the plate back on the table and held out her hand. Her actions were revealing: the nonchalant insult, executed with a certain flippancy, though Maisie understood her manner to reveal a lack of confidence, and something else, a sensation she had encountered already today. *She's afraid of me.*

"A pleasure, Mrs Grant." Maisie paused. "I've been looking forward to meeting you."

"Hmmph!" Noelle sat down next to her mother, in the place just vacated by Maisie. "I'm surprised a woman of your intelligence would get involved in this sort of thing – after all, our family was bereaved by an accident. Mind you, the things that women of supposed intelligence are wont to get up to always did flummox me, eh Georgie?" She looked across at her sister, who had claimed her seat once more, though her father was now holding out his hand for Maisie to be seated, while reaching for a sturdy wooden chair that was not simply varnished but painted in a wine colour, with gold stars embellishing the seat.

"Oh, for God's sake, Noll." The younger sister rolled her eyes.

Though a family row might well have revealed much to her, Maisie did not want to become embroiled in sibling arguments. She stood up, claiming her shoulder bag. "Mrs Grant, I realize that Georgina's decision to enlist my services must have come as a complete shock to you – after all, your family is so recently bereaved, and of course you have broad responsibilities as a justice of the peace here and also in managing your parents' estate. I would very much like to speak with you, especially as, in your role as a JP, you are familiar with the need for detail – is that not so?"

"Well . . . I . . . when you put it like that, I suppose . . ."

"Good." Maisie held out her hand toward the garden, where one could just about make out the path against the dusk. "Let's go for a stroll. It's not as cold as it was and it's only just started to snow lightly. I would value your opinion on a few matters."

"Righty-o." Noelle Grant set down her cup and plate, clearly warming to Maisie's compliments. "I'll whistle for the dogs and off we'll go. Just a tick while I grab a scarf and gloves." She stopped by the window as she looked out. "We'll go out by the back door – I'll find you some gum boots and an old jacket; you'll need them."

Noelle led Maisie to the gun room, which smelled of wet dogs, rubber boots and stale pipe smoke. Once furnished with suitable outdoor clothing, Noelle took two walking sticks from an old clay pot, handed one to Maisie before opening the door and striding forward into the gently falling snow.

"Hmmm, I hope this doesn't settle, you know. Otherwise I'll have to get old Jenkins out with his horses to clear the drive in the morning." She went on, barely glancing at Maisie as she spoke. "The man has a brand-new tractor in his barn and still maintains the shires do a better job. I keep telling him, 'Move with the times, Jenkins, or be done for!'"

Maisie kept up stride for stride as they passed an old shooting brake that she supposed Noelle used to drive herself to and fro between committee meetings and visits to tenant farmers. "There are some folk who are just more confident with tools they know, and he will probably do a better job with the horses than the tractor because of it."

"Hmmph! Well, we'll see about that tomorrow morning, won't we?"

The footpath ahead was barely visible under a layer of snow, so as far as Maisie was concerned, it would have to be a quick walk if she were to get on the main road to Chelstone before the weather made the going difficult for her low-slung MG.

"Mrs Grant, I –"

"Call me Nolly, everyone else does – we're nothing if not informal at Bassington Place."

"Nolly, I wonder if you could tell me about your brother Nick, from your perspective. I'm curious to know more about him – and I understand you may have more insight than most, given that your husband served with him during the war."

Maisie looked sideways and noticed creases form around her companion's mouth as she pressed her lips together. Though she could not see her forehead under her hat, she knew the woman was frowning.

"I don't think Nick was ever as much a flibbertigibbet as Georgie. Yes, they were twins, but Nick was always more single-minded." She paused for just a second or two, then continued. "Now, I know you asked about Nick, but if we go back to the beginning then we have to talk about them both, for they were twins, and although they were always each their own person, there were obvious similarities, and people tended to think of them together."

"I see."

"Georgie could – and still can, I must say – be a bit of a will-o'-the-wisp, a new idea every five seconds – like hiring you, if you don't mind me saying so." She turned toward Maisie, her frown now evident. "Of course, the war calmed her down a lot – a grand idea to do what she did, but she almost bit off more than she could chew. It made her pull her neck in a bit, being in the midst of the horror. Don't get me wrong, I admire her for it, but . . . anyway, you asked about Nick." She paused to negotiate a fallen branch and beckoned Maisie to walk ahead of her for a moment or two before continuing along the path side by side. "Nick had all of Emsy's emotion, all of that feeling, that intensity, but it was tempered by something from my father, a solidity, I suppose you could call it. Of course, they're all an arty lot, my family, but Piers has a bit more – Lord, what would you call it?" Nolly stopped and looked up, taking a moment to call the dogs back to heel.

"Practicality?" suggested Maisie.

"That's it! Yes, Piers may be a creative individual, but he also has a practicality about him – for example, his skill is in making furniture that's both functional as well as artistic; he is craftsman and artist in equal measure. Now, if you take me – I am under no illusions, no illusions whatsoever – I am all practicality, and not a shred of the arty. Nick, as I said, was both. But as boy and man he could and did sail close to the wind."

"Just like Georgina?"

"But in a different way. Georgina didn't care who she upset, whereas Nick was more deliberate. He wanted to shake certain people, certain *types* of people, out of assumptions they may have made. Georgina sprayed her bullets with abandon; Nick always had a target before he took aim. And don't get me wrong, I admired him terribly. I just think . . . oh, I don't know . . . I just think certain sleeping dogs should be allowed to lie, that's all."

"The war?"

"Yes, the war, for a start." Nolly looked up again and across the land now covered with soft, white snow. "We'd better be walking back soon. It's getting dark and this snow is in for the night now. We'll put on the wireless to listen to the weather forecast when we get back."

The women walked for a while, talking about Nolly's various occupations and plans for Bassington Place and the surrounding land. The estate extended for some considerable distance before reaching the first farm. Though much of the land was obscured by snow, there were meadows and woodland where, Maisie imagined, primroses, bluebells and abundant white wood anemones bloomed in spring. A river meandered across part of the land, probably to join the river Rother as it flowed on through the Marshes.

Maisie continued her questioning as they made their way back to the house. "So, tell me about the war and Nick."

"He joined up straightaway, dragging his arty friends with him, even that one who was far too young at the time, what was his name" – she pulled up her collar –"Courtman, that's the one, Alex Courtman. Anyway, they were all sent to different regiments following their training, so it was rather a surprise when Godfrey and Nick found they were serving together."

"I was sorry to learn that your husband was lost in France."

Nolly Grant shook her head. "Nothing *lost* about it. He was *killed*, buried over there. No, he wasn't *lost*, I know exactly where he is. My husband died a hero on a battlefield, fighting for his country – and proud of it, I'll have you know! Let's get down to brass tacks here, none of this 'lost' or 'passed' business. I get so fed up with all this pussy-footing around the truth. People die, they don't get lost and they don't pass anywhere either!"

Maisie raised her eyebrows. "I understand that Nick was close to him when he died."

"Nick was wounded shortly after Godfrey died. I received the telegram informing me that I was a widow, then looked after my brother as soon as he was brought home. Kept me busy. No time to think about it, you know. You have to get on and look after the living, don't you?"

"Of course." Maisie nodded, choosing her words with care. "Nolly, did you appprove of Nick?"

The woman sighed, looking at cobblestones underfoot as they came back into the stable yard. "What did it matter whether I approved or disapproved? This family does what it wants when it wants, without thinking of anyone else. And if they don't let me go ahead with plans for the estate, we'll all be at the doors of the poorhouse!" She paused. "Of course, that's a bit of an exaggeration, but I'm the only one with any sense of the money it takes to run the place or how to deal with the tenant farmers – Godfrey was a sort of de facto manager after we got married and before he went over to France and we ran things together. Now I want to draw people in, you know, visitors. And visitors would never come if two of the Bassington-Hopes – make that three, if Harry has his way – manage to rub people up the wrong way all the time. So, did I approve? No, I didn't. They tried to change things that you just can't change." She looked directly at Maisie. "Did Nick and Georgie really think they could stop a war with their pictures and words? Bloody stupid if you ask me. Frankly, someone should have stopped *them* long ago. Here, use this to pull off your boots."

The women removed boots and coats, and before entering the main part of the house, Nolly looked out of the window to cast judgment on the weather.

"Well, Maisie, I don't think you'll be going anywhere but a guest room tonight. From here I can see that the avenue down to the main road is barely passable now. In fact, you should bring your motor around to the stable yard and get it under cover."

"But I must –"

"Please don't argue. We never allow guests to leave impaired by wine or weather. Now at least Piers can impress you with his 1929 elderflower!"

"NOLLY'S ABSOLUTELY RIGHT, you simply cannot expect to drive as far as Chelstone in this weather – it's probably even worse over toward Tonbridge anyway. No, you must stay, mustn't she, Emsy, Piers?" Georgina looked at her mother and father while her sister poured glasses of sherry from the tray just brought into the room by Mrs Gower.

Maisie acquiesced. "Thank you for your hospitality. I do have to ask a favour, though – I've left my bag at my father's house and I should really telephone him so that he won't worry about me."

"Of course, my dear. Nolly, do show Maisie the telephone. Let's just hope the lines aren't down, you never know. The good news is that, according to Jenkins, who came to the door just after you left, this little lot should clear with ease tomorrow morning. He said – his words – that it was the light fluffy stuff, not the hard stuff, so he'll be over with Jack and Ben to clear the avenue first thing."

"Not the tractor?"

"No, the horses."

"That silly man!" Nolly cursed as she led Maisie to the telephone in the entrance hall.

Having assured her father that she was safe with friends, Maisie moved the MG to a spare stall in the stable block. Originally built to house fifteen horses, the stables were now home to four hunters, with other stalls kept for storage and for horses belonging to the paying guests welcomed by Nolly Grant. Returning to the house, she was shown to a guest room by Georgina.

"Good, the fire's been lit, and Mrs Gower has laid out fresh towels for you. Here, let me show you, there's a bathroom next door. It's a bit old, you could do a lap or two in the bathtub. I'll bring along some nightclothes for you, and a dress for dinner, though it may be a bit big. Nolly likes to keep up appearances and as much as she annoys me, she's stuck down here, so I just go along with it. We never did that sort of thing when we were growing up, so she was always embarrassed to bring friends home. Shame really." Georgina smiled, waving as she left the room. "Drinks in about half an hour, then we'll have dinner. I think it's roast duck this evening."

Maisie looked around the room. The wooden panelling must have once been dark brown, varnished then waxed to a glorious shine. Now it was painted in different colours, a checkerboard of green and yellow with a blue border. In each yellow square, someone had painted a geometric interpretation of a butterfly, a moth or a bee on the flower. Above the blue picture rail, a golden spider's web ran up to and across the ceiling, with the centre of the web at exactly the point at which the light fixture had been added.

"Caught in the Bassington-Hope web!" Maisie smiled to herself as she contemplated the serendipitous assignment of guest room. She walked through to the bathroom, which was mercifully plain, she thought, painted in white, with white tiles surrounding the ancient claw-footed bath and covering the floor. A dark oak chair was situated in one corner and a matching towel rail in another. As she leaned over to turn on the taps, however, she noticed that both pieces of furniture had likely been made to match the room, for the chair had a butterfly carved as if it had just landed on the back, and the towel rail bore a wooden spider climbing along one side. Returning to the bedroom, a closer inspection of the counterpane revealed a patchwork design of garden insects, with needlepoint cushions on the window seat crafted to match. As the bath filled with piping-hot water, Maisie turned to see a poem painted on the back of the door. It was a simple verse, a child's poem. No doubt the room was the work of Georgina and Nick together, the furniture had been made by Piers, with the counterpane and cushions designed by Emma. Was every room in this house an exhibition of the Bassington-Hopes' artistry? And if so, how did Nolly feel about being excluded from the hive of activity, for thus far Maisie had seen no evidence of her involvement.

Maisie found Piers to be most solicitous toward his wife and daughters, formally crooking his left elbow for Emma to rest her hand and be escorted into the dining room, then stepping aside for his daughters and Maisie to enter first. He led Emma to one end of the table, made sure she was comfortable, then waited for the women to be seated before taking his place opposite his wife. Emma was wearing a deep-red velvet gown with a black shawl around her shoulders. Her grey hair had been brushed back, but remained loose, neither braided nor coiled.

"Now you'll be treated to Daddy's wines!" Georgina reached for her table-napkin, then turned to Piers. "What are we having this evening to grace the duck, Daddy?"

Piers smiled. "Last year's damson."

"Fruity with an oakish balance," added Georgina.

"Utter tosh!" Nolly reached for her glass, as Gower, now dressed in formal attire, served a rich blood-red wine from a crystal decanter. "Not the wine, of course, Daddy, but Georgina's description, as usual trimmed with lace!"

"Girls, please! Let's not bicker in front of our guest."

"Hear, hear, Em, hear, hear." Piers raised an eyebrow in mock annoyance, then reached out to place a hand on the hand of each daughter. "They may be grown women, Maisie, but together they can be like cats!"

"And when Nick was here, why —"

Maisie looked from Emma to Piers. The head of the Bassington-Hope household had released his daughters' hands, and now looked down, shaking his head.

"Oh, darling, I'm sorry, I shouldn't have." Emma shook her head, admonishing herself. "It was the wrong moment, with us all together here, and with company."

"If you would excuse me —" Piers placed his table-napkin next to his still-full glass and left the room.

Nolly pushed back her chair, as if to follow her father.

"Noelle!" Emma used her elder daughter's Chistian name, which, Maisie noticed, caused her to turn immediately. "Let your father have a moment. We all feel grief, and we never know when it might catch us. For Piers, it is as a father for his son, and none of us know how deeply that might touch the heart."

"Emsy's right, you know, Nolly, you always think you can —"

"Enough, Georgina. Enough!" Emma turned to Maisie and smiled. "Now then, Maisie, I understand that you are good friends with Lady Rowan Compton. Did you know we were presented at court in the same year?"

Maisie held her wineglass by the stem and leaned aside as Mrs Gower served pea soup from the tureen. She smiled at her hostess. "What a coincidence! No, I didn't know. I bet she was quite a firebrand in her day."

"My goodness, yes. In fact, I think that's why I quite admired her, you know. After all, neither of us really enjoyed that sort of thing, though one was terribly honoured to be presented to Her Majesty. Of course, she went off and married Julian Compton – he was considered quite the catch – when, according to my mother, her mother feared that she might take up with that funny man, what was his name?" She tapped the table, trying to remember.

"Maurice Blanche?" offered Maisie.

"Yes, that's the one. Of course, he's very famous now, isn't he?" Maisie nodded.

"And I – thank heavens," continued Emma, "found an artist who saw the world from eyes like mine, *and* who also had a name, much to my parents' delight."

"Talking about how fortunate you were to bag me, eh, Emsy?"

"Darling, yes I am!" Emma Bassington-Hope's eyes glistened as her husband entered the room once again, taking his place at the head of the table.

"Here we go, ready for a walk down memory lane, Piers?" Nolly rolled her eyes in a conspiratorial fashion.

"A finer walk could not be had – if our new friend could bear to join us." Piers looked to Maisie.

"Of course. And I must say, this is an exquisite wine."

"Yes, and hopefully there will be more of it – where's Gower?" Nolly interjected again.

Two more decanters of Piers Bassington-Hope's carefully crafted wine tempered the family's tensions and, thought Maisie, made them sparkling company. By eleven o'clock they were lingering over the cheese course, Piers had loosened his tie at Emma's request and the two sisters were finally at ease with each other.

"Do let's tell Maisie about the big play. You remember, when Nick almost drowned dear little Harry in the river."

"Should've held his head down a bit longer!"

"Oh, Nolly, come on!" Georgina reached across and tapped her sister playfully on the hand, and they both began to laugh. She turned to Maisie. "Now then, I think Nolly must have been sixteen, because Harry was only four."

"I *was* sixteen, silly – it was my birthday!"

Piers laughed. "Sweet sixteen and we invited everyone we knew for the weekend. How many sixteen-year-olds have two members of Parliament, three actors, a clutch of poets and writers and I don't know how many artists at her party?"

"And not one other sixteen-year-old!" Nolly turned to Maisie, giggling. Maisie thought that she was most like her sister when she laughed.

Georgina took up the story. "We decided to do a river play – all of us."

Maisie shook her head. "What's a river play?"

"A play on the river! Seriously, we had to compose a play that could be acted from the rowing boats, so we thought it would be a good idea to plunder Viking history."

"Pity we didn't know your friend Stig, then, isn't it?"

"Now then . . ." Piers cautioned his eldest daughter, concerned that such a remark might annoy Georgina, who just waved her hand as if swatting a fly.

"There we were, all dressed up in our finery, the actors in boats, thee-ing and thy-ing and throwing hysterical fits of dramatic art back and forth, and Nick decided, on the spur of the moment, to bring some realism into the play. Harry, dear Harry, had just mastered the recorder and had been cast as a court jester – he was always either the dog or the court jester –" Georgina could hardly speak for laughing, aided, thought Maisie, by another glass of the somewhat lethal damson wine.

Nolly continued where her sister left off. "So, Nick picked up Harry, saying, 'I shall cast yonder servant into the sea!' and threw him in the river. Well, of course, Harry went down like an anchor, and there was a bit of laughing, until Emma screamed from the bank, which reminded us that he couldn't swim! Very stupid, when I come to think of it."

"Anyway, Nick leaped into the water – which wasn't that deep – and pulled out poor spluttering Harry." Georgina was now in fits of laughter.

Piers smiled. "Maisie, this is the sort of high jinks our children got up to when they were younger – terrifying at times, thoroughly mischievous in hindsight, but good for a laugh later on."

Maisie inclined her head and nodded agreement, though she wondered if Harry found the experience mischievous, *in hindsight*.

"And," added Georgina, "I remember poor little wet Harry screaming, 'I hate you, Nick, I hate you! Just you wait until I grow up!' Which of course incited Nick to even more teasing, along the lines of 'You and your army, eh, Harrykins?'"

The laughter subsided and Emma suggested retiring to the drawing room for coffee. As they relaxed in front of the fire, Emma brought out photograph albums, telling detailed stories of this event or that. Soon, however, the wine that had aided such mirth an hour earlier now rendered the group more than a little soporific.

Maisie returned to her room, warm and cosy as Gower had made up the fire before retiring. A hot-water bottle had been placed in the bed and an extra blanket folded across the counterpane. She undressed, put on the nightgown left by Georgina and snuggled under the covers. Before turning off the light, Maisie leaned back on the pillows and gazed at the golden threads of the spider's web above. She found the Bassington-Hopes almost as intoxicating as Piers's homemade wine, though she had taken only a few sips at dinner. She was warmed by the intimacy of their stories, the sharing of family events and photographs. But was she captivated by the colour, by the sheer audacity of the family? And if so, could she be blindsided by them, unable to discern something important with her usual integrity?

It was clear that Nick Bassington-Hope was the blue-eyed boy of the family. And despite their differences, Maisie detected a respect between Noelle and Georgina, as if each held the other's strength and bravery in some account. Though Noelle might have thought that Georgina took enormous risks, and clearly disapproved of her way of life, she was proud of her sister's accomplishments as a journalist. For her part, Georgina may well be frustrated by her sister's bossy behavior, the disapproval even of her parents, but she was filled with compassion for the woman who had lost her husband to war, the young man she clearly adored. Georgina, too, was a woman alone, and understood Noelle's quest to rebuild her life, the need to fashion a future with financial security, with companionship and with meaning.

Noelle had been completely honest with Maisie about her ambitions for the estate, and her belief that they should use Nick's legacy to fund repairs and an income foundation based upon more than the leased farms and proceeds from the sale of various crops. It was evident that she considered both Nick and Georgina "troublesome" and Harry a lost cause. *A musician, if you please!*

And as Maisie replayed each and every sentence in their conversation, along with an image of the way Noelle moved when she made a point, or waited for Maisie to complete a question, she was struck by the fact that the eldest sibling – the one who tried, with limited success, to rule the Bassington-Hope roost, who acted more like a matriarch than her mother – had, apparently, never asked to speak to the person who discovered Nick's body, had held back from visiting the gallery and had declined the pilgrimage to a London mortuary to say that final farewell to her brother. While the older sister was recounting events at one of Nick's exhibitions, Georgina – who was more than a little tipsy and leaning toward Maisie on the soft-cushioned settee – whispered, "She didn't even come to see him at the chapel of rest."

No, Maisie had not finished with "poor Nolly" yet, any more than she had with any of the Bassington-Hopes, Georgina included. And then there was Harry. What was it that Georgina's father had said about his younger son, when they were looking at photographs taken of the children in the summer of 1914? It was when he pointed out the photograph of Noelle, Georgina, Nicholas and

Harry, who was about twelve years of age at the time, some ten years younger than the twins, and about half Noelle's age. "And there he is, bringing up the rear. Harry. Always behind, always on the edge, that's Harry."

Burrowing under the covers, Maisie pondered the words before sleep claimed her: *always behind, always on the edge, that's Harry.*

EIGHT

An early morning thaw, together with the efforts of the industrious tenant farmer and his shire horses, meant that the avenue leading to Bassington Place was cleared of snow by eleven, allowing Maisie to leave at noon with Georgina, who had claimed a lift back into London. After a journey that proved to be slow-going, they reached Chelstone. The women conversed comfortably throughout the drive, though in quiet times, Maisie found herself questioning the source of an unease in Georgina's company that had dogged her from the time the woman had first come to her office in Fitzroy Square. At first she had brushed it aside, but now the sensation was hard to ignore. As much as she admired Georgina's strength and felt a compassion for her as she mourned her brother, there was something that nagged at her. It was as they drove through the village of Chelstone that a single word came to Maisie with such power that she almost said it out loud. The word was *doubt*. Her sense of confidence was being undermined by doubt, though she did not know whether it was her ability that she doubted, or her relationship with Georgina and the other

Bassington-Hopes or the case itself. She wished she had time alone to think, to discover the cause of a potentially crippling emotion.

"I say, what a pile, Maisie. And I thought Bassington Place was sprawling! You certainly kept this quiet, didn't you?" Georgina's voice sounded loud to Maisie.

"Oh, we're not going to the main house, Georgina. My father lives in the Groom's Cottage." She turned left down a lane just past the Dower House, where Maurice Blanche lived, and drew up alongside the small beamed cottage that was her father's home. "I shan't be a moment."

"I'm not sitting out here in the freezing cold! Come on, you've met my family. It's my turn now." Georgina opened the passenger door and almost ran to the cottage, rubbing her arms as she went.

Before Maisie could take another step, the door had opened and Frankie Dobbs, expecting to see his daughter, instead came face to face with Georgina Bassington-Hope. Maisie felt her cheeks flush. This was only the third time since her mother died that someone she would introduce as a "friend" had come to the house. There had been Simon during the war, then Andrew last year, but no one else.

"Dad, this is –" Maisie slammed the driver's door.

"Georgina Bassington-Hope. Absolutely delighted to meet you, Mr Dobbs."

Frankie appeared somewhat startled, but was quick to welcome Georgina. "Pleasure to meet you, miss." He beamed as Maisie approached, taking her in his arms as she leaned forward to kiss him on the cheek. "Come on inside, both of you. It's brassy out here."

Once in the cottage, Frankie pulled another chair in front of the fire. "You didn't tell me you'd be bringing a friend home, Maisie. I'd've bought something special for tea."

"It was a last-minute decision, Dad. We'd been snowed in and Georgina needed a lift back to London."

"I'll put the kettle on." Frankie moved toward the kitchen.

"We're not staying, Dad. I've just come to –"

"Nonsense!" Georgina took off her coat and scarf, placed them across the back of an armchair and stood with her back to the fire. "A cup of tea to fortify us for the road would be excellent. Shall I lend a hand?"

Maisie flushed again, annoyed with Georgina for taking liberties – first when she insisted upon coming into the house, and now in assuming that she could just march in and do as she wanted. "No, that's all right. I'll go."

Laughter came from the sitting room as Maisie bustled around the kitchen gathering cups and saucers and setting them on the tray with such energy that she thought they might crack. She knew her behaviour was juvenile, knew that if she tried to explain her mood, she would seem – and feel – churlish, but as she listened to Georgina asking her father questions, drawing him out so that the usually reticent man conversed easily, Maisie wanted to run into the room and stop the exchange immediately. *Why do I feel like this?* Was it possible that she was jealous of Georgina, of her colourful family, of the ease with which she assumed the position of engaging guest? Lifting the heavy kettle from the stove, Maisie filled the teapot with boiling water, realizing, as she pulled away from the rising hot steam, that she wanted to protect her father, wanted to stop the conversation so that no more was revealed of their life together. She set the kettle on the stove again, placed the lid on the teapot and lingered. *I do not trust her.* Yes, that was where the doubt was rooted, in a lack of trust.

Having let her guard down while at Bassington Place, Maisie felt that Georgina was using that knowledge of her, overstepping the mark, giving her father the impression of a friendship that did not – could not – exist between them. She picked up the tea tray and, stooping to avoid the low beam above the door, returned to the sitting room, determined to wrest control of the conversation.

It was a half an hour later that Maisie insisted they should leave, given the possibility of poor road conditions. Frankie Dobbs donned a heavy woollen jacket so that he could wave them off. As she pulled out onto the carriage sweep, she automatically looked to her left before proceeding right and saw Lady Rowan walking across the snow-covered lawn with her three dogs at heel. She waved her walking stick in the air to attract Maisie's attention.

"Who's that?" asked Georgina.

"Lady Rowan Compton. Look, please stay here, Georgina, I really must say a quick hello."

Georgina opened her mouth to speak, but Maisie had already stepped from the motor car and slammed the door behind her before running to greet her former employer.

"I say, lovely to see you, Maisie – though I do wish I had known you were at Chelstone. It's a long time since we sat down for a chat."

"It's a flying visit, Lady Rowan, I needed to collect my case. I was snowed in while visiting a friend and couldn't return to Chelstone until this morning. Now we're back off into town."

Lady Rowan squinted toward the motor. "Is that your doctor friend in the MG?"

Maisie shook her head. "Oh, no. That's the friend I stayed with last night, Georgina Bassington-Hope."

"Bassington-Hope?" Maisie noticed the older woman's posture change with her words, her back becoming straighter, her shoulders bracing. "Daughter of Piers and Emma Bassington-Hope, by any chance?"

"Yes, that's right."

Lady Rowan shook her head. "Well, I never."

"Is something wrong, Lady Rowan?"

"No, no, nothing at all." She smiled at Maisie, then added in a brisk manner, "Better not keep you. It's turned into a lovely day, with the sun streaking across the snow. The roads will be clearer now, so you'll have a good run back into town." The dogs began to bark as they ran in the direction of the Groom's Cottage, for they had seen Frankie Dobbs, whom they knew to be a source of treats. "Oh, dear, just when I thought they were behaving. Cheerio, Maisie."

Maisie said good-bye, ran to her MG and set off. When she looked back before turning onto the Tonbridge Road, she saw Lady Rowan standing with her father, both of them staring after the motor car. Though Frankie Dobbs gave a final wave, Lady Rowan did not raise her hand. Even from a distance Maisie knew that she was frowning.

MAISIE WAS DELIGHTED to return to her own flat to find that the radiators were now warm to the touch. It was enough to contribute to the costs of the central boiler, without adding on a gas fire. Thank heavens the builders had decided not to put in one of the efficient, but so expensive, electric fires.

Sitting in an armchair, her legs curled to one side, she rested a notebook on her knees and jotted some notes. Despite thoughts and feelings that assailed her earlier in the day, there was nothing to convince her that Nick Bassington-Hope's death was anything but an accident. However, if she assumed foul play, she might make progress swiftly. She must look for evidence, motive and a killer. She had not wanted to work in this way at first, for a method based on assumption might lead to misunderstanding, viewing some innocent item as a vital clue, or an offhand comment as the basis for an inaccurate conclusion. She had seen such things happen with the police, when it was obvious that pressure was coming from a higher quarter to make an arrest. Though her approach sometimes took more time, the accuracy of her accomplishments bore out the integrity of her work. But this time, to create momentum, she would take that alternative tack.

Maisie closed her eyes. Envisioning the gallery, she brought to mind the artist working on his platform. He was securing the anchors that would hold the triptych, which must have been quite large. Or was it? The studio in his carriage home would have accommodated a canvas of about eight feet in height, at a pinch, if the canvas were set at an angle for the artist to work. She considered the place where the triptych would hang. Yes, that would have been about right for a centre piece, say, eight feet by four or five feet. Then side panels. She thought back to the mural. Everyone assumed that the lost work comprised three pieces, but what if there were more? Would that make a difference to the outcome? She would study the wall in as great a detail as possible to try to ascertain what preparation Nick was making – indentations in the wall where anchors had been placed might provide a clue to the number of pieces, though the screws and nails used in the construction of scaffolding had also left their mark, despite later renovation work.

A clock on the mantelpiece struck the hour. It was six o'clock, time to get ready for Georgina Bassington-Hope's party. She was dreading it. The truth was that she knew she would feel ill at ease, and not only due to the doubts that had enveloped her earlier in the day. The very thought of a party brought to mind her years at Girton, when she returned after the war to complete her studies. There were occasions when she and other women were invited to parties, usually by men also taking up their studies once again, or younger men embarking upon them. And it seemed as if everyone wanted to dance the past away. For Maisie, such events usually meant an hour or two holding up the wall, a barely sipped drink in her hand, before leaving without even locating a host to thank. She had been to only one party she had ever enjoyed, where she had ever allowed herself to let down her defences, and that was at the beginning of the war. Her friend Priscilla had taken her to a party being thrown by the parents of Captain Simon Lynch, who wanted to give him a joy-filled farewell before he left for France. Memories of that party remained bittersweet. Since then, despite the passage of time along with academic and professional success, she had never managed to garner confidence in such social situations.

Dressing in her black day dress along with the knee-length pale-blue cashmere cardigan and matching stole that Priscilla had given her last year, Maisie brushed out her hair, rubbed a little rouge on her cheeks and added a sweep of colour to her lips. Checking her watch as she dropped it into the cardigan pocket, she took the navy coat from the wardrobe in her bedroom, collected her black shoulder bag, then pushed her feet into her black shoes with the single straps that she'd left by the door.

Maisie had debated the most appropriate time to arrive for the party, which, according to the invitation, started at seven, with a light supper to be served at nine. She didn't want to be the first to arrive, but neither did she want to enter late and miss someone with whom it would behoove her to engage in conversation.

It was not possible to travel at more than a crawl along the Embankment, so dense was the ochre smog that enveloped buses, horses and carts and pedestrians alike – not that there were many of the latter out on a murky Sunday night. Parking close to the red-brick mansions, Maisie was grateful to secure a parking spot from which she could see people enter Georgina's flat, and get her bearings, if only for a moment. It was cold, so she pulled the wrap around her neck and blew across her fingers as she waited for more guests to arrive.

An elegant couple arrived in a chauffeur-driven motor car, the woman – thankfully, observed Maisie – not wearing evening dress but clearly something shorter for what had now become the "cocktail" hour. On her way to Chelsea, it had occurred to Maisie that an evening dress may have been more appropriate, an academic thought, in any case, as she did not own a gown. Another motor car screeched to a halt in front of the wrong mansion, whereupon the driver slammed the vehicle into reverse gear with a grinding crunch, the brakes squealing as he then shuddered to a halt alongside the correct address. Two women and a man alighted, all looking a bit tipsy, whereupon the driver yelled that he was going to find a spot for the motor car, which he drove just another few feet and parked haphazardly before leaving the vehicle with the lights on. Maisie decided that rather than call after him, she would locate the man when she went into the party.

Maisie reached for her bag and was just about to open the door when another motor car pulled up, followed by a second that she recognized immediately. She hoped that her vehicle could not be easily seen from the front of the building. Fortunately, in the darkness, the usually distinctive claret would blend in among other motor cars parked on the street. As she watched, Stratton stepped from the Invicta, whereupon he approached the first motor car just as the man she had seen him speaking to yesterday alighted onto the pavement. They didn't shake hands, so Maisie assumed they had met earlier, or – and this was a new consideration – that they didn't particularly care for each other. A young woman, dressed for a party, followed the man from the first motor, and as both Stratton and the man spoke to her, she nodded. Maisie suspected the woman might be one of the new female recruits to detection working with Dorothy Peto at Scotland Yard. She waited. Soon the woman entered Georgina's building, whereupon the two men returned to their respective vehicles and departed. Maisie ducked as they drove past, hoping, again, that she had not been seen.

She waited as two more motor cars, both chauffeur-driven, deposited party guests at the mansion. Then a man came out of the shadows and swirling smog, walking along the street. He was swinging a cane, his gait suggesting that of a young man, a man who was perhaps singing to himself. He wore no hat, and his overcoat was open to reveal evening attire, with a white dinner scarf hanging rakishly around his neck. Maisie suspected that this was Harry Bassington-Hope. As he walked up the steps to the front door, another motor car emerged from the shadows, and drove slowly past, much as a predator tracked his prey. But just as a lion might stalk for a while just for the sport, so the driver seemed only to be following. The scene suggested to Maisie that this was someone who was simply watching and waiting, someone in no hurry to make his move. *At least, not yet.*

Though the street was dimly lit, as the motor car came alongside, the driver looked directly at the MG. Maisie leaned back into the seat and remained as still as a statue, but at that moment a light went on in the window of the mansion to her left, illuminating his features. Despite the limitations of a sideways glance, she recognized him at once.

"MAISIE, LOVELY TO see you, so glad you're here." Georgina waved a waiter to one side, then linked her arm through Maisie's, a demonstration of affection that unsettled Maisie, though she understood that for the people she was now mixing with, certain social boundaries and codes of behaviour had been eroding in the past ten years.

"Let me introduce you to a few people." Georgina turned to another waiter and took two glasses of champagne, passing one to Maisie, before tapping a man on the shoulder. The family likeness was instantly evident, and he was, without doubt, the same man Maisie had seen walking along the street, cane in hand. Though his coat was now gone, he was still wearing the dinner scarf.

"Harry, I want you to meet Maisie Dobbs."

The young man reached out to shake hands. "Charmed, I'm sure. Always good to meet one of Georgina's Amazons."

"Amazons?" asked Maisie.

"Oh, you know, accomplished independent new women and all that, a fellow marauder abroad. Likes to cut off a man in his prime – don't you, Georgie Porgie?"

"Don't make me sorry I asked you to come, Harry." Georgina shook her head at her brother, then led her guest through the crowded room toward three men standing close to the fireplace. "Come and meet Nick's old friends. It's such a pity you missed Duncan and Quentin in Dungeness – they came up again this morning. Alex, as ever, had already cadged a bed here for a few nights!" As they approached the men, Georgina gained their attention. "Gentlemen, I'd love you to meet an old friend from Girton: Maisie Dobbs. Maisie – allow me to introduce Alex Courtman, Duncan Haywood and Quentin Trayner." Georgina glanced back into the room, then extricated herself from the group. "Oh, do excuse me, the Sandlings have arrived."

They watched Georgina vanish into the gathering throng, then turned to one another again. Maisie was the first to speak. "So, you've known each other for years, I understand."

Duncan reached up to the mantelpiece to press a half-smoked cigarette into a silver ashtray. He was shorter than his friends, with a wiry build, quick in his movements and precise in manner. His features were sharp, with a small slender nose, mouselike eyes and light brown hair swept back away from his forehead. Maisie thought he looked like a vole. He was about to reply when Alex responded to Maisie's question.

"Yes, since before the war, actually. Duncan, Quentin, Nick and I met at the Slade." Alex nodded toward his two friends as he recited their names, and at the floor when he spoke of Nick. "And when the powers that be learned that I was a bit on the young side to have joined up – wanting to follow my compatriots into the fray but thwarted when my mother insisted I was to be sent home, whereupon she boxed my ears for good measure – I was put to work at the ministry. Nick turned up after he was wounded and we both ended up drafting pictures to shake the populace out of its midwar torpor. Then Nick was sent over again for a stint with a paintbrush instead of a bayonet."

"I see." Maisie thought Alex painted an almost romantic picture of the friends' wartime exploits, though was hardly surprised, for he seemed to be something of a romantic figure himself, with dark brown hair combed into place in such a way as to remind her of a poet, or an actor, someone she had seen at the picture house – Leslie Howard, perhaps. He was the tallest of the three, and had retained something of the lanky adolescence of youth. His eyes seemed to narrow into half-moons when he smiled, which was often, and Maisie thought that one could see every one of his teeth when he laughed. Quentin, who was of medium height and stocky, with light brown hair and deep, hooded eyelids, seemed to stand apart, looking down at his feet or across at other guests as Maisie conversed with Duncan and Alex. She felt something akin to fear emanate from him, as if he wanted nothing more than for her to leave the three in peace.

". . . so you should have seen us, raw recruits on the Friday route-marches across London." Alex was speaking of the early days following their enlistment. "We'd be led by the regimental band along the Euston Road, past Lord's, up the Finchley Road, past Swiss Cottage then on to Hampstead Heath. It was a lark, for us lads, because all the shopgirls used to come out and throw cigarettes and sweets at us."

Duncan spoke up. "Frankly, as Nick always said, the most objectionable and insufferable enemies we had to face were mud and rats."

"Oh, and do you remember the anthem?" Alex nudged Quentin, and looked at Duncan before bringing his attention back to Maisie. "Nick would get everyone singing – in fact, I think he wanted a spot at the Artists' Rifles recruiting concert in 1915, but of course, we'd all gone over by then." He cleared his throat and began to sing a verse.

> *"Danger and hardship ne'er can alarm us.*
> *Ready at England's call are we,*
> *The Arts of Peace themselves shall aid us,*
> *We fight for Queen and Liberty."*

A group nearby turned and applauded, calling out for more, whereupon Alex bowed and shook his head. He turned to Maisie. "Actually, I think that's the only verse I can remember, and of course, it's 'Queen' because the Rifles were founded in old Victoria's time."

Quentin spoke for the first time, adding in a surprisingly strong voice, "And we were never ready, any of us, for anything, especially not for France."

The group became quiet, a few seconds of discomfort until a

waiter approached with a tray of glasses filled to the brim with champagne.

"I say, over here!" Alex handed fresh glasses to his friends, while Maisie raised hers to indicate that it was still half full.

"And now you all live down in Dungeness?"

Once again Alex was first to reply. "We're all moving on now, aren't we chaps?" He didn't wait for a response. "Duncan has recently married his long-suffering fiancée, so he's moved to an idyllic cottage in Hythe. And Quentin's in the process of moving." He turned to Maisie and said in a mock whisper, "To live with his thrice-wed paramour in Mayfair."

"That's quite enough, if you don't mind." Quentin's voice signalled a warning.

As the conversation listed toward matters of property in London, Maisie wondered how she might orchestrate a meeting with each man alone, deciding that the party presented neither the time nor the place. For now it was enough to have made the acquaintances necessary to reintroduce herself when they met again, which she planned would be within the next few days.

Maisie chatted to the men for a little longer, then excused herself, claiming a need to catch up with an old friend she had just noticed standing in the corner. As she walked toward the young woman she had seen with Stratton earlier, she was aware of the silence behind her and knew that Nick's fellow artists were waiting until she was out of earshot before discussing the encounter.

"Oh, hello, I think we've met before, haven't we? Was it at the Derby last year?" Maisie addressed the woman as she was reaching for an hors d'oeuvres offered by a waiter.

"I – I – yes, I do believe we have. And yes, it must have been the Derby."

Maisie smiled. "Hadn't you just backed a horse called Murder Squad?"

"Oh, crikey!" The woman all but choked on a vol-au-vent, then shook her head.

"Don't worry, your secret is safe with me, but next time, don't agree to having seen someone at a place you haven't visited. Best to admit that you don't recognize them, then take it from there. A downright lie will always catch you out, unless you're very clever."

"Who are you?"

Maisie smiled as if she really were chatting to an old friend. "I'm Maisie Dobbs."

"Oh, Lord."

"At least you know I'm friend, not foe. Are you working for Stratton?"

She nodded. "I – I can't tell you anything. Look, I really should be going."

"No, don't give up now, you'll likely lose your job – or end up in front of a typewriter at Scotland Yard. Just tell me who you're here to report on. Does our hostess know who you are?"

"No. I came in and latched on to one of those frightful men over there, they were leaning against the door when I came in, it was just the situation I needed."

"Go on."

The woman sighed. "I was seconded to come here by Stratton, and also Vance, from the Flying Squad."

"And who are you watching?"

"Harry Bassington-Hope."

"Why?"

"I don't know."

"You don't know?"

She shook her head. "I'm just here to report back on what time he arrived, who he spoke to, what time he leaves. I'm to note whether he arrived by taxi and whether he takes a taxi when he departs."

"And how were you supposed to know how he arrived here if you were here first?"

"I'd ask him."

"Have you?"

She shook her head.

"What's your name?"

"Doris Watts."

"All right, Doris, here's what you need to know. He came on foot from the far end of the road, possibly having walked or caught a tube from his digs or another engagement – though you can hardly be expected to supply such details, unless he tells you. He's currently drinking and entertaining anyone who cares to talk to him, so why don't you go across and introduce yourself."

"Will you tell Stratton you saw me?"

Maisie glanced around the room to locate Georgina, then replied, "Yes, I probably will, but I will also tell him that you were acting quite inconspicuously and that I would only have guessed that you were with the Yard because I saw them drop you off – now that *was* amateurish, so it's entirely their fault."

Doris Watts was about to speak again, when there was a commotion at the door as Georgina welcomed another guest into the party, the noise level of which had increased in the short time since Maisie had arrived. The hubbub of conversation died down and people began looking at the new arrival, stepping back as their hostess manoeuvred the man into the centre of a group standing by the window. Maisie turned away, for she had grown cold.

"Oh, my goodness, look who it is." Doris Watts placed her hand on Maisie's arm.

At that point, Maisie looked around, her curiosity piqued by the guest who had not only caused the sea of onlookers to part but whose presence had chilled her to the bone.

"Mosley," she whispered.

"It *is* him, isn't it? Wait until I tell D.I. Stratton that she knows Oswald Mosley."

As the man began to speak to the group, more guests edged nearer to him. And with his immediate circle burgeoning to become an audience, what was at first an intimate conversation began to develop into a speech. Maisie, too, was drawn to the clustering guests, though not to listen, but to observe the effect one man could have on the surge of people around him that now encompassed the entire party – with the exception of Alex, Duncan and Quentin, who had quite noticeably moved away, each of them frowning as they looked back and forth from the man, then to one another as they whispered.

Oswald Mosley, the former Labour member of Parliament, was a suave, almost hypnotic orator, with black hair accentuating his piercing dark eyes. Maisie found him cobralike, with a power to beguile that mesmerized those present as he expounded his views on the future of the country.

"The New Party will lead the way, friends. There will be no more unemployment, which has only been increased by our Labour Party's policies. There will be new friendships forged with our former enemies, and never, ever will we march again, to die on foreign lands in defence of our soil. We will build our country and protect our own borders. And we will go forward to take up our rightful place as leaders of the modern age."

The cheers and shouts of "Hear, hear!" and "Hurrah!" escalated around her, with men and women reaching out to touch the charismatic politician as he began to shake hands with those who were queuing up, almost as if he were Midas and one touch would give them the blessing of untold riches. Maisie decided to take her leave. She stopped on the way to the front door to speak to Alex Courtman, who was reaching for another glass of champagne from a waiter's tray.

"I say, Miss Dobbs, not leaving already, are you? The dancing will start in a moment!" As if on cue, the music changed from a background melody to a loud rag. "Oh, jolly good!" Courtman took Maisie's glass and set it on the waiter's tray with his own, and pulled her into the centre of the room, where others were already moving in time to the music. "Just one before you go."

"Oh, no, I – I –"

But before Maisie could object further, she had been caught up in the melee. And though she professed not to be able to dance, her feet found the rhythm and, looking sideways at the other dancers, she followed their lead, and was soon one with the partygoers bent on dancing the night away. She laughed as Courtman caught her around the waist with one hand, clutching her right hand as they stepped back and forth in unison to the ragtime number. She even laughed when she stepped on his toes, a move that caused Courtman to wince in mock pain. Maisie cast the worries of the morning to the side, allowing the music to buoy her spirit and touch her soul. Claiming two more dances before she waved her hands to indicate that she really must leave, Courtman pressed his hand to his heart at her departure, then gave a theatrical bow to signal his farewell. Smiling, she made her way from what had become a dance floor, then looked around just in time to see her partner grab a horrified Doris Watts and pull her to him, while the music grew even louder.

Maisie was still smiling as she searched for her hostess to thank and say goodnight before leaving. The hall was quiet and empty as Maisie turned the corner, in time to hear raised voices coming from a room off to the side. She had glimpsed into the room as she entered the flat, and had seen the journalist's book-lined sanctuary. Now, as she crept closer, she heard Georgina's voice, followed by that of her younger brother.

"Oh, for God's sake, Georgie, you really are a fusspot. In fact, you're getting more like Nolly every bloody day."

"If asking you what in heaven's name you think you're doing is making me like Nolly, then so be it. Do you think I can keep handing over more money to pay off your debts?!"

"Come on, Georgie. You're always flush and this *is* a matter of life and death."

"Don't be dramatic, Harry." As Georgina spoke, Maisie heard paper rustle. "There you are. It's all I can let you have at the moment."

There was a pause in the conversation, then Harry Bassington-

Hope spoke again. "Nick might have nagged the stuffing out of me, but there was always a bit more in my pocket after the upbraiding."

"Well, I'm not Nick! The least you could do is say thank you."

Maisie heard the already ajar door open wider and stepped back so that when she retreated into the hall, there would be no suspicion raised that she had heard the exchange. The front door slammed behind Harry Bassington-Hope, who had not even bid his sister good night.

"Georgina, I'm leaving now, I –"

"Must you go?" Georgina appeared tired, but in the manner of the true hostess began the pretence of being put out by the departure of her guest. As she spoke, she looked over Maisie's shoulder and smiled in the direction of another guest, adding, "In a moment, Malcolm." She turned back to Maisie. "Well, I hope you had a good evening, Maisie, dear."

Maisie nodded. "Yes, indeed, it was. I was rather surprised to see Sir Oswald Mosley here – do you know him?"

"My dear, everyone who's anyone knows Oswald. Future PM, just you watch."

"What do you think of him?"

Georgina shrugged her shoulders, as if there really was no other answer than the one she was about to give. "I think he's a brilliant politician, an amazing man. We're lucky to have his like among us – it was quite a coup, having him come this evening. Everyone wants him at their parties."

Nodding again, Maisie changed the subject. "I'd like us to confer tomorrow morning as early as possible. I have some more questions for you, and there are aspects of the case I wish to discuss."

"Right you are, but let's hope you don't mean too early. How about ten?"

"Of course. Can you come to my office?"

"All right. Ten o'clock at your office."

Maisie smiled. "Thank you for inviting me to the party."

Georgina Bassington-Hope moved forward and pressed her

cheek to Maisie's, then looked around to ensure they were alone. "Maisie, I'm so glad you came. I know it probably seems heartless, having a party when someone you love has died, but . . ."

Maisie nodded. "It's all right, Georgina, you don't have to explain. I do understand." She paused, placing her hand briefly on the woman's upper arm to reassure her. "Your life must go on. I am sure Nick would approve – everyone's having a wonderful time and I have enjoyed myself thoroughly."

Georgina nodded, assured Maisie that she would see her in the morning, then turned aside to indicate to the butler that her guest was leaving. As Maisie departed, she heard Georgina in the distance say, "Not leaving so soon, Oswald?"

MAISIE SLIPPED INTO the driver's seat of the MG and sighed. Despite earlier misgivings that had remained uppermost in her mind, she had seen a vulnerability in Georgina Bassington-Hope and had allowed it to touch her. She was still on her guard, but that did not preclude the compassion she felt for her client when she overheard the conversation with manipulative Harry Bassington-Hope. She understood that the truths that lay between black and white, in the grey areas of experience, were never cut and dried, and though she did not trust Georgina – doubting her in some way she had yet to identify – she had always tried to see the humanity in others.

She started the motor, turned on the lights and pulled out into the street. The smog was even thicker, if that were possible, and once again rendered any speed in excess of a crawl dangerous.

Leaning forward as she drove, Maisie stopped at the junction with the Embankment before turning right to continue her journey. It was then that she saw an unexpected movement by the river wall, an activity that sparked her suspicion and caused her to pull over and turn off the MG's lights. She could barely ascertain what was happening, so thick was the air around her. In the murky light shed by gas lamps, she saw two men talking to a third man who had his back to the wall. One of the first two poked the third man repeatedly on the shoulder, until he reached into his pocket and pulled out something that he passed to the second man. The first man poked him again, whereupon he and the second man stepped into a waiting motor car and drove off. The man with his back against the wall took a few moments to compose himself – he also seemed rather drunk – then he turned and ambled off along the Embankment, as if he were not entirely sure where he was going. The man was Harry Bassington-Hope.

At first, Maisie thought she should offer him a lift, but then decided against such a move. She did not want him to consider that she might have seen what had just transpired, the passing on of money taken from his sister. Even drunks have memories, if unreliable. And she thought that he was probably safe now, seeing as the piper had been paid. But who was the piper? Experience informed her that such men as those encountered by Georgina's younger brother were usually servants to one who was much more powerful, and certainly the conversation she overheard earlier indicated that Nick had baled out his brother before.

Maisie parked in her customary place, close to her flat. As she closed and locked the door, she smiled, remembering the dance, and took one or two steps in rhythm to the rag she could still hear ringing in her ears. But that smile soon evaporated. She stopped to listen, to pay attention to the physical sensation of fear that at once enveloped her, then continued walking. She considered that the sensation might be associated with the scene she had witnessed alongside the Embankment and entertained the possibility that the one to whom Harry Bassington-Hope was indebted might have previously approached Nick directly. Or, if he had not approached him, it was even more likely that he tried to find a weakness he could exploit. She considered the driver of the motor car that had trailed the younger Bassington-Hope to his sister's party, and it occurred to her that she had already discovered the source of Nick's Achilles' heel. It was therefore crucial that she speak to his friends as soon as possible.

With the feeling of dread increasing as she approached the door, Maisie took the flat key from her shoulder bag, then looked toward the brightly illuminated centre stairway and the silhouette of a man pacing back and forth. Now she understood the root of her dread. The appearance of Billy Beale waiting for her late on a Sunday night could mean only one thing.

NINE

Driving at what amounted to breakneck speed, considering that she could barely see three feet beyond the front of the motor car, Maisie was so intent upon getting to Billy's house that she took chances she would never otherwise have taken. Barely missing a horse and cart, the carriage lanterns dim as the man made his way home, she turned into Billy's street with a screech that must have given half the neighbourhood cause to believe the police themselves had come in search of criminals. It was a neighbourhood where to see a motor car was still a rarity, and where residents lived in damp, cramped conditions, most with no running water, and windows that had to be shut tight against the fetid air that came up from the docks.

Billy's wife stood at the already open door as Maisie leapt from the MG, reached behind the seat for what she called her "medicine bag" and rushed into the house.

"We've got her downstairs, Miss Dobbs." Doreen Beale had been crying but followed Maisie as she made her way along the narrow passage through to the kitchen at the back of the house. A pregnant woman sat holding Lizzie Beale, who was whimpering and, it seemed as her eyes rolled back, was on the brink of unconsciousness.

"Clear the table, and set a blanket and sheet on it for me – and Billy, bring over that lamp so that I can see her." Maisie reached for Lizzie, cradling her in one arm as she pulled open the shawl that swaddled her, and then the buttons on her flannel nightdress. "She's burning up and fighting to breathe – and you say you couldn't find the nurse or the doctor?"

Billy shook his head as Doreen laid out a blanket across the table and topped it with a clean sheet. Maisie set Lizzie down.

"No, Miss," replied Billy. "And every time we tried to pick Lizzie up, she screamed, so I knew we'd never get 'er to the 'ospital, that's if they would take the nipper." He paused, shaking his head. "The 'ospitals might be run by the council now, but it don't seem to 'ave changed much, not really."

Maisie nodded, wishing that one of Maurice's clinics were nearby. She reached into the bag that Billy had set on a chair next to her and pulled out a white cotton mask that she placed over her nose and mouth, then secured with ties knotted behind her head. She reached into the bag again and took out a thermometer, along with a wooden speculum that she would use to depress Lizzie's tongue. She also unpacked a small, narrow pan with a handle at each end, which she set on the table and filled with hydrogen peroxide, a makeshift form of disinfection. Taking up the thermometer, she shook it a couple of times before placing it between the soft folds of skin under Lizzie's armpit. Then, leaning closer to Lizzie's face, she lifted each eyelid and studied the child's eyes. She shook her head, gently opening the cherry-red lips a little wider, and pressed down on Lizzie's tongue.

"Closer with the light, Billy."

Billy leaned over, holding the oil lamp close with both hands.

"She's been sick for about four or five days now, hasn't she?" Maisie removed the instrument, and set it down on the table, running her hand across Lizzie's forehead as she did so, then reached for the thermometer, leaning toward the light to study the result.

Billy and his wife nodded together, then Doreen spoke. "At first we thought she was getting better, then she started to get worse, and now this." She pressed a handkerchief to her mouth and leaned against Billy. "What do you think's wrong with her, Miss Dobbs?"

Maisie looked up. "She has diphtheria, Doreen. The tell-tale thick grey membrane has formed across her throat, she has severe inflammation of the tonsils and adenoids, she has a temperature like a furnace and she must be taken to the fever hospital immediately. There is absolutely no time to lose when the disease has progressed this far." She turned to Billy. "If I'm right, I think the nearest is in Stockwell. If we take her to another hospital, we will most certainly be turned away, money or no money. But we must act immediately. Doreen, come with me, we'll go now. I have room for only one passenger, and you're the child's mother. We'll use this sheet and blanket to wrap her." She took off her mask and went to the sink to rinse the instruments, which she wrapped in a clean cotton towel before replacing them in her bag. "Now, here's the important thing: you have got to disinfect this whole house. Normally I would say to burn the sheets, but linen doesn't come cheap, so take all the sheets and blankets and boil them in the copper – and I mean all of them and I mean a rolling boil with disinfectant. As soon as you can, get all the children up and into a tin bath with disinfectant. Scrub everything, Billy, everything. Scrub yourselves, the children, everything and everyone. Throw away any milk in the larder. Keep the windows closed against that air out there. Leave no stone unturned. Boil the children's clothes. You've got four more children in this house, and they're all at risk. Make sure they've all got handkerchiefs, and check for cuts, which you must cover with a clean dressing. Here –" She took a roll of paper-wrapped bandage from her bag. "Children get cuts and you don't even know about them, but it's a way to spread the disease. You'll probably have the inspector around tomorrow in any case, and they may take them in as a precaution. Now, we can't spare any more time." She gathered her belongings, but stopped to issue one last instruction, directed at Doreen's pregnant sister, who was already banking up the fire to heat the water. "You must be doubly careful, madam." She took a clean mask out of her bag. "This may be overdoing it, but please wear this whenever you are with the children. At least until they have all been examined."

It was almost midnight when Maisie sped off once again, this time balancing regard for the comfort of her passengers with the need to get Lizzie to the fever hospital. She had not said as much to Billy and his wife, but Maisie knew only too well that Lizzie's chances of clinging to life would have increased greatly had she been admitted to hospital three days ago. Each day without medical care following onset of the disease increased the mortality rate in young children. The knowledge that one in five children left untreated at five days after first signs of sickness would die caused Maisie to press down on the accelerator. Parking the car in front of the hospital, Maisie put her arm around Doreen's shoulders as they rushed into the dour Victorian building. A doctor was summoned and Maisie gave an immediate diagnosis and details of symptoms and Lizzie Beale was taken away. The women were instructed to remain in the waiting room until the doctor came out to give a prognosis, though Maisie suspected it would be a long wait, for she knew that the child was bound for the operating theatre, where she would be given injections of antitoxin to protect her vital organs from the vicious disease. Without doubt, she would have a tracheotomy to clear the upper airway obstruction, plus removal of her tonsils and adenoids. Would her little heart be able to bear such a dangerous operation?

"Oh, my precious Lizzie. My precious girl." Doreen Beale broke down in Maisie's arms, tears coursing down her face. "We could've sold something, pawned my wedding ring. I blame myself, I should've said to Billy, 'Sell my ring.' I wish I had, I wish I had known. I didn't think." Her heaving sobs seemed to crush her chest, such was the grief and self-recrimination.

"Don't blame yourself, Doreen, you mustn't. It's not your fault. Some children don't display the usual signs until the disease has progressed. It must have looked just like a cold to start with." As she clutched the woman to her, she concentrated on pouring strength into the mother who would need every ounce of resolve in the hours and, if they were fortunate, days ahead. It had been a long evening, and as they stood in the hospital waiting room, Maisie thought back to the party, to those who would never need to think twice about money to help a sick child, or adult, for that matter. Though she had taken an instant dislike to him, she could see why the man whom Georgina predicted would one day be prime minister had begun to appeal to both rich and poor alike. He promised a government that would look after its own first. He promised hope. And the people desperately needed reason to hope.

Maisie's thoughts turned to Billy. "Look, Doreen, Billy should be here with you and Lizzie. The doctor will be out as soon as he has some news, and after he's seen you, they'll likely advise you to leave. I'll go and get Billy, and" – she reached into her shoulder bag –"here's the money for a taxi-cab home."

Doreen began to object, but Maisie countered immediately. "Please, Doreen, take it. I'm too tired to argue my point, and you're too worn out to be proud."

The woman nodded, still sobbing, and Maisie left.

Later, having dropped Billy at the hospital, with an instruction to send word if there was anything else she could do, Maisie returned home. The cold silence of the drawing room barely touched her, for she was as numb now as she had ever been when faced with the prospect of death. She had blamed herself all the way home: she should have insisted on coming to see Lizzie earlier. But now, even in her own home, and even from a distance of some miles, she was not without resources. There was a part she could play to help the little girl win her fight for life. She did not bother to remove her coat, but took her place in one of the armchairs and closed her eyes. With her feet square on the ground, her hands resting on her lap, she allowed herself to descend into a deep meditation, as she had been taught by the wise man Khan, and as he had been taught by his elders before him. She sought the timeless state where, according to her teacher, everything was possible.

Maisie had been so full of doubt in earlier days, wondering what this strange practice was supposed to do, and why Dr Blanche took her to receive instruction in something so embarrassing, so seemingly useless. But later, in her darkest hours, the worth of those lessons was proven to her time and time again, and she had come to hold the word of her teacher in high account. Opening her mind, she imagined the sweet face of Lizzie Beale, the mop of curls, her chuckle when amused, the rosy cheeks and red, red sweetheart lips. She saw her in the hospital and began to speak to the child who was in another part of London. She told Lizzie that her heart was strong, that she could rest now, and that when she awoke, she would be well again. Maisie imagined the child giggling in her bed, her mother and father at her side. And before she opened her eyes, and brought her consciousness back to the room, she petitioned the little Lizzie Beale of her imagination to choose life.

When she finally slipped into her cold bed, pulling the blankets around her, Maisie could not sleep at first, the events of the past week playing over and over again in her mind, with conversations repeated as if the needle were stuck on a gramophone record. To her surprise, the emotion that weighed heavy upon her was anger. She appreciated that her view of the world was blighted by the events of the evening, but even so, she found that, like Billy, she was becoming resentful of the very people who provided both her bread and butter and the roof over her head. Of course, she had been fortunate in life, for hadn't she managed to straddle the barriers of class, of education and opportunity? But when she considered the money that passed hands, the seeming inequity of a society where people would spend thousands on a painting, while a child could die for want of a few pounds worth of medical attention, she was left with a sour taste in her mouth. At the end of the day, wasn't it all about who had money, and who hadn't; who could make money, and who couldn't? And no matter how pleasant the people might be, wasn't it just plain unfair that there were those who had the wherewithal to paint all day, when others knew only the bitterness of unemployment, the gnawing hunger of want?

Turning over yet again, Maisie's divergent thoughts began to blend, with her conscious mind finally giving way to fatigue. She had come to learn that there was often a theme to her work, as if in the dance with fate, cases would come to her that at first seemed unrelated, but were connected, perhaps by emotions raised in the search for truth or by a similarity of circumstance. Since the very day that Georgina Bassington-Hope had retained her services, she had been mindful of the web of connection that existed among that rarified community of people who had money and power. She considered the threads that linked those who wanted high office dearly, and those who would put them there; the relationship between those who wanted something so much that they would pay handsomely to own it, and those who would acquire that object of desire for them.

And couldn't it be argued that the artist wielded uncommon power? One only had to look at the propaganda created by Nick Bassington-Hope. The gift of a creative dexterity gave him the power to move a population to think in a certain way, and to direct the actions of people accordingly. In the moments before sleep finally claimed her, Maisie remembered seeing a group of students clustered around a recruitment bill on the station wall at Cambridge in the autumn of 1914. It challenged them to do their bit for King and Country. GO NOW, BEFORE IT'S TOO LATE! She was a shameless eavesdropper, listening to the to and fro of words as the young men considered a slogan that amounted to a dare. They concluded that it would be a "jolly good show" and left the station bound for the enlistment office. Now that was power, and Nick Bassington-Hope was ashamed of it. And, in truth, wasn't she too a little ashamed? Ashamed that she had used the power available to her to attain a flat of her own, when the Beales were struggling to share their home, their food and the income of one man with another family?

MAISIE WAS NOT in the best of moods when she arrived at the office the following morning. Having risen early, she left the house before six, planning to visit the Beales. As she drove down the narrow cobblestone street with terraced houses on each side, she saw a grey fever ambulance outside Billy and Doreen's house. She parked behind the vehicle in time to see three children being brought out wrapped in red blankets. Already a clutch of local street urchins formed a standing audience to the scene, holding their collars and chanting:

> *"Touch collar,*
> *Never swallow,*
> *Never catch the fever!*
>
> *Touch collar,*
> *Never swallow,*
> *Never catch the fever!"*

Billy came from the house to send them on their way, shaking his fist as they ran up the road, still singing. He seemed as grey as the vehicle into which his middle child had been gently placed, along with Doreen's sister's two children. Turning to go back into the house, he saw Maisie.

"You didn't 'ave to come, Miss. You did enough last night."

"What's happening, Billy? Do you have news of Lizzie?"

"I came 'ome a couple of 'ours ago; Doreen stayed. They didn't like it, at the 'ospital, but she weren't leaving with our Lizzie so ill. And what with the poor little scraps all lined up in cots, it's a wonder they can keep an eye on all of 'em, though Lizzie is in a special ward, because of the operation." He paused and rubbed his eyes.

"They operated as soon as she went in there, had to do the cut 'ere." He drew a finger across his throat. "Took out 'er tonsils. And she's been given injections of antisomething or other."

Maisie nodded. "What do they say?"

"It's touch and go. They say they're surprised she's still alive, still fighting. What with 'er bein' so young. They said they thought they'd lost 'er in the operating theatre, but she started to pick up again. Shocked all of 'em, it did. Like I said, it's touch and go though. And now they're taking the others, all except the eldest, who's not showing any symptoms. Inspector said that was because 'e's older and in school. They pick up something there to protect 'em, what did the man call it?" Billy shook his head, his exhaustion plain to see.

"He probably has an immunity, Billy. And the others aren't as far gone as Lizzie. Do you want a lift back to the hospital?"

Billy kicked his foot against the step. "But what about my job, Miss? Can't afford to be out of work, can I?"

Maisie shook her head. "Look, let's not worry about that now. I'll drop you at the hospital. Mind you, I daresay the matron will give you your marching orders; they don't like family waiting. Our matron used to complain all the time about family getting in the way, and that was at visiting time. Even the doctors were terrified of her. Anyway, come back to work when you're ready, Billy."

Later, as Billy was about to get out of the MG at the fever hospital in Stockwell, he turned to Maisie. "There's many an employer would 'ave put me on the street for this little how-d'you-do. I won't forget it, y'know."

"It's not important, Billy." She sighed. "Just keep imagining Lizzie at home, back to her old self. Don't see the sickness. See the life in your child. It's the best thing you can do."

MAISIE COULD NOT help but reflect upon her thoughts from the night before. Certainly there was plenty to inspire her, for as she made her way around London she could see men on their way to join the lines for assistance, or queues at factories where it was said a man could find work. And there were those who predicted that the situation would get even worse before it got better.

Feeling the anger, and shame, rise again, Maisie tempted her thoughts even more as she watched the exodus out in search of a job. Many of the men limped along, others bore scars on their faces or wore the expression of those embattled to a point where any last vestige of optimism had been lost. These were men – and women – whose country had needed them but who were now without a means to support themselves. They were the forgotten heroes now waging another battle for honour.

Slamming the door of her office, Maisie was in high dudgeon as she picked up the telephone receiver and dialled Scotland Yard. She asked to be put through to Detective Inspector Stratton.

"Yes!" The detective sounded rushed.

"Detective Inspector Stratton, I'd like to have a word with you this morning. Can you be at the usual caff, at around half past eleven?" She was aware of her clipped tone, but did nothing to correct her manner.

"All right. I assume it's something important."

"Important, Inspector? Well, you can tell me when we meet whether Harry Bassington-Hope is important or not." She did not wait to hear a response before setting the black telephone receiver back in its cradle.

Maisie looked at her watch, then the clock. Georgina Bassington-Hope would arrive in approximately half an hour. There was time to compose herself before the meeting, which she was dreading, so much so that part of her did not want to become settled at all, but wanted to encounter her client with the fury that had been building since she arrived home last night. The telephone rang.

"Fitzroy –"

"Maisie."

"Oh, hello, Andrew."

"You don't sound pleased to hear from me."

Maisie shook her head, even though the caller, Andrew Dene, could not see her. "No, not at all. Just a bit pressed, that's all."

"You're always pressed, if you don't mind me saying so."

As far as Maisie was concerned, it was the wrong comment, at the wrong time, the match that lit bone-dry tinder. "Well, Andrew, perhaps I am. Perhaps a dying child is a pressing thing, or a murdered artist. Perhaps you should go back to whatever you were doing and leave me alone to my pressing things!"

"Maisie, that was absolutely uncalled for. You are not the only person in the world with demands upon them, or the only person who's ever had to deal with death – come down to my neck of the woods and you'll see that!"

"Andrew, I –"

"We can talk about this when we meet. In fact, as far as I'm concerned, there's much to be laid on the table."

"Yes, of course, you're right."

"Well, I'd better go, Maisie. You're busy – and I know from experience that this is not the time to extend our conversation. I'll be in touch."

There was a click on the line. Maisie slammed the telephone down in frustration and pinched the bridge of her nose between thumb and forefinger. It was not how she had intended to end her courtship. She knew that she had been curt, her manner unforgivable. She had allowed her sadness regarding the sick child to become anger, which didn't help anyone. But she had to put the exchange to the back of her mind – there was a morning of work to get through.

Another woman might have waited by the telephone, expecting the ring that would herald the start of a conversation where contrition was expressed on both sides. Or she might have picked up the receiver, poised to utter *I'm sorry*. But Maisie was already considering the comment she had made. *A murdered artist.* Though she had wanted to keep an open mind for as long as possible, and despite the fact that she had suggested to Billy that to accept the Bassington-Hope case as a murder investigation would move their work along, she had not until this moment made a declaration of her personal feelings about the matter. And now she had. Burdened by emotion, had her intuition spoken? Andrew Dene was almost forgotten as Maisie leaned over the case map and prepared to meet Georgina Bassington-Hope, who, she thought, was not quite above suspicion herself, despite the feelings expressed, hand on heart, when they first met.

Maisie was about to make a notation on the map when the telephone rang again. She was inclined not to answer it – she wasn't ready to speak to Dene yet; she didn't really know what to say – but when the caller did not give up, she relented.

"Maisie, I am glad I've caught you." Lady Rowan spoke before Maisie could give her number.

"Lady Rowan, how good to hear from you. Is everything all right?"

"Yes. Well, no, not really, that's why I've taken the liberty of telephoning you at your office."

Maisie sat down at her desk. "It's not a liberty, Lady Rowan. Is there something I can help you with?" She ran the telephone cord through her fingers.

Lady Rowan continued. "Actually, I hope I am about to help *you*. Look, I know this is none of my business, and I did think that perhaps I ought not place the call, but – you know me – I have to speak as I find." She paused, and when Maisie did not respond, went on. "It was seeing you with the Bassington-Hope woman, I just wanted to know – are you good friends?"

"She's an acquaintance. I was invited to Bassington Place for tea on Saturday, and when the weather closed in, they insisted I stay until the following day."

"Yes, I'm sure."

"What do you mean?"

The woman sighed. "I've known the Bassington-Hopes for years, since before Piers and Emma were married. You could say it was a marriage made in heaven, two art lovers coming together. I know that sounds all very romantic, but I wanted to warn you."

"About what?"

"Oh dear, this is so hard to explain without seeming terribly narrow, but I felt you should know what type of people they are – how they work, so to speak."

"Work?"

"All right, I am just going to launch in – it's my way and at least I will have said my piece."

"Go on."

"The Bassington-Hopes have always been spoiled, both before their marriage, and afterward. Their way of life is completely indulgent, and it's rubbed off on their children. Now, I know there's no law against all that; however, such people can be dangerous – not in an aggressive manner, you understand – but in the way they use people." She paused. "I've seen it happen. They seem to collect people, people who interest them – even artists can get bored with one another, after all. It is as if they suck upon those who are chosen to entertain them, then spit them out when they are done – then they move on to someone else."

"Oh dear . . . Lady Rowan, if I may say so, that sounds rather harsh."

"I am not saying that there's something terrible in the way they do things, Maisie, and one feels desperately sorry for them, losing their son in that accident – I read the obituary. Awful business, that accident." She paused, taking a deep breath before speaking again of the reason for her telephone call. "And you know, they can be enormous fun. But when they are no longer interested, when they've taken what you have to give, they drop you. One can never feel safe with them."

"I see."

"Do you, Maisie? Have my comments made me sound like an old fusspot? I was worried because I feared such a thing might be happening to you. I know you are terribly clever and can see this sort of thing for yourself, but I wanted to make sure – you're just the sort of person they would draw into their circle, someone interesting, someone with something to say. Then when you were comfortable, you'd find that their curiosity had waned, and someone you thought to be your true friend wasn't, after all. I don't think that makes them bad, or even that they do it consciously. As I said, you can see it in their children, except perhaps that older girl – she must be forty by now. Didn't she lose her husband in the war? Poor dear. I remember we were invited to a party when she was sixteen or thereabouts. The house was full of all sorts of people – like puppets in a play, I felt – but there was no one there for her, none of the younger set. Instead there were all those supposedly bright lights with new ideas – politicians, writers, artists, professors – even a royal presence."

"I understand – and I know it isn't like you to speak out of turn, so I appreciate your candour. Thank you for your concern, Lady Rowan, and for taking the trouble to telephone."

"And I haven't poked my nose where it doesn't belong?"

"Of course not. I hope you always draw my attention to such things. And the conversation will remain between us."

"Yes, I know that, Maisie. I can trust you."

MAISIE SET THE telephone receiver back on the cradle and remained seated and still for some moments. Lady Rowan's warning had illuminated a dark corner in Maisie's understanding of the Bassington-Hope family, a blind spot where feelings of doubt and a lack of trust had been seeded. *Now I know why I could not feel safe.* She had been an audience to the Bassington-Hope show, a performance that went on despite the shadow of death. She thought about Nick and Georgina, and could see where the traits described by Lady Rowan had manifested in the children. Nick using real people in his paintings, despite the fact that he risked causing pain or embarrassment to another – yet, for the most part, those same people were drawn back to him. Then Georgina, throwing a party full of "interesting" people, inviting a controversial politician, drawing energy from the bright lights she gathered around her.

To her surprise, Maisie felt a wave of tenderness for Georgina. Where Lady Rowan saw a woman who used others, Maisie saw one who hungered for the attention and associations that would define her. Could it be that her past accomplishments meant little to her now? Maisie stood up and began to pace back and forth. She looked at her watch. Georgina would be here soon, and she wanted to consider the conversation with Lady Rowan before meeting her client. The Bassington-Hope offspring clearly had flaws – *don't we all*, she thought – but how might such flaws have contributed to Nick's death? That was her main concern, as was building respect between Georgina and herself. She remembered a discussion with Maurice, years ago, when there was an obvious disconnect between her mentor and a new client. Maurice discussed the issue of character with Maisie. "I don't particularly like the man. However, I do respect him. I suspect his feelings toward me are the same. I've come to the conclusion that liking a person we are required to have dealings with is not of paramount importance, Maisie. But respect is crucial, on both sides, as is tolerance, and a depth of understanding of those influences that sculpt a character."

The doorbell rang. Georgina Bassington-Hope had arrived.

TEN

"Lovely to see you at the party, Maisie. I feared you might have had more than enough of us." Georgina eased into a chair by the gas fire. "Everyone had a smashing time – and Nick wouldn't have wanted life to grind to a halt, you know. In fact, he would have said to party away merrily."

"It was a colourful evening – a lot of fun," replied Maisie, as she placed the woman's coat on a hook behind the door. "I had an opportunity to speak to Nick's friends, and to meet Harry. Thank you for inviting me, Georgina. Would you like tea?"

"No, thank you." Georgina looked around. "Where's your man this morning?"

Maisie seated herself close to her client. "His children are rather ill, so it seemed only right that he should be with his family. All being well, he'll be back at work tomorrow."

"Oh, dear. I am sorry. . . . Now then, to Nick."

"Yes, *Nick*." Maisie was surprised that the plight of Billy's family had been brushed off so quickly, though she allowed that perhaps Georgina did not want to linger on illness, which might be interpreted as akin to loss. "I'd like to ask some more questions of you, if I may."

"Fire away." Georgina fidgeted in her seat and crossed her arms.

"First of all, I'd like to have a more detailed picture of Nick's relationships with those he was closest to and those who had an effect on his life. Let's start with his work, and Stig Svenson."

Georgina nodded. "Yes, indeed, Stig. He was a supporter of Nick's work right from the beginning, more or less as soon as he left the Slade. At first he would exhibit a piece of work here and there, as part of a larger exhibit, and always encouraged Nick to develop his range. He made it possible for Nick to go to Belgium; then, after the war, to America."

"How did he make it possible? Contacts? Financially?"

"Both. He believes in nurturing new talent along with close hand-holding. He's very good at his job, steering his clients toward works that not only reflect their tastes but that prove to be lucrative investments. He knows his market and he understands his artists."

"I see. And does he represent Nick's friends as well?"

"Yes, to some extent. They are certainly at the gallery on and off. They've all known Stig for years."

"How did Mr Svenson react when Nick enlisted?"

"The Viking vapours, a sort of hot sweaty state that he gets himself into when things run out of control or if he's about to lose money. He was furious, telling Nick that he was ruining his career, that he was on the cusp of fame, how could he . . . and so on. But when it led to such stunning work, Stig was amazed. He couldn't wait to get out and sell to the highest bidder."

"So, Svenson has done quite well out of his relationship with Nick?"

"Oh, yes, I'll say, very well indeed. I don't think he loses money on anything."

Maisie nodded, stood up and paced to the window, then back to the fireplace, where she leaned against the mantelpiece to continue the conversation. "Georgina, it's important for me to have a true sense of who your brother was in his heart." She touched her chest as she spoke. "I know the war affected him deeply – how could it not? But I would like you to recall conversations, perhaps, that might lead me to have a greater understanding of him."

"Is this necessary?"

Maisie remained calm at her place by the fire. "Hmmm, yes, it is. If I am to establish a motive for murder, then I must inhabit the victim, as far as that might be possible. It is my way."

"Yes, I know." Georgina Bassington-Hope paused, then rubbed her hands, whereupon Maisie leaned down and turned up the gas jets. The woman continued.

"To say that Nick lost an innocence in France would be too light an observation, but the description serves to explain what happened to him."

Maisie spoke softly. "Yes, I understand. Very well. Go on."

"It wasn't so much that first time, when he was wounded – though that was bad enough. But going back disturbed him deeply."

"Tell me about the wounds first."

"To his shoulder, a shrapnel wound that effectively gave him a 'blighty.' He was also gassed, and . . ." She paused. "He wasn't unbalanced, not like some of the shell-shock cases I wrote about, but he was *disturbed*. Then they drafted him to work in propaganda. No choice about it."

Maisie was thoughtful. "I'd like to go back to him being disturbed. Does anything stand out from your conversations immediately following his repatriation?"

"What stands out was his silence, though within that reserve, there were stories here or there, if you happened to be with him."

"Stories?"

"Yes." Georgina paused, her eyes narrowing as if she were looking into the past. "He saw some nasty things. Well, didn't we all? But these were more disturbing, from what I can gather, than the shocking things that you or I experienced. And he didn't say much, but I knew he remembered things . . ."

"Are you all right?" Maisie sensed her client had weakened.

Georgina nodded. "As an artist, Nick saw events as messages, if you know what I mean. He would see a man killed and at the same time, in the melee, look up and see the dot that was a skylark overhead. It was something that touched and intrigued him, the reality of that moment."

Maisie said nothing, waiting for the woman to continue her reflection.

"He told me that he had seen overwhelming acts of terror and, on the other side of the coin, acts of compassion that touched him to the core." She sat forward. "I wrote about one of the stories, you know. This is the sort of thing that you would never have heard about in *The Times*, but I managed to sell it to an American magazine. There was a man, not someone he knew well because he had just joined a regiment following training with the Artists' Rifles. It was after a big show, and the man had completely lost his mind, running here and there, uncontrollable. Nick said that he thought there would be compassion for him, understanding, but no, something quite different happened." She paused again, as if choosing her words with care. "Someone called him a shirker, then another said, 'What shall we do with him, boys?' to which it was decided that he would be sent out alone in broad daylight to check the wires. So the man staggered out toward the line and was cut down by an enemy sniper in short order."

Maisie shook her head and was about to speak when Georgina went on.

"And that's not the end of it. His body was brought back and hung from a post above the trench, whereupon the soldiers used the dead man's remains for target practice, having daubed the letters 'LMF' on his back. Now that's the sort of thing you'll never hear about in an official record."

"LMF?"

"Low Moral Fibre."

Maisie tasted the salty saliva that flooded her mouth. She swallowed before continuing her questioning. "Georgina, I know you said Nick had just joined the regiment, but did he know the men who committed this dreadful act, or their commanding officer?"

Frowning, Georgina replied. "Well, that's the thing, I believe he must have, because I can just remember him saying that it was terrible what war could do, to change a man, to bring about a sort of anarchy where soldiers – human beings – would do something out of fear."

"Fear?"

"Yes, that fear we have of someone who was one of us, but who has now changed. Nick always said that he wanted to show how people were joined, how they were the same, that it was something sacred. And he said that's what scared people – people like those men – seeing something terrible that could so easily have been them, so they have to destroy it. Mob rule." She shook her head. "And isn't it funny, that 'sacred' can be 'scared,' if you jiggle the letters around a bit."

"Did he paint this scene?"

"I'm sure he did. I looked for it when I went to the carriage after he died. In fact, I looked for work that depicted some of his stories and found only those general war sketches that you must have seen."

"I'd hardly call them general."

"Yes, I know."

Maisie checked her watch, taking a seat next to her client once again. "And what about compassion? Did he draw those episodes?"

"I can see no reason why he wouldn't have. I believe there's a whole body of work that we haven't seen, to tell you the truth, and I believe that Nick kept those sketches and detailed pieces safe away from view because they were like a rehearsal for the big show – the piece we can't find, the triptych."

Picking up her notes, Maisie knew she must make progress. "I'd like to come back to Nick's work next time we meet. However, I do have a few more questions for you now. To get straight to the point, had Nick had any arguments with anyone lately? I know I have asked this before, but I must ask again."

"Well, though they all lived in Dungeness, the boys – Quentin, Alex and Duncan – weren't quite as close as they once were. They're all pretty much moving away now. In fact, I understand that Duncan and Quentin are going down again on Wednesday – they're both moving, you know, I think they have to pack and such like." She paused, for a second. "And Nick was distancing himself from everyone, it seemed, though that isn't unusual for someone like my brother, an artist preparing for months for a major exhibition."

"And within your family?"

"Nick had argued with Harry. You have probably guessed that by now. Harry is both man and boy, with the boy being more obvious most of the time. And he gambles with a nasty losing habit, so he's come to both Nick and me for help. No good going to Nolly. Nick took him to task last time he got into big trouble."

"What do you call big trouble?"

"A few hundred pounds."

"And Nick could help?"

"He had reached a position where his art commanded a good price. Since Nick died, Harry has come to me twice. I was careful with my money, and I invested a bequest from my grandmother very wisely and managed to pull it out of stocks just in the nick of time, but I can't fritter it away on Harry. Mind you, I have helped him out just lately."

"Where does he work?"

"Various clubs, you know – the Kit Kat, the Trocadero, the Embassy, that sort of thing."

Maisie didn't know, but needed to locate Harry. "I'd like to talk to him, Georgina. May I have his address?"

"I – I don't actually have it."

"I see. Well, then, a list of the clubs, perhaps?"

"All right, I'll scribble a few down. I always depend on Harry to turn up when he needs something, to be perfectly honest. And he never disappoints me."

Maisie flicked through some notes. "Now, then, how about Nick and Nolly?"

Georgina sighed. "As you know, Nolly can be terribly difficult. And she hasn't always been like that, though she wasn't quite like the rest of us. She adored Godfrey, her husband, and is bent upon cherishing his memory as a war hero."

"Yes, she said as much to me."

"It's sad, really. I mean, he was a delightful chap, but a bit bland. We all joked that it was her quest to breed some common sense into the line – you know, a few farmers, accountants and solicitors. Being a Bassington-Hope must have been so terribly hard on her, when I think of it. Mind you, she and Nick were very close when he came back."

"Really?"

"Yes. Of course, I was still away, and Nolly visited him just about every day in hospital and convalescence, then remained in London with him, just to make sure he was all right when he started work at the Office of Information. I think the fact that he was with Godfrey when he died –"

"Nick was with Nolly's husband?"

"Didn't you know? I was sure . . . well, anyway, he was with him when he died. Godfrey was in the regiment that Nick joined – just a fluke, but that sort of thing happened all the time." Georgina was thoughtful, then she looked at Maisie, frowning. "It's just awfully sad that Nolly and Nick fell out and didn't really put their differences behind them."

"What were their differences?"

"I'm trying to think when things deteriorated. I do know that she took an intense dislike to his work, said that he should forget the war, that it was idiocy to dredge it all up just for the sake of a picture."

"When was that?"

"They were on the outs just before he went over to America. Yes, that's it, I remember her saying, at lunch, just after he sailed, 'Let's hope the cowboys and Indians capture his imagination instead of the bloody war!' Daddy agreed with her – mind you, Daddy always tries to see Nolly's side of things. She's the eldest and he's really rather protective of her, endeavours to understand what makes her tick, though I think he's as flummoxed as the rest of us. I say, Maisie –"

"I'm sorry, Georgina. I was listening, but just thinking about something you said." Maisie was pensive for a moment. "And how about you and Nick? Were you on good terms when he died?"

"Of course. I mean, we had our little differences of opinion, perhaps about a play we'd seen, or about something in the newspaper. But Nick and I were terribly close, not fighters."

As she spoke, Maisie watched as Georgina systematically pressed down the cuticle of each finger with the thumbnail of the opposite hand.

"Now then, just two or three more questions today. Was Nick seeing anyone, did he have a sweetheart?"

Georgina smiled. "Such an old-fashioned term, *sweetheart*. Nick's mind was on his work most of the time, and when it wasn't he played the field in a dark horse sort of way. There was always a girl here or there for him to squire along to a party, if he wanted someone with him. And I do mean *girl*. No one of note, though, and certainly no one I can remember."

"What do you know about Randolph Bradley?"

Georgina shrugged, and as she looked away, Maisie noticed the faintest colour rise to her cheeks. "Typical American businessman. Pots and pots of money, and he's managing to hold on to it, which is a feat – I hear the economic woes are worse over there than they are here. He's been one of Stig's clients for years, so he began collecting Nick's work some time ago. I understand he has a gallery at his house dedicated to Nick's work – these trade millionaires do like to show off their acquisitions to one another, don't they?"

"Do they?"

"Oh, absolutely! I've heard that Bradley will stop at nothing to get a piece he wants."

"And he wants the triptych?"

"Yes, but when it's found we're not selling. Nick didn't want to. After he died, Nolly thought it would be a good idea to get rid of everything. Which is strange, as at one point she wanted to have all of Nick's work hidden away. Change of heart caused by impending financial doom on the estate, I shouldn't wonder. Plus the fact that it would go overseas. As I said, she hated Nick's war work, said that it shouldn't be allowed to hang anywhere in Britain or Europe."

"I see." Maisie consulted her watch again. "You know, I do have one last question – for now, anyway. You hinted that if Nick was murdered, then your life might be at risk. What caused you to say that?"

Georgina shook her head. "I think I was being overcautious. It's just that Nick and I did the same kind of work, the same things were important to us. It's hard to explain, but we both wanted to *do* something with our chosen fields. I didn't want to just doodle away with words, I wanted to write exactly what I saw when I was driving an ambulance in France. Nick wanted to do the same thing with his art, whether it was to show the beauty of nature or the violence of men and beasts."

"Yes, I see that."

"Do you think he *was* murdered?" She looked directly at Maisie.

"There is compelling evidence to support the pathologist's conclusion that his death was the result of an accident, though I have a feeling in my heart – as you do – that the truth is not quite as straightforward. I believe we have made progress this morning, Georgina. I will be leaving for Dungeness again on Wednesday, but I would ask you not to tell anyone else that I will be there. I plan to go to the gallery again, and to pay a visit to Mr Bradley. But, I cannot continue to feign a passing interest in Nick for much longer. Inevitably, others outside your family will learn that I am investigating your brother's death."

"And what tack will you take in these meetings?"

Maisie tapped the index cards with her pen. "If Nick sought to illustrate personal or universal truths, there are many who must have been touched by his work. Some might have been grateful for such enlightenment, but as experience taught Nick in the trenches, people do not always like to see *what is so*, especially if they see themselves reflected in the brutal honesty of the artist. I'm curious to know how he touched his more immediate audience – friends and associates – with his work. You see, if Nick was the victim of a crime, it is more than possible that he knew his killer. Which means that you are likely known to that person too."

"INSPECTOR, I'M SORRY I'm late. My first appointment of the day went on a bit." Maisie took off her scarf and placed it on the back of the chair facing Stratton, who was already sipping tea. "Another cup?"

"No, thank you, this will do."

"Then you won't mind waiting while I just fetch myself some."

Maisie returned with a cup of strong tea from the urn and a plate of toast and jam, setting them down before taking her place at the table.

"So, Miss Dobbs, what is it this time?"

"Inspector, as I said before, I am most grateful to you for supporting Miss Bassington-Hope's decision to seek my help – though, as we have established, the purpose was to keep her occupied and out of your hair. However, what has become clear to me is that something else is going on. Now, I appreciate that your investigations are your own business, but you must have known that I would stumble across the fact that you – and the Flying Squad chappie – have an intense interest in the activities of Harry Bassington-Hope."

Stratton shook his head. "I told them you would find out."

"Vance?"

"I even told them you would know his name in short order."

"And whose idea was it to deliver Doris to her place of surveillance without regard for who might be watching?"

Stratton sighed. "All right, so you know there's been an interest in young Harry."

"You're going to have to tell me more than that, Inspector. I seem to have become enmeshed in your work without being asked if I minded!"

Stratton shook his head, and took a sip of tea. "Harry Bassington-Hope, as you probably already know, has got himself involved with some rather undesirable people. In fact, undesirable is an understatement. Typical story, the odd flutter on the gee-gees or seat at the card table became something of a regular pastime, and the gambling habit, together with some of the types he meets in those clubs, led him deeper into debt with people one should never be indebted to."

"How does this all connect to his brother?"

"I'm getting to that, though we doubt if there's a direct connection, apart from the elder Bassington-Hope bailing out the younger from time to time. No, the reason why there was a collaboration between departments, between myself and Vance, is that a small-time punter one step shy of crooked – another Harry Bassington-Hope type – was found dead a couple of months ago, we believe murdered by the very same men that Harry is indebted to."

"Harry's the mouse to catch the big cat, is that it?"

"Yes. We are simply watching and waiting."

"So, again, Inspector, the connection – or not – to the death of the artist?"

"Nick Bassington-Hope tripped over his feet on scaffolding, *as we know*. However, the timing was dreadful as far as our investigation was concerned. The last thing we wanted was that hot-headed sister – with her connections in Parliament, and unable to believe her beloved perfect brother could be so clumsy as to kill himself – running amok in search of a killer, ruining months of solid police work in the process."

"I see. But what if there was no accident?"

"You mean our criminal element? No, they would have no interest in Nick Bassington-Hope. As far as we know the men at the top would not have even made a connection. Art isn't their game."

"What is?"

"They make a lot from the clubs – protection, that sort of thing. They're fencing jewellery – diamonds, gold. They are involved with bank robberies. The crime barons of London, you could call them. It's like a pyramid, from the little weasels on the ground tucking away a pound or two here and there, right up to the top, the men who run the show."

"I see . . ."

"You see what?"

"Oh, you know . . . it's clearer to me why you kept things quiet, though I do wish you had told me more a week ago."

Stratton sighed. "Well, I must say, you're doing a good job of keeping that woman quiet."

"Am I, Inspector?"

"Yes. I'm sure we'll have the string-pullers behind bars soon enough. We just have to keep very close to young Harry, and at some point we will nab them in the process of committing a crime."

"Hmmm . . ."

"What's that supposed to mean, Miss Dobbs?"

"Nothing, Inspector. Nothing at all." Maisie took one last sip of tea, finished the toast, then set her cup on the saucer and reached behind her for her scarf. "By the way, how is Doris?"

"Well, I don't think we'll be using women in detection for a while. Wasn't quite up to the job."

Maisie stood up, her chair scraping against the bare floorboards. "Oh, I wouldn't write off the likes of Doris just like that, Inspector. You never know what a woman might be able to uncover that you've completely missed."

MAISIE FOUND BILLY and Doreen Beale in the waiting room of the fever hospital. "What news of the children? And Lizzie?" She had hurried into the building and was unwrapping her scarf and removing her gloves as she spoke.

Billy had his arm around Doreen, comforting her. Their faces bore the signs of strain, the skin around their eyes lined and drawn. Billy shook his head. "We've been waiting all night again, what with one thing and another. The eldest is at 'ome, with Doreen's sister, and right as ninepence, and the other nippers – our Bobby, and Jim and Ada's two – are all doin' all right. But Lizzie . . . it's still touch and go, like I said before. And we was just about to go in to see the little lass again, and they turfed us out, said there was an emergency."

Maisie nodded, then looked around for a nurse or doctor to speak to. "Have they told you what the emergency was?"

"The poor little mite is in trouble all over 'er body. I reckon they've shoved some more of that antiwhatsit into 'er." Billy faltered. "And it's not just 'er breathin', no, it's 'er 'eart, her kidneys, it's everything. She's fighting though, by God she's fighting."

"I'll see if I can find out anything more for you." Maisie placed a hand on Doreen Beale's shoulder, nodded at Billy, and went in search of a nurse. She had barely reached the door when a doctor came into the waiting area.

"Are you Mrs Beale?"

"No," replied Maisie, "I am Mr Beale's employer, and I have come to see if I might be of assistance to them. I was a nurse, so I have an understanding of the situation, and I brought their daughter in."

"Good, it's quite troublesome talking to the parents at times, especially from the East End, you know – words of one syllable, if you know what I mean."

Maisie glowered. "No, I don't know what you mean. The parents are perfectly capable people, but they are distraught – and they depend upon your compassion and honesty, if I may say so. Now, perhaps you would be so kind as to give me the details, and I will talk to them."

"I'm sorry, I didn't mean . . . we've just had a lot of children brought in overnight. Half the time the poor souls haven't had a good meal because the father can't get work, and the whole situation isn't getting any better. They haven't the heart for the fight."

Noting his waxen skin and the way he rubbed a hand across his forehead, Maisie softened her tone, which she realized had been rather too harsh, still bearing some residue from the earlier conversation with Stratton. She had seen such strain years ago, in France, though the frontline fight was against the weaponry of war, not diseases left to flourish amid decay and want. "How is Lizzie Beale?"

The doctor sighed. "I wish I had better news. How that child is still alive beggars belief. She clearly didn't present early signs of diphtheria, and of course it progressed until it came down hard on the poor little wretch, like a wall of bricks. As you know, we proceeded with an immediate tracheotomy, tonsillectomy and adenoidectomy, so the risk of infection is terribly high. Antitoxin was administered, but she's fighting to keep vital organs functioning. There's little more we can do except watch, wait and keep her as comfortable as possible."

"And your prognosis?"

"Well, every minute she's alive is like money in the bank. I can't promise she'll still be with us by this time tomorrow, though."

Maisie felt the lump in her throat grow. "And the other Beale children?"

"Got it in time; early stages, so they are expected to make a full recovery."

"Can the parents see Lizzie?"

The doctor shook his head. "Strict rules, you know. Matron would have my entrails for garters if she thought I'd let family in at this time."

"Doctor, I know all about matrons. You have cause to feel as you do. However, the child is clinging to life, and the parents in turn are grasping for a shred of hope. Why not allow them to be together, just for a few minutes?"

He sighed again. "Good Lord, you will have me shot! But . . . oh, all right. Go and get them, then come with me."

Nurses shook their heads as the doctor led the Beales along the corridor, first into a small anteroom where they were instructed to wash their hands and put on masks, then into a ward where the most serious cases were quarantined. Austere, iron-framed cots were lined up, each with just a sheet and rough blanket to cover the feverish body of a child. The vapour of disinfectant barely masked another lingering smell, the foul breath of death waiting for another victim to weaken.

"I'll wait outside, just in case Matron comes along," said Maisie. "I can bear the brunt of her temper if she finds the rules have been broken."

The doctor nodded and was about to take the Beales to their child when Maisie spoke to the couple. "Don't be afraid to touch her. Hold her hands, tell her you're there, rub her feet. Let her feel you. It's important. She'll know . . ."

Maisie departed the hospital a half hour later, leaving the Beales to wait for an opportunity to see young Bobby before returning home. Billy maintained he would be at the office the following morning. Rearranging her plans as she drove to the Ritz, where she would call on Randolph Bradley, Maisie decided that a visit to Stig Svenson would be more effective tomorrow, before her visit to Dungeness. If Billy were with her at the gallery, it would provide an introduction to conversation with the caretaker. And she didn't want to arrive at the coast too early. No, she needed to be there at dusk. To wait.

ELEVEN

The clerk, with perfectly oiled, swept-back hair, pushed a pair of tortoiseshell spectacles to the bridge of his nose and peered at Maisie's calling card. "And Mr Bradley is not expecting you?"

"No, but I am sure he will see me as soon as he knows I am here." She reached for the card. "Look, let me scribble a quick note for him on the back. Do you have an envelope?"

Maisie wrote on the card and slipped it into the envelope, then passed it back to the clerk, along with a coin. "I'm sure you can arrange for him to receive this directly."

The man executed a short bow, then turned to another clerk, who nodded, then went on his way. Twenty minutes later, as Maisie stood waiting in the foyer, a tall, distinguished man walked toward her. She estimated him to be about six feet two inches and probably forty-five years old. His suit was impeccably tailored and indubitably English. A royal-blue kerchief had been placed in his breast pocket with a flourish and matched his tie. His shoes shone. He had one hand in his trouser pocket as he walked across the foyer and waved to the clerk with his free hand. His smile was engaging, his blue eyes sparkled. This was a very successful man, a man who seemed to excel at cultivating Englishness, though in his ease of manner, it was clear that the British Isles was not his home.

"Miss Dobbs?" The man had taken the hand from his pocket, and now held it out to her. "Randolph Bradley."

Maisie smiled. She had only ever met one American, and that was Charles Hayden, Simon's doctor friend, in the war. She remembered that same relaxed style, despite the gravity of his work. "It's very good of you to see me, Mr Bradley."

The man looked around, clearly searching for a place conducive to private conversation. "We'll have coffee in there." He pointed to the dining room, where it appeared the waiters were preparing for lunch. Undeterred, Bradley simply strode to a table, stood as a waiter pulled out a chair for Maisie, then took a seat, ordering a large pot of fresh coffee as he did so.

"So, Miss Dobbs. You want to know more about my interest in Nick Bassington-Hope's work?"

"Yes. When did he – and his work – first come to your attention, as a collector?"

Bradley reached into the inside pocket of his jacket and pulled out a packet of cigarettes and a lighter. "Let me ask a question before I say anything. Are you helping the boys in blue?"

"I beg your pardon?"

"The police?"

"No, I am not. I work privately, as I said in my note, and as you can see from my card."

"So, who're you working for? Who's paying you?"

"I have been asked by Georgina Bassington-Hope to conduct a limited investigation into her brother's death. She felt that there were a few unanswered questions. In order for her to put the family's loss behind them, Miss Bassington-Hope retained my services."

"So are you investigating me?"

Maisie smiled. "Mr Bradley, you are an avid collector of Mr

Bassington-Hope's work, so he obviously spent time with you – any artist would be anxious to keep the buyer happy, is that not so?"

Bradley nodded. "Yep, you've knocked the nail on the head there. Nick was nobody's fool, and knew where his bread and butter came from. He may have had his garret on the beach – I never went there, but heard all about it – but he knew how to sell his work."

"What do you mean?"

The American acknowledged a waiter who came bearing a silver coffee pot, setting it on the table with a matching jug and sugar-bowl. He did not speak until the waiter had left the table after pouring coffee for Maisie and himself.

"Cream?"

Maisie declined. "You were talking about Nick, his understanding of the business of art."

Bradley took a sip of coffee, and went on. "A lot of these folks, artists, have no idea when it comes to selling their work. They have an agent, a guy like Svenson, and that's it, they leave it all up to him. But Nick was interested – interested in *my* interest in his work. He wanted to meet me, and we talked a lot, got to know each other."

"I see." Maisie nodded as she spoke, setting her cup in its saucer.

"You see what?"

She cleared her throat, not quite used to conversing with someone so forthright, and embarrassed to recall that Stratton had challenged her with exactly the same words. "It's a figure of speech. I've been trying to build a picture of who Nick Bassington-Hope was, and I find that he was something of a chameleon. He was an artist, and people sometimes jump to conclusions about artists, that they don't have their feet on the ground, that sort of thing. Yet Nick was a most sensible person, someone who had seen unspeakable things in the war, and yet who did not draw back from depicting them. And he wasn't afraid to use real people in his work either. So, when I say 'I see,' I am simply seeing more of the man than I did before. And seeing the man Nick Bassington-Hope was is essential if I am to submit a comprehensive report to my client." Maisie did not miss a beat before putting another question to Bradley. "So, when did you first learn of his work? How did you go about building the collection?"

Bradley stubbed out his cigarette, went to reach for another, and changed his mind. "Remind me to hire you next time I want to check into the background of someone I'm about to do a deal with." He paused and continued. "First let me tell you that I served in the war, Miss Dobbs. I'd already built a business by then, but was drafted in by our government to advise on supply of, well, you name it, anything and everything, before the first doughboys went over in '17. I could've stayed in the States, but I shipped over to France myself, to make sure the job was done right. Didn't come back until after the Armistice. So I saw the war, Miss Dobbs, saw what the boys went through. And your boys went through it all for a lot longer."

Maisie said nothing, knowing that at this point in the meeting it was best to simply allow the man to speak. He had leaned back in his chair, not too far, but enough to indicate that he was letting down his guard. He reached for that second cigarette, poured more coffee for both Maisie and himself, and continued as he put away a silver monogrammed lighter, half closing one eye against a lingering wisp of smoke. "Svenson came to see me, oh, must have been in '22. Nick had a few pieces in an exhibition at the gallery – of course, it was a much smaller outfit then. I reckon Svenson has made a mint off Nick Bassington-Hope, and those old masters he buys from Europeans on the brink of ruin. Anyway, he tipped me off early, so I came along – I was in England anyway – and saw, right there and then, that this was an artist I could appreciate. I'm not the kind of collector who will buy anything just for the heck of it, Miss Dobbs. No, I have to like the piece I'm buying. But . . ." he paused and looked at her directly, "I go all out for something I want. And I wanted this boy's work."

"Why?"

"It was just darn amazing! So simple, so – Lord, what did Svenson say? Measured, that's it, *measured*. Nick didn't just serve up blood and guts, no, he could touch the . . . the . . . *essence* of the scene. And he didn't draw back from the horror of it all, in his war work, and that's what I saw, at first. But he added something else, something . . ."

"Truth?"

"Right. He could touch the truth."

"So you started buying."

"There and then, like I said. And I wanted to see what he'd done before, and I wanted everything he painted that was for sale later. His American period is a departure, but has all the hallmarks that he's known for – and remember, I know the place, done business all over."

"So what about his latest collection? You've bought all but the main piece, I understand."

"Yeah. Bought it all, didn't even have to see it. I know what I'm buying with this boy – and it's worth a heck of a lot more now that he's dead. Not that I'll sell."

"But you didn't procure the main piece?"

"Nick didn't want to sell. But I'll get it, you'll see. When they find it, I'll get it."

"I understand there was another bidder."

Bradley shrugged. "Small fry. I'll get it, like I said."

"Do you know anything about it, apart from the fact that it's supposed to be more than one piece?"

"That's what I've been told, Nick said as much to me, and it's what I would have expected."

"Why?"

"Well, you look at his other work; it has a serial quality to it. So I'm pretty sure this one is a triptych. And I'm sure the subject is the war. That's why I want it."

Maisie made no immediate response, whereupon Bradley stubbed out his cigarette and leaned forward, his elbows on the table.

"I believe that this piece, whatever it is, will distill – yeah, I reckon that's a good word – *distill* everything he thought and felt about that war. Remember, I've collected him for years, watched him grow, change, sort out his life with his art. I think that once it was finished, this final piece, he was ready to let the past be the past, you know, step forward to whatever was next. I predict that whatever he moved on to would be an example of . . . of . . ."

"Resurrection? Rebirth?" Maisie offered, almost absentmindedly, for her mind had wandered, thinking about Nick Bassington-Hope and the work that had caused his death.

"Yeah, that sounds about right. I like that. Yeah. It was there, to some extent, in his American period. But even that seemed to show an exploration, a journey, not an arrival." He nodded again, and looked around the room, now filled with guests taking luncheon. He looked at his watch. "Any more questions, Miss Dobbs?"

"Oh, yes, just one or two if you don't mind. I'd like to know how long you've been doing business with Stig Svenson, and – I promise this is confidential – what he's like to deal with."

"I've known Svenson since before the war, when we were both starting out. I'd made some money and I wanted to indulge myself. When I was a boy, an English *fellow*" – he grinned, checking that Maisie had caught the quip –"lived on our street. He wasn't rich, none of us were in that neighbourhood, but every day he left that house dressed as if he were going to the Bank of England. His clothes weren't new, but they were good. I didn't know anything about him, except that he was dapper, as you would say. *Dapper*. I wanted to be like him, and when he died his family – turns out he had kids in the city – came out and sold up everything. And you know what? He worked in a factory. Not a fancy office, but a factory. And he spent money on art, all sorts of pictures from artists you'd never even heard of. I was only young, but I bought a couple I liked, cheap. So, that set me on my path, my love of art. I came to see Svenson in '19, when I was in London before shipping back home. I bought a couple of pieces from him – cut price, you guys weren't in any position to haggle then – and we kept in touch. My business boomed and I was over here as much as I was at home." He paused, once again reaching for a cigarette, then reconsidering before he continued talking, looking directly at Maisie. "Now, even though I've known Svenson a while now, I believe he'd take the shirt off my back if he could. We respect each other, but I know what he's about. He's sharp, understands what sells – and right now, that's European art, all your rich dukes and counts and princes selling off the family heirlooms. God only knows where he's getting it from – *and* he knows who wants to buy. Make no mistake, if there is a pie with money anywhere in London, Paris, Rome, Ghent or Amsterdam, Stig Svenson's finger is in it." He stood up and came around to pull out Maisie's chair for her. "And Nick had his number. Knew Svenson could pull a buyer, but watched him like a hawk all the same."

Bradley accompanied Maisie into the foyer of the hotel.

"Thank you for seeing me, Mr Bradley. You have been most helpful, most kind to allow me so much of your valuable time."

"My pleasure, Miss Dobbs." He handed her a calling card. "Call me if you need any more information." He laughed. "In fact, call me if you find that darn painting. I want it and I'll pay the family whatever they want for it – Nolly Bassington-Hope knows that – in fact, she can't wait to get it out of the country!"

Maisie drew a breath to put another question to the American, but he had turned and walked away. And though he appeared to move in an easy fashion, he walked with some speed, for in an instant he was gone.

MAISIE KNEW SHE was struggling with the case. Already the loose threads threatened to unravel before she could even distinguish a pattern. There were points she was missing and she understood that all the thinking in the world wouldn't make the task any easier. She had to continue working away, trusting that each step taken would be like another drop of water on stone, gradually wearing down the hard shell that time and circumstance had wrapped around clarity.

Except that she didn't have time for *gradually*. Of course, it would have helped had she been able to set out right from the start with a letter of introduction from Georgina to the effect that she was investigating Nick Bassington-Hope's death with her permission. But Georgina had not initially wanted her to reveal the nature of her inquiry, thus she had left the first interview with the caretaker to Billy, rather than question him herself. However, that might have been a good strategy, though she must speak to the man personally tomorrow, with Billy there to ease the path of conversation.

Nick's three closest friends, according to Georgina, were still in London and, as far as she knew, Alex Courtman would be at Georgina's flat this afternoon. As she traveled to Kensington, Maisie was struck by the fact that all three men were moving on, with two of them appearing to have recently become financially better heeled, which was interesting if one considered that an artist created something to be acquired on the basis of sheer desire, not need. On the other hand, thought Maisie, she had already seen that there were plenty of people who could still afford such luxuries and perhaps those people who bought art were viewing this as a time to build their collections at a lower cost than might otherwise be the case. She shook her head as she walked, wishing she understood the art world a little better.

The places where Nick Bassington-Hope chose to live were desolate. His past was desolate, as were the natural landscapes that drew him. There were women – *girls*, as Georgina described them, but his work was his life, his true love. And he too seemed to be financially secure, to have enough money to help Harry with his debts. Georgina said that Nick's art was selling well, and of course Maisie knew that Bradley had spent a considerable amount feathering Nick's nest. But could there be another source of revenue? And what was the relationship between Nick, Harry and the man who drove the motor car that followed the younger brother to the party? She knew the man by appearance already, and suspected – though she had no hard evidence – that Stratton was wrong when he assumed that the underworld known to Harry Bassington-Hope had not beaten a path to Nick's door.

She parked the MG, walked to Georgina's flat and rang the bell. A housekeeper answered, then showed her into the drawing room and went to summon Alex Courtman.

"Ah, Miss Dobbs, *the dancer*. How charming to see you again." Alex Courtman held out his hand. He appeared even more youthful today, dressed in gabardine trousers, a white collarless shirt with the sleeves rolled up and a reddish-brown cable-knit pullover. He did not wear a tie and did not seem unduly concerned about his casual appearance, which was exaggerated by unruly dark hair that appeared not to have had the benefit of a comb that morning.

"I wonder if you would be so kind as to oblige me with a moment or two of your time, Mr Courtman?"

"Of course." He extended his hand toward an armchair, then sat down on the end seat of the chesterfield, close to Maisie, who glanced around before turning to face him. There had been so many people at Georgina's party, she had hardly looked at the room, which now seemed quintessentially bohemian, though perhaps not as outlandish as the Bassington-Hope family seat. There were antique pieces that immediately suggested a connection to old money, but instead of the gravity an ill-lit room might inspire, this interior was bright with windows flanked by heavy swags of pale gold silk. In one corner a carved screen was draped with fabrics from Asia, and a collection of masks from around the world were displayed on a wall.

Maisie felt comfortable in the room, now that she was able to pay attention to the details. The walls were painted a pale yellow, the picture rails and mantelpiece white; nondescript colours chosen to provide an accommodating backdrop for the works of art. There were three paintings by Georgina's brother, and several others by artists unknown to Maisie.

"How may I help you, Miss Dobbs?"

"As you know, I am working on behalf of Miss Bassington-Hope to discover more about the circumstances of her brother's death. To that end, I must find out more about his life. You were one of his dearest friends, so I thought you might be able to" – she smiled – "paint a picture of him for me, by answering some questions?"

"Fire away!" He leaned back into the chesterfield, a move that caught Maisie's attention. It occurred to her that she felt as if she were on a stage with Alex Courtman, who, having just read his words from a script, was now waiting for her to play her part. Instinctively she wanted to unsettle him.

"You're all moving on now. Nick's dead, of course, but Duncan has his house in Hythe, Quentin's bought a flat 'with his thrice-wed paramour,' and you're spending more time here than in Dungeness. It couldn't have all been planned since the accident."

Courtman answered calmly. "Well, these things tend to happen all at once, don't they? It just takes one to step off the boat and everyone else gets itchy feet. Duncan was courting for ages, poor girl must have wondered if he was ever going to make an honest woman of her. Then Quentin grasped his opportunity to make a dishonest woman of someone else – the woman's still married to husband number three – and I found myself up here more and more." He looked out the window, then back at Maisie. "I'll probably get my own flat soon."

"You've all done very well with your work, haven't you?"

He shrugged. "Nick's work sold very well, and I do believe we were affected simply by being associated with him, as if some of that stardust flaked off onto us. And, frankly, Svenson makes the most of the friendships. If you stick around him long enough, you'll hear him talk about the 'Bassington-Hope school' and how our work was influenced by Nick."

"And was it?"

"Not at all. We're all quite different, but if I can go up the ladder hanging on to Nick's coattails, then that's what I'll do."

Maisie paused before continuing. "You said at the party that you met some years ago."

He nodded. "Yes, as I told you, we all met at the Slade, though I knew Duncan better than I knew Nick and Quentin, to tell you the truth. Not that you would guess, but I'm a bit younger than the others, a latecomer to the group. It doesn't make much difference now, but in those days I was definitely the new boy. Then we joined the Artists' Rifles together, more or less, which sealed the friendships, though Nick, Duncan and Quentin are – were – something of an exclusive trio. But when it comes to a move such as the one to Dungeness and away again – it only takes one and we all fall in."

"And who was the one?"

"Nick. He's the one who said that we ought to do our bit in the war. Seemed as if that's all people said then, you know, do your *bit*. Trouble was, it was a bit too much to have bitten off, if you ask me. Old men always tell the young to do their bit, and half the time it isn't anything they'd want to do themselves."

"Indeed." Maisie nodded, familiar with the stream of disillusion that formed an undercurrent to conversations concerning the war. Sometimes the emotion came from angry defence of the war, but more often, she realized, it was inspired by an inability to understand how and why the war happened, and why so many who fought were now all but abandoned, or so it appeared. Hadn't Mosley exploited the situation at Georgina's party? And hadn't so many been drawn to his words, as if he could provide answers to their own deepest questions? She continued. "Perhaps you can tell me about the Rifles. Was this where you got to know each other really well?"

"In training, not over in France. We were all assigned to different regiments. Nick ended up in the same regiment as his brother-in-law, much to his dismay, though I understand he came to rather like the old chap." Courtman stared out the window, his eyes blankly focused across chimney pots and into the distance. "He said in a letter that he'd always thought the man was a bit wet, but came to regard him as simply *kind*. Nick was quite shattered when he was killed."

"Do you know the circumstances, specifically?" Maisie had not expected the conversation to take this turn and was intrigued enough to allow the man to reminisce.

Courtman turned to Maisie. "Circumstances? You mean other than two lines of men with guns pointed at each other?"

"I meant —"

"Yes, I know what you meant. I was being facetious. Talking about the war does that to me. How did Godfrey Grant die? As far as I know it was during a cease-fire."

"Cease-fire?"

"Yes. I mean, you've heard about the Christmas truce and all that? Well, there wasn't just one truce, you know. It happened fairly often. In fact, it wasn't unusual for there to be a quick truce for both sides to whip out, collect their wounded and bury their dead. Imagine it, men like ants scurrying back and forth, trying to honour their own before some smart-aleck officer calls them all back to their own side for another round."

"Nolly's husband was killed in a truce?"

"Yes, as far as I know. Not sure what happened, of course. Probably didn't get back to his trench before they were under starter's orders again, something like that."

"I see." Maisie made note of the conversation on an index card, shuffled a fresh one into place and looked up. "So, back to Nick. What was your training like? Did he continue with his work?"

"Never saw him without a sketchbook. Mind you, we're artists, we all had our sketchbooks, even though it was Nick who was on a quest to render those drawings into something more substantial."

"You've never sold your war paintings?"

"Miss Dobbs, I have never completed any war paintings. Even though Svenson might like to say that my work is of the Bassington-Hope school, I would rather draw everyday life here and now than bring those scenes to mind every time I put brush to canvas. In any case, I've just got a new job. Commercial artist, that's the place to be now. . . ." He paused, choosing his words with care. "Nick's art was his exorcism, in a way. He painted the war out of his soul and into the open. Every time a picture was born of his memory, it was as if something dark was laid to rest. And if that darkness made one of the higher-ups hot under the collar, it was icing on the cake for Nick."

"What do you know about the triptych?"

He shook his head. "If you know it's a triptych, then I know about as much as you."

"Do you think it was the last of his war paintings?" Maisie leaned forward.

Courtman was quiet for some moments, then he looked up at Maisie. "You know, I think it was. I hadn't thought about it like that before, but when I consider his work and the way he spoke of that piece – he never said anything *specific* about it, by the way – I do believe it was the last of his war paintings." He paused once more, just for a moment. "Yes, very intuitive of you, Miss Dobbs. How very astute you are."

"No, not me. It was something suggested by Randolph Bradley, actually."

"Hmmph! The American moneybags, eh? Well, he should know, shouldn't he? He all but bought Nick himself, the way he snapped up his work. He was furious about that triptych, or whatever it is. Furious! He came to the gallery when we were setting up Nick's scaffolding – and, let me tell you, we knew what we were doing, that scaffolding was solid, absolutely solid."

"What did he want?"

"He called Nick aside. They started talking quietly, you know, backslapping from Bradley, lots of congratulatory comments, that sort of thing. Then there was a pause and the next thing you know, Bradley is saying, 'I'll have that painting if it's the last thing I do – and if I don't, your career is dead, pal!' Makes you wonder, now that I think of it. Not that he would have done anything really. In fact, that's what surprised me, you know, he's always such a gentleman, as if he set out to show us how being British should be done. Bit of a cheek, for a bloody colonial."

"Then what happened?"

"Oh, Svenson came out in a bit of a lather and everyone calmed down. Bradley apologized to Nick, to Duncan and me. He said that it just showed the sort of emotion Nick's work inspired."

"Did Nick say anything?"

"Oh, yes, that's when he really let the cat out of the bag."

"Yes?" Maisie inclined her head, in a manner that suggested simple curiosity, rather than the excited energy Alex's words had inspired.

"He smiled, as if he'd really got the upper hand now. Then he said, quite calmly – you know, I'm surprised Georgie didn't tell you this –"

"She knows the story?"

"For heaven's sake – she was there! Anyway –"

"She was at the gallery, when this was going on?"

"Well, she came with Bradley." He grinned. "Come on, you must have known about Georgie and Bradley?"

Maisie shook her head. "No. I didn't." She paused a moment, then was quick to go back to the conversation. She'd consider Georgie and the American later. "But, Mr Courtman, how did Nick let the cat out of the bag?"

"He announced his intention for the piece – we're all assuming it's a triptych, but I don't know, could have been more pieces –"

"And?"

"He said that this piece would not grace a private home, but instead he was going to give it to the nation, to the Tate or the National or even the war museum at the old Bethlem Lunatic Asylum in Lambeth – rather an appropriate place for a museum of war, don't you think? A disused lunatic asylum? Anyway, Nick said, to everyone there, that it was his gift to the dead of war and those who would have us go to war in the future, so that we may never forget who we are."

"Never forget who we are? Did he say what he meant?"

"Yes, in fact, Bradley asked him. 'And who the hell are we, god-damn it?' Bit embarrassing, to tell you the truth, but Nick wasn't at all unnerved by it, even though the man spent a fortune, a *fortune*, on his work. He didn't smile – his face said nothing about his mood – but he said, quite simply, "We are *humanity*." And then he turned back to the scaffolding, and Duncan and I looked at each other and did the same, just carried on with our work, you know, shuffling Nick's map of where the anchors for the painting – or paintings – should go, and getting down to it. Everyone went on their way with a bit of muttering here and there, as you can imagine. But Svenson never came back to tackle Nick, as far as I know, to give him a lecture about the purse strings. At the time I assumed he'd wait until everyone had calmed down before playing the diplomat, but . . ."

Maisie said nothing. Alex leaned back on the chesterfield and closed his eyes. He sat that way for some moments, until Maisie spoke in a soft voice. "You've been most helpful, Mr. Courtman." She stood up, collected her black document case and checked her watch. "I really must be going now."

"Righty-o." Courtman came to his feet. "Hope I didn't put my foot in it, you know, spilling the beans about Georgie and Bradley. You won't tell her . . . well, if you do, please don't let on that it was me who told you."

"No, of course not." Maisie held out her hand to Courtman. "I have one more question for you, if you don't mind?"

"Yes?"

"Were Georgina and Nick on good terms when he died?"

"Oh, lummy, here we go." He sighed before answering. "They had been having some spats before the opening. Nick was upset about the affair with Bradley – the American's married, you know, has a wife in New York who doesn't like coming over to Europe – and said as much to Georgie. I think there were some other things going on in the family as well. Harry played them off against each other a bit, to tell you the truth. Then on the day we left to go set up the scaffolding, I was in the guest room with Duncan and I heard Georgie and Nick at loggerheads. Yelling at each other – you this and you that, back and forth." He shrugged. "I feel sorry for Georgie, actually. Must feel awful, now that Nick has gone. In fact, it's a wonder she came to you, really, isn't it?"

"Why?" Maisie had reached the door, and Courtman leaned past her to grasp the handle.

"Well, if I were a detective, I'd wonder about that temper of Georgie's."

Maisie smiled. "That's the interesting thing about detection, Mr Courtman. Things are rarely as they seem, and when they are, we tend to overlook them. I will keep our conversation in confidence and trust that you will do the same."

"Absolutely! No problem there, Miss Dobbs. Let me know if there's anything more I can do to help."

"Oh, before I forget" – she turned back – "will Duncan and Quentin be here later?"

Courtman shook his head. "No, they both went back down to Dungeness, actually. I think Duncan has a buyer for his carriage, probably another forlorn artist, eh? And Quentin is still packing up. They said they both had a lot to do down there, so off they went."

Maisie thanked Courtman again, waved, and was soon on her way. Now there were even more threads for her to gather up and spin onto bobbins. It was as if she were herself an artisan, standing before a giant loom with her skeins of wool, each one held ready to form part of the finished scene, the picture that would reveal the circumstances of Nick Bassington-Hope's death. All she had to do was create the warp and then the weft, her shuttle flying in and out, up and down through the threads, laying her hands across the panel, her fingertips testing for tautness and give, the comb pushing the weft down to ensure close weaving without the hint of a space.

The thing that intrigued her, as she walked down the street, was that if Alex Courtman was as tethered to the roots of the case as she thought he was, why had he been so forthcoming during their meeting? Even more interesting was the fact that the two other friends had returned to Dungeness, a move that underlined the need for her to keep to her plan to drive down the following day – and to ensure that she was doubly careful.

TWELVE

Maisie passed the parked Austin Swallow upon her return to the flat that evening. *Oh dear*, she thought, as she manoeuvred the MG into its customary place. She locked the motor car, then turned to face Andrew Dene, who was walking toward her, his overcoat flapping and his hair swept up by a sudden whip of cold wind. To smile was his way, and he did so as Maisie greeted him, though she could see tension revealed in his hunched shoulders. He placed a hand on her arm and kissed her on the cheek. An onlooker might have thought them cousins or friends and would never have guessed at the intimacies shared in the now-floundering courtship.

"This is a surprise, Andrew." Maisie searched for her keys, her hands shaking in anticipation of the looming confrontation, then walked to the main entrance of the block of flats. "Come on, I'll put the kettle on."

Andrew Dene followed her into the foyer, then to her flat, where she selected a second key to enter. "I thought it was about time we sorted things out," he said, as she pressed the key into the lock.

Opening the door, Maisie turned and nodded, then automatically reached to feel the radiator before placing her hat and gloves on a small table. She took off her mackintosh. "Yes, of course, you're right. Here, let me take your coat. Go and make yourself comfortable." She waited as Dene removed his overcoat and scarf, then placed both coats over a chair in the box room.

"Shall I make a pot of tea?"

Dene, already seated in one of the two armchairs, shook his head. "No, thank you. I doubt I shall be staying long, Maisie."

Maisie nodded as she made herself comfortable on the second armchair. At first, she thought better of removing her shoes, then, silently reminding herself that she could do as she pleased in her own home, she kicked off the shoes and tucked her legs up, rubbing her ever-cold feet as she did so.

"I thought we ought to talk about *us,* Maisie."

She said nothing, allowing him to speak uninterrupted. She had learned early, from Maurice, that it was always best to allow a person who had something important to say – perhaps a declaration, or a complaint – the courtesy of an uninterrupted statement. To interject might only inspire the person to begin again, thus repeating themselves. And as she had already observed signs that Dene was unsettled, she would not give reason for the conversation to become inflammatory, for she wanted him to think well of her, if that were possible.

"I had hoped, when we first began seeing each other, that you might one day become my wife." Dene swallowed deeply, causing Maisie to think that he would have done well to accept refreshment before embarking upon the conversation. "Despite appearances to the contrary, Maisie, I have not been lucky in love and am not the Lothario that some have thought me to be. I've just been waiting for the right girl, someone who would have an understanding of my background, what it takes to move up, so to speak, from one's given station in life. And I thought that girl might be you." His voice wavered briefly as he pushed back the hair that had fallen forward, and went on. "I know your work is so very important to you, but I trusted that it might, in time, take a second place to our courtship. Now, I don't know." Dene turned to her, his eyes glistening. "I have to say, Maisie, that I was flummoxed by your manner when we last spoke on the telephone. But even before that, buying this flat" – he swept his hand around, indicating the room – "it sort of put me in my place, even though I held out hope."

Still Maisie said nothing, instead keeping her attention focused on the man in front of her. She was not without emotion, cradling in her heart a melancholy that it had come to this. But she knew well that another sensation lingered inside her: the bittersweet ache of relief. And she was sadder for knowing it.

"So, before I say anything else, I want to know, Maisie, if there's any hope for me – for us, as a couple – if I proposed?"

She said nothing for some seconds. Even though she had practiced this conversation at night, tossing and turning, wondering how she might reveal herself and be understood, she felt incompetent with words where personal matters were concerned. Her voice was soft, measured. "Andrew, you are, and have been, a wonderful companion. I enjoy your company, so how could I ever fail to be charmed by your presence?" She paused. "But the truth of the matter is that . . . oh, this is so hard to explain." Dene opened his mouth to speak, but Maisie shook her head. "No, please let me try, Andrew – I must try to say what I mean, so that you understand." She closed her eyes as she searched for words. "After my . . . my breakdown last year – for that is what it was, I know that now – I have struggled to see the path ahead. I know both you and Maurice said I should rest longer, but it's not my habit; I feel that I have some . . . some sort of mastery over circumstance when I am working. That command – oh, that's not the right word." She bit her lip. "That *order* makes me feel safe, gives me battlements and a moat. And the truth is, Andrew, my business takes all the stamina I have at the moment – and you deserve more." She cleared her throat. "I have found myself fearing that as time goes on there would be pressures upon us to conform to the accepted role of a doctor and his wife, and that would mean I would have to choose. So, I have chosen now, Andrew. Now, instead of later." Maisie paused. "I have seen how the joys of our courtship have been compromised by my responsibilities to the people who come to me for help, and my choice has often been the source of great angst for us both. Even though you have been in London every fortnight, and I have journeyed to Hastings in between . . . it hasn't been conducive to a happy courtship, has it?"

Dene inspected the palms of his fine hands, the long fingers stretched out before him. "Don't mind me saying so, Maisie, it's all very well you saying that, but you could have been more honest from the start. You must have known all this, and that I wasn't prepared to sort of drift along – in fact, I came here to end our . . . our . . . courtship. At least I'm the one with the courage to face the –"

With tears blurring her vision, Maisie interrupted Dene, having not expected the angry response. "I believe I have been responsible toward you, and respectful, I –"

"You haven't been honest with *yourself* – until now, I suppose. I'm sure you never intended to prolong the courtship, and in the meantime, I might have met someone else, been able to get on with my life. In fact, I have met someone, only I wanted to find out where we stand."

"Well, Andrew, you should do as you please. I believe I have been sincere in my dealings with you, and –"

"Dealings? Sincere? Maisie, you surprise me, really you do. I have been a handy diversion for you, a weekend here, a dinner there, walks when you want them and the ball in your court."

Maisie stood up, shaken. "Andrew, I think it's time for you to go. I wish we could part on better terms, but in light of this conversation, I fear that isn't going to happen."

Andrew Dene, now on his feet, responded in a tone laced with sarcasm. "So be it, Miss Dobbs, psychologist and investigator." He sighed, adding, "I'm sorry, that wasn't called for."

Maisie nodded, and without saying more she led the way to the box room, gathered Dene's coat and opened it for him. "Drive carefully, Andrew. It's an icy night out there."

"I'm in hospital digs tonight, I'll be all right."

"Good luck, Andrew."

"You, too, Maisie." Dene turned, and walked away.

MAISIE WENT DIRECTLY to her bedroom, switched on the light and opened the wardrobe. At this point she did not want to think about Dene or consider the consequences of the end of their courtship. Having pulled out several items of clothing, she slumped on the edge of the bed, clutching her blue cashmere cardigan and stole. She pressed the soft fabric to her cheek and wept. In spite of the sense of relief, she already felt the cool breeze of loneliness cross her heart. Knowing Andrew had been a barrier between herself and an isolation that seemed to so readily envelop her, but to use him as a buffer between herself and the ache for close companionship was not fair. He was a lively suitor who had clearly adored her, but she did not have confidence enough to relinquish her work. And, she reminded herself, it would have come to that.

Turning back the bedclothes, Maisie curled up and pulled the eiderdown around her body, yearning for a few moments of comfort before she had to face the evening ahead. She shivered, though it was not cold in the room. As her tears gradually abated, she confessed to herself that there was something else, a truth she may never have considered had she not met the Bassington-Hopes – and it had given her a clue to that quality she was seeking in life that she could not define, the illusive unknown that she knew she would never find with Andrew Dene as her partner. She realized that she had come to love colour, both in the landscape of character and quite literally – on fabric, canvas, clay or a room. Andrew was fun, buoyant, but the world she had entered by dint of working for

Georgina was bursting with something fresh: there was a potency, a fire that made her feel as if she were cracking open her cocoon and waiting, waiting for her wings to dry before taking flight. And how could her wounded spirit be born aloft if she tethered herself now? That was at the heart of her discontent. There was something in those words. . . . She clambered from the bed and searched for the book again, to the place she had marked. *"He would create proudly out of the freedom and power of his soul. . . ."* Could she do that with her life? And if she could, would she come tumbling down to earth like Icarus? What was it Priscilla had said to her last year? "You've always kept to the safe places!" Now she was among people for whom such a conservative approach was anathema. Maisie felt her head spin with thoughts that plunged her from excitement to despair as she castigated herself for such self-absorption, when the troubles faced by the Beale family and thousands like them were so desperate. And the very thought of Priscilla brought sadness anew, for she missed the honesty and depth of their friendship. Visiting her in France last year had brought a realization that she ached for the proximity of a close friendship.

After her breakdown, she had felt a return to the aloneness that had shrouded her when her mother died. Being with Andrew had helped her throw a line out into the future, an anchor she would use to pull herself away from the war, away from the loss of Simon, the terrible images that haunted her – and into the present so that life could go on. But now she was tentatively lifting the anchor, ready to cast off toward the light emanating from Georgina, her family and friends. She shivered again, cold to the core, remembering the doubt and Lady Rowan's warning. Could she be more like Georgina than she thought, if she took energy, took life, from those who lived in a world of colour, of words, of artistry? Might she become the sort of person that Lady Rowan described, someone who used people?

Maisie leaned back, exhausted. Maurice had instructed her to not take on anything too taxing, given the fragility of her recovery.

Though he was in favour of a move to a flat of her own, he had suggested that it might not be the right time, that she should avail herself of the opportunity to live at the Comptons' Belgravia mansion for at least another three or four months. But she had forged ahead, wanting to take advantage of a well-priced property, and – she knew this – she harboured a desire to underline her singularity, her ability to continue as she had begun, standing firmly on her own two feet. Even though those same two feet had crumpled under her not so long ago.

Realizing that she was stepping into a spiral of self-recrimination, she galvanized herself, drying her eyes and taking a deep breath. "It was for the best," she said aloud, thinking of Dene. Then she smiled, as Priscilla came to mind once more. She knew exactly what her friend would recommend, ash dropping from her cigarette as she waved a hand to emphasize advice delivered in a clipped tone: "If I were you, Maisie, I would wallow until I couldn't squeeze out one more drop of salt water, then I'd buck up, powder my nose, put on my very best clothes and hit the town – and I do mean *hit*."

Rubbing a hand across her eyes, she stepped in front of the mirror, wrapping the stylish blue stole around her. Yes, together with the black dress, it would do quite well for a woman out alone in the evening – even if she was working.

MAISIE LEFT THE flat at ten o'clock, yawning as she did so. It wasn't completely unusual for a woman to go out alone anymore. In fact, it had become quite acceptable, especially as there weren't enough men to accompany them. Based upon her experience since the end of the war, she thought many bachelors were quite caddish anyway, making the most of the surfeit of women with an easy-come, easy-go flippancy. Certainly, Nick Bassington-Hope appeared not to have been above such behaviour.

Clutching her list of clubs, Maisie planned to simply pop her head around the door of each, act as if she were there to see her friend Harry Bassington-Hope and then leave as quickly as possible if she couldn't immediately confirm his presence at the establishment. Fortunately, now that Joynson-Hicks was no longer the home secretary, she had little fear of being on the premises of a club when it was raided, a game of cat and mouse played by so many of those referred to as "bright young things" before Jix was relieved of his position.

Chelsea for two of the clubs, Soho for another two, and one in Mayfair were on her list. By the time she arrived at Stanislav's, an establishment in Soho, Maisie thought she was becoming more accomplished in the act of nonchalantly walking into a club, sweet-talking the man or woman at the door, and then leaving when the reply was to the effect that Harry was expected later, or on another evening. Clearly he had several engagements each night, and worked at different places, though she certainly had no intention of lingering unless he was without doubt expected shortly at a club.

She had finally put the black dress aside, settling instead on a pair of black trousers and a long sleeveless blouse with a boat neckline and a matching sash at the hip. The outfit had been a castoff from Priscilla, who had bundled it up and sent it along with several other items in a brown paper parcel. It had arrived just before Christmas, with a message that read, "Having children has ruined, simply ruined my waistline. These are a bit old-fashioned but am sure you can use them." The trousers had barely been worn, and seeing as women who donned trousers were still in the minority, they were not as old-fashioned as Priscilla had suggested. Maisie thought the blouse was made with room to spare, though she would concede that, had Priscilla not sent the clothes to her, they would probably have languished at the back of her wardrobe. Now she was grateful for the ensemble, which she thought did not suit her at all well, though it was perfect for the evening's subterfuge.

She took a deep breath and pushed against the door of Stanislav's, whereupon a well-built man stepped forward to hold it open. A young woman smiled from behind a black and silver counter framed by a series of square silver lampshades, the lights providing the only illumination in the foyer. Maisie blinked, then smiled in return at the young woman, who was wearing a long black velvet dress with sequins along the hem, hipline, collar and cuffs. Her blond hair was tied back into a small chignon, and her eyes were accentuated by kohl, her lips blood-red.

The woman greeted her cordially. "Are you a member?"

"Oh, no – but I am a guest of Harry Bassington-Hope. Is he here yet?"

The woman inclined her head. "I'll find out. Just a moment, please."

The woman opened a door behind her, poked her head into a room that Maisie couldn't see, and said, "Oi, is 'arry 'ere yet?" There was a delay of several seconds before she closed the door and addressed Maisie again, the cut-glass accent restored. "He should be here at any moment, madam. Please follow me. We have a small table where you can wait."

Maisie was relieved to see that the table was situated in the corner of the room, close to the back wall, a perfect position from which to observe the comings and goings of people in the club. A waiter came to the table, and Maisie ordered a ginger beer with lime cordial. Someone had once told her that it was a popular drink in American cities, where prohibition required one to banish all evidence of alcohol from the breath, so Maisie ordered it, not because she intended to drink, but because it might give the impression that she was a seasoned club goer who would order something stronger later. The harmless cocktail was delivered and Maisie settled back to observe the room.

A series of tables of varying sizes, seating from two to eight people, were placed several tables deep around three sides of a small parquet dance floor. On the fourth and farthest side, a quartet had just started to play and already a few couples were dancing. Maisie tapped her foot and sipped her drink. Though she was tired when she first set out, she had since picked up and decided that it would be quite fun to come with friends to such a place. If one *had* a clutch of friends to come with, that is.

Her eyes scanned the room, looking for any faces she recognized. It wasn't long before she noticed Randolph Bradley and Stig Svenson at a table close to the bar, the Swede leaning forward, intent upon the conversation, while the American relaxed against the back of his chair, his grey silk suit with even darker grey tie and kerchief punctuating his wealth. Maisie wondered if Georgina would appear and moved her chair farther back into the shadows. She watched as the American raised an index finger to the waiter, who came to his table in haste. Bradley stood up, pressed a note into the man's hand, slapped him on the back. He shook hands with Svenson and left. Stig Svenson stared into his cocktail for a few moments, then raised the glass and finished the drink in one mouthful, leaning his head back as he did so. He wiped his mouth with a handkerchief pulled from his trouser pocket, then he, too, left the club.

As she scanned the room a second time, Maisie noticed another man, a man she had never seen before, watching Svenson leave the club. She closed her eyes and, in her mind, replayed the scene when she had first glanced around the room. She knew he had been there when she came in and that he had been carefully watching Svenson and Bradley. Who was he? She squinted into the dark as the man stood up, pulled a note from his trouser pocket and checked it against a wall light before placing it on the bar. He took his hat from the seat next to him and left the club.

"Care to dance, Miss Dobbs?"

"Oh, my goodness, you made me jump!"

Alex Courtman pulled back a chair and sat down at the table. "Now, I can't for a moment believe that you are here for anything but business. I must say, you look ravishing, by the way."

Maisie raised an eyebrow. "Thank you for the compliment, Mr Courtman. Now, if you don't mind, I'm waiting for a friend."

"Oh, a friend? Then I am sure your friend won't mind if I steal you away for a dance, will he?"

"No, thank you, Mr Courtman. I'd rather not."

"Come on! You don't go to a club unless you are up for a dance or two." Courtman reached over, took Maisie's hand and led her, blushing and protesting, to the dance floor. The popular tune had drawn many more couples from their tables, so there was hardly room to move, but that didn't stop Courtman from swinging his arms from side to side with the beat and, embracing the music, and occasionally Maisie, with gusto. Maisie, too, began to swing her arms, following her partner's lead. Seeing her enthusiasm, Courtman took her by the waist and swirled her around. As the music reached a crescendo, a trumpet joined the rag, wheeling in with a high-pitched long note, to the accompaniment of piano, bass, drums and trombone. The dancers roared, applauding as they continued to move around the floor. Harry Bassington-Hope had arrived.

Courtman claimed Maisie for two more dances before, breathless, she held up her hands in mock surrender, and returned to the table, her partner following her.

"I say, you can dance when you like, can't you?"

Maisie shook her head. "To tell you the truth, apart from Georgina's party last week, I don't think I've danced since . . . since . . . well, since before the war, actually."

Courtman raised his hand to summon a waiter, then turned back. "Don't tell me, you danced with the love of your life and he never came home from France."

The smile left Maisie's face. "It's none of your business, Mr. Courtman."

He touched her hand. "Oh dear, I'm terribly sorry. I didn't mean to offend you, it's just one of those wartime stories, isn't it?"

Maisie nodded to acknowledge the apology, withdrawing her hand. She changed the subject. "So, are you a regular here?"

"I come occasionally. But especially when I'm owed money."

"Harry?"

Courtman nodded. "He's Nick's brother, after all. He tapped me for a few pounds on Sunday. Said he'd repay it in just two days, so it's time for me to receive my due from him."

"Was it just a few pounds?"

He shook his head. "No, a bit more than that – twenty, to tell you the truth. But I'm not exactly flush, so I wanted it back today. And I'll get it too."

Maisie looked toward the dance floor, which was still packed, and then at Harry Bassington-Hope, his legs splayed, his bow tie pulled loose, as he leaned back again, his trumpet held high, teasing another impossibly high note from the shining instrument.

"If he looked after his money like he looks after that trumpet, he'd be a rich man." Courtman reached for the cocktail the waiter had just set before him.

"It's gleaming," said Maisie. She turned to Courtman. "When does he stop, or take a break?"

"In about another fifteen minutes. You can leave a message with the waiter – along with the appropriate monetary accompaniment – and he'll pass it on to Harry, telling him to join you."

Maisie followed his instruction, slipping a couple of coins into the waiter's palm as she gave him the folded piece of paper.

"Shall I wait until he comes?" Courtman smiled at Maisie with such sincerity that she could almost forgive his lack of manners just a few moments ago.

"Yes, thank you, Mr. Courtman. I am not really accustomed to such places, to tell you the truth."

"I know. Mind you, I'm only staying on one condition."

"Condition?"

"Yes. I want to claim the first dance after trumpet boy gets back up there."

HARRY BASSINGTON-HOPE SWAGGERED off the stage and over to the bar, stopping on the way to receive backslaps, shake hands with customers and to lean over and kiss women on the cheek, receiving a few lipstick prints on his face as he did so. Maisie watched as the waiter approached him and whispered in his ear, whereupon Harry looked around to locate Maisie's table. He nodded to the waiter, reached for the drink that had already been placed on the bar in front of him and made his way over to Maisie.

"Miss Dobbs, we meet again, though I must say, I would never have pegged you for a night owl." He pulled out a chair, turned it around and sat down, his arm resting on the chair back as he set his glass down on the table. He saw Maisie look at the clear liquid. "Soda water. Never drink anything stronger while playing, though I try to make up for lost time when I'm off duty." He turned to Alex Courtman. "Alex, old chap, still taking up room in my sister's flat? I would have thought the Yankee would have kicked you out by now."

Alex Courtman stood up. "Moving on next week, Harry, to new digs over in Chelsea."

Harry Bassington-Hope turned back to Maisie. "What do they call an artist without a girl?"

Maisie shook her head. "I haven't a clue."

"Homeless!" He chuckled at the joke, while Maisie smiled and shook her head.

"The old ones are the best, aren't they, Harry?" Courtman stood up and drained his glass. "I'll be back to claim that dance when trumpet boy here starts playing again."

Georgina's younger brother watched as Courtman strode toward the bar, then brought his attention back to Maisie. "So, what can I do for you, Miss Dobbs?"

Maisie thought Harry Bassington-Hope did not look like a man who had lost his only brother just a month earlier. "As you know, Georgina has been unsettled regarding the police assessment of the circumstances of your brother's death and believes be may have been the victim of foul play. She asked me to look into the matter, and –"

"And it's usually someone close to the victim, isn't it?"

"Not always, Mr Bassington-Hope. Though, family and friends tend to have a transparent relationship with the victim, in which they are not always consciously aware of anything unusual going in the months and days leading up to death. In asking questions, I find that the memory is ignited, to some extent, and even a small recollection can shed light on a meaningful clue as to the truth of the incident."

"I suppose it's no secret, then, that my relationship with my brother – as dear as he was to me – was really rather poor."

"Was it?" Maisie said only enough to keep Bassington-Hope speaking.

"I was still in school when he went into the army, so he was very much the big brother, and as for the girls, Georgie and Nolly, well, Georgie was off on her own adventure anyway, and Nolly barely noticed me. I was a sort of fly in the sibling ointment. Mind you, I rather liked Godfrey, Nolly's husband. He was always up for a game of cricket, you know, much more of a big brother type than Nick, actually."

"And what about when Nick died?"

"Stupid accident, very stupid accident, wasn't it?"

"Was it?"

"Of course. Now if he'd just let his pals help him a bit more and hadn't been so secretive, then it wouldn't have happened." He shook his head. "No, I can't imagine anything but an accident, and it could have been avoided."

"Hadn't you and Nick argued over money?"

"Hmmph! I suppose that must be common knowledge." He paused, checked his watch, then went on. "My brother and I lived different lives. Yes, I had hit a spot of trouble financially, and Nick helped me out, but you know, with Nick there always had to be a bit of a lecture. God knows why, it's not as if his halo wasn't a bit tarnished."

"What do you mean?"

"Oh, nothing really. He just wasn't the blue-eyed boy that Georgina would have you believe. Didn't think twice about who he'd upset with his work, you know, and believe me, he could upset people."

"Who did he upset?"

He looked away, toward the stage, where the other musicians were taking their places, stood up and drained his drink before replying. "You could start with the family. Had a habit of upsetting everyone at some time or another. Father had to calm Nolly down a couple of times – to think he could upset her so much after all she'd done for him."

"How did he upset –"

"Sorry, Miss Dobbs. I really have to go, the boys are waiting for me." He turned and hurried around the perimeter of the room so as not to be waylaid by admirers and was up on the stage with a single leap, taking up his trumpet and coaxing another wail into the rafters, the band joining him as the note changed mid-climb for a slide down the scale. The dancers were up and moving, and as Maisie collected her bag, she felt a pressure on her elbow.

"Oh, no you don't! You promised one more dance." Alex Court-man had loosened his tie while sitting at the bar, waiting for Harry Bassington-Hope to depart.

"But –"

"No 'buts' – come on."

IT WAS ANOTHER hour before Maisie left the club to make her way through cold, smog-filled streets to her flat. She parked the MG, checked the lock and walked toward the main door of the building. It was as she opened the door that she looked around be-hind her. A shiver had slithered along her spine, and she closed the door behind her with haste, then hurried to her ground-floor flat. Once inside, she locked the door and, without turning on the lights, went to the window and looked out at the small front lawn and sur-rounding trees that separated the flats from the street. She stood there for some time, but there was no one there, though she felt, instinctively, that she had been watched.

Clearing her mind, she sat on a pillow, cross-legged in meditation before going to bed, hoping that her practice would leave a path free of conscious thought for some fresh connections to reveal themselves to her. She had not been able to question Harry Bassington-Hope as thoroughly as she had wanted, though she had not come away empty-handed. From a practical perspective, she had procured a list of the clubs where he was employed and knew broadly how and when to find him again – if she needed to continue the conversation that had been so abruptly brought to a close. She had not pressed any point that might have alerted him to her knowledge of his underworld dealings – and she knew already that one of his attackers the previous Sunday was also known to Nick.

The conversation had shed even greater light on the Bassington-Hope family, and though it was not something a well-mannered woman would do, she now planned to drop in without prior notice when she made her way back from Dungeness this week. She suspected she'd be welcomed anyway. Nick alienated members of his family from time to time, and in the weeks before his death it appeared that he had argued with both sisters and his brother – he had had little in common with the latter in any case. He had upset the man who was not only the source of a considerable amount of money, but his sister's lover. And the dynamics of those relationships seemed as if they were about to give Stig Svenson peptic distress – he had a lot to lose when Nick Bassington-Hope refused to toe the line. Alex Courtman was an interesting case – not as close to Nick as the other two friends and bluntly honest about his ability as an artist. He was also quite forthcoming in terms of sharing information with Maisie. Was he deliberately misleading her? And why did he seem to be on the edge of the "inner circle"?

Maisie decided to push the case to the back of her mind, and instead concentrate her thoughts on Lizzie Beale. Billy might be back at work in the morning – she hoped against hope that the news of his daughter was encouraging. Having lain awake for some time worrying, it distressed her when she tried to summon an image of Lizzie and found that she couldn't. She *could* see her little red coat, the lace-up leather boots on her feet, her mop of curls like those of a rag doll and her dimpled hands. But not her face.

THIRTEEN

As Maisie packed her suitcase for the journey down to Dungeness the following day, the earthy smell of new leather reminded her of Andrew Dene, from whom the suitcase was a gift just a few months earlier. She fingered the straps, running her hand across its smooth top as she closed it. Today would challenge her, she understood that already, and she knew it would have been heartwarming to think that, at the end of the day, she could turn to someone who loved her, someone who would say, "You're home now, let me hold you until tomorrow comes."

Though there was no rain, no sleet, the sky above Fitzroy Square was gunmetal grey, shedding a deep silver light across equally grey flagstones. It was as if all colour had been drained from morning's promise, as if time would be suspended until tomorrow, and the tomorrow after that. As she unlocked the front door, Maisie checked the watch pinned to her jacket pocket. Even though she was a few minutes late, she knew she would be surprised if Billy were at the office. He would not come today. She moved toward the staircase, and stopped. *Why am I even going up the stairs?* Then she turned, locking the door behind her again, and made her way back to the MG.

Rain had started to fall lightly, that fine mist of a shower that would continue now for the remainder of the day. Maisie did not drive to the hospital in Stockwell, for she knew there was no need. Instead she drove straight to the Beales' small house in the East End.

She saw that the curtains were drawn as she parked her motor car on the street outside the house, and as she stepped from the driver's seat, she was aware that the thin, worn fabric at the windows of other houses on the street had flicked back and forth, as neighbours watched the comings and goings. Maisie knocked at the door. There was no answer, so she knocked again, hearing footsteps become louder until the door opened. It was Doreen's sister. Maisie realized that she had never been introduced to the woman, so did not know her name or how to address her.

"I came . . . I hope . . ."

The woman nodded and stepped aside, her eyes red-rimmed, the bulk of her pregnancy weighing upon her, causing her to clutch her back as she made room for Maisie to enter the narrow passageway.

"They've been talking about you, miss. They'd want to see you."

Maisie touched the woman on the shoulder, and walked to the kitchen door, where she closed her eyes and petitioned herself to say and do the right thing. She knocked twice and opened the door.

Billy and Doreen Beale sat at the kitchen table, both with untouched cups of cold tea in front of them. Maisie entered and said nothing but, standing behind them, rested a hand gently on each of their shoulders.

"I am so sorry. I am so, so sorry."

Doreen Beale choked, pulled her pinafore up to her swollen eyes and wept, pushing her chair back as she slumped over. She clutched her arms around her middle, as if trying to stop the pain that came from the very place where she had carried Lizzie before she was born. Billy bit into his lower lip and stood up, allowing Maisie to take the seat he vacated.

"I knew you'd know, Miss. I knew you'd know she was gone." He could barely form words, his voice cracking as he spoke. "It's all wrong, all bleedin' wrong, when something as beautiful as our little Lizzie can be taken. It's all wrong."

"Yes, Billy, you're right, it's all wrong." She closed her eyes, silently continuing the plea that she be given words that might soothe, words that would begin the healing of bereaved parents. She had seen, when she entered the kitchen, the chasm of sorrow that divided man and wife already, each deep in their own wretched suffering, neither knowing what to say to the other. She knew that to begin to talk about what had happened was a key to acknowledging their loss, and that such acceptance would in turn be a means to enduring the days and months ahead. Oh, how she wished she could speak to Maurice, seek his counsel.

"When did it happen?"

Billy swallowed as Doreen sat up, wiped her eyes with her pinafore again and reached for the teapot. "We're not minding our manners, Miss Dobbs. I'm sorry. I'll put the kettle on."

"I'll do that, Dory." Doreen's sister stepped forward.

"No, you sit down, Ada, you need to take the weight off."

Doreen Beale busied herself at the stove, stoking the fire. She was about to pick up the coal scuttle when Billy stepped forward.

"No you don't. I'll do that."

"Billy, I can do it! Now then" – she snatched back the coal scuttle – "you talk to Miss Dobbs. It's very kind of her to call."

Maisie remembered the days that followed her mother's death, days when father and daughter could barely speak to each other. They kept busy, both of them going about their daily round without talking about their loss, avoiding contact because neither could bear to see despair feasting upon the other. And it had taken years to heal the wounds of the soul that mourning had visited upon them.

"We went back to the 'ospital yesterday evening, early-ish. Turns out she'd taken a turn for the worse, so we went in to see the poor little mite – there was nothing of 'er, Miss. Poor little scrap." Billy paused and reached for the cold tea, just as Doreen turned to pick up his cup. She nodded for him to continue talking as she took the cup and washed it in the sink. The air in the kitchen was smoke-filled and stale, steam from a kettle adding to the damp discomfort. "The doctor was there, and the nurses, and they tried to make us leave, but we wouldn't go. 'ow can they expect you to leave when it's your own flesh and blood lying there?"

Maisie whispered thanks to Doreen as cups of fresh tea were set on the table, and she patted the chair so that Billy's wife would sit down again. Ada remained seated next to the fire, silently rubbing her swollen belly.

Billy continued. "Seemed to go on for 'ours, the waiting, but it was – can't remember the time now, to tell you the truth –"

"Eleven. It was eleven o'clock. I remember looking up at the clock," Doreen interjected as she stirred her tea, and then continued stirring without stopping to drink.

"Anyway, at eleven o'clock, the nurse comes to get us, and when we got to the ward, the doctor told us she was on 'er last. That there was nothing more that could be done." He choked, putting his hand to his mouth and closing his eyes.

They remained in silence for some moments, then Doreen sat up straight. "We just stayed there, Miss Dobbs. They let me hold her until she was gone. I reckon I won't forget that, you know, that they let us in to hold her, so that she didn't go alone." She paused, then looked at Maisie. "They said she never would've known anything, at the end. They said she wasn't in pain. Do you think she knew, Miss Dobbs? You were a nurse, do you think she knew we'd come, that we were there?"

Maisie reached for Doreen's hands, looked at Billy, then his wife. "Yes, she knew. I know she knew." She paused, searching for the words that would say something of what she had come to feel, to know, when in the presence of death. "I used to believe, in the war, that when someone dies, it's as if they've shed a thick woollen coat that has become too heavy. The weight those men released was a result of wounds caused by guns, by shells, by terrible things the dying had seen. Lizzie's weight was a disease that was stronger than her body, and even though the doctors did everything they could to help her overcome the attack, the fight was too much for her." Maisie's voice cracked. "So, you see, I believe she knew you were there, that you'd come to hold her as she took off that heavy coat. Yes, she knew you'd come. And then her little spirit was free of the struggle and she slipped away."

Doreen turned to her husband, who knelt down beside her. They clutched each other, weeping together, as Maisie quietly stood up, signalled to Ada that she was leaving and stepped lightly along the corridor to the front door. She turned to Ada as she opened the door and stepped out onto the pavement.

"Tell Billy not to come to work until he's ready."

"All right, Miss Dobbs."

"Has your husband found a job yet?"

She shook her head. "No, though he thinks he might get some work down on the docks at the end of the week. Mind you, what with the unions . . ."

Maisie nodded. "When will Lizzie be laid to rest?"

"Not for a few days yet, might even be over a week, what with one thing and another."

"Please send word to me. And if you need anything . . ." Maisie handed her a calling card.

"Right you are, miss. You've been good to Billy and our Doreen. They're lucky he's in work."

Maisie smiled, then said good-bye. She left the East End with her hands firmly on the steering wheel, her attention on the road, her eyes smarting. But instead of going directly to Fitzroy Square, she was compelled to make her way toward the Embankment, where she parked the MG and walked down to the water. She leaned on the wall and watched the Thames, an even deeper grey today as it reflected clouds overhead. The damp smog had barely lifted and Maisie pulled up the collar of her mackintosh and rewrapped the scarf around her neck. She closed her eyes and remembered Lizzie Beale, felt her head in the crook of her neck when she had taken her in her arms on the day that Doreen had come to the office last year, her worries, then, about Billy. Maisie folded her arms around her body, felt herself fighting the tears that she knew would come, as she pushed back from the abyss that might draw her in all too quickly if she succumbed once again.

She stood watching over the water for some moments longer, then turned to walk back to her motor car. That Billy and Doreen had reached out to each other gave succour to her aching heart, and she found herself wondering about Emma and Piers Bassington-Hope. Had Nick's mother and father turned to each other upon hearing of his death? The character of an artist suggested an ability to demonstrate emotion and that both were artists supported an assumption that they had readily shared the joy and heartache that comes with bringing up a family. But in terms of the heart, what if they were mired in the behaviour of their parents before them and given to sheltering their innermost feelings from each other? Was that why Emma had broken down in Maisie's company, searching for the arms of a complete stranger to comfort her? If that were true, and the Bassington-Hopes had created a wall of silence between them regarding the loss of their son, then the weight of their bereavement must be intolerable, especially given that their daughter had cast suspicion on the circumstances of his death.

SLUMPING DOWN IN her office armchair, Maisie looked at the cold, damp weather outside and felt a wave of fatigue wash over her. Yes, it was still early days. If Maurice were with her, she knew she would be admonished for pressing on so soon following her recovery. She leaned over to ignite the gas fire, then reached into her old black document case for her diary. Flicking through the pages, she reconsidered her week. Georgina Bassington-Hope was paying her handsomely to compile a report in which she would list evidence that either supported the fact that her brother was killed in an accident of his own causing or that he died as a result of a deliberate act by another. Knowing that few outcomes were a case of black-and-white, a case of guilty or not guilty, Maisie allowed that the artist's death might well have been an accident, with the actions of another being the cause. And it was possible that fear of the consequences kept that person from coming forward. There again, Nick Bassington-Hope's death might well have been premeditated murder, which begged the question as to whether such an intention was connected with the seedy element that Harry – *always on the edge, Harry* – had taken up with. Or, if it was murder, what if it had nothing to do with Harry's activities and everything to do with Nick's connections or his work?

His work. Maisie pondered Nick Bassington-Hope's work, from those early days at the Slade, then in Belgium, to the graphic depictions of patriotism evident in the propaganda he developed for the Office of Information. Instinct told her she had barely seen the tip of the iceberg in terms of his war paintings, and from what she had been told, Nick had almost made it his business to upset people since he returned to France as a war artist. Had America really saved his soul? Or had the fire in his mind been only temporarily tempered by the grandeur of a natural environment that clearly captivated him? Was Randolph Bradley correct, when he suggested that, in the piece that was missing, Nick was laying the war to rest? Had the path he'd taken placed another relationship at risk? Maisie knew that when people changed, when something conspired to render their path different from those who were closest to them, those others often felt abandoned, left behind. Was the fact that he would not compromise the integrity of his work – as he saw it – a reason for his death?

She sat in front of the fire for a moment or two longer, then, sighing, she moved to her desk, reached for the telephone receiver and placed a call to Duncan at Georgina's flat. As luck would have it, he was there alone and agreed to see her in an hour. She was sure that

Duncan and Quentin would recount their respective conversations with her to each other, so she took the liberty of inquiring as to where she might find Quentin and was directed to the Chelsea Arts Club, where he would most likely be playing snooker all afternoon.

As Maisie replaced the receiver, she wondered if Alex had confided details of their meeting to his friends. She was still uneasy upon recalling their conversation and the leisurely way he shared confidences. Was she being manipulated? She reconsidered the conversation at the party, the manner of Haywood and Trayner in particular, keeping quiet as Alex Courtman regaled her with tales of the past. It occurred to her that he was perhaps too keen to deflect her attention back to earlier times.

Turning the knob at the side of the gas fire, Maisie shut off the jets and looked around the office. Everything was tidy, all notes and files were neat and not one single item was out of place. She stood for some time, thinking of Billy and Doreen Beale, the rush to admit Lizzie to the hospital, the raging fever that was a portent for what was to come and the anguish of losing their child. How was it, then, for them to return home, for them to touch her clothes and, given the circumstances of her death, to burn everything that was hers?

Closing the door, she secured the room, turning keys in two locks and checking the handle once to ensure that it was safe. As she stepped out into the square, the cold caught her cheeks and she slammed the door behind her, again taking care to check the lock – she might not come back to the office until tomorrow morning when, she hoped, Billy would return to work. Thoughts of work brought her firmly back to the case of Nick Bassington-Hope, whereupon she looked at her watch and set off toward the MG, which she'd parked around the corner in Warren Street. Had she waited just one more moment, Maisie would have seen two men walk across the square to the building she had just left and open the door with ease. One of those men she would have recognized, though she did not know his identity.

DUNCAN HAYWOOD OPENED the door before Maisie had a chance to knock. As at their first meeting, Maisie thought he resembled a small creature that scurried back and forth, squirreling away supplies for a long winter. His clothing was precise: a well-tailored but well-worn tweed suit, a clean shirt and tie and polished shoes. Had he made the effort to ensure a good impression during her visit? Would he usually be more relaxed, perhaps like Courtman, or Nick Bassington-Hope? Though the thought had not occurred to her in such a way before, Maisie concluded that Nick had been very much the leader of the group.

"Miss Dobbs, lovely to see you again." He reached forward to take her hand. "May I take your coat?"

"Thank you for agreeing to a meeting – and no, don't worry about my coat, I'm still a bit cold." Maisie smiled, shook hands and entered the flat, taking up the same seat as before, with Duncan settling onto the chesterfield in the same place that Alex had previously chosen.

"I take it that Alex and Georgina are both out today?" She slipped her gloves off, laid them in her lap and unwound her scarf.

"Yes, Alex is looking at a studio-*cum*-bed-sitting-room to rent, and Georgina is probably with Lord Bradley."

"Lord Bradley?"

Duncan smirked. "A joke, Miss Dobbs. It's a nickname we have for him, Quentin, Alex and I, and of course, Nick, when he was alive." He paused, as if to gauge her sense of humour. "After all, the man is trying to be British to the core, what with his suits for the City, tweeds for shooting and you should see him on a horse! Tailored jodhpurs, hacking jacket, the lot, and he rides to hounds with the West Kent, and occasionally with the Old Surrey, you know. Then, of course, he opens his mouth."

Maisie thought the man's manner snobbish and felt like saying as much, but instead put a question to him. "Duncan, I wonder if you can tell me more about your relationship with Nick, and about your life down in Dungeness – even though you live in Hythe now, and are newly married." She smiled. "Congratulations, by the way."

"Thank you." He smiled in return, hesitating in a manner that suggested he was measuring his response to the question. "I've known Nick since before the war, as you know – so I won't repeat old news."

She inclined her head, acknowledging his subtle reference to her information gathering and her understanding that there were few secrets between the friends. But *few* did not eliminate the possibility that there might be one or two important facts not shared, and Maisie suspected that Alex might not have revealed all the details of the meeting to Duncan.

"I was as close as one could be to Nick, to tell you the truth. Georgina was his closest confidant, though a chap can't tell his sister everything, can he?" The question was rhetorical; there was no pause for a reply. "We were all in the same boat, frankly. A bit broke, wanting some peace and quiet, and the coast provided exactly the environment we were looking for, plus there was the added attraction of railway carriages being sold off on the cheap and a community of artists coming together in Dungeness. Most have gone now, not everyone can hack that weather and the coast can be bleak. Of course, Nick was really coming back and forth a lot to London, as he began to enjoy a level of success that we three could only dream of, to tell you the truth. Mind you, 'success' is a loose term to an artist, Miss Dobbs. Success is when you can afford food on the table, your canvasses and oils and to put a new shirt on your back. But Nick was just making it, just getting to that point where the money was coming through in larger quantities."

"But I thought Bradley had been purchasing his work for years."

"He had, but not only does Lord Bradley drive a hard bargain – I think it's in the blood – Svenson also takes a cut, then there's all sorts of others to pay when you have an exhibition. And you obviously know that Nick was more or less bankrolling the activities of his brother."

"I knew he helped him out."

He smirked again. "Oh, to have that kind of helping out!" Standing, Duncan moved to lean against the mantelpiece, but instead kneeled down to light the paper, kindling and coals already set in the grate. The fire did not catch immediately, so for a few seconds longer Duncan's attention was drawn to the kindling. Maisie looked on, noticing that an old packing crate had been put to good use, the black lettering still visible across one or two shards of splintered wood. Almost mindlessly, Maisie read the word: *Stein*. As Duncan struck yet another match, Maisie looked around the room, drawn, as she was nowadays, to the paintings. A new landscape had been added to the wall above the cocktail cabinet, a rather modern work not to her taste. She wondered, once again, what it would be like to have sufficient funds to part with money for something that wasn't actually useful.

The wood began to catch now, and reaching for the bellows, Duncan turned to Maisie, then went on with his response to her question. "Living out there in Dungeness was an adventure, but I'd had my eye on Hythe for some time, and it seemed quite logical to move there permanently when the right house came up."

"You must have eventually become fairly successful then." Maisie knew the comment may have gone too far, prying into the man's financial situation. In any case, he seemed not to notice.

"I cheat, you know. Teaching art at two schools, and in the evenings at the church hall. It helps enormously. And my wife's family helped with the house."

"How very fortunate for you." Maisie went on with barely a pause. "You were with Nick and Alex on the night of Nick's death, weren't you?"

"Yes – look, Miss Dobbs, you know all this already, so why are you asking me? Do you think I had something to do with Nick's death? If you do, then let's get it out on the table and do away with all the fancy footwork. I have nothing to hide and will not be peppered with questions in this way." His outburst was sudden and, Maisie admitted to herself, warranted. It had been her intention to push him.

"Do you think he was murdered?"

"Put it this way, he was not generally a careless person, and he had planned the exhibition down to the last nail in the wall. That, however, does not give an answer either way. He was tired, he had been working feverishly hard, and he wanted this to be the best, the most talked-about art opening in London."

"Would it have been?"

"I saw all but the main piece, and I thought it was brilliant. Bradley's got the bulk of the exhibit now, though. And as we all know, he would kill to get his hands on that triptych, or whatever it is."

"You don't know what it is?"

"No."

"Did Nick work on it in Dungeness?"

"If he did, I never saw it. Hasn't anyone told you how secretive he could be?"

"Did Nick ever receive visitors at his carriage?"

The man shrugged his shoulders. "I wasn't his keeper, you know. Despite the fact that we all lived in the same place, I think I can count the times on one hand when we were there together in the past year, so, no, I cannot give you any information about his social life, I'm afraid."

"Did Harry visit, as far as you know? Even if you didn't see him, did Nick mention it?"

"He came down a few times."

"When was the first time?"

He shook his head. "Can't remember."

"Did Harry's London friends ever come to the coast?"

"Now why would they do that? Far too uncomfortable for the club crowd, you know. Strange people, they spend their evenings in sooty, sordid clubs, then go back to their palatial surroundings."

Maisie did not take her eyes off him, but kept up the pace of her questioning. "Do you know the Old Town, in Hastings?"

"Been there. All jellied eels, whelks, Londoners on their days off and slums down on Bourne Street."

"Have you ever spoken to the fishermen?"

"What?"

"The Draper brothers, perhaps?" Maisie pressed, before he had time to conceal the shock his widened eyes revealed.

"I – I, well I have no idea what you are talking about."

Maisie checked her momentum. "Tell me what you know about the mural in Nick's carriage."

He shrugged again. "Dr Syn. He loved the myths and legends of the Marshes, loved the stories of smuggling gangs, of devil riders, and of course he'd met Thorndike, the author."

"What about the Draper boys?"

"What about them?"

"In the mural."

Another shrug. "I have no idea what you are talking about."

"Don't you?"

"No."

Maisie paused before speaking. "I wonder if you wouldn't mind explaining something else to me." She leaned forward. "At Georgina's party, when Oswald Mosley came into the room, he was almost immediately surrounded by admirers, yet you, Alex and Quentin all but turned your backs. Now, I am no follower, but I'm curious to know what you think of him."

Haywood lost no time in replying. "God, that man makes me sick. Look at the way he postures, the rhetoric – and the fools can't see through him, any more than people can see through that tyrant in Germany – Herr Hitler. If you ask me, they are cut of the same cloth – and we should all keep an eye on them. I cannot believe Georgina invited him or even thinks he can do half of what he says – the man's power hungry."

"I see. That's a strong opinion."

"I have friends in Heidelberg, Munich and Dresden, and to a man they have the same opinions about their leader – we must watch his type, Miss Dobbs."

She smiled. "Mr Haywood, thank you so much for your time, you have been most accommodating."

"But –"

"But?"

"I thought you would have some more questions, that's all."

She shook her head. "Not at all. I only ask questions when I am still seeking the answers – and you've been an invaluable help to me. Thank you."

Maisie wound the scarf around her neck once again and stood to warm her hands by the fire for a moment before plunging them into her gloves. "Now, I had best be off. I'm hoping to catch Quentin at the Chelsea Arts Club."

Duncan had risen to his feet as Maisie stood in front of the fire. "Yes, quite." Without adding further comment, he led her to the front door and bid her farewell. As the MG's engine rumbled to life, Maisie watched his silhouette move with haste to the telephone table.

For her part, Maisie was in no hurry. Of course, she would go to the club, just in case, though she knew the purpose for her visit would have departed before her arrival. In fact, she knew that, even as she drove toward Chelsea, Quentin would be apologizing to his companions for deserting such a cracking game of snooker. He would rush into the cloakroom, take his coat and, upon leaving, hail a taxi-cab to take him to the home of his mistress. And in a curt manner, he would probably instruct the driver not to dawdle.

AS SHE TURNED the corner into Fitzroy Square, she was surprised to see Sandra, one of the maids at the Belgravia mansion of Lord and Lady Compton, waiting on the doorstep.

"Sandra, whatever are you doing here?" Maisie had always straddled a fine line when it came to addressing the staff at Ebury

Place. None of the skeleton staff now retained there had worked at the house when she herself was in service as a girl before the war, but they knew of her early days. Through trial and error she had forged a relationship blending respect with amiability, with Sandra being the one who was the most forthcoming, always ready to engage in a "chat" with Maisie. But now, with Sandra's ready smile gone, it seemed that something was amiss. "Is everything all right?"

"I wondered if I could have a word with you, miss." She was twisting her fingers around the handle of the shopping bag she carried. "I thought you might be able to help me."

Maisie understood that it must have taken more than a spoonful of courage for the young woman to come to her. She turned to press her key into the lock, but was surprised when the door simply opened at a light touch. "That's strange. . . ." She looked back at Sandra. "Come up and tell me what's troubling you." Distracted, Maisie shook her head. "One of the other tenants must have forgotten to lock the door."

Sandra looked around. "Probably those two men I saw leaving as I crossed from Charlotte Street."

Maisie shrugged. "I suppose they must have been visiting the professor who has an office above ours."

"Didn't look like professor types to me."

"Oh, it's probably nothing." Maisie shook her head again and smiled at Sandra. "Now, come along, let's get into the office and you can tell me everything." She led the way up the stairs. "This is the first time you've seen our office, isn't it? Of course, my assistant – you remember Billy – isn't here at the moment. It's very sad, but – oh, my God!"

There was no need for Maisie to turn her key in the lock, no need for her to twist the handle, lean on the door and then enter her office. The door was already wide open, the lock forced for someone to gain entry. Someone who had no thought for the faithfully maintained system of index cards or the detailed files kept in a cabinet alongside Maisie's desk. The room was strewn with paper, with letters and cards. Drawers were pulled open, a chair was on its side, even a china cup had been broken as those who had gained unlawful entry had gone through in search of – what?

"Crikey, miss." Sandra stepped forward and reached down, unbuttoning her coat as she did so. "This won't take –"

"Don't touch a thing!" Maisie surveyed the scene. "No, leave everything as it is."

"Shouldn't you call the police?"

Maisie had already considered that the two men might well have been police themselves, given Stratton's strange behaviour recently and the fact that he was working with the other man, Vance. No, she would deal with this herself. She shook her head. "I don't think I will." She sighed, appraising the task ahead of her, wondering how she might bring order to the chaos. "Sandra, do you know anyone who could fit a new lock, someone handy?"

The young woman nodded. "Yes. I do. Sort of why I came to you."

"I'm sorry, Sandra. Look, let me deal with this first, then –"

"You stay right here, miss. I'll be back as soon as I can."

"Where are you going?"

"Well, Eric don't work at Ebury Place anymore. He's working for Reg Martin, at the garage, now. He can turn his hand to anything, can Eric, so I'll get him up here. He'll put in a new lock for you." Sandra pulled on her gloves and stood with her hand on the door frame. "And if I were you, miss, I'd close this door and shove that desk in front of it until I get back. Won't be long."

Maisie heard the door slam as Sandra left the building. Negotiating papers strewn across the floor, she stepped over to the table where she had worked on the case map with Billy. Usually the map was locked away each time they left the office, but this time . . . this time, she had slipped up, leaving the diagram of their progress on the Bassington-Hope case laid out ready to resume work when Billy returned tomorrow. Now the map was gone.

FOURTEEN

Maisie was exhausted by the time she arrived home. Once inside the empty flat, she collapsed into a chair without taking off her coat. The death of Lizzie Beale had taken its toll and now the burglary at her office added to her fatigue. She reached to ignite the gas fire, then leaned back into the chair again. The child's passing had touched her deeply, and she knew it was not only because the death of one so young is always particularly wrenching – certainly she was not the only one to wonder what picture it painted of a country, of a government, when the life of a child was allowed to slip away, when a parent could not summon medical help for want of the money – but she remembered the first time she held Lizzie. The way in which the child buried her face into the crook of her neck, her dimpled hand holding on to a single button on her blouse, had left Maisie feeling bereft when she was taken from her. It was the child's warmth and closeness as she clung to Maisie that had caused her to realize she was lonely, that there was a longing for a deeper connection in her life.

Slipping to the floor, Maisie rested against the seat of the chair and held her hands out toward the fire. She felt vulnerable, invaded. The image of the broken lock flashed through her mind; the memories of shredded wood where the door had been forced and the paper and cards strewn across the floor conspired to unsettle her even further. *Who has stolen our case map?* Could it have been those men she had seen with Harry Bassington-Hope? Surely they would not have taken the case map. Was it a consolation prize snatched by intruders who didn't know what they wanted but were simply led by instinct? Could they have been hired by Bradley, perhaps expecting to find a clue to the whereabouts of the triptych? Might it have been Duncan and Quentin whom she had so recently unsettled? *They've something to hide.*

Or could it have been Nick Bassington-Hope's killer? Sandra said she had seen two men. Could two men have killed the artist? She asked herself again if Harry's gangland associates could have taken the life of his brother. Maisie rubbed her eyes and slipped the coat from her shoulders, reaching behind her to drape it over the seat of the chair. *Sandra.* She'd never discovered why Sandra had come to her; instead, distracted by the vandalism of her property, the young woman's offer of help had been accepted with little more said.

By the time Sandra returned with Eric, who carried a bag of tools and a new lock, Maisie had cleared the office and begun to file papers and cards. The door was soon repaired. With every bone aching for rest, Maisie returned home. It was only when she sat gazing at the gas jets that she realized she hadn't discovered the reason for Sandra's visit, although she remembered, as the couple made their way toward the Warren Street underground station, her former maid's arm was linked through that of the young man at her side.

Despite checking and double-checking the integrity of locks on the front and back doors and the windows, Maisie could not settle and slept fitfully. Though she had loved the idea of a ground-floor flat, with a back door that led out onto the postage stamp of a lawn, she now wondered if her choice of home were not somewhat precarious for a woman in her line of work. Not that she expected to have much to do with those who would cause her harm, though perhaps the fact that she had no such expectation demonstrated a naïveté on her part.

MAISIE WAS ON her hands and knees in the office the following morning when she heard the front door thump closed against the wind and Billy Beale's distinctive footfall on the stairs. She clambered to her feet as her assistant entered the office.

"Bloody 'ell . . ."

Maisie smiled. "I've broken the back of the job, but we've got our work cut out for us today." She smiled and came toward him, touching him lightly on the sleeve. "Do you feel up to it, Billy?"

With the semblance of a man in his sixties, not his thirties, Billy nodded. "Got to earn my keep, Miss." He paused, taking off his coat and hanging it on the hook at the back of the door, along with his flat cap and scarf. A black cloth band stiched around the upper arm of his jacket signalled his state of mourning. "And to tell you the truth, what with one thing and another, it's best for me, is this. Doreen's sister started with the baby this morning, so there's no room for me – or for Jim, 'e's out looking for work again. So, it's best if I'm out of it. Give something for Doreen to think about. They've got to get ready for the other nippers bein' allowed 'ome soon as well. Anyway, the woman from up the road, the one who's there for all the babies 'round our way, was just coming in the door when I was leaving, so I'm in no 'urry to go back there."

"Is Doreen coping?"

"I should say she's keepin' 'er 'ead above the water, Miss. Just. It's all a bit strange, to tell you the truth. There we are, you know, just lost our little girl, and there's a baby about to come into the world. And what to? What sort of life is it? I tell you, Miss, I wasn't goin' to say nothin', but me and Doreen've been talkin' and we've laid it out for ourselves, for our boys."

"Laid out what?"

"Plans, Miss." Billy shook his head and leaned back against his desk. "There ain't nothin' 'ere for us, is there? Look at the place, look at it. I've got a trade, Miss, I've got this work with you, doin' inquiries, under me belt, and look at me, I can't keep me nippers safe. No, Miss, we've decided. We're savin' up, you know. To emigrate."

"Emigrate?"

"Well, Miss, mate of mine in the war, 'e went over to Canada afterward. It was them Canadian boys tellin' 'im all about it, you know. Took 'im until '21 to afford passage." Billy shook his head, recalling his friend. "Me mate wasn't one to write, not the sort, but I got the odd postcard, you know, with 'Hands Across the Miles' on the front, and 'e says there's a good life for men like me, men what ain't afraid of a bit of 'ard graft, men what'll work to make a better life for their families. I reckon we can put a bit by, me and Doreen — it'll be easier when we ain't got the extra mouths to feed — and we'll go over there. Fred's doin' well, you know, got work, nice place to live, not all cramped up like we are in the East End, with all that river filth."

Maisie was about to say something about acting in haste, about waiting for the weight of their loss to lift before leaving home behind them, but instead she smiled. "You're a good father, Billy. You'll do what's best. Now then, unless you're planning to sail to Canada this afternoon, we'd better get on. I have to leave for Dungeness later, but I want to ensure this is all put away and clear again before I go." She turned to the desk. "Oh, and you'll need these — keys for the new lock."

Billy caught the set of keys Maisie threw to him. "Did we lose anything important, Miss?"

Maisie nodded. "The case map."

SOME TWO HOURS later, Maisie and Billy had brought order to the chaos and were now sitting at the oak table in front of a length of pristine white lining paper of the type usually used by decorators, which they proceeded to pin to the wood.

"There, clean slate, Billy. We might see some links, some clues that have evaded us thus far."

"I 'ope so, Miss. Bloomin' lot of 'ard work down the drain if we don't."

Maisie took a red pen and began to draw a circle with Nick Bassington-Hope's name in the center. "I want to see Arthur Levitt this morning, Billy, and I also want you to talk to your Fleet Street friend this afternoon, if you can."

"Right you are, Miss."

"All right then, let's get on . . ."

They worked on the map until ten o'clock, whereupon the length of paper was rolled up and secured with a piece of string. Both Billy and Maisie looked around the room.

"Like I've said before, Miss, my old mum always said to 'ide somethin' in plain view."

"Well, in my haste I already did that, and look where it got me! No, we need a very safe place – and I don't want to take it home."

"I've got an idea, Miss." Billy walked over to the fireplace, carefully edged out the gas fire that had been fitted to stand in front of an original grate designed for logs and coal. "Long as we don't weaken the old gas line by pulling the fire back and forth, this should work for us, the old 'up the chimney' trick."

"Seems a bit obvious to me, Billy, but until we think of something better, it will have to do. Here you are."

Billy pushed the case map behind the gas fire, moved the fire back into position and checked to ensure the fuel line was not compromised by the exercise.

Scrutinizing the door several times to check the integrity of the lock, the pair were finally satisfied that the office was secure.

"Of course, you know the irony of all this checking and double-checking, don't you?"

"What's that, Miss?" Billy pulled up his collar against the wind.

"The men who broke into the office may well have what they want. And if they don't, they're going to try somewhere else."

"Reckon you should get that Eric bloke 'round to do the lock on your flat."

"I will. As soon as I get back from Dungeness."

Slamming the passenger door of the MG behind him in a way that always made Maisie cringe, Billy added a final two-penn'orth of advice. "Of course, you know what you need, a woman alone in your position, don't you, Miss?"

"What's that?" Maisie might usually have reminded Billy that she was quite capable, thank you very much, but she was mindful of his fragile state and allowed him to continue.

"A bloomin' great dog. That's what you need. A big 'airy thing to mind you from these 'ere criminal types."

She laughed as she drove toward Albemarle Street.

SEEING BILLY'S ARMBAND, Arthur Levitt removed his flat cap. "Everything all right, son?"

Billy pressed his lips together and Maisie could see him struggling. She knew that every time he uttered the truth of the family's bereavement, the anguish wrenched his heart as if for the first time. He shook his head. "We lost our youngest, Mr Levitt."

"I'm sorry, son."

"We're not the first, and we won't be the last. My old mum lost four babies, all of 'em under two. You'd think all that'd be in the past, wouldn't you? Anyway, just got to get on. There's the boys to look after, and my wife's sister is about to 'ave another one, so she's got plenty to take 'er mind off it." He changed the subject quickly. "Arthur, this is Miss Dobbs, my employer."

Maisie stepped forward, extending her hand. Levitt raised an eyebrow but was courteous.

"What can I do for you, Miss Dobbs?"

"Mr Levitt, I am conducting an informal inquiry on behalf of Miss Georgina Bassington-Hope into the death of her brother at this gallery. Miss Bassington-Hope feels that there are a few places where information regarding the events leading up to his death is rather thin, hence my interest in speaking to you – in confidence."

"Well, Miss Dobbs, I don't know." He looked around. "Mr Svenson isn't here, and he won't like it, I'm sure."

"I've already spoken to Mr Svenson." It was true enough, though Maisie was quite aware that her words suggested that he had given her leave to speak to his caretaker. "And I know you've given a statement to the police regarding the discovery of Mr Bassington-Hope's body, but I'd like to ask you a few more questions."

Levitt looked back and forth between Billy and Maisie, then sighed. "Right you are. Probably no harm in it, and if it helps Miss Bassington-Hope, then it's all to the good."

"You liked Mr Bassington-Hope?"

He nodded. "Very nice man. Always thoughtful, always respectful. Not like some of them, the airy-fairy types who flap back and forth like a finch in a thunderstorm. No, Mr Bassington-Hope was more of your feet-on-the-ground type. Not afraid to do the heavy lifting – mind you, he preferred to do it, was very protective of his work, you know."

"Yes, so I understand." Maisie glanced at Billy, who was busy taking notes. She saw that his hands were shaking, and wondered when he had last taken food. Turning her attention to Levitt again, she continued. "Mr Levitt, perhaps you could tell me what you remember about the day Mr Bassington-Hope died."

He was silent for a moment, squinting as he looked out the high window of the storeroom at the back of the gallery.

"He was here early. Came in a van."

"Was that unusual?"

Levitt nodded. "He came on his motorbike, as a rule, kept it spick-and-span, he did. It was a Scott Flying Squirrel. He and Mr

Courtman – I'm sure you know who he is – would be in here josh-ing with each other about who had the best motorbike – his Scott, or Mr Courtman's Brough."

Billy looked up. "Very nice, I'm sure," he muttered.

Levitt noticed the sarcasm, but continued. "He didn't use the bike that day because he had too much to carry, his tools and so on, so he came in an old van he'd borrowed."

"I see. Go on," Maisie encouraged the caretaker.

"I was here before seven, so I reckon he came at about eight. There was a lot of unloading. He'd picked up Mr Haywood on the way, from his sister's, so I understand, and Mr Courtman followed on the Brough."

"I thought Mr Bassington-Hope had been at his sister's flat the night before." Maisie looked down, directing her words to the ground, rather than to Billy or Levitt.

"Yes, miss, that's right, but apparently he'd left early to go to his lock-up, where he loaded up, then came here. He reckoned he'd go back again later to pick up the final piece, what everyone's been call-ing a triptych."

"How did he spend the day?"

"First of all they all got stuck in and put up the main part of the exhibition, which was easy, to a point. I reckon it would've been a very good show, but there was nothing there for anyone to purchase, on account of Mr Bradley buying up the lot."

"So I understand. Tell me about the scaffolding and what hap-pened next."

"Well, as soon as they had put up the works that had been brought over in the van, Mr Bassington-Hope went back to his lock-up to collect more paintings, and the other two went out for a bit of something to eat. Mr Courtman did ask if he needed help, but he said that he didn't. There was more preparation, and then the wood and so on for the scaffolding was delivered, and they all worked for the rest of the day on that."

"Were there visitors?"

"Well, yes. There was family dropping in throughout the day, and, of course, Mr Svenson was flapping a bit, giving everyone directions. Mind you, he always drew his neck in a bit with Mr Bassington-Hope. Could be sparky, he could – you know, get touchy if he was told to do something he didn't want to do, and he wasn't shy when it came to telling Mr Svenson off. Saw him do it in company once, which was a bit strong. Between us, it embarrassed Mr Svenson – made him fume, to tell you the truth. I thought to myself at the time that one day he would push Mr Svenson too far. No, Mr Bassington-Hope never pulled back from anything. He was a bit like his brother in that regard. And those two sisters of his, come to that."

"You knew his brother?"

"I've been here years, miss. Seen all the family paintings one way or another. The mother is very talented, of course. I think it's only that older sister who can't wield a brush to save her life." He scratched his head, remembering the question of Harry. "As far as the brother goes, I'd seen him come and go a couple of times when Mr Bassington-Hope was here for an opening or when his work was exhibited." He pressed his lips together, as if weighing how much to reveal. "What you've got to remember, Miss Dobbs, is that Mr Svenson holds the purse strings, so if that younger one wanted some money from his brother, he'd be more likely to get it if he was standing in his bank, if you know what I mean."

Maisie nodded. "Yes, I do. So, tell us about the scaffolding, about what they did next."

"Meticulous, I would say. Mr Bassington-Hope was very careful, measuring, testing the strength of the trestle. He knew that, once it was up, he'd be here on his own working on placing and securing the pieces. He said to me, 'Last thing I want is to break my painting arm, Arthur.' Mind you" – he looked at Maisie to ensure she was listening carefully – "mind you, he also knew the scaffolding was temporary, that it would probably only be used again to dismantle the exhibit, so it's not as if it were made like you were building a house underneath. You couldn't go jumping all over it with a hod of bricks or anything. But it was sturdy enough for the job, and with a barrier along the back, so he could lean – lightly, mind – and check the placing of the anchors and, of course, the paintings."

"When did everyone leave?"

"Well, there was that dust-up in the afternoon, and I'm sure you've heard all about that, what with Mr Bradley doing his nut because Mr Bassington-Hope wouldn't sell that main piece. Then they left, and the men worked on until, oh, must've been eight o'clock."

"And do you know when Mr Bassington-Hope intended to collect the main pieces?"

"Now, I leave at nine, as a rule, only I stayed a bit, but Mr Bassington-Hope said he'd lock up and I should get home, because the next day would be a long one. I asked if he was sure, what with having to lug the pieces up the stairs on his own, and what have you –"

"Lug the pieces up the stairs?"

"You see these here staircases?" He pointed to a staircase at either side of the storage room, in the centre of which was a tunnel-like corridor that snaked through to the main gallery. "They lead out onto the balconied landings in the gallery. There's a door at either side. He would have had to carry the pieces up these stairs, then lift them over the balcony to the scaffolding. Then he'd either hop on over or climb up from below, but this would definitely have been the easiest way to do the job. And he wanted the downstairs door to the gallery locked, didn't want anyone coming in to disturb him."

"What time did Haywood and Courtman leave again?"

"Reckon about eight. Courtman wanted to get going, had a lady-friend waiting somewhere, and so Haywood asked for a lift on his motorbike."

"And no one else came to visit between eight and the time you left?"

"Mr Svenson came in again, but eventually he left before me. He was very anxious, but he's also very good with his clients, you know. He works with their temperaments, I think you would say. And he trusted Mr Bassington-Hope."

"Could anyone have entered the gallery?"

"The downstairs door was locked, definitely, but the upstairs door was unlocked – but you'd've expected that, what with him having to go back and forth."

"Did he pull the van in?"

"The van was on the street. And of course he hadn't collected the main pieces. I can only think he was running behind a bit, though he would have wanted to bring them in late, I would have thought, on account of him wanting to keep them a secret."

Maisie paced back and forth. "Mr Levitt, tell me about the morning when you found Mr Bassington-Hope."

"It was long before seven, and I expected him to be here to make sure that no one could eyeball the exhibition before the opening. The van was parked on the street here and the outside door was unlocked, so that's when I thought he was already in. I put the kettle on" – he pointed to a small gas stove – "and I went down the corridor here, where the door was still locked, with the key in it on the other side. I banged on the door to let him know it was me, only there was no answer. So I went upstairs, hoping he'd left that door unlocked, and he had. But when I opened it and went out onto the balcony, that's when I saw him. The scaffolding had broken where the poor man had lost his balance and fallen back." Levitt choked. Maisie and Billy were silent, waiting for him to settle into the story again. "I ran downstairs as quick as I could to get to him. He was stone cold. I could see straightaway that it was a broken neck. I opened the door to the back – keys in the lock as I thought – and I ran into Mr Svenson's office, it's off the corridor there, I have a spare key – and telephoned the police. That's when Detective Inspector Stratton came to the gallery."

Maisie cleared her throat. "Do you know what happened to the van?"

"The chap he borrowed it from found out what had happened and claimed it from the police. They released it after a day or two. Nothing in it but a few tools, though."

"And what about a key or set of keys? Mr Bassington-Hope must have had a key to his lock-up."

Levitt shook his head. "You'd probably be best to ask Miss Bassington-Hope. But to tell you the truth, I don't know if there was anything."

"Why do you say that?"

"Well, I was standing there, talking to Detective Inspector Stratton while two other policemen were going through Mr Bassington-Hope's belongings, you know, patting down his body. And there was no key there or I would have heard them. You see, I was listening for that. I'm a caretaker, Miss Dobbs. You'd sometimes think I'm the chief jailer, with a key for this and a key for that. And, apart from a key to the van, which he'd put on that shelf over there, there was no other key found that morning, or since then."

"Does that strike you as strange?"

The man sighed. "To tell you the truth, Miss Dobbs – and I haven't said as much to anyone else – I thought the whole thing was strange, something about it just didn't sit right with me. But there again, if you were there, you'd've probably thought it was an accident too."

Maisie inclined her head. "Would I, Mr Levitt?"

MAISIE AND BILLY took a brief sojourn in a pie and mash shop, where a hearty helping of eel pie, mashed potato and parsley "likker" brought some colour back to Billy's hollow cheeks. As they stood on the street ready to part company, he declared himself "well up" for the afternoon ahead.

As soon as she was back in the office, Maisie set about catching up with her work. There were some bills to prepare, and planning for the following week to complete. The post had to be dealt with, and she was pleased to see two letters of interest with regard to her services.

With about another half hour before she needed to leave for Dungeness, she moved to the table but did not remove the case map from its hiding place. She took a seat and doodled with a pen on a blank index card. She thought there might be something going on in Dungeness – based more upon her understanding of Nick's mural, than anything else – that suggested knowledge on his part of some underhanded dealing. But how deep was his personal involvement? She felt that Haywood and Trayner had something to hide, but Courtman seemed on the periphery of the group, probably not part of an inner circle.

Harry Bassington-Hope? Her mind drifted back to the dilettante musician, and the words came into her mind: *he knew what was going on.* But Maisie considered Harry to be someone caught in a web of his own making. She knew his type, had seen it before. Harry's actions had led him to the slippery slope, and she knew he would not draw back from dragging someone else down with him – be it a friend, a brother or sister. His addiction was to the highs and lows of the gamble, that intoxicating thrill of risk blended with chance – and those who had something to gain from his weakness had lost no time in using him to their advantage. *But how did they do it?* Maisie shook her head and ran her hands through her hair. *No, they weren't after just family money alone.* She scraped back her chair and wandered to the window. *What did Harry get from his brother that someone else wanted?* She ran her finger across the condensation on the window pane, then watched a rivulet of water drizzle down to the wooden frame. *And did Nick die as a result of it?*

Maisie turned, ready to collect her belongings, to prepare herself to leave. She had always spoken with Maurice at times such as this, when she was about to move ahead into the darkness. She depended upon his counsel at that point in the case where she, too, was playing with risk, leaving so much to chance. *Am I as much of an addict to the thrill my work sometimes brings?* Was it the thought of possibly giving up that *edge*, that contributed to dissatisfaction in her courtship with Andrew Dene? Maisie put her hand to her mouth. She had always told herself that she did this job because she wanted to help others; after all, hadn't Maurice told her once that the most important question any individual could ask was, "How might I serve?" If her response to that question had been pure, surely she would have continued with the calling to be a nurse – and perhaps help children such as Lizzie Beale in the bargain. But that role hadn't been quite enough for her. She would have missed the excitement, the thrill – and it was a thrill – when she embarked on the work of collecting clues to support a case.

Hadn't she felt that fountain of expectation rise within her at the nightclub, while waiting, ever watchful, for Harry Bassington-Hope? There was the prickle across her skin when she saw the man at the bar leave, perhaps to follow Svenson and Bradley. Then at the gallery, that familiar excitement building as she questioned Arthur Levitt. Or outside Georgina's flat, when she arrived for the party, there was that compulsion to wait, to watch, to remain alert, to uncover a truth that had hitherto been hidden. Of course, Georgina was the same, though in her case, the urge to seek adventure played out in capturing the fabric of truth she would fashion for her stories. And she was involved with a married man. *There's a gamble.* And Nick too – didn't he sail close to the winds of disapproval with his work? Didn't he risk losing his supporters?

Truth. Wasn't that why she took on the case? That bolt of recognition when Georgina placed her hand over her heart and said, *"A feeling, here,"* even though she did not know the woman well, had not established an acquaintance; she was drawn by her declaration. She had stepped forward, laid her hand on the woman's shoulder, the voice in her head saying, *Yes, this I understand.* That was the thrill, and that was the quest for which she took her risks. *The search for truth.* But what if she were wrong? What if all the supposed clues were simply unimportant connections: the wayward brother, the wealthy sponsor, friends who appeared to have something to hide. Heavens, didn't everyone have something to hide? Maisie sighed, knowing her thoughts had taken her along a less than welcome path, the way of doubt. She had never been blind to the reality of her obsession with her work, but she had certainly been less than honest with those who deserved more from her – Andrew Dene for one.

Almost instinctively, she reached for the telephone receiver, then drew back. No, she would not place a call to Maurice. She had forged her independence from him. The business was her own now, there was no need to seek his counsel, his voice, his opinion of her reasoning, before setting off.

Checking that she had everything she needed, Maisie put on her coat, hat and gloves, and took up the black document case, along with her shoulder bag. She reached the door, and as she held out her hand to grasp the brass handle, the telephone began to ring. She was determined to ignore the ring, but it occurred to her that it might be Billy trying to contact her before she departed for Dungeness, so she reconsidered and lifted the receiver.

"Fitzroy –"

"Maisie."

"Maurice." She closed her eyes, and sighed. "I thought it might be you."

"Were you about to leave your office?"

"Yes. I'm off to Dungeness."

There was a pause. "I sense you've reached that point in a case where you must take a risk or two. Am I correct?"

Maisie closed her eyes and sighed. "Yes, as always, Maurice."

"Ah, I hear just a hint of impatience, Maisie."

"No, not at all. I was just leaving, my hands are full."

Another pause. "I see. Then I will not detain you. Take care, remember all you have learned."

She nodded. "Of course. I will be in touch soon, Maurice."

The click as the receiver met the cradle seemed to echo against the walls, the short finality of the conversation reverberating across the silent room. Maisie stood by the desk for just a few seconds, nursing a regret that she had not been kinder. Then she left the office, double-checked the lock and made her way to the MG.

It was as she was about to slip into the driver's seat that Maisie saw Billy running along Warren Street toward her.

"Miss! Miss! Wait a minute!"

Maisie smiled. "You've built up a head of steam there, Billy. What's wrong?"

"Nothing wrong, Miss, but there's something come up, you know, that sort of – what is it you always say? Oh, yes – sort of *piqued* my interest."

"Yes?"

Billy caught his breath and held his hand to his chest. "Gaw, I thought I'd miss you there. 'old on a minute." He coughed, wheezing and looking around him as he did so. "Right then. This is what my mate down Fleet Street 'ad to say today. There ain't nothing on our 'arry B-H to report, nothing on Nick, or the sisters. So, generally, it's all clean, nothing to report. So, I says to 'im, 'So, what else 'as been comin' down the blower this week, mate?' and 'e says that the only thing 'e's got a lead on, though it ain't much, is that these 'ere villains that 'arry's been in cahoots with, 'ave been suspected of getting into the minin' business."

"Mining? What on earth do you mean?"

"Manner of talking, Miss." Billy grinned. "Now, what do you think *minin'* means?"

"Coal?"

"Close. Very close. Turns out that my mate is following a lead that they're into diamonds, as in the moving around of the same."

"But aren't these criminals always into whatever can be stolen?"

"No, not stolen as in a rotten little tea-leaf 'aving it away with 'er Ladyship's tiara.' No, we're talking raw diamonds, brought in from somewhere else and fenced over 'ere."

Maisie was silent for a moment or two. "Yes, yes, that's very interesting, Billy. I'm not sure how that might have anything to do with Harry and this case, but . . ."

"What, Miss?"

"Just a thought. Anything else?"

Billy shook his head. "Nah, nothing much. My mate says 'e's been keeping an eye on what's going on over there on the Continent, says that it's a bit more interestin' at the moment, so there ain't much that can affect the B-Hs."

Maisie settled into the MG, winding down the window as the engine grumbled to life. "And what has been happening in Europe, then?"

"Well, my mate says, all the usual stuff. Been a few burglaries, old money's 'eirlooms bein' pinched, that sort of thing."

"Good work, Billy – I'll consider everything you've said on my drive to the coast. Hold the fort until tomorrow afternoon, won't you?"

"Right you are, Miss. You can depend on me."

Maisie looked into Billy's almost lifeless grey-blue eyes and smiled. "I know I can, Billy. Just *you* take care of yourself – and your family."

BILLY STOOD WATCHING as Maisie drove off toward Tottenham Court Road. She hadn't confided in him regarding her plans for the evening, and what, exactly, she wanted to accomplish in Dungeness. He knew she hadn't wanted to worry him, which worried him even more. In fact, he knew her well enough by now to know that she had – as near as damn it – worked out *what* had happened to Nick Bassington-Hope on the night of his death even if she might not know who else was involved. She probably had two or three possible suspects lined up, and if he was right about it, she was just waiting for someone, somewhere, to put a foot wrong.

FIFTEEN

Maisie made a snap decision that there was no need to begin her journey to Dungeness for another hour or two – she certainly didn't want to arrive *too* early. Much of the planning was based on supposition anyway. She had no firm evidence that this evening, under cover of darkness, she would find out if her suspicions concerning the activities of a few residents in the small coastal community were well-founded; all she had to go on, truly, was a tale of derring-do, a colourful mural on a former railway carriage and the history of a desolate place – the case was all loose ends and no skein of yarn. But she could confirm one or two facts, and those facts might indicate that the time was indeed right for her to go to Dungeness today, especially as it would be a clear, moonless night.

Maisie parked alongside the entrance to Georgina's flat and checked her appearance before making her way to the front door. She rang the bell and the housekeeper came within seconds, smiling when she recognized Maisie.

"Miss Dobbs. I'll tell Miss Bassington-Hope that you're here." She showed Maisie into the drawing room as she spoke.

"Thank you." Maisie removed her gloves and scarf and waited without taking a seat.

"Maisie, what a surprise. Have you news?" Georgina entered the room several minutes later. Her hair was drawn back in a loose chignon, which exposed her pale skin, the almost juvenile freckles on her nose and grey circles under her eyes.

"No, but I wanted to ask you some questions, if you don't mind. I'd like to clarify my understanding of certain events leading up to the death of your brother."

"Of course." As she held out her hand toward the chesterfield, Maisie noticed a circular ink stain against the upper joint of the middle finger of her right hand.

"I see you've been writing, Georgina. Have I disturbed you at an inopportune moment?"

The journalist shook her head. "I wish I could say that you had. In fact, I welcome any disturbance, to tell you the truth – it saves me sweating over a blank page for the rest of the day."

"Blank page?"

Georgina sighed, shaking her head. "The call to write hasn't been answered by words yet. I usually compose with my typewriting machine these days, but I thought that if I took up the fountain pen again, it might ignite inspiration's touchpaper."

"Is there something specific you want to write?"

She shook her head. "I've been assigned to write something about Oswald Mosley for an American journal, but I can't seem to get going."

"Perhaps it's your subject, rather than your ability."

"Hardly. The man elicits excitement wherever he goes. I can't think why I cannot get the words on the page. I can't seem to describe the honesty, the integrity of his mission."

Maisie smiled. "Could that be because, in truth, such qualities are not truly present?"

"What do you mean?" Georgina sat up. Her spine, previously curved under the weight of a burdensome task, was now erect with indignation. "He is –"

"It was simply a question to consider. Have you experienced such an issue with your work before?"

"No." She curled a stray wisp of hair behind her ear before leaning forward and resting her elbows on her knees. "Sorry, that's a lie. To tell you the truth, even though I've done quite well – especially with the bound collection of my wartime reports – I haven't been really inspired since the peace conference in 1919." Georgina shook her head, slapped her hands on her knees and stood up, folding her arms and walking to the fireplace, where she reached down, took up a poker and plunged it into the fire, moving the hot coals around to stoke the flames. "I think I need a war to write about, to tell you the truth. I should really just leave the country and look for one."

Maisie smiled, though it was not a smile of mirth but one that she knew was rooted in an emotion akin to that expressed by Billy when he first met the Bassington-Hope woman. Her resentment was growing, but she was mindful that even though she knew the woman a little better now, she was still a client.

"As I said, Georgina, I'd like to ask a few questions. First of all, are Nick's friends still with you?"

"No, Duncan left this morning. As far as I know, he and Quentin have gone down to Dungeness, as planned. They both have loose ends to deal with." She paused, looking at Maisie. "I thought you were going again this week."

"Yes, that's right." She did not elucidate with more information. "They've been here for a week or so, haven't they?"

Georgina poked the fire once more, then replaced the cast-iron tool in the holder next to the coal scuttle. "Yes, I think they were down for just a day around about the time you visited. I remember thinking that it was a shame you hadn't met then. You must have just missed them."

"Of course." Maisie was thoughtful. *I am right. Today is the day.* "Georgina, may I ask some personal questions?"

The woman was cautious, her chin held a little higher, betraying a reticence she would likely not have wanted to reveal. "Personal questions?"

"First of all, why did you not tell me of the encounter between Mr Bradley and Nick at the gallery on the afternoon before he died?"

"I – I – I forgot. It wasn't terribly nice, so I wanted to forget, to tell you the truth."

Maisie pushed harder. "Might it have anything to do with your relationship with Mr Bradley?"

Georgina cleared her throat and Maisie, once again, watched as she pushed down the cuticles of each finger, moving from her left hand to her right as she answered. "There was no *relationship*, as you put it, at that time."

"There was an attraction."

"Of – of course. . . . I mean, I had always got on with Randolph – I mean, Mr Bradley. But we weren't close at the time of Nick's death."

"And what about you and Nick? I have asked you this question before, however, I understand that you went back to the gallery after the row in the afternoon – of course, it was a row during which you took Nick's part. I realize you supported his refusal to sell the triptych."

"Yes, I supported his decision. We always supported each other."

"And why did you go back?"

"How did you –" Georgina sighed, now cupping her hands, one inside the other, on her lap. "I shouldn't ask, should I? After all, I'm paying you to ask questions." She swallowed, coughed, then went on. "I went back to talk to Nick. We'd left under a cloud and I couldn't leave it on such terms. I wanted to explain."

"What?"

"Nick knew that Randolph and I were attracted and he didn't like it. Randolph was his greatest admirer, and Nick didn't want complications. He also heartily disapproved of our interest in each other – which, I have to say was a bit rich, when you consider his peccadilloes."

Maisie said nothing.

"He'd had an affair with Duncan's wife-to-be," continued Georgina, "and he'd had a bit of a fling with a married woman years ago, so he wasn't so pure as the driven snow as Emsy would have you believe. Of course, my father knew what Nick was like, truly, and had upbraided him on more than one occasion."

"Really?"

"Yes. But that was ages ago." She waved her hand as if to dismiss a triviality. "I went to Nick to make up, to let him know that I supported him, and I wanted him to accept me too."

"And he didn't?"

"Not with Randolph, no. We'd argued about it before." She paused, looking straight at Maisie. "My brother could be pretty bloody-minded when he liked, Maisie. On the one hand you had the easy-going brother, and on the other, a man with the morals of a vicar and actions that fell shy of the sort of behaviour that Harry is capable of."

"I see."

"And he never forgot – and sometimes the things he saved in his mind turned up in his work – so you can imagine how I felt. I imagined a mural of star-crossed lovers with my face depicted alongside Randolph's. So we had words both on the morning and on the evening of his death, and I left without saying good-bye, or sorry, or . . . anything, really." Georgina began to weep.

Maisie said nothing, allowing the tears to fall and then subside before continuing.

"And you do not think that the argument might have rendered Nick so unsettled as to make an error of judgment with his step?"

"Absolutely not! Nick was too single-minded to allow such a thing. In fact, he was probably so hardened in his response to my appeal because he had only one thing on his mind – exhibiting the triptych."

Maisie reached for her scarf, beside her on the chesterfield. "Yes, I understand." She stood up, collected her gloves and bag and turned as if to leave, though she faced Georgina. "And you didn't see anyone else after you left the gallery that evening?"

"Well, Stig came back. I saw him turn into Albemarle Street as I left the gallery. Frankly, I didn't really want to see him and fortunately a taxi-cab came along at just that moment."

"About what time was this? Had Mr Levitt gone for the day?"

"Yes, Levitt had left." She closed her eyes, as if to recall the events. "In fact, I know he'd left because I had to bang on the front door for Nick to open it. The back door was locked."

"And did you leave by the front door?"

"Yes."

"Do you know if Nick locked it behind you again?"

"Um, no, I don't." She bit her lip. "You see, he told me to just leave him alone, that he just wanted to get on with his work. I could barely speak to him, it was just so unlike us to be at odds with each other."

Maisie sighed, allowing a pause in the questioning. "Georgina, why did you not tell me about the affair with Bradley sooner? You must have known how important such information could be."

Georgina shrugged. "Having an affair with a married man is not something I'm proud of, to be perfectly honest with you."

Maisie nodded thoughtfully and walked to the painting above the cocktail cabinet. "This is new, isn't it?"

Georgina looked up, distracted. "Um, yes, it is."

"From Svenson?"

"No, I'm looking after it, for a friend."

"Lovely to have it for a while."

She nodded. "Yes. I hope it won't be too long though."

Maisie noticed a wistfulness about her client, a blend of regret and sadness that possession of the piece seemed to have brought with it. She continued to look at the painting, and as she did so, a fragment of the jigsaw puzzle that was Nick Bassington-Hope's life fell into place – and she hoped it was exactly the right place.

Maisie did not question Georgina Bassington-Hope further, satisfied – for the moment, in any case – with her responses. She was dismayed, however, that she had not learned of the unlocked front entrance to the gallery before.

As the women stood on the threshold, Georgina having waved her housekeeper away, saying she would see Miss Dobbs out, Maisie decided to throw a grain of possibility to the once-renowned journalist.

"Georgina, you mentioned that you needed a war to ignite your work." Maisie made the statement without inflection in her voice.

"Yes, but –"

"Then you need look no farther than the boundaries of the city in which you live, though you will have to risk travelling beyond your chosen milieu."

"What do you mean?"

"Mr Beale and his wife have lost their youngest child to diphtheria. In a house that barely contains one family, they have taken in a family of four – almost five, a new baby will be born before the end of the day – because his brother-in-law has lost his job. And the Beales are among those who consider themselves better off. Your friend, Oswald Mosley, has lost no time in using such circumstances for political gain; however, I am unaware of any real understanding among those who *have* of the plight of those who *have not*. The war is being waged, Georgina, only the war is here and now, and it is a war against poverty, against disease and against injustice. Didn't Lloyd George promise something better to the men who fought for their country? You would do well to consider igniting your pen with that for a story! I'm sure your American publisher would be happy with the unexpected view you put forward."

"I – I hadn't thought –"

"I'll be in touch soon, Georgina. Expect to hear from me within two days."

Georgina nodded and was about to close the door when Maisie

turned to her one last time. "Oh, by the way, are you acquainted with a Mr Stein?"

Georgina frowned and shook her head rather too fiercely as she replied, "No. The only Stein I know is Gertrude."

MAISIE WONDERED IF she had gone too far with Georgina. *What do I know about journalism, to be advising her?* Then she reconsidered. The woman was clearly grief-stricken over her brother's death, but wasn't it also true that her actions since that time reflected a need to have some of her old power back? Bullying the police had led her, in frustration and anguish, to Dame Constance, who had in turn led her to Maisie. And now, of course, she was fuelling her emotions with an adulterous affair. Georgina had been known as a maverick in the war, a young woman who went too far, who pushed as hard as she could – indeed, she had been something of a cause célèbre among the alumnae of Girton College. Her bravery had inspired a notoriety that even her detractors could not fail to admire. But now, with no cause to champion, no passionate call to arms to draw out her skill with words, no treacherous game of risk to excite her, her language had become flabby, her interest in her assignments minimal. It did not take an expert in journalism to understand what had happened.

Maisie continued to consider Georgina as she drove south toward the Romney Marshes. She had succumbed to the same failing that she had warned Billy against, having become resentful of those with greater means, their ability to indulge themselves when so many were vainly clutching at any semblance of hope. As she watched the new suburbs give way to the frost-laden apple orchards of Kent, she recalled the nightclub, the dancing and the home that she returned to each night, and Maisie flushed. *Am I not becoming such a person?* And she wondered, again, whether her chosen service truly amounted to a contribution of some account.

DUSK WAS ON the verge of night as Maisie drove from Lydd along the road to Dungeness. Though the land was barren, with few houses and a cold wind blowing up from the beach, she managed to park the car on the side of the road, where it was shielded by an overhanging tree. She wrapped her scarf around her neck, pulled her cloche down as far as she could and took her knapsack from the passenger seat, then set off in the direction of the beach. She had taken a small torch from her knapsack but did not use it, preferring to stabilize the night vision she would rather depend upon, along with her memory of the route to Nick Bassington-Hope's railway carriage home. She walked as quickly as possible, but took care to be as light of step as she could.

Reluctantly, she flicked on the torch every fifty or so yards to get her bearings. Finally, with salt-filled sea air whipping across her face, she came up to the front door of the cottage, having taken care to move into the shadows as the lighthouse beam swung around onto the beach. Her gloved fingertips were numb as she removed the key from her coat pocket. She sniffed against the chill air and wiped the back of her hand across her eyes and squinted. Turning against the side of the carriage so that the glow of her torch could not be detected, she flashed the light to illuminate the lock, pressed the key home and gained entrance, extinguishing the torch as she stepped into the carriage. Closing the door behind her, she moved with speed to pull down the black blinds, though she would not use the lamps. Even a sliver of light might give her away.

With the torch, she inspected the cottage to see whether there were any signs that others had been there since her previous visit. The stove was as she had left it, the counterpane seemed untouched. She moved into the studio, directing the beam to the walls, to the chair, the paints, the easel. The greatcoat was still in the closet and as she touched the thick woollen fabric once again, Maisie shivered. She returned to the main living room, this time using her torch to inspect the mural once again. Yes, Nick Bassington-Hope was a talented artist, though she wondered what others had thought when they looked at the mural. Did they note what she had seen, ask themselves the same questions? And what of Amos White – had Nick ever invited him in? Could he have seen the mural? If so, he must have felt threatened. Nick Bassington-Hope told stories with his work, transposing images of those he knew onto his depiction of the myths and legends that inspired him. She touched the faces and thought of the triptych. *But what if the story were true, and the faces known to others as well as to Nick?* That, most definitely, would constitute a risk.

Maisie pushed one of the armchairs close to the window, then pulled the counterpane from the bed. She would have loved to light the fire but could not risk even a wisp of smoke being seen from the beach, so she settled into the chair, wrapping the counterpane around her body as she did so. She reached into the knapsack and took out cheese and pickle sandwiches and a bottle of R. White's Dandelion and Burdock. The set of the blind allowed the barest snip of a view out to the beach. It was all that she needed, for now. She tucked into her food, stopping to listen between each mouthful. Then she waited.

Fearing the magnetic pull of sleep, Maisie went through the entire case in her mind, from the moment of that first encounter with Georgina Bassington-Hope. Admittedly, she was intrigued by the group of friends – she had never engaged with such people before – though at the same time she felt ill at ease with the company her client kept, and it was not simply a matter of money, upbringing or class. No, these people did not live by the same rules; their behaviour both fascinated and intimidated her. The house in Tenterden came to mind. There was none of the familiarity that inspires a sense of security. Everything she touched seemed to challenge the accepted way of living, with colour and texture assaulting the senses in a way that she had never before experienced. Had she not felt seduced by the audacity of the family, by the fact that they dared to be different? She sighed. This case resembled

Stig Svenson's Gallery, the exhibition hall designed so that only one piece was truly visible at a time, so the attention of the viewer was not distracted by the next piece or the next. She seemed able to consider only one clue, one item of evidence at any one time.

Feeling the gritty sensation of fatigue in her eyes, Maisie squirmed in the chair, pulling the counterpane around her again to fight the cold. It was then that she heard the crunch of boots on the pathway that led down to the shingle bank and then the beach. Moving to the gap between window and blind, Maisie squinted to see better. The shadowed figures tramped toward the bank, drawn by an ever-brighter light that beamed up from the beach. She heard raised voices, then the heavy rumble of a lorry. It was time for her to make her move.

Replacing the counterpane and chair took barely a minute. She checked both rooms once with her torch, and then left by the back door. Though it seemed as if each footfall reverberated into the night air with an increasingly loud echo, she knew that the men would hear nothing, the sound caught up and carried away by the cold wind. Maisie stepped forward with care, using old barrels, the sides of other cottages and any fixture available to disguise her approach toward the activity, which was now illuminated by lanterns.

Maisie took her chance, leaning around the corner of an old shed to ensure her way was clear. Then, stooping, she ran to cover alongside the remains of an old fishing boat, its clinker-built sides having given way to rot as it languished, spent and broken, until someone deemed it ready for the fire. She caught her breath, the bitterly cold air razor sharp in her throat and chest, then closed her eyes for a second, before she took a chance to look out from her hiding place.

A large fishing boat had made landfall and been winched up the beach. On the boat, the Draper brothers from Hastings, together with Amos White, moved back and forth, easing large wooden containers from the deck onto the shingle, where Duncan and Quentin took the contraband and carried it to the waiting lorry. Barely a word passed between the men, though when a voice was raised, it was invariably that of the fourth man on the boat – the man who had instigated the beating of Harry Bassington-Hope, the man whose face was depicted in the mural on the dead man's carriage wall. Maisie remained in place for another moment, observing, working out who was who, which man wielded power. Clearly the fishermen were mere puppets, doing what many had done for centuries to augment the meagre income of the fisherfolk. The artists seemed confident, knowing exactly what they were doing, and the other man, the man who came from the underworld of London – what was his role? Maisie watched closely. *He isn't a lackey, and he isn't the boss either – but he does have power.* It was time to leave, to move on, to be ready for what she anticipated would come next. And as she moved, she knew the dice had just rolled from her cupped hand across the table.

Maisie made her way back toward the path that led out onto the Lydd Road. Then she ran to the MG, unlocked the door and took her place in the driver's seat, her teeth chattering against the bitter cold. She sat in silence for a moment, to ensure she hadn't been seen or followed, then she rubbed her gloved hands together and started the motor car, setting her course toward the road the lorry had taken when she had observed it before. Only this time, she planned to reach the destination first.

She'd had no time to conduct an initial reconnaissance, depending instead upon her supposition that the route taken by the lorry would lead to a barn, or some other building where goods could be stored until later, when – as the saying goes – the coast was clear. Or perhaps the barn took the role of a clearinghouse, where booty was divided between the man from London and the artists. Again she chose a spot where the MG would be hidden by one of the leaning trees common to the Marshes, and made off on foot. Unlike the beach, this road was muddy underfoot, and even as she walked, Maisie could feel the cold wet earth squelch through her brown leather walking shoes. Her toes were beginning to tingle and, after a brief respite, her fingertips were once more becoming numb. She lifted her hands to her mouth and blew warm air through her gloves. A dog barked in the distance, and she slowed her pace, listening to the quiet of the night as she made her way along the farm road.

Though the night was pitch-black, she could ascertain the outline of a barn set among the fields. She ran the last few yards to the side of the barn and waited for a minute. The upper walls seemed as if they had been constructed of old ships' timbers centuries before, though Maisie guessed that, once inside, the bones of the building would reveal a medieval beamed structure, wherein each piece of wood would be identifiable with roman numerals scratched into the grain by the original artisans. Panting now, and rubbing her arms for warmth, Maisie knew she had some time before the lorry rumbled along the road. She must find a hiding place.

Though double doors had been added at each end of the barn, Maisie suspected there would be a smaller doorway, designed for a man to enter if he were coming in alone, with no bales on his cart or livestock to herd. Locating such a door, she listened, then pulled it open. Without waiting to survey the surroundings, she closed the door and, flashing the torch once, she saw that an old delivery van was already hidden inside the barn. She stepped quickly toward the rough ladderlike staircase leading into the loft and rafters. Climbing up, she found a cubbyhole space under the eaves, alongside bales of hay from summer's harvest. From her vantage point she would be able to see any activity at the far end of the barn where she expected the men to enter. The van was clearly parked in such a way as to be ready to have crates transferred from another vehicle. *Yes, it's all going according to plan.* She breathed a sigh of relief – she had gambled upon there not being anyone waiting for the containers to arrive and was glad to discover that she had been correct. Now she would wait, again.

Silence. Was it a half an hour that passed? An hour? Maisie waited, her heartbeat slowing to a pace that was almost normal.

Then, in the distance, the sound of an engine revving, a bump, a rumble, the lorry coming closer along the rutted road. The occasional roar as the driver accelerated to clear a mudhole suggested that the vehicle was being manoeuvred in reverse gear. Soon she would have another piece of the puzzle. Soon she would know what Nick had known.

With a shudder the lorry stopped, then after some manipulation of forward and reverse gears, was brought into position, finally scrunching to a halt beyond the doors at the far end of the barn. Men's voices were raised for a moment, then the double doors were pushed open. The canvas flap at the back of the lorry was drawn back, and Duncan and Quentin jumped out. Though she didn't recognize the driver when he joined the men, Maisie thought that it might have been one of those she had seen with Harry's assailant.

The wooden containers were unloaded. As expected, each container resembled those she'd seen at the back of Svenson's Gallery, where Arthur Levitt unpacked and shipped artwork.

"Right then, you two, we'll take what's ours and we'll be on our way. You know which one our stuff's in, so get a move on," instructed the driver.

Quentin pointed to two of the containers, and as he did so, Maisie noticed that the top of each was numbered in black paint and also bore a name. She managed to read only three names: D. ROSENBERG, H. KATZ, and another marked STEIN. Quentin took the crowbar that Duncan held out to him and ripped the slats of wood apart. She craned her neck as he reached inside and pulled out what was clearly a painting, but wrapped in a light linen cloth, and then a layer of sacking. Duncan helped Quentin to unwrap the work. They both hesitated for a moment as they caught a first glimpse of the painting.

The gang leader prodded Quentin. "Get a bleedin' move on, for gawd's sake! You can admire the fancy bits later."

The artists exchanged glances and together laid first sackcloth, then linen, on the floor to protect the painting, which they placed on top of the cloth, facedown. Maisie leaned forward, trying to see what was happening yet without making a sound.

Duncan took a knife from his pocket and handed it to Quentin. "Be careful, old chap."

Quentin smiled. "Of course." Then he leaned down, with his knife piercing the heavy paper at the back of the painting. He laid a hand against the frame to steady the blade, then proceeded to remove the backing. *Ah, it's false.* Maisie chewed her bottom lip as she watched the scene unfold before her. From the place between the original cover at the back of the painting and the false cover, Quentin pulled out a small pouch. He threw the pouch to the gang leader and then repeated the exercise with the second selected piece.

"There, you can tell your boss that that's the last one, Williams. There will be no more *deliveries* for a while, if at all. We've done all that we can, for now."

The man shook his head. "Nah, you don't expect me to believe that, do you, my little artsy-fartsy darlings? Mr Smith don't like to be lied to. Anyway, that German fella ain't finished yet, no, not by a long chalk, so I reckon them heirlooms will keep on coming. Only just started, he has, so there'll be a lot more where that came from, wanting to be tucked away safely."

Quentin shook his head. "The point is, Williams, that we aren't doing this anymore. It was more or less straightforward until you came along, and now it isn't. Makes it tricky for everyone – especially our friends in Germany and France."

"Well, I ain't got the time to chin-wag about this with you boys. But I'll be in touch. Oh, and here's another little something, just for your trouble." Williams took a roll of banknotes from his pocket and threw it to Duncan. "Thanking you." He smiled, nodded to his driver, and turned as if to go. Then he looked back. "And if I was you, I wouldn't leave it long before you move this little lot. Never know who might be watching you, you don't."

The two men left in the lorry, which rumbled away along the

road. Duncan and Quentin remained in the barn a moment longer.

Quentin became agitated. "Damn that stupid Harry. And damn Nick for telling him about what we were doing. He had no right –"

"All right!" Duncan held up a hand. "The fact is that he did talk, and Harry got us into this. Now we have to get out of it. Bloody shame that we can't help out Martin and Etienne and their people any longer though." He sighed. "Anyway, let's pack up, and get out of here."

Maisie watched as they repacked the opened crates and made a mental note of the black numerals used for some sort of identification. Once the loading up was completed, the men were quick to depart. The van was secured and Duncan stood by the doors while Quentin reversed out of the barn. The doors were locked again, though Maisie did not move until she was sure she could no longer hear the van's engine.

EASING HER WAY down the wooden staircase, she brushed hay from her clothes and began to step into the area where the movement of crates and the handover of other contraband had taken place. She had managed to catch a glimpse of the work as it was uncovered by the men, and though the light was insufficient for identification, she knew that even if it was not the work of a venerable master, the piece was clearly valuable. But who owned it? And if bringing the piece into the country wasn't completely illegal – she had no proof, but the conversation between Duncan and Quentin suggested something other than acquisition of art for financial gain – why was it being brought into the country at all?

Maisie took an index card from her knapsack and made a note of the identification markings she'd observed on the containers. *Did the markings indicate ownership or possibly value? Could they be a clue to a route from the point of departure until the container reached its final destination?* She considered these questions while making additional notes about the rough dimensions of each container. It was as she began to pack away her pencil and notes, that she ceased all movement, barely daring to breathe. Voices outside became louder, so she hurried toward the stairs again, but was only halfway up when the doors flew open and a long-haired Alsatian dog burst through. He made a beeline for Maisie, though the men who came behind the beast could not see his quarry. For her part, Maisie became still and silent, sitting down on the middle step and closing her eyes. She relaxed every muscle, as if to meditate, calming her mind and body so that she felt no fear. The bounding dog halted his gallop. Instead he stood before her, as if weighing instinct against training, then lay down at her feet, subdued. She used the moment to her advantage, slipping the index cards into the gap between two beams.

The panting dog was soon joined by a man. "And what have we here, Brutus?"

Another man, clearly more senior given his manner and tone of voice, was close behind. He was dressed completely in black, with a black pullover and cap, black trousers and black leather gloves. In fact, as other men came into the barn, Maisie noticed that they were all dressed for stealth at nightfall, with two men in uniform, but it was not the uniform of the police. She said nothing, though she recognized the second man immediately. He was the man who had been at the bar in the nightclub where Harry Bassington-Hope was appearing, who'd left to follow Stig Svenson and Randolph Bradley. She was beginning to understand who he was and knew that his powers far exceeded those of the police.

"If you're mixed up with these little shenanigans, Miss Dobbs, you should be wrapping a worried look across your face."

Maisie stood up, determined not to show any surprise that her name was known to the man. As she spoke, she reached down to rub the dog's ear. "I am not involved in *these little shenanigans*, though, like you, I was curious to know what was going on here."

"Jenkins!" The man called over his shoulder to a colleague, one of the men currently searching the barn. "Escort this young lady to HQ for questioning." He turned back to Maisie and, as if he had forgotten something, addressed Jenkins again. "Oh, and while you're about it, get this bloody useless specimen of a dog out of my sight and back into the training kennels. My wife's Jack Russell's got more gumption than this lug. Brutus, my eye!"

Maisie was silent while being escorted to a waiting motor car. It would not have done any good to complain about lack of warrants or any other required documentation. The powers of Customs and Excise officers were well known and predated the founding of the police. As Maisie knew well, they were of prime importance to the government, having been founded in times when all manner of revenue was crucial to a country saddled with outstanding war debts.

The officer ensured that she was seated securely, if not comfortably, in the van.

"Excuse me, sir, will you be able to bring me back here to collect my motor car?"

The man smiled, his grin eerie in flashes of light shed by torches and the headlamps of other vehicles. "The little red motor? No need, miss. We've already got an officer taking it in for you."

"I see." Maisie sat back in the van and closed her eyes. Even if she did not sleep, she must regain some energy for the inquisition that surely awaited her. She knew she would have to appear to be giving information, though she would, she hoped, with some subtlety be seeking facts to add to those already gathered. And she knew she would have to be very, very careful. Without a doubt these men were operating independently of Stratton and Vance, who were probably themselves being manipulated with some dexterity, so that their investigation did not interfere with that of the Customs and Excise. Maisie smiled. She had to be the one to pull the strings in the hours ahead.

SIXTEEN

Maisie was surprised. Instead of being led into a bleak white-washed cell for questioning, she was shown into a comfortable sitting room where she was served tea and plain arrowroot biscuits. She was tired, which was hardly surprising, for it was now past three in the morning. Anticipating a long wait, she removed her shoes and lay down on the settee, pulling a cushion under her head for comfort.

"Nice little forty winks, miss?"

Maisie awoke with a start, as an officer touched her shoulder.

"Time to see the boss, if you don't mind."

She kept her silence as she leaned over to claim her shoes. Pushing her feet into the cold, mud-encrusted leather, she took time to tie her laces before standing to follow the officer, who was not wearing a uniform.

"Ah, Miss Dobbs, do come in." The man held out his hand toward a chair, then flicked open a file from which he took several sheets of paper. "Now then, a few questions for you, then, all being well, we can let you go."

"Where's my motor car?"

"Safe as houses. Just needed to give it a bit of a once-over. Nice little motor car, cost a young woman like you a bob or two."

Maisie did not rise to the bait, though she inclined her head and smiled at the man in front of her, who was clearly a senior officer. She lost no time, however, in demonstrating her knowledge of the department's reach.

"I believe it's not only my car that has been the subject of one of your once-overs, Mr . . . ?"

"Tucker. The name is Tucker." The man paused, gauging his response. "And you mean your office?"

"Yes, my office. Your men broke in and turned over my records with little consideration for my property."

"Let's just say that you were keeping company with persons who were subject to investigation. My officers and I decided that in the interests of the country, it was a good idea to see what you'd gathered, and we had to be quick about it. As you know, I do not have to explain myself to you."

"You might have asked, instead of costing me a new lock."

"And we might not." He referred to his notes again and pulled a wad of folded paper from the file. "I think we should start with this, don't you, Miss Dobbs?"

Maisie made no sudden move toward the desk; instead she leaned back in the hard wooden chair, just enough to underscore her detachment from the outcome of the questioning. She didn't want this man to think she was concerned.

"I was thinking, while being brought here, that I might see that particular item again today."

"So, what is it?" The man snapped.

Maisie cleared her throat. *Good, he's just a little off balance.* "It's what my assistant and I call a 'case map.' Clearly you have knowledge of my profession, and why I might want to keep track of clues uncovered and items of evidence that might contribute to the conclusion of my work on a given case." Maisie paused deliberately to exhibit an ease as she answered the questions put to her. "We draw up a chart where we ensure that every single aspect of our investigation is available to us in this graphic form. Pictures and shapes, even if constructed with words, can tell us more than just talking back and forth, though I think a blend of such conjecture always works very well – don't you, Mr Tucker?"

The man was silent for a moment or two. "And what does this map tell you – what have your little patterns led you to?"

"I haven't finished yet," she countered with an edge to her voice, which led to more fidgeting on the man's part. Her interrogator clearly wasn't used to the sense that control of a conversation was slipping from his grasp.

"Right then, what about the boys down in Dungeness?"

"What about them?"

"What do you know, Miss Dobbs, about their activities on dark and windless nights?"

"I should say you know more than I, Mr Tucker." She shrugged her shoulders. "I was merely interested in the two men, given their relationship with Mr Bassington-Hope – Nicholas, not Harry, that is. You know that I was retained by his sister simply to corroborate the police findings, that his death was an accident."

"Are you aware what was going on in Dungeness?"

"Smuggling."

"Of course it's smuggling – don't be deliberately obtuse with me, Miss Dobbs."

"Far from being obtuse, I am as in the dark as you, Mr Tucker. If you must know, I think Duncan Haywood and Quentin Trayner are a long way from being seasoned smugglers, and embarked upon the operation with only the best of intentions. However, the underworld element clearly found a means of using the situation to their advantage."

"You know about the diamonds, then?"

"I guessed." Maisie leaned forward. "Now, how long have you been watching them?"

Tucker threw his pen onto the desk, splattering ink across the edge of the manila folder. "About three months – and you keep this under your hat, mind. I've looked into who you are, and I know which side you're on, though I wish you'd keep your nose out of it. I'm not interested in these little bits and pieces of art coming across. For crying out loud, they might as well have sent them via any above-board carterage firm, though I am sure the French and German authorities would have their noses put well out of joint if they knew." He gave a cynical half laugh. "No, we're after what you call the 'underworld element,' though we're waiting to catch the blighters red-handed. But we've been too slow about it." He closed the file.

"So, what do you know about the paintings?"

Tucker smiled. "Now it's my turn, Miss Dobbs – you know very well what the importation of the paintings is all about. You don't need me to tell you."

Now calmer, he explained that his interest was not in the artists, but in those who had taken advantage of the wayward Harry and his brother. For her part, Maisie explained that Nick would have done anything to keep Harry safe – even if it meant submitting to the demands of criminals. Tucker agreed, nodding as she spoke, whereupon Maisie shared her knowledge of the diamond smuggling operation. When it was clear that there was nothing more to be gained by detaining her, she was allowed to leave.

Collecting her motor car, she returned to Dungeness. It was all falling into place. Soon every single clue would be set on the case map she carried in her head, the one that no one could steal. She often thought it was like a child's game in a colouring book, where tracing a line between dots on a page would reveal a picture to be filled in with crayons or paint. But one had to be careful to ensure that each dot was connected in the correct sequence, or the completed image might bring to mind something else altogether.

MAISIE HAD NO fear of lighting the fire and warming water on the stove in Nick's cottage. If she were seen, it was of little import now.

The former railway carriage was soon warm, and as the kettle came to the boil, Maisie used a fork to toast her remaining sandwiches in front of the open stove. Once she had eaten, soothed by food and hot tea, fatigue enveloped her again, and she knew that, before she embarked upon the several tasks she wanted to complete prior to leaving the cottage for the last time, she must sleep. The blinds had remained closed against a winter sun just beginning its climb into the now clear coastal sky, so all Maisie had to do was draw back the counterpane and curl into Nick Bassington-Hope's bed.

It was past ten when she awoke, rested and ready to set out on her quest to discover the location of the lock-up, for she was convinced that she would find the information she wanted here, in the artist's home. Using the china jug from Nick's dressing room, she brought water from the barrel outside the back door, shivering as she splashed her face and washed her body. The change of clothes in her leather case was welcome and would be more appropriate than her current attire for the return visit to Bassington Place. Refreshed, she was ready for her search, and stepped back into the studio.

The image that had presented itself to her on the previous visit, a slip of paper hidden somewhere in the recesses of the chair, had nagged at Maisie. From her earliest lessons with Maurice she had been taught to trust her intuition. She was blessed – and sometimes, she thought, cursed – with a keenness of insight. Trust and skill had enhanced her ability to see where others were blind, and confidence in herself and others had led her time and time again to that which she was seeking.

Removing cushions from the chair, she pushed her hands deep into the edges of the upholstered seat. Her fingers scraped against the wooden frame and, though she felt her knuckles grow raw, still she searched with her fingers. Another coin, some crumbs, a pen and a cork. *Blast!* Her fingers would only stretch so far. Frustrated, Maisie heaved the chair over with a thud. Linen had been stretched across the bottom of the chair to cover the frame and finish the piece. Though old and stained, and with a couple of small tears, the square of fabric had remained in good condition, so nothing that had fallen down into the chair could have been lost. Slipping her finger into one of the tears, she ripped the fabric back to reveal even more lost trinkets. There was a collection of dusty coins, a paintbrush – she marveled at how it must have worked its way into the base of the chair – and another pen. She pulled the linen off completely and cast the torch's beam deep inside the skeleton of the chair. There was nothing there. She began to lower the chair, but her hands were moist with perspiration from the effort of holding up its weight. The chair began to slip, and with a sudden thud, landed on the wooden floorboards and bounced up again.

"Damn!" said Maisie, in anger as well as shock, for the last thing she wanted to do was to damage the carriage and the weight of the chair had caused a floorboard to push up. "Oh, that's all I need!" She knelt to inspect the splintered floorboard, but as she leaned closer, she realized that the piece of wood had become dislodged because it wasn't a full-length floorboard but a shorter fragment that was already loose. She hadn't noticed it before, because it was covered by the chair. Taking hold of the torch, she shone the light into the dark narrow recess below. When she reached in, her fingers brushed against a piece of paper. She extended her hand farther, and, between finger and thumb, pulled out an envelope of some weight.

Sitting back, Maisie turned the envelope and drew the torch across to reveal the words FOR GEORGINA. She bit her lip, considering the question of integrity, then shook her head and opened the envelope. A key wrapped in a piece of paper fell out, with an address in southeast London. She allowed her hands to drop and breathed out a deep sigh. *Intuition was all very well, but luck held the trump card!*

After completing a quick repair of the floorboard and setting the chair on top so that the damage was not immediately visible, Maisie packed up her belongings. For the last time, she checked the cottage to ensure that she had left it as she had found it. It was just as she was about to leave, her hand on the doorknob, that she set down her bags and returned to the wardrobe in the artist's dressing room. There was no logical explanation for her actions, and she preferred not to question what it was that inspired her to do such a thing, but she opened the wardrobe and pulled out the army greatcoat. With the sound of waves crashing onto the beach outside, and gulls whooping overhead, Maisie buried her head in the folds of rough wool, breathing in the musty smell that took her back to another time and place.

There was much she understood about Nick Bassington-Hope, even though they had never met. Having lived through death, he had discovered life again, but with war's horror still so present, he had searched for peace of mind, finding hope amid grand landscapes, and in the rhythm of life unfolding in nature. She had seen the heavy hand of anger in his work immediately following the war. But later, when he had achieved the equilibrium he'd travelled so far to find, he had surely been able to return with a new dexterity, a lighter touch, a broader view. Maisie understood that Nick had seen his message clearly, that maturity had provided him not only with skill but with insight, and that he had been able to touch the canvas with his most potent images but held his message close until the work was complete. And though she had never met Nick Bassington-Hope, she knew that this case, like so many before, contained a gift, a lesson that she would draw to her as surely as the coat she now held to her heart.

Carefully replacing the garment in the wardrobe, Maisie smiled. She patted the material one last time, acknowledging an essence caught in each thread, as if the fibres had absorbed every feeling, every sensation experienced by the owner in a time of war.

NOLLY BASSINGTON-HOPE WAS surprised but nevertheless extended a warm welcome to Maisie when she arrived at the house unannounced. She explained that her mother and father were out walking, sketchbooks in hand, making the most of a bright day, even though the cold snap continued.

"They may be getting on a bit, but it's their habit, and the walk does them good. They'll be back soon." She showed Maisie into the drawing room, then excused herself for a moment to speak to the staff.

Maisie wandered around the room, grateful for time alone, time that allowed her to stop and look more closely at a painting or inspect a cushion embroidered in shades of orange, lime green, violet, red and yellow, invariably with a design that was outlandish in comparison to anything she had seen at Chelstone. She reflected upon how the house must have been before the war, with colourful, buoyant gatherings of artists and intellectuals drawn like moths to the bright light of possibility encouraged by Piers and Emma. She imagined gregarious friends of Nick's and Georgina's voicing opinions at the dinner table, encouraged, she thought, by the free-thinking elders. There would always be swimming in the river, picnics alongside the mill, impromptu plays composed on the spot, perhaps with the boy Harry and his trumpet entertaining the group – when he wasn't being teased by his siblings. And Noelle? What about Noelle? Georgina had described her sister as an outsider, though Maisie had come to understand that she was, perhaps, simply just different, and loved all the same by Piers and Emma. The conversation with Noelle during her previous visit had been, she thought, too brief, and she was left with an incomplete picture of the eldest sibling. Now she must add colour to her outline.

A sideboard bore a collection of family photographs in frames of silver, wood and tortoiseshell. Maisie was drawn to the photographs, for there was much to learn from facial expressions, even in a formal picture posed in a studio. Her attention darted from one frame to another, for she knew Noelle would return shortly. There was one photograph, at the back, of a young couple on their wedding day that drew her attention. Indeed, she was surprised it was still there and wondered if the image of the younger Noelle and her fresh-faced new husband gave solace, reminding Georgina's sister of happier, more carefree times. Maisie picked up the photograph, holding a finger to cover the lower faces of both man and wife. Looking into their eyes, she saw joy and hope. She saw love, happiness. The photograph mirrored so many cherished photographs still dusted every day by women in their middle years, women widowed or who had lost a sweetheart in the war. Maisie replaced the photograph just in time.

"I bet you wish you hadn't taken on this assignment from my sister, don't you?" Dressed in a woollen walking skirt, silk blouse and hand-knitted cardigan, this time Noelle wore a red scarf at her neck, a colour that seemed to highlight hair that was not as coppery as Georgina's but now seemed less mousy and equally striking.

"On the contrary, it's led me into some interesting places."

Noelle held out her hand to a Labrador, who heaved himself up from a place beside the fire and came to his mistress. "Ah, you must have been out in search of Harry again. That would have taken you to some interesting places."

Maisie laughed. "Oh, they're certainly entertaining, those places where your Harry performs."

Noelle softened and laughed along with Maisie. "He's actually quite good, isn't he?"

"You've been to see him?"

"Curiosity, you know." She paused. "And more than a touch of big-sister surveillance."

"Ah, I see."

"Yes, so did I. And I knew there and then that there was nothing I could do for Harry, though I do still try to get him away."

"I don't think he's going to audition for the philharmonic."

"No, not Harry." Noelle sighed. "Is he in trouble again? Is that why you came?"

"I came because I've been to Nick's cottage a second time, and I have some questions, if you don't mind."

They were interrupted by the housekeeper, who brought tea, biscuits and cake. Noelle continued after pouring a cup for Maisie.

"And how can I help?"

"I understand that three people went to the cottage after Nick died. I assumed the visitors were you, Georgina and your father."

Noelle nodded. "Yes, that's right. Frankly, it was so upsetting that we only stayed for a short time. We thought we'd go back again in a few weeks. The cottage will be sold, obviously, but frankly, Emma just wants everything left as it was, for now – and I must respect her wishes." She leaned forward to set her cup on the tray. "To tell you the truth, if it were completely up to me, I would have everything sold immediately, no hanging on, get it over with and get on with life. Now *that* is what Nick would have wanted."

Maisie nodded, acknowledging the practicality of Noelle's approach. "So, nothing much was taken?"

"Well, Georgie was in no fit condition to see the cottage, let alone think of what should be removed. I couldn't just crumble like that, but Georgina fell to pieces." She looked at Maisie directly. "Not what one would expect from the valiant reporter, is it?"

"The cottage was left as you found it, then?"

"For the most part. Piers looked around more than I, to tell you the truth. Nick was actually quite a tidy person, liked a certain order. Of course, the army does that for you. Godfrey was the same, though I only saw him on one leave before he was killed, but I noticed it, that order, so to speak."

Maisie saw that when she spoke of her husband, Noelle's jaw tightened. She placed her cup on the tray and waited for Noelle to continue.

"Piers began to go through some of the sketchbooks, but found it too hard, though he did take a couple or three with him."

"Your father took Nick's sketchbooks?"

The woman nodded. "Yes, though I couldn't tell you where he's put them, probably in the studio." She paused. "Is it important?"

Maisie shrugged, an air of nonchalance belying her instinct. "No, I doubt it, though it would be interesting to see them. I have leafed through the remaining sketchbooks, so I would be curious to see the work that your father considered worthy of keeping. Your brother's art is compelling, to say the least."

Noelle gave a half laugh. "As you know, I'm not an artist, though one cannot live under the Bassington-Hope roof and be completely untouched. Yes, as you've seen, my brother touched a fuse every time he lifted his brush or wielded a charcoal. If you saw his work, you saw what he was thinking, how he saw the world. He wasn't afraid."

"I know. But were there others who *were* afraid?"

"Good question, Miss Dobbs. Yes, others were afraid." She paused again, taking a biscuit from the tray and breaking it in pieces, which she fed to the Labrador one by one before turning back to Maisie. "Look, I know Georgina has told you that I'm a tweedy old widow before my time, but I am not without eyes. I have seen people come to shows where Nick's work was exhibited, only to reveal absolute relief not to see their own faces somewhere on a canvas. As I said before, I thought he took chances, really he did. You never knew when someone might get bloody-minded about it. On the other hand, look at those landscapes, the mural work. I admired him enormously – and make no mistake, Miss Dobbs, I admire my sister as well. Georgina is terribly brave, though we don't always agree. But she should never have come to you, there is nothing suspicious about Nick's death and this dredging up of the past can only prevent us from coming to terms with the fact that he's gone."

"Yes, of course, but –"

"Oh, look, here's Piers." Noelle went quickly to the doors that led into the garden and opened them for her father to enter. Maisie realized that when she had seen Piers and Noelle on her previous visit, Georgina and Emma were there. She had not seen the patriarch alone with his eldest daughter before, and was immediately struck by the concern and affection demonstrated between them. In the moments that followed, as the dog barked a greeting, and Noelle took her father's coat and handed him a much-worn cardigan that had been draped across the corner of a chair, she understood the place that each held in the other's world. Maisie remembered, years ago, a book. Why had she read that book? Perhaps it was given to her by Maurice, or had she taken it up herself, drawn, perhaps by the author's reputation? What was it? *The Rainbow*, yes, that was it, the novel by D. H. Lawrence. There was one image that remained with her, had caused her to think about her own life and wonder, *How might it have been if* . . . yes, it was *The Rainbow*. Hadn't the father, Will Brangwen, taken the eldest child, Ursula, as his own when more children were born? And hadn't the girl sought out Will to be both mother and father to her? Was that what she saw now, in Piers and Noelle? When the twins were born, Emma Bassington-Hope had perhaps immersed herself in the new babies, leaving Noelle to turn to her father for comfort. Piers loved all his children, of that there was no doubt, but it was Noelle, sensible Noelle, whom he had taken under his wing.

Was it her father who comforted her when she learned of her widowhood? Maisie imagined his suffering as he held the grief-stricken young bride, the daughter whose hand he had placed in the hand of the kindly Godfrey Grant, the words "Who giveth this woman?" echoing in his ears. Had Piers stepped forward as her protector, even as she pushed despair to one side to care for the injured Nick when he came home from France? And now Noelle had taken on the responsibility for her aging parents, knowing that there would never be another marriage, there would never be children and that if she was to be of account in her own eyes, she must make something of herself in her community.

"Lovely to see you again, Maisie, my dear. Emma has stopped in the studio, a pressing need to immerse herself in her work." Piers turned to Noelle as she passed a cup of tea to him with one hand, while shooing a warmth-seeking Labrador away to the corner with the other. "Thank you, Nolly."

"I hope you don't mind me dropping in to see you, I was passing through town," Maisie explained.

Piers leaned back. "Remember, our children's friends are always welcome, Maisie, though I do wish Georgie hadn't got you involved in questioning Nick's accident."

"That's what I said." Noelle offered cake to Piers, who raised an eyebrow as if taking forbidden fruit and helped himself to a slice. She placed a plate on his knee, along with a table-napkin. "Though I am sure Maisie has come to the same conclusion as the police, that Nick's death was an accident. But if Georgie's got more money than sense . . ."

Maisie turned to Piers. "I understand that you have some sketchbooks that belonged to Nick. Noelle said you took two or three from his cottage. I'm fascinated by his work, I'd love to see them."

"I – I – good heavens, I have no idea where I put them." Having finished his cake, Piers reached forward to set his plate on the tray, his hand shaking. "That's the trouble with age, one forgets." He smiled at Maisie, but the restful ambiance of the drawing room had altered. Piers became unsettled and Noelle sat forward, the language of her body indicating concern for her father.

Maisie softened her tone. "Well, I would love to see them, when you find them. I have come to hold your son's work in some regard – that's one advantage of my profession, I am able to learn so much about subjects I have never before encountered. I confess, before meeting Georgina again, my knowledge of the art world was limited, to say the least."

Noelle stood up, so Maisie reached for her shoulder bag. "I really must be on my way. My father is expecting me this evening, and I'm sure he has cooked me a wonderful supper."

"You know, you must forgive me for not inquiring before, but is your father alone, Maisie?" Leaning on the arm of the settee, Piers rose to his feet.

"Yes. My mother died when I was a girl, so there's only the two of us."

"I'm sorry." He smiled, reaching for her hand. "That's the trouble with us Bassington-Hopes, we're so involved with ourselves, we forget to ask about our guests."

Maisie smiled, returning the affectionate squeezing of her hand. "It was a long time ago, though we still miss her very much."

She bade farewell to Piers and Noelle, asking to be remembered to Emma as she left the house. The MG spluttered to life, and as she drove away, she glanced in the mirror to see father and daughter standing together for one final wave. Then Noelle put her arm around her father's shoulders, smiled up at him and they turned into the house.

Though the conversation had been benign – an unexpected, but nevertheless welcome guest, afternoon tea by the fire – another piece of the puzzle had slipped into place. With or without the sketchbooks taken from Nick's cottage, she believed she knew something of what they contained and why Piers Bassington-Hope might have wanted them out of harm's way.

SEVENTEEN

The time with her father proved to hold news that was surprising, though it explained Sandra's visit to her office. The Comptons had decided to close the Belgravia house completely until their son, James, returned to London from Canada at a future date. Though it was inevitable – the costs incurred in retaining a London home were not insignificant – the move indicated to Maisie that her former employer and ever-supportive patron, Lady Rowan Compton, was finally relinquishing her position as one of London's premier hostesses. During the early morning journey back into London, Maisie felt both uneasiness and excitement. On the one hand, the door to part of her past was closing and with that came a sadness. The house she had been sent to as a motherless girl was now empty, not to be opened, perhaps, until the property's heir returned with a wife and family. On the other hand, it was as if, finally, a tentacle that gripped her to what had gone before was being drained of strength. Slipping into a lower gear to push the motor car up the notorious River Hill, Maisie felt as if the past were losing its claim on her, that even though her father lived in a tied cottage on the Chelstone estate, it was his cottage, his work, that benefited him. The house in Belgravia was all but gone for her now, and it was as if she were being set free.

According to Frankie, events had progressed with speed following Maisie's move and conjecture by the staff of what might happen next had been "bang on the money". The Belgravia household staff had been offered new positions at Chelstone, though only two accepted. Eric had found a job with Reg Martin, who, despite the economic depression, was doing well with his garage business. Eric and Sandra had become engaged, so Sandra had declined the job in Kent to stay in London, though no one knew what she was going to do for board or living until the wedding, when she, too, would live in the one-room flat above the garage. Now Maisie understood that Sandra had likely come to her for advice, and wondered how she could possibly help.

Drawing into Fitzroy Street, Maisie parked the MG, and as she looked up at the office window, she saw the light, indicating that Billy was at the office already.

"Mornin', Miss. Well, I 'ope?" Billy stood up from his desk and came to Maisie to take her coat as she entered.

"Yes, thank you, Billy. I've a lot to tell you. Everything all right here?"

"Right as rain, Miss. Shouldn't say that, should I? Looks like it's fit to pour down out there." He turned from an inspection of the sky outside the window back to Maisie. "Need a cuppa, Miss?"

"No, not at the moment. Let's get down to work. Fish the case map out of the chimney – though I have to tell you, here's the old one!" Maisie held up the crumpled wad of paper returned by the Customs and Excise.

Billy grinned. "Where'd you get that, Miss?"

"I'll explain everything. Come on, let's get set up over at the table."

Five minutes later, Maisie and her assistant were seated in front of both the old and new case maps, pencils in hand.

"All right, so you say that Nick B-H and 'is mates were all in this smugglin' lark?"

"It appears that Alex Courtman was probably not involved, though I don't know why. Could be because he met them later at the Slade, that he was a bit younger and therefore wasn't part of that earlier camaraderie. Let's keep an open mind about that one, though."

Billy nodded. "So, what was it all about?"

Maisie opened her mouth to reply when a continuous ring of the doorbell suggested an insistent caller.

"Go and see who that is, Billy."

Billy hurried to the door. She hadn't inquired after Doreen, or the other children, knowing that there would be time for them to speak of the family. Asking the question as soon as she walked into the office would pressure Billy in a certain way; Maisie had decided it was better to wait until he had warmed to the day, making it easier for him to respond to inquiries about his wife and children. The cold light of dawn must always bring with it a sharp reminder that his daughter was gone.

Maisie looked toward the door as Billy returned to the office with visitors.

"Inspector Stratton." Maisie stood up and stepped forward, though she stopped by the fireplace when she saw the man who accompanied him.

"I don't believe you've formally met my colleague, Inspector Vance." Stratton introduced the other man, who was his equal in height, if less solid in stature.

With his choice of clothing, Stratton could have been taken for a moderately successful businessman and, to the casual observer, there was nothing to distinguish him from the man in the street. Vance, on the other hand, seemed rather more flamboyant, a brighter tie than one would expect with a blue serge suit, and he wore cufflinks that caught the light in a way that revealed them to be made of something less valuable than a genuine precious metal. She was neither impressed with Vance nor in awe of him, and she thought he probably wanted those around him to have a sense of the latter.

"Inspector Vance, it's a pleasure." Maisie extended her hand, then turned to Stratton. "And to what do I owe the pleasure, at such an early hour?"

"We've got a few questions for you, and we want answers." Vance interrupted, his voice pitched at the level he doubtless employed when interrogating those he suspected of gangland associations.

Stratton glared at Vance, then turned to Maisie, who was intrigued to see the men jockeying for position to establish seniority. "Miss Dobbs, as you know, we have been conducting investigations into the activities of Harry Bassington-Hope and, moreover, those he is connected with. We believe you have knowledge that may be of interest to us in our inquiries. I would advise you to share any and all information that you've uncovered, even if you consider that it may not be pertinent – we must judge such details ourselves against intelligence we already hold." Stratton completed his explanation with a look that suggested to Maisie that he would not have called on her in such a way if he were working alone. She nodded once in return to acknowledge the hint.

"Inspectors, I am afraid I have some news for you that will be most unwelcome, for you have not only been pipped to the post, but you are effectively working in the dark with others sniffing along the same trail."

"What do you mean?" Vance made no attempt to conceal his irritation.

"Look, do take a seat." Maisie glanced at Billy, who brought chairs from behind the desks. He understood that she wanted to remain standing and he followed suit. "What I mean, gentlemen, is that the Customs and Excise have cast their eyes in the same direction, and though the nature of their investigation is not exactly the same, it overlaps your own, and they are digging the same plot of land, so to speak." She paused, gauging the effect of her words before she went on. "I am surprised you didn't know, for I'm sure it would make more sense if you all worked together." Her eyes met Stratton's and he shook his head. Maisie's observation was the equivalent of a jab in the ribs with the tip of her sword. She had let him know she was aware of his difficult relationship with Vance, and he knew there was more to come.

"How the hell —" Vance stood up as if to move toward Maisie, who was standing with her back to the gas fire. The second he began to step forward, Billy edged closer to him.

"Please, Mr Vance, I am about to tell you all that I know, though it is precious little, I'm afraid." She had deliberately undermined him, addressing him by the common "Mister", but to correct her would make him seem churlish.

"Continue, Miss Dobbs, we are anxious to hear what you have to say." Stratton remained calm.

"Let's take them down to the station, that's what I say." Vance flashed a look at Maisie, then Billy. Then he sat down again.

Maisie ignored the comment and continued, directing her explanation at Stratton. "The Excise are interested in the same people, though perhaps for different reasons. I know only that they are keeping Harry Bassington-Hope in their sights, along with those who would use such a naive person for their own ends. His gambling debts have left him — and his family, without their knowledge — vulnerable. I would imagine —"

Vance leapt to his feet. "Come on, Stratton, we haven't got all bloody day to listen to her. We'll find out more on our own, now that we know the Excise boys are on to them."

"I'll be there in a moment, keep the engine running." Stratton turned toward Maisie as Vance left, waiting until the footsteps receded and the front door banged shut before speaking, his tone subdued. "What has all this to do with Nick Bassington-Hope's death? You must reveal anything you've discovered. I realize my reputation may be compromised, but if his death was a result of his brother's fraternization with these hard nuts . . ."

Maisie shook her head. "I do not believe there was a direct link."

"Thank God. At least his sister will rest when she hears that you've come to the conclusion that it was an accident after all."

"That's not what I said, Inspector." She paused. "You'd better be off, it sounds like Vance is rather impatient, with that insistent motor horn. I will be in touch."

Stratton was about to speak again, then seemed to think better of it. He left with a nod to Maisie and Billy.

"BLIMEY, MISS, I was amazed, the way you 'andled them two coppers." Billy shook his head. "Mind you, you don't reckon you let the cat out of the bag a bit soon, you know, showed your hand premature?"

"Billy, I barely told them a thing. They can fight it out between themselves, and then with the Customs and Excise. Revealing something of what I know gets them off my back for now – no, let them all come off their high horses and put their cards on the table, then they might achieve something instead of treading on one another's shoes or being afraid that one department will bag the laurels first."

"So, what's been going on – and what do we do next?"

Maisie returned to the table by the window and looked down at their original case map. She picked up a pencil and struck a line through words and scribbled ideas that pertained to the smuggling operation, then she circled the notes remaining, looping them together with a red pencil. Billy joined her and ran his finger along the new lines that charted the progress of her thinking.

"I would never 'ave guessed that, Miss."

Maisie frowned, her eyes clear, her voice low as she responded. "No, neither would I, Billy. Not at first, anyway. Come on, we've got work to do. I won't be able to prove this without more legwork on our part." She walked to the door and reached for her mackintosh.

"Oh, I didn't tell you, did I? I know where the lock-up is. We're going there now, then we'll go to see Svenson again."

Billy helped her into her mackintosh, took his coat and hat from the hook, and opened the door. "Why do we need to see 'im again?"

"Corroboration, Billy. And, if I'm right, to organize a very special exhibition."

THE LOCK-UP WAS in what Maisie would have called an "in-between" area. It was neither a slum nor was it considered a desirable neighbourhood, but it was instead a series of streets with houses that, one might think, could have gone either way. Built a century before in a convenient location on the south side of the river by a wealthy merchant class, the houses had been grand in their day, but in more recent years many had been divided into flats and bed-sitting-rooms. Once-tended gardens were gone, though there were some patches of green from an abandoned lawn here or a rose turned to briar there. Pubs and corner shops were still well frequented, and people on the street did not seem as down-at-heel and wanting as those in the neighbourhood where Billy lived. Another year of economic strife, though, and life could change for the locals.

They saw only one other motor car, a sure sign that they had left the West End. A coster went by atop his horse-drawn barrow, calling out the contents of his load as he passed. He waved to other drivers – of carriages, not motor cars – as the horse lumbered down the street.

Slowing the MG to a crawl, Maisie squinted to read the street names on the right, while Billy, clutching a piece of paper with the address they were seeking, looked out on the left.

"It should be along here, Billy."

"'old up, what's this?"

They had just passed a corner pub, and on a strip of land before the next house, a one-story brick building with double doors at the front was partially hidden behind an overgrowth of grass and brambles. A broken path led to the doors and a number had been painted on the wall.

"Yes, this is it." Maisie drew the MG to a halt and looked around. "I would rather no one knew we were here."

"Let's park the old jam jar back there, nearer where we made that first turn. There was a bit more traffic there. Little red motor like this stands out a bit round 'ere."

Maisie drove to the spot suggested by Billy and they walked back to the lock-up.

"Who do you reckon owns this place?"

"Probably the publican, or the brewery. I would imagine Nick walked around looking for a place like this, and the rent would have been welcomed by the owners if it was sitting here unused."

They stepped carefully along the path, where Maisie knelt down and opened her black document case. She removed the envelope found under the carriage floorboard and took out the key. She leaned closer to the lock, pressed the key home and felt the tumblers click.

"Got it, Miss?"

She nodded. "Got it!"

Together they pulled back the doors, entered the lock-up and closed the doors behind them again.

"I imagined it would be darker in here."

Maisie shook her head. "I didn't. The man needed light, he was an artist. And I doubt if those skylights were there when he rented the place – look, they seem quite new, and raising them up like that would have cost a penny or two. He intended to use this for a long time."

They spent a moment inspecting the skylight, which ran the full length of the lock-up – a not insignificant thirty-odd feet – and both commented on the way it had been raised first, then constructed into a pointed roofline. Maisie looked around the room, for it certainly seemed more like a room than a glorified shed.

"In fact, I would say he put quite a bit of money into this place."

She pointed to indicate her observations. "Look over there, the way the crates are stacked and held back. And the shelving for canvases and paints. There's a stove and cupboards, an old chaise, the carpet. This was not only a place where he worked on the larger pieces, but this was his workshop – that's a drafting table, look, with plans for exhibits. If Dungeness was his coastal retreat, then this was his factory. This is where it was all put together."

"And everything's in its place." Billy's eyes followed Maisie's hand. "I tell you, Miss, I bet there's more room 'ere than in our little 'ouse. In fact, I wonder why 'e didn't make a bit of a garden out there? Doesn't seem like 'im to let it stay wild like that."

She shook her head. "A garden would have attracted attention. I suspect he wanted to come in, go to work, leave again . . . and all on his own time." Maisie took off her gloves and surveyed the room again. "Right, I want to search every nook and cranny, and I want to ensure we're not disturbed. We've good light, thanks to those" – she pointed to the skylights – "and I've brought my small torch with me. Now then, I'm anxious to see if my suspicions are right about those crates over there."

They walked over to a series of crates of differing sizes, though each was approximately eight inches wide.

"Let's see how many there are first." Maisie nodded to Billy, who already had his notebook in hand. "And keep your ears open for voices. We have to be as quiet as we can."

"Right you are." Billy nodded in agreement, then shrugged as he touched a number on the top of a crate. "What d'you reckon these are for?"

Maisie scrutinized the numbers, which were marked 1/6, 2/6 and so on until the final crate, which was marked 6/6. "All right, this looks fairly straightforward, though we won't know until we get inside. This has to be the main piece for the exhibit and the numerals suggest that it comprises six pieces."

"So, it's not a triptych then?"

"We'll soon find out."

"Are we going to open all of them?"

"Perhaps. Then we must search this place for anything pertaining to the placement. Nick gave Alex and Duncan a guide to positioning anchors and other fixtures that would secure the works, though he didn't reveal how many pieces, or in what order they should be put in place. There must be a master plan here somewhere, something he worked on . . . and there has to be a cache of sketchbooks that contain the preliminary drawings and roughs that he used to create the work."

"What about all those books you saw down in Dungeness?" Billy asked Maisie while studying a tool rack. "Gawd, even 'is tools're kept neat and tidy."

"The sketchbooks were revealing in that I could see his progress, the images that moved him, right from his early days as an artist. But even though they contained his reflections upon the war, I think there are books, somewhere, that definitely pertain to this collection."

"Crowbar, Miss?"

"That'll do, but take care."

"Which one shall I start with?"

Maisie touched the first crate. "This one. It's one of the largest, and it's on the outside, so let's be logical and open it first."

Billy shimmied the crowbar between two slats of wood, pulling them apart. With each crack as a nail came free, both Maisie and her assistant stopped all movement and listened to ensure they had not drawn unwanted company. Finally, the crate was opened, and Maisie reached to pull out a painting that had been packed in a similar manner to those she had seen unloaded by the smugglers. Billy helped her stand the work against another crate before removing a hopsack covering, followed by a clean linen cloth, which, when pulled back, revealed the painting.

In a plain wooden frame, the piece appeared to be a horizontal panel measuring approximately eight feet by three feet.

"Blimey."

Maisie said nothing, feeling the breath catch in her throat.

Billy reached to touch the piece, and though she thought it would be better to stop him, Maisie found that she couldn't, for she understood the action as a reflex of memory.

"It's got me right 'ere, Miss." He touched his chest with fingertips that had lingered on the painting.

"Me too, Billy."

The panoramic scene depicted two armies marching toward each other, with every last detail so clearly visible that Maisie felt that she could focus on the face of a soldier and see into his soul. Across and through the barbed wire they ran forward to meet the enemy, then, to both left and right, men began falling, with wounds to head, to leg, arm and heart taking them down. In the mural, so full of movement that it appeared animated, the two armies were not shown in combat, for instead the foot soldiers had become stretcher-bearers, running to their wounded, caring for the dying, burying their dead. Ants in khaki going about the business of war, the toil expected of them. The work suggested no victor and no vanquished, no right side and no wrong side, just two battalions moving toward each other with the terrible consequence of death. Blending skill with passion, Nick Bassington-Hope had revealed the landscape of war in all its darkness and terror – the sky lit by shellfire, mud dragging down those who remained unfelled and the stretcher-bearers, those brave souls who hurried across no-man's-land in the service of life.

"If that's just one of 'em, I'm not sure I can look at the rest."

Maisie nodded and whispered, as if to speak aloud would dishonor the dead. "I just need to see one or two others, then we'll pack them all up again."

"All right, Miss." He lifted the crowbar and began to open the next crate.

THE TASK COMPLETED, Maisie and Billy leaned against shelving to rest for a moment.

"Does anyone know what Mr B-H wanted to call this 'ere masterpiece?"

"Not as far as I know. People don't even know what to call it, and because he was so interested in the triptych form while in Belgium before the war, they all assumed that's what it was."

"I don't reckon I ever want to 'ear the word *triptych* again, not after this."

"I don't think I do, either. Now then, if you search through those shelves over there, I'll attack this chest of drawers."

Both began work in silence, as a bladelike shaft of sunlight piercing through the clouds came to their aid with a shimmering beam onto the glass above. Taking up a series of papers and rough sketches, Maisie looked over at her assistant, who was pulling out a collection of completed but unwrapped canvases. "Will your boys be home soon, Billy?"

"Reckon by the weekend. The 'ospital talked about convalescence somewhere on the coast – you know, fresh air to clear the lungs. Of course, if Doreen's brother-in-law 'adn't decided to throw in 'is lot to come up to London, we could probably 'ave done it, but not now. Costs money, does that. But the boys will be all right, you'll see." He hesitated, just for a second. "Of course, they know about their sister now, that we've lost Lizzie."

"I see," Maisie said as she pulled a collection of thick sketchbooks from a drawer. Of quarto dimension, they were each numbered in the same manner as the crates in which Nick had identified his masterwork. "Oh, look . . . one, two, three, four . . ." She leafed through each one in turn. "These are the sketchbooks where Nick did his preparatory work for the pieces, but –"

"What is it, Miss?"

"Two are missing."

"P'raps Mr B-H put them somewhere else, took them down to 'is cottage in Dungeness."

"Yes, of course, they must be down there."

"Do you remember seeing them?"

"No, but –"

Billy was silent, then, for his thoughts had kept pace with Maisie's. She set the sketchbooks to one side.

"Those are coming with us. I think we can go now."

"Don't we need to find the diagram thing that shows how all the bits of art are put together on the wall?"

Maisie shook her head. "No. From the pieces I inspected, each segment has a certain shape and will only fit logically in one place, just like a puzzle. It shouldn't be difficult to work out."

They ensured that everything in the lock-up was left as they had found it, then secured the doors and walked to the MG. Billy glanced sideways at Maisie and cleared his throat, ready to ask a question.

She responded before he uttered a word, her eyes filled with tears. "I'm all right, Billy. It's just those paintings . . ."

EIGHTEEN

It was midafternoon before Maisie and Billy arrived at Svenson's Gallery, opening the main door to a flurry of activity as the Guthrie collection was in the midst of being taken down and packed for shipping to new owners. Svenson was ever dapper in another well-cut suit set off by a rich-blue cravat and bright-white silk shirt. He called across to Arthur Levitt, instructing him to oversee the movement of one particular piece, and as the visitors stood to one side waiting for him to notice them, he reprimanded a young man for having "fingers like sausages and a grip like a wet fish", adding that the painting in his hands was worth more than his granny's portrait over the mantelpiece at home.

"Excuse me, Mr Svenson!" Maisie raised her hand to attract the gallery owner as he moved on.

"Ah, Miss . . . er, Miss . . ." He turned and smiled, giving additional orders as he approached.

"It's Miss Dobbs, and this is my colleague, Mr Beale."

"Charmed to see you again, and to make your acquaintance, Mr Beale." He inclined his head toward Billy and brought his attention back to Maisie. "How may I be of service to you, Miss Dobbs? I trust that all is well with our friend Georgina."

Maisie nodded. "Quite well, though it's still early days, isn't it?"

"Yes, poor Nicholas's death hit Georgie particularly hard." He paused, then remembering that there was clearly a reason for her visit, spoke again. "Forgive me, Miss Dobbs, but is there something I can assist you with?"

"May we speak in private?"

"Of course." Svenson held out his hand in the direction of his office, then called to Levitt. "Make sure those gorillas are careful with that portrait!"

The office was, like the gallery, a bright room with white walls and furniture constructed of dark oak and shiny chrome. There was a cocktail cabinet in one corner, a system of filing cabinets in another, and in the center, a large desk with two trays of documents, one on either side of a leather blotting pad. A set of two crystal inkwells was positioned at the top of the pad, along with a matching container with a clutch of fountain pens, each one of a different design. A black telephone was within easy reach. Though there were two chairs in front of the desk, Svenson directed his guests to the right of the door, where a coffee table was surrounded by a matching settee and two chairs in black leather.

"So, what can I do for you, Miss Dobbs?"

"First of all, I have to make a confession. My first visit to your gallery was not in the context of my friendship with Georgina. We were, indeed, both at Girton, though her purpose for being in touch with me was in connection with my profession. I am a private inquiry agent, Mr Svenson, an investigator –"

"But –" The colour rose in Svenson's cheeks as he began to stand.

Maisie smiled. "Let me finish, Mr Svenson, there is no cause for alarm." She waited for a second or two, then, satisfied he would not interrupt again, she went on. "Georgina came to me several weeks after Nick's death, essentially because she felt, in her heart, that his passing was not the result of a simple, unfortunate accident. Given

my work, and my reputation, she wanted me to make some inquiries, and to see whether there might be any reason for doubt –
she understood that her emotional state might render her unable to
see the facts with clarity." Maisie chose her words with care, so that
Svenson felt no undue pressure from the weight they carried – after
all, the man in question had died on his premises.

Svenson nodded. "I wish she had confided in me; I could have
helped her, poor girl."

Billy stole a glance at Maisie and raised his eyebrows. Maisie
nodded in reply, then continued speaking to Svenson.

"Please, do not take this as an indication of my suspicions or
findings, but I do have some questions for you. I understand that
you came back to the gallery later in the day that Nick died, to speak
to him – is that so?"

Svenson sighed. "Yes, I did. I came back."

"But you did not tell the police?"

He shrugged, waved his hand to one side as if brushing away a
troublesome fly and shook his head. "To tell you the truth, no one
asked me. When Mr Levitt found the body . . ." He rubbed a hand
across his mouth. "I still cannot believe our beloved Nick is gone. I
expect to see him walk in that door at any moment, full of some
new idea, a piece finished, a complaint about the manner in which
another piece is exhibited." He paused. "Levitt summoned the police first, then placed a telephone call to my home. I reached the
gallery shortly after the detective, Inspector Stratton, who seemed
rather annoyed that he had been called to a clear-cut accident. The
pathologist made an initial examination and away they all went,
taking Nick with them. The silence after they had left was extraordinary. So much activity, then nothing." He held out his arms. "A
man dead and his legacy all around us – it was unbearably strange,
such a vacuum."

"So, you weren't asked when you last saw Nick, that sort of
thing?" Maisie was quick to bring the conversation back to her original question.

"Not specifically. To tell you the truth, I can barely remember. It was such a blur. There was much to do, the family had to be informed, the newspapers contacted, an obituary to compose – I was Nick's agent, after all."

"But you saw Nick on the evening of his death, didn't you?"

Svenson sighed again. "Yes, I did. There was something of a contretemps between Mr Bradley – who as you know was Nick's most fervent supporter – and Nick, here in the gallery, earlier in the day. It was in connection with the triptych, a piece that Nick's secrecy suggested would become a work of significant value and import. Nick, as you have no doubt gathered if you've been making inquiries, had announced that the piece would not be put up for sale, would not be offered to Bradley first, as it should have been, by rights. No, out of the blue, Nick declared that the piece would be given to the war museum in Lambeth, and if they weren't interested, then the Tate or some other such national institution. His decision presented something of an anathema to Bradley, and their words were fierce and heated."

He had been rubbing his hands together as he spoke, but now he looked up at Maisie, then Billy. "I returned with the express purpose of cooling the eruption, so to speak. It was crucial that the two men remained able to do business, that there was respect on both sides, each for the other. If Nick wanted to make a gift of the piece, all well and good, but I was intent that we should take the appropriate steps toward reconciliation, perhaps by allowing Bradley to purchase the piece, then place it with the museum for permanent exhibition, a bequest in his name. I have brokered such arrangements in the past."

"And Nick didn't accept your proposal?"

"Dismissed it immediately. Of course, the budding liaison between Georgie and Bradley did not help matters. Nick was furious with her."

"Did you enter by the front or back door?"

"I entered by the front."

"Did you lock the door upon leaving?"

"I . . . I . . ." Svenson frowned and fell silent.

"Mr Svenson, do you remember locking the door?"

He shook his head. "That I do not recall turning the key in the lock does not indicate that I didn't actually secure the door. It is something I do all the time, it is a habit." A hint of his Scandinavian accent was revealed as he spoke, indicating to Maisie that he was less than sure of his facts.

Maisie pressed on. "Did you see anyone lingering outside, as you departed the gallery?"

Svenson closed his eyes, his words deliberate, as if trying to remember the details. "I closed the door . . . raised my umbrella to summon a taxi-cab that had just turned into the street. It was a fortuitous arrival and –"

"Mr Svenson?"

"Oh, dear. Oh, no!"

"What is it?"

"I rushed to the taxi-cab! It had started to rain again. I didn't take a second glance at the passenger alighting on the other side of the motor car. I remember thinking that I was glad he or she had stepped via the left-hand door so I could just dive in and be on my way, and – I have now recalled – oh, my dear. . . . I may not have locked the door. The taxi-cab's arrival just when I needed it distracted me, made me hurry, I –"

Maisie placed a hand on Svenson's forearm. "Don't worry, Mr Svenson. If someone wanted access to the gallery, they would have found it whether the door was open or not. It's just another piece of information to help me in my work."

"But, do you think Nick was *murdered*?"

Maisie and Billy exchanged glances again. As Maisie questioned Svenson, Billy had been taking notes. Now it was time to move on to the second reason for their visit.

"Mr Svenson, I'm also here with some news, news that, for the meantime, we must keep between just we three. In addition, I have a proposal for you, and I need your help."

Svenson shrugged. "My help? How?"

"I know where the masterwork is, and I want to exhibit here, at your gallery. I —"

"You know where the triptych is?"

"It's not a triptych. And yes, I know where it is. Let me finish, Mr Svenson. I want informal invitations sent to a select group of people – Nick's friends from Dungeness, his family, Mr Bradley, perhaps a representative from each of the museums. I am sure you will have an opportunity for an open exhibition later, perhaps to show other works found by Georgie and Nolly following Nick's death – to my untrained eye, it would appear that even his sketchbooks would draw good money – though that would have to be with permission granted by the family and by his sisters, as executors."

"Oh, my God, my God, we must make arrangements. I must see the work, I must!"

Maisie shook her head. "No, Mr Svenson. I have to make a request I hope very much that you will grant, for it is crucial to my work, and to the purpose of this special exhibition."

"What do you mean?"

"Not only do I require you to keep the arrangements confidential, only releasing information in the manner I stipulate, but I will need to have private access to the gallery. I want only men of my choosing to assist with mounting the pieces. There will be a timetable to follow, a specific period during which – to all intents and purposes – the gallery will appear to be unattended. I cannot emphasize enough that my instructions must be followed to the letter."

"What about Georgie? Will she be told?"

"I will see her this afternoon. As my client she must be kept apprised of my progress, but she also understands that in my work I cannot be expected to account for or inform her of every decision, if I am to be successful."

"You ask much of me, Miss Dobbs."

"I know. But you, in turn, asked much of Nick, and though he could be fractious at times, your reputation has increased a thousandfold as a result of that relationship. I think you owe him this, don't you?"

The man was silent for a few moments, then regarded Maisie again. "Tell me exactly what you want me to do."

GEORGINA BASSINGTON-HOPE WAS, fortuitously, at home when Maisie arrived. When informed by the housekeeper that Miss Dobbs was waiting in the drawing room, Georgina emerged from her study with the now-familiar ink-stained fingers.

"My apologies if I have disturbed you while working, Georgina."

"It's the curse of the writer, Maisie: I am both annoyed and relieved upon being interrupted. I can spend much time cleaning the keys on my typewriter or rinsing the nib and barrel of my fountain pen – in fact, anything that constitutes a writer's work without actually stringing two words together." She smiled, pulled a handkerchief from her pocket and rubbed the stains. "Tell me, have you news?"

"I think we should sit down."

Georgina sat down on the armchair, continuing to clean her fingers with a handkerchief, though now her hands shook. She looked at Maisie, who had taken a seat on the chesterfield at the end closest to her. "Go on."

"First of all, Georgina, I want to ask you about the painting above your cocktail cabinet, the one that belongs to Mr Stein."

"Maisie, I told you, I don't know a –"

"Georgina! Please do not lie to me. You must have known that my work on your behalf, would lead me to unearth the truth of what has been going on down in Dungeness."

Georgina stood up and began to pace. "I didn't think it had anything to do with the investigation."

"Didn't think it had anything to do with the investigation? Have you lost all grip, Georgina?"

The woman shook her head. "I just knew Nick's involvement had no link to –"

Maisie stood up to face her client. "That is as may be, Georgina, but I had to follow the lead I discovered and that has taken valuable time – it was a distraction that had to be explored before I was able to conclude that it was of no import regarding Nick's death."

"I – I'm terribly sorry. But what they're doing *is* all in a good cause."

"Yes, I know that. But you realize that Harry is in deep water, and Nick must have been at risk too."

"And you don't think it had anything to do with his death?"

"No, Georgina, I don't." Maisie sighed. "But if you wish to help Harry, as well as Duncan and Quentin, then you must locate them soonest and tell them I want to speak to them as a matter of urgency. I have advice that I think will help them, though they have taken enormous risks."

"Of course. I –"

"And I do have some news for you."

"About Nick's death?"

"Not exactly. I have located the lock-up where Nick kept much of his art, including the missing work."

Georgina reached out to touch Maisie's arm. "You've found the triptych?"

"There are six pieces, actually."

Georgina faced Maisie squarely. "Then let's go then, I want to see it."

Maisie shook her head. "Please sit down, Georgina. There are other plans already in motion, plans that I request you follow."

Georgina took her seat once again, though her tone was short. "What do you mean? What gives you the right to execute 'other plans' without first requesting my express permission? If anyone should be making plans, it should be –"

"Georgina, please!" Maisie raised her voice, then reached out and clasped both the woman's hands in her own. "Be calm, and listen."

Georgina nodded, snatching back her hands and crossing her arms.

"You are absolutely right to be put out, and right to want to see your brother's work," continued Maisie. "However, in the interests of developments in my investigation, I had to move with some speed."

"But I'm your bloody client! I'm the one paying your fees, and a pretty penny they are too!" Georgina leaned forward, her body tense.

"Quite right, but there are times in my work when my allegiance has to be to the dead, and this is one of them. I have thought long and hard about what to do in this case, and I must ask for your trust and your blessing."

There was silence in the room. Georgina Bassington-Hope tapped her right foot several times, then gave a final deep sigh.

"Maisie, I don't know why you are acting in this manner, or what has inspired your 'plan,' but . . . but, against my better judgment, I trust you. At the same time, I am extremely annoyed." She reached out to Maisie, who held her hand once again.

"Thank you, for your trust." Maisie smiled at Georgina. "My work does not end when a solution to a given case is found, or the grain of information sought is discovered. It ends only when those affected by my work are at peace with the outcome."

"Whatever do you mean?"

"What I mean is something that my clients can never really understand until I have achieved the aim of the investigation."

Georgina stared into the fire for some moments, then turned to Maisie. "You'd better tell me your plans."

MAISIE LEFT THE flat just as it was getting dark, a wintry smog swirling around outside. By the time she reached the MG, a dark

sense of sadness had enveloped her, a feeling that she had anticipated and knew presaged the devastation that awaited Georgina
Bassington-Hope and her family. She wondered if she had another
choice, whether she could turn back the clock and lie to protect others. She had made such decisions before, but . . . she rested in the
driver's seat for some moments, considering her position. There it
was again, the game of risk and chance, only this time her loyalty
was to the dead artist, and to the truths that moved him. Would it
have been different had the paintings not touched her so? She
would never know now, though she understood that even from beyond the grave, it was as if Nick Bassington-Hope's dream of his
work being viewed by the widest possible audience had caught her
imagination, and now she was a conspirator, a speculator with the
lives of others, in the quest to make that wish come true.

HAVING STOPPED AT a telephone kiosk to leave a message at
Scotland Yard for Detective Inspector Stratton, it was no surprise to
see his Invicta motor car waiting upon her return, parked on the
flagstones in Fitzroy Square. She tapped on the window as she
passed, whereupon Stratton stepped from the motor and followed
her up to her office.

"I do hope you have something I can use, Miss Dobbs."

"I've some more information for you, Inspector; however, I need
some assistance in return. I think you'll find it a fair exchange."

Stratton sighed. "I know I won't hear a word unless I agree, so –
against my better judgment, and in the hope that your request will
not compromise my position – you have my word."

"Far from compromising your position, I think you might expect
some congratulatory comments later on. Now, here's what I've
learned about the smuggling operation in Kent." Maisie pulled two
chairs in front of the gas fire and ignited the jets. When they were
both settled, she began.

"Let me start at the beginning. The artists, Nick Bassington-Hope, Duncan Haywood and Quentin Trayner, have all been involved in the smuggling operation on the coast. They were helped in their quest by three fishermen – two from Hastings, men with a boat large enough for their purposes, and one from Dungeness, an older man with, I am sure, a knowledge both deep and broad when it comes to the coves, caves and other secret places along the coast. And of course he was the linchpin, the go-between who recruited just the right locals for the job."

"Go on." Stratton did not take his gaze from Maisie.

"Now, the thing about this operation is that there was nothing strictly illegal, so to speak – not in the way you may think. Of course, this is conjecture on my part, gleaned from various sources and a sense of the mission – and I mean exactly that – taken on by the artists." Maisie paused to see how her words were being received. "As you may know, the most valued art collections here in Britain and across the Continent are being plundered by a select group of American buyers, those who still have money, and who are keen to take advantage of an aristocracy weakened by war, by economic disaster and by the fact that lines of succession were effectively cut off for so many of the families that owned those collections. And investment in art is currently looking a good deal safer than stocks and shares, so a lot of valuable and beloved works of art are making their way across the Atlantic, and our museums can only afford to save so many. Then you have the artists, people like Bassington-Hope, like Trayner, like Haywood, artists who have seen an exodus of the paintings that inspired them as young men. Nick, especially, was touched by the power that the wealthy wielded in the art market. Of course, he did well from such expenditure, but was also angered by what was happening. And that's not all." She paused, assessing Stratton's interest. "There are others who have good reason to fear for the future of their property. I am not sure, to tell you the truth, which group came first for the artists, but it is of no great consequence." Maisie pressed her lips together, choosing her words with care. "As you know, politics in Germany have become increasingly influenced by the new party, the one led by Adolf Hitler. There are those who have become fearful, who have, to all intents and purposes, seen the writing on the wall. They predict that their property will be taken from them. And there are others who want to help. I have discovered that valuable works of art are being distributed throughout Europe, taken to safety until such a time as they can be returned in confidence to their owners. And the owners know it may be years, possibly decades, before that sense of safety returns once more. The artists have two contacts, one in France, one in Germany, and possibly more, who receive and prepare the items for evacuation. Once in safe hands, the valuables are then placed with sympathizers who will keep them hidden until claimed by their rightful owners when this unsettled time has passed. There is no law against that, but they obviously do not want the departure of the paintings to be observed by those who might want them, whether that person is an investor intent upon ownership against the wishes of an extended family or a political party set upon disenfranchisement of a segment of the population."

"That's all very well, Miss Dobbs, but the men we're after aren't interested in paintings." Stratton leaned forward, holding out his hands toward the fire.

"I know, but they are interested in diamonds, aren't they?" Maisie replied as she leaned down to turn up the jets.

Stratton was silent.

"As I said, much of what I have gleaned came from a comment here, an overheard conversation there, perhaps an observation that led to a lucky guess, but here's what I think happened to interest the men you're looking for."

"Go on." Stratton pulled his hands back, and pushed them into his coat pockets.

"Harry Bassington-Hope was in trouble —"

"For goodness sake, we know that!"

"Bear with me, Inspector," continued Maisie. "Harry was in trouble – a not uncommon occurrence. His back against the wall, he revealed a secret that, at some point, his brother must have confided in him: that the artists were moving paintings and other artworks from the Continent across the Channel for safekeeping. Such things are of little consequence to criminals who prefer to trade in what they already know, and who deal only with that which can be handled easily via contacts who can move the goods and make money on them. One thing they know is the market in precious stones, particularly diamonds. Bringing in the gems from their own overseas contacts therefore became a much easier proposition – lean on Nick Bassington-Hope, make it clear that his brother will suffer if he doesn't play the game and you have a leader who will see that his partners acquiesce. In short, Nick had already created the means to traffic valuables, he had the system in place, so your criminal element simply piggybacked on the scheme – and the threat to Harry Bassington-Hope's life ensured that mouths remained shut. And once the system was proven to work, steady payments from the men pulling Harry's strings ensured that everyone was well and truly ensnared in the net."

"Assuming you're right, Miss Dobbs – and that remains to be proven – how the hell did you discover all this?"

"I paid close attention, and of course, I was lucky in places – being in Dungeness at the right time, seeing the operation first-hand. And my assistant and I have spent hours at the Tate, learning about art. Ultimately, though, one has to take that leap of faith, that risk. It's a bit like placing a bet." Maisie paused, smiling. "And of course, I saw the diamonds being removed from the back of a painting, and handed over, so I knew what was happening. And so did the Excise, yet – as far as I know – they haven't yet caught your criminals. But they will soon be there first with the bracelets. I should add that I was questioned in some detail by your fellow government servants, and I think I may have told them just about everything I've told you."

Stratton was silent for a moment, then he turned to Maisie. "Anything else, Miss Dobbs?"

"One more thing." She paused. "I have left word for Nick Bassington-Hope's friends to be in touch with me. When I speak to them, I will press them to see you as soon as possible. I trust that their willingness to assist you will result in a tempered view of their activities."

"Dealing with me is one thing. When the villains get wind of this, those men will likely need some sort of protection."

"I've thought about that. They were pressured into collaboration, Harry Bassington-Hope's life being the bartering point. With Nick dead and Harry owing money right, left and centre, both Haywood and Trayner were ready to throw in the towel."

"The gang made sure they were in it up to their necks though, by giving them money – and, as high and mighty as their intentions were, they didn't turn it down, did they?"

"Who would, in the current circumstances?" Maisie shook her head. "I know it's a stumbling block, but surely if they assist you with your inquiries and help you to make arrests . . ."

Strattton sighed. "I'll do what I can." He paused, shrugging his shoulders and looking down at his hands, then brought his attention back to Maisie. "Now – how do you want me to help you?"

"I think what I have in mind will help you too." Maisie spoke quietly. "This must be handled with the utmost care, Inspector."

SVENSON ARRANGED FOR scaffolding to be erected at the far end of the gallery on Saturday, while, for her part, Maisie gathered the men – and one woman – who would assist her on Sunday afternoon when construction had been completed. Though the original layout plans were not available, and Maisie did not want to request assistance from Duncan Haywood and Alex Courtman, Arthur Levitt acted as foreman, instructing the men to position trestles at a certain height from the ground to facilitate correct positioning of each piece. From her inspection of Nick Bassington-Hope's masterwork, Maisie had been able to sketch a layout for her helpers to follow, though she did not share its contents with either Svenson or Levitt.

In the meantime, per her instructions, Svenson had prepared letters bearing news that the "triptych" had been discovered and that, following work on the exhibition throughout Sunday, a preliminary viewing would take place during the following week. Formal notification of the reception would be sent shortly. The letter acknowledged the unusual nature of the invitation, which, he surmised, would no doubt be understood by all who knew Nick. The decision to have a reception for a limited, select group to honour the artist was impromptu and presented an opportunity for the gallery to pay respects to a man of uncommon depth. It was also noted that, in accordance with the known wishes of Nicholas Bassington-Hope, representatives would be invited from London's leading museums.

At her request, Maisie was handed the letters to post. They would have been received on Saturday morning by each member of the Bassington-Hope family, though there was some discussion as to the best address to use for Harry. Envelopes were also prepared for Quentin Trayner, Duncan Haywood and Alex Courtman, and it was anticipated that when Randolph Bradley's breakfast tray was delivered to his suite on Saturday morning, the letter would be set on top of a copy of the *International Herald Tribune*.

Maisie and Billy spent most of Saturday assembling the people and equipment they would need to execute their part of the production. Svenson had stepped forward to cover all costs involved in setting up the exhibition on Sunday evening as well as for the exhibition itself. Billy's brother-in-law would be working for the first time in months, and Eric had asked for and been given use of Reg Martin's van. Sandra assisted Maisie with procurement of all manner of nails, screws, hooks and pulleys. The plans were falling into place. Sunday loomed almost too quickly.

MAISIE, BILLY, ERIC, Jim and Sandra entered the gallery as the men put final touches to the construction of wooden struts, trestles and ladders that would be used to position the pieces of Nick Bassington-Hope's creation.

"That's all for now, Mr Levitt. We can manage from here."

Levitt nodded. "You'll need the keys."

"Thank you."

As soon as they heard the caretaker leave, Billy ensured the back entrance was secure and the front door was locked. Together Eric and Jim pulled screens across so that the back wall could not be seen from the street, while Maisie and Sandra covered the floor with heavy cotton dust-sheets of the type used by housepainters.

"Ready for us to unload the van, Miss?"

"Ready, Billy."

Maisie and Sandra opened a box they had brought in with them and took out tools they would need for the next part of the plan. The men returned with six panels, which they laid on top of the dust-sheets, before returning to the van for more equipment. In the meantime, the women set to work, each taking care to don a pair of overalls and cover her hair with a top-knotted scarf before commencing.

Some three hours later, Maisie checked her watch and caught Billy's eye.

"Time to let Stratton in, Miss?"

"Yes, it's time. Then you go up to the landing."

"You'll be all right?"

"Of course."

As Maisie took up her place behind a screen, she felt a churning in her stomach. There was always the chance that she would be wrong. She swallowed. Yes, this was her gamble.

AT HALF PAST nine, according to Maisie's watch, illuminated for just a second with her torch, she heard the rumble of a motor car in the alley, followed by the sound of a latch at the back of the gallery being rattled. Any sense of movement was suspended as she raised her head to listen. Deliberate steps echoed, as if the person entering the gallery were carrying a heavy load. Soon there was a distinct creaking noise as the door leading into the gallery was opened, and the steps came ever closer. Then a pause. The intruder's breath came heavy and fast. There was a whine, a mournful aching sound that came from someone clearly struggling with a burdensome weight.

There was a deep sigh and a metallic sound echoed into the air. And something else, a distinct smell. Maisie almost choked. *Oil. Paraffin.* Back and forth, the footsteps moved faster now, the sound of the inflammable liquid slopping across the floor beneath the pieces that Maisie and her helpers had worked so hard to install on the wall. The scaffolding would ignite in a second, though she could not make her move yet. She knew she had to wait, had to linger long enough to hear the interloper speak. There would be a declaration – at least she hoped she was correct in her sense that such destruction would be accompanied by words spoken to Nick Bassington-Hope, as if the artist were in the room himself. Finally, as the fuel's vapour became overwhelming, a voice spoke loud and clear. Maisie pulled the kerchief from her head and held it across her nose and mouth, all the time listening.

"You disappointed me, Nick. You just didn't know when to stop, did you? I pleaded with you, dear boy. I did all I could to prevent this, but you couldn't draw back, eh?" The can rattled with the dregs of paraffin, and Maisie heard a second can being opened. "Couldn't believe you wouldn't listen. Couldn't believe you just stood there. I didn't mean to hurt you, Nick, didn't mean for this . . . but you couldn't be allowed to do it, couldn't be allowed to dishonour your own flesh and blood. . . ." The soliloquy drifted into a whisper, as the man upended the can, then fumbled with a matchbox drawn from his coat pocket.

"Damn!" The match failed to ignite, and as he tried to take out another match, the box fell to the ground, its contents scattered in the pungent liquid. "Damn you, Nick. Even dead you're trying to save that monstrosity, even dead I cannot stop you."

Maisie stood up and began to walk toward the man who had come to destroy the work of his beloved son.

"Piers . . ."

Now partially illuminated in a half shaft of light from the street-lamp outside, the man frowned, as if not quite able to comprehend what was taking place. "What the hell – ?"

She could wait no longer; the risk was too great. "Billy, Stratton!"

Soon the gallery was filled with movement as Stratton's men rushed in with sand-filled fire buckets, and Piers Bassington-Hope searched for anything that could be used to ignite the flammable liquid.

"It was his fault, you know, it was Nick. I didn't mean it to happen, I didn't want –"

"You can save that for the station, sir," instructed Stratton. He nodded to a sergeant, who pulled the older man's arms behind him, the loud click of a handcuff lock echoing in Maisie's ears as the killer of Nick Bassington-Hope was led away.

"I – I wanted to talk to him, I –" Maisie looked around. The fire brigade had been summoned to secure the gallery.

"It's too dangerous here and there's no need for you to remain anyway, Miss Dobbs. You'll have to come down to the station, of course."

"Yes, indeed – but I'll have to telephone Svenson first, and I want to wait until the gallery is safe before I leave. I don't think either of us expected this sort of damage."

Stratton looked up at the painting. "Pity he didn't get rid of that thing, if you ask me."

Billy, who had been talking to both the police and fire brigade, joined them at that moment.

"You talking about that valuable work of art there, Inspector?"

"I am indeed."

Maisie rolled her eyes. "Let us just say, gentlemen, that my endeavours with paint might have saved a great work of art this evening."

They all turned to look at the six pieces of plywood that Sandra had whitewashed earlier, and that Maisie had proceeded to use as a background for her own masterpiece.

"Thank heavens he came without a torch!"

MAISIE FELT HEAVY in body and soul as she drove slowly back to her flat in Pimlico in the early hours of the morning. Piers Bassington-Hope had trusted that one beloved child would understand the plea he'd made on behalf of another; his actions, borne of a deep disillusionment, had caused the death of his eldest son. Yet he had not considered, as Maisie had, that the child he cared for so deeply might be strong enough to endure any depiction of life or death created by her brother.

NINETEEN

As if angels had conspired to clear the heavens for Lizzie Beale, a low, bright winter sun managed to sear through morning fog on the day her body was committed to earth. A service in the local church, its buttresses soiled by smoke and green lichen growing upon damp sandstone, moved all who came. It seemed that the whole neighbourhood had turned out to say good-bye to the child whose smile would never be forgotten. Maisie looked on as Billy and Doreen, bearing their daughter's weight between them, carried the small white coffin topped with a posy of snowdrops into the church.

Later, at the graveside, Billy's quiet stoicism provided strength for Doreen as she leaned against him for fear her legs would not support her during the final farewell. And cradling her newborn child swaddled in blankets, Ada stood alongside her sister, knowing the warmth of their sisterhood would be sustenance on grief's barren journey. A clutch of relatives gathered around the Beale family, so Maisie stood to one side, though Billy had beckoned her to come closer. She watched the coffin as it was lowered into the ground and pressed a hand to her mouth as the minister, with a gentleness that can only be borne of strength, said the words, "Ashes to ashes, dust to dust . . ." and followed with another prayer for the dead child. Then Billy reached down to lift a fistful of cold brown earth. He looked at the dirt in his hand, then took the rose from his lapel and threw it into the chasm that would soon be filled. It was only when the rose sat between the pure white snowdrops that he threw down the first clod to signal his good-bye. Doreen followed, then others stepped forward. Having waited until last, respectful of those closest to the Beale family, Maisie walked slowly to the edge of the grave, remembering, once again, the softness of Lizzie's head, of the curls that brushed against her chin, and the small dimpled hand that grasped her button. She, too, took up a handful of earth and heard the thud as it splashed across the coffin. Then she bade Godspeed to dear Lizzie Beale.

ON THE PREVIOUS day, instead of driving straight to Scotland Yard following the arrest, Maisie had gone immediately to Georgina Bassington-Hope's flat, where she broke the news that her father had been taken into police custody in connection with the death of her brother.

"Georgina, I am sure you want to be with him. I will take you now, if you wish."

"Yes, yes, of course." Georgina placed a hand on her brow, as if not sure what to do next.

"I'll get your coat, Georgina." Maisie summoned the house-keeper, who left, then returned with her employer's coat, hat, gloves and handbag.

"Do you need to inform anyone before we leave?"

"I – I think I will . . . no, I'll see him first. No good talking to anyone before I've seen Daddy, and Inspector Stratton. Nolly will have a fit if I don't have every last detail at my fingertips. I think that's what made me a journalist, you know, having Nolly for a sister!" Georgina gave a half laugh, then looked at Maisie, her eyes dark, her skin ashen. "Fine mess I've got the family into, eh? I should have left well enough alone."

Maisie silently opened the door for her client, steadying her as she descended the steps to the waiting car. She said nothing to Georgina about truth, about the instinct that had inspired her to seek Maisie's help. It was not the right moment to speak of the inner voice that instructs us to move in a given direction, even though we know – even though we know and might never admit to such intuition – that to continue on our path is to risk the happiness of those we hold dear.

GEORGINA BASSINGTON-HOPE ALL but fell into her father's embrace upon entering the interview room at Scotland Yard, her sobs matching his own as they held each other. Having escorted her to the room, along with a woman police auxiliary, Maisie turned to leave, only to hear Georgina call to her.

"No, please, Maisie – stay!"

Maisie looked to Stratton standing behind Piers Bassington-Hope, who gave a single nod. She could remain in the room.

Sitting close enough to see Georgina's hands shaking, Maisie was silent as they spoke, Piers repeatedly clearing his throat and running his hands back through his silver hair as he recounted the events that led to his son's death.

"I'd gone along to Nick's cottage, must have been early in November. We hadn't had much time to . . . to talk, as father and son, alone, for ages. You know what your mother's like, always fussing around Nick, so that I hardly had time with him when he came to the house." He swallowed, then cleared his throat again. "Nick had gone to fill the kettle with water from the barrel, so I sat down – next to a pile of sketchbooks. I began leafing through them – as always, stunned by your brother's work." He paused. "I was so proud of him."

Georgina reached out to her father, then withdrew her hands to pull a handkerchief from her pocket, with which she rubbed her eyes.

Piers continued. "Nick was taking his time, so I continued – ready to put them down when he came in, you know how secretive he could be, and I wouldn't want him to think I was snooping. And that's when I found them, the sketchbooks. . . ." He held a hand to his chest, heaving a sob, then coughed, so much so that the woman auxiliary left the room to bring a cup of water.

"I – I recognized the subject of the work immediately, no mistaking it. And I asked him what the hell he thought he was doing. How could he do that, how could my son . . . do that? He told me that the piece was the most ambitious undertaking of his life, that he could not compromise. Georgina, I begged him to choose an unknown model, but Nick declined, saying that in his work he must honour truth, and that he had thought long and hard about his decision, and felt it only right. I tried to make him understand, tried to make him see – but he just waved me away, told me I was an old man who didn't understand what art was all about these days, that I should stick to ivy-clad walls." Piers clenched his teeth, trying to stem the tears. "My son thought I was spent as an artist, and my pleas were met with disdain – there's no other word for it." He held out his hand to Georgina. "You know how Nick could be, Georgie; you know how stubborn he could be, how intractable." He leaned back in his chair. "I came again over the following weeks, came to ask him to reconsider, to petition him to stop, to think again, to . . . to be kind in his work. But he wouldn't give an inch."

Piers sipped from the cup of water, then began to describe the final bid to change his son's mind. He had come to the gallery on the eve of the exhibition when everyone had left, knowing that he was the only person who had any knowledge of the paintings and knowing that success in his plea was imperative. Entering by the front door – left open by Stig Svenson – Piers saw his son was on the trestle and, wanting to face him, rather than look up at him – a desire that Maisie understood immediately, though Piers would not have been able to explain his motivation – he went to the stairs leading to the landing and was soon on a level with his son. Still agile, Piers had climbed over the railing and onto the scaffolding so that he could press home the importance of his request. Nick began to turn his back on his father, going about his work as if he were not there.

Piers Bassington-Hope sobbed as he continued. "I had seen, then, the cold refusal in Nick's eyes. He infuriated me. After all, how could he be so indifferent, so oblivious to what he was doing? I could not help myself, I could not –"

Georgina handed her father a fresh handkerchief, which he pressed to his eyes. "I am so terribly sorry." He shook his head, then went on. "I – I could not help myself. I raised my hand and struck him across the cheek, then again with the back of my hand. I struck my own son." He swallowed deeply, placing a hand on his chest once more in a bid to control his emotions. "Then the trestle began to move. We both became unsteady, barely able to stand upright, then . . . then . . . Nick turned around and swore at me, and I – I lost control of my senses. It was as if I were blind. I could not see, could only feel this . . . this welter of anger that rose up from my feet and exploded in my head. I felt my hand connect with the side of Nick's face, then I reached out to grab hold of the scaffolding, anything to steady myself. Then Nick was gone. It happened before I could stop it. One second he was there, a look of complete disbelief on his face." Piers looked directly at Stratton. "I had never raised a hand to any of my children, Inspector. Never." He was silent for a moment. "Then Nick was gone. Before I could reach out, before he could gain a foothold, he was gone, the barrier broken as he fell. And I heard a terrible, terrible thud as he hit the stone floor." Piers Bassington-Hope leaned sideways, moaning, as if he would collapse. A police constable stepped forward to support him.

"When did you know your son was dead, Mr Bassington-Hope?" Stratton spoke with a steady voice, neither soft nor confrontational.

Piers shook his head. "I thought he might cry out, might get up and begin to berate me for challenging him. I wanted him to shout at me, to argue, to yell – anything but that silence."

"So, you left the gallery?"

Piers looked up, indignation evident in his eyes. "Oh, no, no. I rushed to his side and I . . . I knew he was dead, could see the life gone from his eyes. So I held my son in my arms until . . . until his body was cold." He explained that it was only as dawn broke that he panicked, his thoughts now of his wife and daughters and the anguish they would feel upon learning that Nick was dead. The last words he spoke before Stratton brought the meeting between Georgina and her father to an end were, "He was my son, Inspector, *my son*. And I loved him."

NICK BASSINGTON-HOPE'S FINAL exhibition at Svenson's Gallery took place in early February 1931, with a select group of family and friends invited to preview an event that was also a memorial to the artist, who – as Svenson made a point of telling everyone who came – would be remembered as an interpreter of both the human and natural landscape. There were those who were surprised to see Piers Bassington-Hope escort his wife from the Invicta motor car that drew up outside the gallery, and as guests entered, Harry Bassington-Hope, at first tentatively, then with more confidence, lift his trumpet to play the heartrending lament he'd composed after first seeing the work his brother had named *No Man's Land*.

Duncan and Quentin arrived together, furtively nodding an acknowledgment toward Maisie, who had helped broker their freedom with a full description of the events she had witnessed at the barn on Romney Marsh and a statement to the effect that she considered

them "tea boys" in the diamond smuggling operation. Alex Courtman stepped into the gallery and joined his two friends, then looked
around the room as if searching for someone. He saw Maisie, raised
his hand to greet her, only to have his attention drawn to the door:
Randolph Bradley had arrived, his shining American Du Pont Mer-
rimac Town Car eliciting gasps from onlookers as it pulled alongside
the entrance to the gallery. Bradley made an entrance wearing a
stylish English double-breasted suit, and Maisie saw just a hint of
disapproval from Nolly when he approached her sister, who gave a
half smile as she raised a cheek to be kissed by her lover. Soon Harry
leaned back, pressing his lips into a piercing final note and the low
murmur of those gathered ceased as Stig Svenson climbed the steps
onto a plinth, beside which was the cord that, when pulled, would
open the thick, blood-red velvet curtains to reveal the completed *No
Man's Land*.

Svenson pressed a white handkerchief to his eyes as he stood behind the lectern to address the guests, who edged forward to hear
him speak.

"Thank you, all of you, for coming today. As those closest to
Nick, I know you would not have missed this opportunity to view *No
Man's Land* before the work is available to a broader audience, as it
most surely will be in the future. It was no secret that Nick's most
fervent wish was for a bequest to a public institution, and I am
proud to announce that Mr Randolph Bradley has most generously
purchased *No Man's Land* as a gift to the Imperial War Museum, in
perpetuity." There was a round of applause during which Svenson
cleared his throat, holding a hand to his mouth for a second before
speaking again.

"We all knew Nick. We all knew that he journeyed to the very
edge of convention in his quest to tell the truth of what he saw, of
what he felt in his very soul, with his skill as an artist. You've seen his
early work, seen the Flemish villages, abundant landscapes, the murals, works of utmost complexity, and every one marked by an acute
sense of place, or perhaps an appreciation of love, of hatred, of

war, of peace. He was a man of and beyond his time, a man of sensitivity almost crushed by the weight of his experience in the years 1914 to 1918. This piece is, perhaps, his most telling. It is a work of art that will leave not one of you with an opinion steeped in the gray mist of ambiguity. Be prepared to hate it, be prepared to love it, but do not expect to leave untouched by the message of Nicholas Bassington-Hope."

It seemed as if everyone in the room held their breath at the moment when Svenson turned to the pulley and drew back the curtains concealing the masterpiece sought since the night of the artist's death. As silence followed the collective gasp, Maisie opened her eyes, for she had closed them when Svenson reached for the cord. No one uttered a sound. She had seen the complete work in the days leading up to the opening, yet none of the impact was lost with familiarity, in fact, as the artist intended, at every viewing another scene seemed to come to the fore, giving rise to a new emotion.

The segment that had stemmed Billy's desire to see more when they first visited the lock-up formed the base of the exhibit. Each and every face was clear and distinct, the artist achieving a level of detail reminiscent of the masters he'd studied in Brugge and Ghent. Three large pieces – the anticipated triptych – formed the next level, and were deliberately shaped to resemble the stained glass windows of a grand cathedral. The column to the left mirrored part of the scene below, the soldiers' expressions even clearer now, filled with fear, terror and determination as they marched forward. Then the magnificent giant centrepiece that had every person in the gallery transfixed. Maisie felt as if she were part of the scene, as if her feet were caught in the mud and blood of *No Man's Land,* and she were close enough to reach out and touch the ground upon which men had fallen.

The scene depicted required no explanation. A cease-fire had been called, and, as was the custom, stretcher-bearers from both sides had been sent forth to bring back the living, while others toiled with shovels to bury the dead. Soldiers brushed shoulders with those against whom they had fought, and every man knew that it was not uncommon for friend to help foe commit a countryman to the earth. There was much for the battle-weary to accomplish as the guns would be alive with shells and bullets before too long and men would be marching upon one another's trenches with bayonets fixed, intent upon killing before death could claim them. Nick Bassington-Hope had seen that moment, had recorded the instant when two infantrymen, one British, one German, had come upon their own, the dead having fallen to the ground next to each other. With mud and blood smeared across their faces, exhaustion writ large in eyes that had looked into the furnace of hell, the soldiers had reacted with instinct and, instead of taking up arms, in that terrible moment had reached toward each other for comfort. And there they were captured in time, almost as if a camera had been used, rather than oils. The men were kneeling, locked in a raw embrace, one clutching the other, as if holding on to that other human being was to hold on to life itself. The artist had caught, in eyes, in mouths, in lines across foreheads, in white-knuckled hands, a depth of grief, a futility that came when man recognized man, not as an enemy with a gun, but as a reflection of himself. And it was clear to anyone who knew the family that the British soldier offering succour to the German was the dead war hero Godfrey Grant.

Noelle had already seen her brother's work. Without faltering, she had stood in front of the painting, recognizing now why Piers had sought to protect her. Maisie remained with the woman, as her eyes moved from the centre panel to the one on the right, the panel that spoke the truth of her husband's death. Nick Bassington-Hope could never tell his sister that her husband was murdered, that he was tortured, then shot, by the very men with whom he had served. The gentle Godfrey, who had turned to his enemy and seen, instead, his brother, had made his way back to the British front line, to a silence in the trench that was broken only by taunting. He stood next to men who, afraid of what it meant to see the enemy as human, instead saw a foe in their fellow man. His life ended with the letters LMF scrawled in blood across his forehead. LOW MORAL FIBRE.

With his brush, Nick had told a story no words could recount. The two final pieces, triangular-shaped segments to the upper left and right of the triptych, designed so that the collection of paintings would form a rectangle when displayed together, revealed something of what he had come to sense as a pilgrim in the wild places that healed him, that before there was barbed wire and trenches there were verdant fields and thick green forests, and, after the battle, so the grass would grow again, the land belonging not to man, but to nature, to love. No matter what claim there might be on this soil or that, the artist knew it all to be no man's land.

While some moved forward to study the pieces in detail, others, including Piers and Emma Bassington-Hope, moved back to view the work as a whole. No one spoke, there was no discussion of light or depth, of a brushstroke here, the use of a palette knife there. Maisie recalled something that Dr Wicker, the expert who had been so helpful at the Tate, had said in response to a question: "With a true masterpiece, there are no words required. Discourse is rendered redundant. That's why the work of a master transcends all notions of education, of class. It rises above the onlooker's understanding of what is considered good or bad, or right and wrong in the world of art. With the artist who has achieved mastery, skill, experience and knowledge are transparent, leaving only the message for all to see."

Maisie remained in the gallery for just a few moments longer, then left to return to her office, for she wanted to complete final notes on the written report she would hand to Georgina Bassington-Hope when the time was right, along with her bill. She bade good night to the two policemen in plain clothes who waited by the door to escort Piers Bassington-Hope back to the cell where he awaited trial on a charge of manslaughter. Though the detective sergeant held a pair of handcuffs, they would most likely not be used until the prisoner stepped from the motor car upon arrival at their destination. As Maisie emerged from the gallery into the freezing night and made her way toward the MG, she realized she was glad to be leaving.

LATER, HAVING COMPLETED her report, Maisie leaned back, put the notes in an envelope, tied the two strings together to seal the flap and placed the envelope in her drawer. Trusting time to be the most efficient editor, she would check the notes in a few days, then the closing bill would be calculated for presentation to her client when they met. In the days that followed, she would undertake the process she referred to as her "final accounting," a period of time during which she visited the places and, where appropriate, the people she had encountered as she worked on a given case. It was a method learned in her apprenticeship with Maurice Blanche, and one that had served her well, enabling work to begin on the next investigation with renewed energy and insight.

Before leaving the office, Maisie completed an overdue task, that of writing a letter of thanks to Dame Constance Charteris at Camden Abbey. She acknowledged the referral that had brought Georgina Bassington-Hope to her door and gave a brief description of the outcome. The Bassington-Hope family had been through a tumultuous time: shock, sorrow, regret and anger – at both Piers and Nick. There had been arguments and compassion, alliances had swung back and forth, then the family had come together to support the patriarch, even though true forgiveness eluded them, for now. She described the way in which the trial had brought Noelle and Georgina together, perhaps with more understanding than before. In her letter, Maisie suggested that Dame Constance might be seeing Georgina again soon, and added that she herself would love to visit in due course.

She drove home at a low speed, taking special care in the night-time smog. Making her way past Victoria, she turned, on a whim, toward Belgravia. She was soon parked outside 15 Ebury Place. Houses on either side of the Comptons' mansion showed signs of life, with lights in upper windows, perhaps a door opening to reveal a butler showing a visitor out into the night. But the house that had once been her home reminded her of an old, old woman gone to bed early because even a short day was long. There were no lights, no signs that a family was in residence. Without closing her eyes, Maisie thought she could hear the voices that echoed back and forth when she was young, of Enid cursing, of James gamely stealing biscuits when he came back to England to go to war. She could hear Mrs Crawford, Mr Carter and, as the years sped by in her mind's eye, she imagined the staff who were new to the house and to her when she had come back, this time to live upstairs. It occurred to her that the ritual of her final accounting was rather like closing up a house, for wasn't she checking each room before securing the door, looking out of a window to recall the view and then moving on? And wasn't there always a new case, a new challenge, something fresh to ignite her appetite for excitement, just as there was now the flat in Pimlico? She smiled, took one last look at the mansion, pushed the MG into gear and began to slip away, back toward her new home.

MAISIE TRAVELED TO Dungeness the following day, parking the motor car close to the railway carriages that had been Nick Bassington-Hope's home. Already a FOR SALE sign had been set up, nailed into a thick stake that had been hammered into the ground. She walked alongside the carriage and cupped her hands around her eyes so that she could see inside. Just a few pieces of furniture remained, enough to make the property seem welcoming when another soul came looking for a windswept retreat.

The sun shone, though the air was crisp, and as she was dressed for a meander along the beach, with a woollen thigh-length coat atop walking skirt and boots, gloved hands and a cloche set well down to protect her ears, she set off, pulling up her collar as she turned away from the carriages. On toward the lighthouse she tramped along, pebbles scrunching underfoot as she made her way past fishing boats pulled up onto the shingle. Nets had been emptied and left in neat piles, and gulls wheeled down from overhead as fishermen gathered in twos and threes to gut the fish or mend their nets. There was no sign of Amos White, and though the men raised their heads, then muttered together as she passed, she smiled and continued on her way. With the sting of salt on her cheeks, her eyes smarting against the chill wind, Maisie was glad she had decided to walk, for she loved the water, loved to be here, at the boundary of sea and land. What had her friend Priscilla called her just a few months ago? *A mudlark!* Yes, a mudlark who found treasure on the beach, though the banks of the Thames were a far cry from this. She stopped, drawn to the edge of the water, so that waves almost, though not quite, reached her shoes as they crashed into the shore.

The sea lapped even closer, though Maisie remained in place, her hands holding her collar to protect her neck. *It's because it's the beginning, and also the end.* That was what she loved about the place where the water met the land – the promise of something fresh, a suggestion that, even if what is happening now is to be suffered, there is an end and a beginning. *I could sail away on that beginning,* thought Maisie, as she turned to leave.

Driving through Hastings Old Town, she knew she risked seeing Andrew Dene, but knew too that it was important to bid her own farewell. The MG was too conspicuous to drive down the street where he lived, so she parked close to the pier, then walked back toward Rock-a-Nore. She watched day-trippers and even stopped for a cup of strong tea served by a fisherman's wife at a beach-side hut. It was when she turned, ready to go back to her motor car, that she saw them, a couple running across the road toward the East Hill funicular railway. They were laughing, hand in hand. Though her breath caught in her throat, Maisie was not saddened to see Dene with a woman, a woman who seemed so at ease in his company, no shred of doubt upon her face. Knowing they had eyes only for each other, she watched the funicular ascend to the top of the hill, then whispered "good-bye" as she walked slowly back toward the pier.

She drove through Winchelsea, and then Rye, and reached Tenterden by lunchtime, though she did not stop to see Noelle or Emma but simply decelerated the car as she passed the gates that led to the estate. There had been a healing of familial wounds at the preview of *No Man's Land*, though it would be some time before Piers would be home again. It was as if, in some way, Nick were still with them, living on through the body of work he left behind. Maisie looked through the gates and thought that, one day, she might be back, perhaps with Georgina. Or she might be invited to tea on a Saturday afternoon, drawn in, once again, to the Bassington-Hope web. Something had been ignited within her in that house. If her soul were a room, it was as if light were now shining in a corner that had been dark. And she'd been touched by something less tangible, something she'd found among people who saw nothing unusual in painting trees on walls. Perhaps it was the freedom to strike out on one's own path, seeing not a risk in that which was new, only opportunity.

A night at her father's house provided a brief respite from the pressures of recent weeks. With the memory of her breakdown still uppermost in her father's mind, Maisie took care not to concern him further, keeping conversation light. They spoke of horses, especially new foals expected, and of the closing of the Comptons' Belgravia house. Then, after they had enjoyed a supper of rabbit stew, with dumplings and fresh crusty bread to mop up the broth, they sat by the fire, where Frankie slipped into sleep, his daughter looking on before fatigue claimed her. It was past twelve when she felt an eiderdown envelop her and was aware of the lamps being extinguished so that she could dream on undisturbed.

Maisie left early the following morning, going directly to the office, where she began to read, once again, the final report she would soon deliver to Georgina Bassington-Hope. Billy had left a note with a list of the tasks he hoped to complete by the end of the day, mainly jobs that would bring other cases up-to-date, especially as the duo's attention had been elsewhere in recent weeks. The funeral had been a turning point for the Beale family. Jim had several sources of steady work, a day here, a day there, but it all helped, all added up, according to Billy. There was talk that the visitors might return to Sussex, seeing as the situation was no better in London than any-where else. According to Billy, he and Doreen had weighed up leav-ing the East End, talked about getting out of the Smoke.

"But when it comes down to it, it's me roots, ain't it? O'course, they ain't Doreen's roots, but, well, you never know, do you? We're still thinking about goin' over there, when we've got a bit put by." He paused, looking at Maisie for encouragement. "What d'you reckon, Miss?"

"I reckon, Billy, that there's such a thing as serendipity, that if you are meant to move on, you will. And I believe that if you imagine, and keep on imagining, a better life for your family, then events will conspire to present the opportunity to you. And when that time comes, you will make your decision, one way or another."

"Bit of a gamble, though, ain't it?"

"So is staying in one spot."

EPILOGUE

It was late February before Maisie made an appointment to visit Georgina Bassington-Hope at her home in Kensington. Arriving at the flat, she was surprised to see Nick's Scott motorcycle standing outside, now with panniers added.

As she waited while Georgina was informed that her visitor had arrived, Maisie heard the unmistakable rat-tat-tat-tat-tat of typewriter keys hitting a paper-filled platen. The journalist was having a productive day. The housekeeper left Georgina's study, beckoning Maisie to enter. The book-lined room resembled a beehive, such was the level of energy generated by the woman who seemed unable to tear herself away from her work. Maisie was still until, finally, with a forefinger resting on a key, Georgina turned to her.

"One second, just one second while I finish this thought . . ."

Maisie took a seat next to the desk. Finally, Georgina released the platen, rolled out the sheet of paper and added it to a manuscript alongside the typewriter.

"Maisie, how are you?" She reached out and grasped Maisie's hand. "Come along, let's sit by the fire."

The two women moved to chairs set beside the blazing coal fire.

"I'm well, but more to the point, how are *you*?"

Drawing back her thick copper hair, Georgina wound the waves into a chignon at the nape of her neck, and secured it with a pencil. "I thought I'd never climb out of the hole I'd dug for myself, to tell you the truth. What with the terrible, terrible outcome of your investigation – and I'm not blaming you, no, I blame myself – I thought it would be best if I just went away, take a leaf out of Nick's book and go off to America or something."

Maisie's expression betrayed her thoughts.

"Oh, you are just like Nolly! You'll be delighted to hear that it's all over with Randolph Bradley. I'll get to that in a minute. However, you must know that Piers is expected home in just a few months. What with the verdict of manslaughter, and considering his age, and the circumstances of the crime, he'll be home by the autumn, according to the solicitors."

"I'm glad. Are you all coping? What about Emma and Noelle?"

Georgina sighed. "We're making progress, patching things up, you know. Rome wasn't built in a day. Nolly's been a great help, an absolute brick – mind you, she always was. She's done wonders with Piers and Emma. And with me – and she's sorted out Harry, come to that."

"You can tell me about Harry later. What about your sister?"

Georgina shook her head, pausing to gaze into the fire before she spoke again. "Piers was the only one who realized, really understood, that Nolly's wall of tweedy organization was all that stood between her and the tide of sadness that came with Godfrey's death. When she went on about him being a war hero, and so on, it was herself she was trying to convince, and I think that none of us really understood her. It was so easy to think that Nolly was all right, you know, 'Good old Noll!' " She sighed, looking into the flames as if for answers. "But what Piers didn't grasp was that Nolly might be better than any of us when it came to dealing with the truth, that even though she was devastated when she first saw the paintings, it was as if she knew, as if she understood right there and then why Nick had chosen to use Godfrey as a subject for the piece. You know, people think that Nick and I were close – and of course, we were, we were twins, after all – but Nolly is the eldest, and that's almost like being another parent. She nursed Nick when he came home wounded, and even though she could moan and groan about him, about his work, she was very forgiving, when it came down to it."

"Yes, I can see that."

"She's both worried and delighted that Harry seems to be sorting himself out."

"And what's he going to do?" Maisie was warmed by the conversation and by Georgina's unexpectedly buoyant mood.

"You'll never believe this, but Harry has joined a shipboard band, entertaining passengers on their way from Southampton to New York." She shrugged her shoulders. "I just hope that staff are banned from the gaming tables! Seriously, he said he'd wanted to go to New York for ages, that it's where his kind of music was born, and that's where he should be."

"Following in his brother's footsteps?"

"It's where Nick heard the sound of his drummer, so perhaps it'll be the same for Harry."

"And what about you, Georgina?" Maisie gestured toward the typewriter. "You seem to have found your muse."

"My muse is Nick. Come along, I'll show you." Georgina returned to her desk, followed by Maisie. She reached for a series of large black-and-white sketches that had been laid out for her to view as she worked at the typewriter.

"Oh, my . . ."

"Only sketches, but brilliant, aren't they? So detailed. They're good enough to exhibit."

Maisie nodded, pulling a lamp across so that she could better see the work. Nick Bassington-Hope had depicted everyday life on the streets that were home to those who knew only want. Scruffy street urchins, lines of men waiting for work, women struggling to wash laundry at a cold-water street pump – the forgotten of London seen through the eyes of the artist.

"It's as if he had taken a photograph, as if someone like Frank Hurley were behind the camera, not an artist with charcoal and paper."

"I know." Georgina nodded, the colour rising to her cheeks.

Maisie lifted her gaze from the sketches and looked at Georgina. "What are you going to do with them?"

Georgina began to speak quickly, her excitement mounting. "After you gave me the keys to the lock-up, I went over on my own to have a look. That's when I found these, the sketches. I just sat there and wept, not just because they're Nick's and I miss him terribly, but because of what they represent." She swallowed, looking at Maisie intently. "You were right, Maisie, this *is* war, this *is* a battlefield, and I have to do something about it. But I have only one real gift, and that is my skill with words. I can draw a bit, but this is what I work with." She pulled the pencil from the chignon and held it up to emphasize her point, her unclasped hair cascading across her shoulders. "So, here's my plan – and let me tell you, I not only have the promise of an exhibition from Stig, but I have a contract from my publisher!" Georgina splayed the sketches across the desk. "There's a story in each of these, a history, a person whose life others will want to read about – someone who I will *make* them want to read about. And I'm not going to stop there." She was speaking faster now. "These are all of London, with some of rural poverty in Kent, but Nick hadn't finished. I'm going to travel across Britain, from London to Birmingham, to Newcastle, Leeds, Sheffield, up to Scotland, and I'm going to tell the story of what's happened since 1929, what's happening now. I can't wait for bloody Mosley to become king – or whatever it is he wants – and rise to the occasion and save everyone, for heaven's sake!"

"Is that why you ended the liaison with Bradley?" Maisie risked the impertinent question.

Georgina shrugged. "It began to end almost as soon as it started.

To tell you the truth, I hadn't been really inspired since the war – you hit the nail on the head there, Maisie." With her hands still resting upon her brother's sketches, Georgina looked out the window and, it seemed, into the past. "I took such huge chances out there in the war, but – oh, it is so hard to explain – there was this thrill, this feeling here" – she touched a place just above her belt buckle –"that told me that what I was doing was right, that I might be taking a risk, might even be killed, but it was a gamble for a good reason. I would have something to show for it." Her words began to slow, and she shrugged her shoulders. "I missed that feeling, and I think I tried to get it back by having an affair. But it was never right. You see" – she turned so that she and Maisie were face-to-face – "you see, I realized that even though there was the risk, the thrill of an affair with a married man, and an exciting married man at that – it was completely false. Completely without substance. There was no . . . no . . . no truth, no solid, meaningful reason to play with that particular fire. Do you understand?"

"I do, yes; I do understand."

"So now, with this work, with Nick's sketches there to challenge me, I've found that reason again, that old voice saying, 'Do it, it's worth it.' And I can feel it inside me, that the chance, the challenge of taking off on my own is a worthwhile endeavour."

Georgina spoke for some moments longer, while Maisie encouraged her with a ready smile, leaning forward to show excitement about the expedition and that she was keen to wish her well. Then having submitted her written report, Maisie gathered her belongings, ready to leave, but Georgina touched her on the arm.

"I've something for you. Call it a gift from Nick." She held out a parcel wrapped in brown paper and string. "No prizes for guessing, it's a painting. But one you will find quite extraordinary, I think."

"A painting, for me?"

"Yes. I found it in the lock-up. A completed watercolour. Quite extraordinary, you know, because he had rolled a note along with it, explaining the subject. It reminded me of you, and I remembered you saying something about bare walls in your new flat, and I thought you might like it so I had it framed for you. Of course, if it isn't to your liking, you can give it away."

MAISIE UNLOCKED THE front door of her flat and called out. "Anyone home?"

Sandra emerged from the box room, a duster in her hand.

"Settling in, Sandra?"

"Yes, miss. I can't thank you enough. I hope me being here won't be too much of an imposition."

"Not at all. We can't have you living in a hostel until your wedding in June, can we?"

Sandra smiled, beckoning to Maisie. "Come and have a look. Eric helped me move a bed and dressing table in. Got them cheap we did – at a house sale, you know."

Maisie looked into the room that had already been made cosy by the new lodger.

"And now that I've got a job in that dress shop, I can do night classes as well – typewriting's the thing, you know. I was just about to go and sign up."

"Right you are, Sandra. I'll see you later." Maisie smiled as the younger woman gathered her coat and hat and left the flat. Though she had wondered about her decision to extend the offer to Sandra to live with her until her marriage, she was delighted to lend a helping hand, as others had in turn helped her in the past. And in the way that fortune and providence gravitate toward each other, Sandra had found a new job soon after accepting Maisie's offer.

LATER, AFTER SHE had hung the painting on the wall above the fireplace, Maisie dragged one of her two armchairs and set it in front of the fire. Sipping tea from a tin mug, she read the note that

Nick Bassington-Hope had left with the painting he'd completed a year before.

Winter, but you would think it's the first day of spring. The sun is shining, and everything has that look of readiness for rebirth. I had just returned from Lydd when I saw the subject for this painting, and something made me want to paint her. Despite the freezing cold, she walked along the beach and stopped to look out across the Channel, almost as if she were looking into the future. Can't explain it, but I had the feeling that this was a woman on the brink of something fresh, something new, a woman leaving the past behind. So, what with the promise of spring in the air, I came straight back to the cottage and began to work.

Maisie wondered what Nick had seen on that day, for the picture could well have been a photograph taken on her last visit to Dungeness, as she walked on the shingle and looked out to sea. She finished her tea and sat for some time, studying the painting, thinking about the man who had caught a moment of reflection. Her moment of reflection. She read the note again and closed her eyes. *Readiness for rebirth.* Winter warming to spring; the land new again after battles have raged; a child dead, and a baby born. It was time to move on, to dance with life again.

ACKNOWLEDGMENTS

As always, deepest thanks to my writing buddy, Holly Rose, for keeping me on track with my writing, and for limitless encouragement. More especially, Hol, thank you for your yellow highlighter – where would Maisie and I be without it? Gratitude must also go to my "old china plate", Tony Broadbent: thank you for our wonderful conversations about "old London" and for giving me even more research materials with which to breathe life into Maisie's time and place – my bookshelves runneth over! In addition, my Cheef Resurcher (who knows who he is) has once again been on his toes, bringing golden nugget of historical significance to my attention.

The Imperial War Museum has fascinated me since childhood, and continues to inspire and intrigue me, not least when I am using the archive and library – thanks must go to the ever-helpful staff, who so efficiently find books and correspondence to support my understanding of the Great War and its aftermath.

To my agent, Amy Rennert – love and gratitude for your powerful blend of experience, knowledge and grace; to my editors, Jennifer Barth (in New York) and Anya Serota (in London), thank you both for your skillful and sensitive editing, for your insights and that shared uncanny ability to read my mind.

And thanks to my family – for everything: my husband, John Morrell; my brother John and sister-in-law, Angella; my wonderful parents, Albert and Joyce Winspear, who visited Dungeness with me, tramping across the shingle on a bitterly cold day while I made notes for *Messenger of Truth* – that's what you call support!

Read more ...

Jacqueline Winspear

MAISIE DOBBS

Maisie Dobbs takes on her first investigation in 1920s London

Young, feisty Maisie Dobbs has recently set herself up as a private detective. Such a move may not seem especially startling, but this is 1929 and Maisie is exceptional in many ways.

Having started as a maid to the London aristocracy, studied her way to Cambridge and served as a nurse in the Great War, Maisie has wisdom, experience and understanding beyond her years. Little does she realise the extent to which this strength of character is soon to be tested. For her first case forces her to uncover secrets long buried, and to confront ghosts from her own past.

'Jacqueline Winspear's Maisie Dobbs is a welcome addition to the sleuthing scene. Simultaneously self-reliant and vulnerable, Maisie isn't a character I'll easily forget' Elizabeth George

'Readers sensing a story-within-a-story won't be disappointed. But first, they must prepare to be astonished at the sensitivity and wisdom with which Maisie resolves her first professional assignment' *New York Times*

Order your copy now by calling Bookpoint on 01235 827716 or visit your local bookshop quoting ISBN 978-0-7195-6622-6 www.johnmurray.co.uk

Read more . . .

Jacqueline Winspear

BIRDS OF A FEATHER

The extraordinary Maisie Dobbs returns in her second case

London, 1929. Joseph Waite is a man who knows what he wants. With his Havana cigars and Savile Row suits, he is one of Britain's wealthiest men. And the last thing he needs is a scandal. When his daughter runs away from home, he is determined to keep the case away from the public eye. So he turns to a woman renowned for her discretion and investigative powers – the extraordinary Maisie Dobbs.

Maisie soon discovers that there are reasons why Charlotte might have left home. Instinctively she feels that Charlotte is safe. Yet, suddenly, she finds herself confronting a murder scene.

'In Maisie Dobbs, Jacqueline Winspear has given us a real gift. Maisie Dobbs has not been created – she has been discovered. Such people are always there amongst us, waiting for somebody like Ms Winspear to come along and reveal them. And what a revelation it is!' Alexander McCall Smith

'A terrific mystery . . . Both intriguing and full of suspense, it makes for an absorbing read' *Observer*

Order your copy now by calling Bookpoint on 01235 827716 or visit your local bookshop quoting ISBN 978-0-7195-6624-0 www.johnmurray.co.uk

Read more ...

Jacqueline Winspear

PARDONABLE LIES

Much-loved Maisie Dobbs returns to investigate her third case, a thrilling story of family tensions and mysterious deaths in the First World War

London, 1930. Maisie Dobbs, the renowned psychologist and investigator, receives a most unusual request. She must prove that Sir Cedric Lawton's son Ralph really is dead.

This is a case that will challenge Maisie in unexpected ways, for Ralph Lawton was an aviator shot down by enemy fire in 1917. To get to the bottom of the mystery, Maisie must travel to the former battlefields of northern France, where she served as a nurse in the Great War. As her investigation moves closer to the truth, Maisie soon uncovers the secrets and lies that some people would prefer remain buried.

'Feisty, working-class heroine Maisie is a deliberate throwback to the sleuthettes of old-fashioned crime writing. The well-plotted story, its characters and the picture of London between the wars are decidedly romantic' *Guardian*

'For readers yearning for the calm and insightful intelligence of a main character like P. D. James's, Maisie Dobbs is spot on' *Boston Globe*

Order your copy now by calling Bookpoint on 01235 827716 or visit your local bookshop quoting ISBN 978-0-7195-6736-0
www.johnmurray.co.uk